The l... ... their
tragedie... ...gle to
establis...

Through Maggi and Beau the reader, too, lives life on the backside, experiencing first-hand

what it takes to be a trainer, groom, jockey,
owner, and how each interrelates with the other
the rules and regulations of horseracing.
the good and bad in horseracing
improvements, changes and developments
in over twenty years of horseracing
the techniques and tools of racing
racetrack jargon.

THIS IS THE FIRST TIME THE TRUTH OF LIFE ON THE BACKSIDE HAS BEEN TOLD!

NOTHING HAS BEEN "CHANGED TO PROTECT THE INNOCENT" . . . YET, THE INNOCENCE OF THE READER WILL BE CHALLENGED.

BEAU. Stubborn and talented, a diamond-in-the-rough. Soft-hearted, easy going and honest, always. Maybe the best trainer in the business, anywhere. A non-conformist . . but he needed Maggi like nothing else in his life.

MAGGI. Forceful and dynamic. Thrived in her life on the backside. She was driven to be successful . . . but she saw success only in Beau.

TENDERNESS ... BITTERNESS ... TOGETHERNESS ... CONFLICT

Their deep love and devotion and attraction for each other was born on the backside. Together, they built one of the largest businesses of its kind in all of horseracing.

To Shirley & Richard, Best Wishes, Margie Hazelton 9-29-02

"BACKSIDE"

This title can be ordered directly from the publisher.

Teeny Weeny Publishing
Route 2
P.O. Box 2672
Seymour, MO 65746

Teeny Weeny Publishing
Route 2
P.O. Box 2672
Seymour, MO 65746

Printed in U S A
ISBN 0-930380-08-8

TO:

The Backside People—who make racing possible

The Claiming Horse—without him, there would be no racing

The Owner—who picks up the tab

Management—who oversees it all

*Richard—for without him I would never
have known the backside*

Prolog

This is a true story but told in novel form. It lets you pass through the   stable gates of racetracks, into the restricted barn area, where only licensed personnel are allowed.

Be up at 5 a.m. with Beau and Maggi, working with their horses. Learn the skills it takes to be a successful trainer. The problems it entails, the hardships that no one ever hears about. The good and the bad of this wonderful life.

Don't put this book down! For every page tells you more truth of racing. What it is like to be an owner, trainer, jockey, pony girl or boy, jock's agent, dispels the myths of the past that have been unfair to the people who make their living on the **BACKSIDE**.

A fact . . . Most people refer to the barn area as the backstretch. Not so. The backstretch is the far side of the racetrack itself. The proper name for any stable area at any track is BACKSIDE.

1 Late Fifties

Beau and Maggi were shocked to see Bert Maddox standing in their driveway as they drove in, and Beau braked the pickup to an abrupt stop. "Thank God you're home!" Bert blurted as his voice cracked.

"Why what's wrong, Bert?" Beau asked, as Bert ran toward the pickup.

"There's a fire at the fairgrounds, in the barn area! We just heard it on the ten o'clock news!"

"Come on, get in my car quick, and I'll tell you the rest on the way over there." Beau and Maggi jumped into Bert's car. Bert's wife Rhoda was crying bitterly, "Oh, Maggi, I hope they can save my little Annie . . ."

"I'm sure someone will get her out of the stall," Maggi said trying to ease her mind.

"No, they said Barn 6A and 5A were the barns involved in the fire, and Annie is in barn 6A, Ohoooooooo . . . my little pretty Annie."

"Get a hold of yourself and don't think about it," Bert commanded her. . .

Maggi felt so helpless as she listened to her sobs. It made her sick to think the beautiful mare might be killed in the fire, as well as the other horses in the same barn. Then she remembered Rip, her dog. "Oh, Beau, Rip has been locked up in the house for hours."

"He'll be okay till we get back," Beau stated. But Maggi felt bad she hadn't had time to let him out . .

3

Mrs. Maddox's continual sobbing brought her back to what was happening..

She whispered to Beau, "I hope their barn can be saved."

"Me too," he said.

Phoenix was still a small town, so the traffic at this late hour was nil, and it took them just ten minutes to get to the fairgrounds.

As they swung into the fairgrounds' entrance, Maggi gasped, "Oh, Beau, look!"

Roaring red and blue flames were shooting hundreds of feet up into the black sky, entangled with ugly gray clouds of smoke.

Frantic horses were running crazily through the barn area, bumping into objects as though they didn't see, others running back into their stalls, looking for the only security they know. Silhouetted human figures with halters were chasing after the horses, trying vainly to catch them.

A horse ran by with his night blanket in flames.

"Oh, that poor horse!" Maggi cried out.

"You stay here," Beau told Maggi as he jumped from the still running car.

"It's my barn, all right," Maddox confirmed.

"Goddamn it to hell !" he cussed as he parked his car away from the fire.

The flames were licking higher as they engulfed the dried wooden stable. The heat was so intense, Maggi could feel it on her face even though she was a good distance away.

Then! A dramatic crash! The noise made several other horses break out from their stalls at a nearby barn, as the barn crumbled like a volcano of fire and sparks. Maggi knew there was no hope of any horse surviving in that barn!

"Oh, my little Annie, my beautiful little mare!" Mrs. Maddox cried out.

"Oh, don't look at it anymore," Maggie told her, trying to comfort her as best she could, with the tears streaming down her face.

Beau was the first to come back. "All forty head burned up," he said grimly. "There just wasn't time for anyone to save a horse."

Bert Maddox came up to the car and said, "There's nothing we can do now, we just as well go home until daylight."

As the car rolled out of the barn area backside, Maggi stared out of the window. A veil of tears distorted her vision as her thoughts went back to one year ago.

* * * *

She left California for a position in Arizona. As she drove, she felt an excitement of her new job at the Maddox ranch training show horses. Something she always wanted to do was work with horses. She fell in love with Arizona's vastness and mountains instantly! She brushed her thick black curls from her forehead and rubbed her brown eyes, burning from the strain of driving so long.

She stopped for gas in Wickenburg for the last time. The station attendant glanced with male appreciation at her well-formed body as she got out from under the wheel to let her dog, Rip, out for a spell.

"It will be my first time to go so far from home," she told Mr. and Mrs. Bert Maddox. They insisted that she come to live with them on their ranch and train their show horses and teach their daughter how to ride.

Bert Maddox was a big, stout man, not looking his fifty years and with a crew-cut hair style showing his salt-and-pepper hair to its best advantage. He wore nothing but snap-button Western styled shirts, Levi's, and cowboy boots regardless of where he went. He was a kind man and a good husband and father. He knew the dairy business better than anyone in the valley when it came to buying dairy cows to yield a top milk base.

Rhoda Maddox was pretty, fat, jolly, kept a spotless home, and set a bountiful table. She adored Bert and he idolized her. Maggie loved both of them and was adopted into their family circle instantly.

Maggi loved her job and was capable of doing it well. While growing up, she had learned from the best horsemen in California. She had won her honors in the show circuit and also in certain rodeoing events. She became the best girl calf roper in California, even winning in competition against the men.

She brought her German shepherd dog, Rip, with her. She couldn't have left him behind. He had been too much a part of her early life and was company for her on the long trip to Arizona, giving her no trouble...lying in the back seat quiet and patient, yet eager to respond to her command.

On the weekends, when there were no horse shows going on, Maggi went to a local jackpot roping. One Sunday, after having just roped her calf in 14 seconds, she was tying up her horse to her horse trailer, when she heard a deep, smooth voice.

"Hello, I'm Beau Witlow," it said. She looked up and saw a tall tanned cowboy sitting on a big sorrel horse. She felt weak!

"Hey, you're damn good with that rope, and the best girl roper I have ever seen."

"Thank you," Maggi answered.

"How about heeling for me in the next team roping jackpot?" he asked.

"Sure," she answered.

"I'll be right back; I'll go put our names down," he stated and rode off.

She liked the way he sat his horse, and he was so good looking, she thought: clean-cut features, black hair, and a nice body. His Levi's fit him in the right places. As he came riding back toward her, she dropped her head. She didn't want him to see her staring at him.

He got off his horse and came up close to her. "You're sure pretty," he said as he grabbed a thick loose curl on her shoulder.

"I'd like to kiss that sexy mouth of yours," he stated with a grin, showing a mouthful of beautiful white teeth. Maggi felt a flush as his hand brushed her shoulder. She even liked the smell of his shaving soap.

They won the team roping. While waiting for the next one, they spent the time talking, Maggi enthusing about her job at the Maddox ranch and Beau describing the cow ranch and dairy herd he ran with his father.

"When the roping is over," Beau said, "I hope you like Mexican food, 'cause that's where I'm taking you to dinner."

"Sure do," she answered.

"Great! You follow me," he said.

Later on, she followed his horse trailer through traffic, and knew she was in love with this cowboy.

They became inseparable, sharing every secret...Beau told of his childhood, a divorce and his son, Stevie, who was being raised by his father, Buck, and stepmother, Jan.

"I promised never to take Steve away from them. I want you to understand why he could never live with us, when we get married."

7

"But you can have him on weekends and for holidays?" she asked.

"Sure," Beau said. "Anytime we want. Why not?"

Two months passed when Beau stated, "Looks like we'll have to get married. We're not getting any rest, and I want to be with you all the time. I'll get someone to milk the cows this weekend and we'll drive to Lordsburg, New Mexico and get married. That way we don't have to wait for any blood tests."

It was a simple exchange of wedding vows in the living room of the justice of the peace. A highway patrol officer was best man, and the justice's wife was the best girl.

The bride and groom were dressed in Levi's.

They left with a huge marriage certificate, with old fashioned scrolled print. Even the shabby motel where they spent their wedding night seemed beautiful to the two lovers. Beau was so gentle and tender with Maggi that her responses were immediate and without fear. Daylight awoke them in one another's arms, and tender caresses and love fulfilled them again.

As they drove back toward home, each whispered softly to the other.

Within a month, they bought an acre of land with a tiny two-room house on it. Maggi had a way of fixing it homey and cozy.

> *When the one man loves the one woman and the one woman loves the one man, the very angels leave heaven and come and sit in that house and sing for joy.*
>
> *Brahma*

* * * *

8

A sudden stop startled Maggi back from her daydreaming. They were home already! It seemed to her they had just left the fairgrounds and the fire.

"Come on in," she said to Mr. and Mrs. Maddox, "It's been a terrible night, I'll make some coffee and breakfast. We all need it."

Poor Rip was so glad to see Maggi—and he had to go!

After the Maddoxes left, Beau lay down for a hour. Maggi was too upset to sleep.

At six the next morning, Beau and Maggi were waiting for Mr. Maddox at Barn 6A in the State Fairgrounds. There were several loose horses still running about. Three came trotting through the smoldering mass of black ashes and charred carcasses. The carcasses were an ugly sight: stumps for legs, bowels ejected, seared hides, eyeballs cooked to an opaque white. Maggi grimaced.

"Oh God, how awful!" she told Beau as the horses trotted off out of sight behind another barn.

A mammoth scoop lift was forcing its way into the wet mess, dumping its load into a huge truckbed to be hauled off. There were so many dead horses and so much debris that a long line of trucks stood, with motors running, waiting to be signalled. Each time the loader picked up a carcass it also picked up chunks of mud and burned beams. Three men had the grotesque job of pulling out these pieces of charred wood. The plopping of the dead horses as they smacked against the bed of the truck was sickening to Maggi. It was especially so as each truck lumbered away, showing charred limbs flailing wildly about as the vehicle lurched and swayed out of the barn area.

"Come on, let's get away from here," Beau insisted and they walked toward the car. Mr. Maddox was talking with the fire chief.

"These barn fires are bad," the chief stated. "But then, stable fires usually are, because the barns are old dried wood, and drafty. They're way out from good water supplies and sometimes what equipment there is isn't in good shape. And, look at the stuff you've got around here —tack rooms, feed rooms, and straw and hay. And you've got visitors who don't know all the hazards of barn fires and are careless. And look at all the straw used for bedding the horses. You've got a dozen things just waiting for the least spark."

By now, several horsemen had bunched around the chief to listen to what he had to say, as he continued.

"You'll find a lot of common hazards in practically all stable areas at every race track—combustible materials, smoking, housekeeping, poor fire brigade training, and even car parking keeps us from getting close to the fire. It's the people who are to blame. Grooms overloading a light plug, cooking and lighting heaters. Most of these barn fires start between 3 and 5 a.m., when everone is sleeping. Damp straw takes time for the heat to build up—then everything goes up—SWOOSH!"

"Just keep in mind," he continued to explain, " a straw or hay fire actually produces more heat energy for spreading fire than gasoline. A horse standing in a bed of straw may as well be standing in a pool of gasoline. Straw burns three times as fast as gasoline, with temperatures from 1800° to 2000° F."

"If you get to a fire in one minute, a water variety fire extinguisher would probably put out a hay or straw fire. After that, you'd need a regular hose...maybe up to about four minutes. From four to ten minutes is crucial to save the horses and building. If you've got a private trained fire brigade equipped with hydrants and a large hose, with water at good pressure, you have a good chance of *stopping the fire before the entire stable and horses are destroyed. But you have to rely on the public fire department getting here quick. That means they have to be close by and have unimpeded access to the fire."*

"It would take at least four to six fire streams to stop a stable fire if water is applied within ten minutes. By twelve minutes after ignition, the average stable is so heavily involved in fire that there is little hope of saving the animals or the structure," he finished. *"You folks will have to excuse me. I have to tend to my men now."*

"Thanks a lot," Mr. Maddox said, "for your efforts to save the barn."

"Come on, honey, let's go home," Beau spoke. Maggi was ready to leave. As they drove home, she was thinking of all the beautiful horses, little Annie, and the groom. When Beau spoke, he broke into her thoughts.

"Hey, you're out of a job, do you realize that?" he asked.

"I never even gave it a thought till now," she answered.

Mr. Maddox soon found her a good job working with a saddle factory, acting as their salesman. She liked the pay, the hours, and best of all, she was her own boss.

2

It is not what you have lost,
but what you have left that counts.
Harold Russell

Six months, and more bad luck followed. The cattle market dropped. Beau's wages were cut to $180 a month.

"This is just enough for us to get by on," he told Maggi. But things got tougher. Maggi figured they could save hers and Beau's gas money if she quit her job and they moved out to the ranch into the bunkhouse.

It was a happy time for all of them: Beau, Stevie, and Maggi, especially one evening as Beau told of Stevie's encounter with the milk aerator.

"I heard this hollering from the milk barn, and it was coming from the milk room," he began. "When I walked into the milk room, there was Steve...with his tongue stuck fast to the frozen aerator," he said, laughing out loud, and the whole family laughing with him.

"I poured some water over the frozen milk, and his tongue came loose," he kept laughing.

"He likes that frozen milk, and is always chipping it off, but this was the first time he tried that," he said, rumpling Stevie's hair. "Bet you won't do that no more!"

"Uh, Uh!" said Steve.

Even Rip enjoyed bringing in the milk cows.

Maggie got to know Buck Witlow better during their stay at the ranch. She liked him. He was as good-looking as Beau, but a bit heavier. And she respected him as a cowboy, the best she had ever been around! Cattle and race horses he knew well. He was a strong-willed man and the head honcho in the family. Even Beau was intimidated.

The third crisis came when Beau came in from the milk barn, a month later,and told Maggi, "Daddy has to sell out or he'll go under. And they insist we take Stevie, since I'm married now."

"What will you do?" Maggi asked. For the first time since they married, she was scared!

"The only other thing I know is go back to the race track," he answered.

"Doing what?" she asked.

"Galloping horses for a start," he replied, "until I can get some horses to train." Maggi tried to be confident as Beau spoke, but inside, she cringed at the thought of Beau being on a racetrack...with gamblers, bums, gangsters! That's all she had ever heard about the kind of people on the racetrack.

But to Beau it was different. He was raised on the backside, riding horses for his Dad since he was eight, a successful jockey till World War II came along and shut down all the race tracks.

"Look, I can make us a living, at least. Don't worry, honey. We'll make it. Besides, this is all I know besides ranching and milking cows," he told her, and put his arms around her.

"Honey, I don't care as long as we're together," she said.

Beau went straight to the little Arizona Downs meet and within a week he was galloping fifteen to twenty horses a morning at a dollar a head. Maggi got her old job back and Steve moved in with them.

3

"Honey, I've got a steady job breaking colts for Doc
Hardy," Beau told Maggi. "I'll make more money than I
have these past three weeks."

"Great!" Maggi answered. "Where does he live?"

"I'll take you over there Saturday, okay?" he told her.

"That will be a good day, because I don't have to
work," she added.

"You'll get a kick out of old Doc!" Beau chuckled.

Maggi wasn't prepared for Doc. He was a giant of a
man, with a big nose. It was the first thing she saw on his
face. He was bigger than two John Waynes and enhanced
his height even more by wearing a six-inch brim Stetson
with the high crown unshaped, just like it came from the
hatbox. His gruff voice matched his bulk, yet when he
spoke he was gentle and polite in his manners. She liked
him instantly.

"I find him fascinating to listen to," she told Beau.

"He's something, all right. He used to be the auctioneer
at the livestock sale," Beau told her. "Whenever a dog
would stray into the sale ring, Doc would always say,
'Somebody kick that dog so that we'll know who the
owner is'. . . it always got him a laugh," Beau stated.

14

While Beau rode the colts, Maggi looked over the little ranch of ten acres. Some brood mares, colts and three well-bred studs were Doc's source of income. Maggi marveled at the strong, rough timber he had made his corrals from, as though he were matching his own sturdiness.

Maggi didn't see Doc coming up behind her, and he scared her when he blurted out, "Young lady, that husband of yours is the best damn colt breaker around Arizona. The best pair of hands on a horse since Earle Sande," he told Maggi.

"Who was Earle Sande?" she asked.

"The greatest jockey that ever lived," Doc answered. "He got killed in a spill ... a darn shame, too," he added. "He had so much talent!"

Beau was happy working with the new colts. He loved teaching them and seeing them progress daily, responding to his gentle handling. He took his time with babies . . . getting their confidence first, them introducing himself and the saddle and bridle, and then, their learning how to carry the weight and line out—turning left and right at his command. It all took time as Beau didn't believe in riding colts longer than twenty or thirty minutes at a saddling, and he always gave them a nice bath afterwards to make them feel good and help gentle them.

It was one Saturday, while he was giving a colt his bath with a hose that Maggi noticed Beau had on his best and only dress shoes. She mentioned it to him.

"Why your good shoes ... out here?" she asked.

"Cause my boots are too bulky and big, and my feet could get caught in the stirrups," he stated.

It made sense to Maggi about the stirrups, but she

thought, "Why couldn't he have bought a pair of riding boots instead?" It wasn't till they stopped for a bite to eat that she found the answer.

Beau spoke up, "I know I'm too damn big to be riding these colts. I'll have to quit in a few more years. And I guess that's what bothers me. My feet look so damn big, I feel like a moose on a horse. And the dress shoes make my feet look smaller," he added. "All jocks try to look as slim as they can, and that's where I got the damn complex, I guess—when I was race riding. I damn near killed myself dieting. Hell, I took boxes of Ex-lax a day," he continued to tell her. Maggi listened with compassion. "I'd sit in the hot box all morning—anything to try and keep my weight down, but I was tearing up my stomach, and I knew eventually I would have to hang up my tack. But it was hard for me to give up something I loved, so I deliberately got myself ruled off."

"How did you do that?" Maggi asked.

"Easy," he grinned. "During a race, I was laying second coming down the homestretch, and I deliberately reached over and grabbed the saddle towel of the horse who was in front of me. This will hold a horse back, get him off stride. Hell, everyone saw it . . . the officials on the grandstand roof. I was immediately disqualified and placed last in the race. And later the racing commission ruled me off permanently from race riding. Because the foul was intentional. I know it was a crazy thing to do, but I was fifteen and knew I could never just quit on my own.

Maggi put her hand into his and spoke softly, "I love you." Beau smiled down at her and squeezed her hand.

16

The following few weeks were sublime, but Maggi soon learned that when you're involved with racehorses on any scale, nothing is permanent!

"We're taking the colts to the fairgrounds tomorrow morning," Beau told Maggi one evening during dinner.

"How come? Why can't you stay at Doc's place?" she asked.

"Because the colts have to learn to break from the starting gate and get used to galloping with other horses," he explained.

Maggi felt a pang in her stomach because of his going to the race track, but she said nothing. She felt so insecure all of a sudden ... not over money, but of Beau!

* * * *

The track quickly changed their lifestyle. With her working hours and his, Maggi hardly saw Beau till evening, except on weekends.

One Saturday afternoon, Beau brought home a lifelong jockey friend.

"Maggi, this is Pee Wee Foy," Beau said.

"Pleased to meet you," Maggi replied. As she reached out for his hand, she was surprised at his strong grip. He was less than five feet tall but perfectly proportioned with broad shoulders, well-muscled and narrow hipped. His complexion was ashen, and his skin was drawn tight over his cheekbones. As he smiled, she knew he was wearing dentures because the coloring was so artificial.

"Boy, you are little! How much do you weigh?" Maggi asked him.

"Oh, 105 pounds," he answered.

"My foot! More like 125!" Beau interjected into their

conversation.

"Okay, 115," the jockey admitted.

"You mean *you* have trouble keeping your weight down, as little as you are?" Maggi asked.

"I'm fighting my weight all the time. I can fill up to 130 pounds if I don't watch myself," he stated. Maggi shook her head in sympathy.

"Yep, I make good money riding, yet I have to starve myself to death, ain't that the pits?" he grinned.

"Can you have a cup of coffee and some cake?" Maggi asked.

"Coffee, but no sweets," he answered. As they drank their coffee and talked, he asked Maggi, "How do you like being around the race track life?"

"It's okay, the little I know about it, even though I've been around horses all my life," she replied. "And I see it's totally different from what I know about horses. It's another world."

"Yeah, we're different all right," he grinned at Beau. "Beau tells me you're a good calf roper and a good hand with a horse yourself."

"Well, thank you," she answered and smiled a thank you toward Beau.

Beau turned his head toward Pee Wee and asked, "Where's your wife?"

"She's getting a divorce. You know me and my drinking and running around. She just couldn't take any more of my shit. Especially the last drunk I was on. . ."

"How's that?" Beau asked.

"I came home plastered one night, and she wouldn't let me in our house trailer. So, I just backed up my car to the trailer hitch, hooked it up, jammed it into second gear, and pulled the house trailer right out of the trailer court! Plumbing hoses, water hoses, awnings, steps, wiring

18

shooting sparks—right down Nineteenth Avenue! The wife and kids were inside, screaming to stop, and pounding on the windows," he laughed. "But I kept right on driving down the street."

"What happened? Where did you end up?" Maggi asked, spellbound.

"Oh, a cop finally stopped me, and I was taken to jail. It cost me $500 and my license for sixty days," he added. "But Emmie got even with me. She was going to the store one afternoon and because I was so drunk, she wouldn't let me come with her," he stated. "So, I just jumped up on the hood of the car. Man, she grabbed rubber, and darn near threw me off the hood. But I got a hold of the windshield wipers just in time," Pee Wee said.

"Well, she was trying to knock me off, so I started kicking out the windshield," he continued. "I finally kicked and shattered the glass to where she couldn't see out, and she had to stop the car," he grinned. "That's when she went and got the divorce."

"I don't blame her," Maggi added as she looked at Beau, thinking, what kind of a friend is this?

Beau changed the subject, "Come on, you two, I have to go back and feed at the track."

After they fed the colts and left Pee Wee with some race track friends, Beau told Maggi, "Pee Wee is crazy, and wasting his talent. The bottle has ruined him. When he first showed up on the race track he was eight years old. He wanted so much to be a jockey. He mucked out stalls, walked hots, shined shoes, washed dishes in the track kitchen, until he finally got good enough to gallop racehorses." Beau continued. "Before long, trainers started giving him mounts to ride in a race. He was, and is, one of the best race riders around. But he can't handle prosperity. As long as he's broke, he's trying—but let him make a few bucks, and he hits the booze. What do you think of him?" he finally asked Maggi.

"Well, I don't like his drinking problem, but he seems a nice enough guy sober," Maggi said hesitantly.

"There will never be another one like him," Beau confirmed as he drove into their driveway and parked the truck.

Steve came out the door to greet them.

A few days later, Beau glanced at the clock behind the bar. It was eight already. He knew he should go home, and that Maggi would be mad, but he didn't want to leave. He was having a good time with all his old race track buddies, playing pool and swapping stories of different horses. He decided he had better leave when someone called, "Hey, Beau, come over here and have another beer with us." As Beau walked over toward the booth, he knew he would stay till they closed the bar.

Maggi cleared the table and put Steve to bed. She was furious by now and worried. "Where in the devil was Beau?" she thought. This was the first time he had ever done this sort of thing since they had been married, and she didn't like it one bit.

Every time she heard a car she just knew it was he driving in. By midnight, she gave up and went to bed. When she woke up, it took her a second to realize that Beau had not come home. She sent Steve off to school and headed for the race track at the fairgrounds before she went to work. She found Beau at his barn, brushing one of the colts.

"Why didn't you come home last night? And where were you?" she blurted out.

"I was late getting my work done, and they locked the stable gate, and I couldn't get my truck out," was his story.

"You don't expect me to believe that stupid story?" she answered. She was really angry now, for she could see he was going to make light of the whole matter. "Well, if you think I'm going to put up with this—like Pee Wee's wife has—you're sadly mistaken!" she snapped, leaving for her car.

Beau came home early that night. Maggi was in the kitchen, and he said, "Honey, I'm sorry about last night. I won't do that again. I promise."

"I know you won't 'cause I'm getting a divorce! No husband of mine is staying out all night," she said.

"Oh, come on now—you're being silly. I didn't mean to hurt you. Hey, I love you," he stated as he put his arms around her and kissed her softly and wiped away her tears.

Maggi knew she never intended to go through with any divorce!

4

Maggi was glad to hear that Pee Wee had left for New Mexico and the Silver City race track. He was a bad influence on Beau and had caused her nothing but trouble since he showed up.

Just when Doc's colts were about to run, he decided to take them all back home to his ranch. Beau was upset over the change in his plans.

"He has always done that," he told Maggi. "Just hates to run a two-year-old. He'll end up selling them; he believes in letting someone else have all the problems and expense."

"Now what will you do?" Maggi asked.

"Gallop and break more horses," he answered. "What else can I do?"

"Can't you get some horses to train?" she asked again.

"Hey, I've been away a long time, and it takes time to get a stable back together. On the race track, they forget you the day you leave," he added.

"Well, don't get so mad, I don't know these things," she remarked.

* * * *

Two weeks had gone by and the State Fair was almost over, when Beau came home and told Maggi, "I got a small stable to train for . . . a nice old couple I've known for years. Mable and Bud Owens. They have four cheap claiming horses and want me to take them over right now and then maybe on to Ruidoso, New Mexico for the summer," he said.

"How come they don't train them?" Maggi asked.

"They're getting old and can't hack the work anymore," Beau explained.

"How much will they pay you?" she asked again.

"Five dollars a day per horse."

"Twenty dollars a day—not bad," Maggi remarked.

"Hey, wait a second! The feed, hay and grain, and leg medicine comes out of that also," Beau explained. "We won't be getting rich, but it's a living."

Taking care of four head and galloping meant long hours for Beau. Maggi and Steve both missed him being at the dinner table. One night after Steve had gone to bed, she asked Beau, "Hey, how about me helping you out at the barn?"

"You don't know anything about taking care of race horses—cleaning out stalls," he kidded her.

"You can show me, can't you?" she asked.

"I guess so. We'll see. Come on, fix me something to eat. I'm starved!" As she dished up his plate, she had already made up her mind she would quit her job and work with her husband.

Beau was full of surprises as Maggi was finding out each day. One evening, he came home and told her, "I bought us a three-year-old filly on the cuff for $200."(Pay as he wins)

"What kind of a racehorse can that be for $200?" Maggi remarked.

"Oh, she'll win a race just off her racing conditions

alone. . . and some good care," Beau remarked. "The old gyp I got her off of hasn't been feeding her half the time. She's poor as a rail."

"What is a Gyp?" Maggi asked.

"Usually some old guy with one or two bad-legged horses trying to eke out a living. And they will steal hay and grain and even sift out dirty straw bedding for their stalls so they don't have to buy any," Beau explained.

"Where did they get the name Gyp?" she asked again.

"Hell, I don't know. From being a gypsy, I guess. This poor filly hadn't been galloped all year. The old man just gyped her on a forty-foot lunge line, to save paying a gallop boy."

"How's that?" Maggi asked.

"Oh, they find an open area somewhere on the backside and stand in the center and let the horse run in a circle on this lunge line for about an hour each day," he told her. "And this is all the excercise they get, till they run. Hell, they do all right—most of them—and they're pretty shrewd old duffers. I like 'em. The race track wouldn't be

gyping a horse!

the same without them," he grinned.

Maggi spoke up, "I have seen a lot of show horse people lunge their horses just for a little exercise, but I didn't know you could train a racehorse like that!"

With another horse in his barn, Beau decided he could sure use Maggi at the barn. They made arrangements with their next door neighbors to get Stevie off to school.

That first morning at the track, Beau tacked up (saddled and bridled) one of the horses, and as he led the horse from its stall, he told Maggi, "Okay, you can muck out his stall while I gallop him."

She grabbed a pitchfork and stepped into the stall, and stuck the fork into the bedding straw. The straw was soggy from urine and manure and packed down. She couldn't lift it. She tried again, this time getting the fork under a corner of the bedding. The whole mat of bedding came up as she lifted the fork. "Christ, this is harder than it looks," she said aloud. She kept stabbing at the stubborn mass, just tearing up little tufts of loose straw. She was getting hot and had started to perspire. Suddenly, she heard a burst of laughter and saw Beau sitting on the horse in front of the stall.

"I told you you couldn't do it. I wish I had a picture of this!"

"I'll muck this damn stall if it takes me a week!" Maggi sputtered. "But you're right about one thing -- it's a smelly messy job!"

"Well, let that go for now. I'll do it later. Come over here and hold this horse for me while I give him a bath." After he'd washed the horse off with hot soapy water, rinsed him off and scraped him down, Beau threw a cooler blanket over him and tied it securely.

Then he told Maggi, "Get on the saddle pony and cool

out this horse by walking him in the circle in front of our barn for forty-five minutes. I'll go clean the stall before I take the next horse.''

Within a few days, they had a simple routine going. Maggi was a good organizer. Beau got the stalls cleaned while she walked hots (cooled out the horses). She washed out their feed tubs and water buckets while she waited for Beau to come back from galloping the horse. She saw to it that the buckets of hot water were ready and that the cooler blankets, halter, and shank were laid out by the time Beau came back.

She liked being with Beau and working with the horses and thought, ''This race track life isn't so bad.''

WALKING HOTS HORSEBACK

26

To make a few extra dollars, Beau galloped outside horses as soon as he was done training his own. Maggi wasn't one to sit still long and she noticed other gals ponying horses for a dollar a head once around the mile track.

Beau tried to talk her out of doing it. "You'll ruin your saddle pony; it's one of the hardest things on a saddle horse who isn't used to it," he told her. "And you'll get some rank sons-of-bitches that'll pull you right out of the saddle and run away."

"But I can do it. I'm no dummy," she remarked.

"Okay, go ahead. You'll learn what I'm trying to tell you," he told her.

Maggi led her first horse onto the training track. He lunged forward with such a burst of speed, he almost pulled her clear out of the saddle, and during all of this, her saddle horse tried to run off also.

She was busy for the next four jumps, reeling in the long leather shank strap on the racehorse and trying to get her pony horse back under control. She knew she was a good hand, but she didn't know just how good till right now!

She was glad there were no other horses on the training track because she was all over it, swinging back and forth getting the two horses under control. She snatched the thoroughbred's head back behind her right leg and held him there. He was lunging high in the air, jerking, see-sawing back and forth, crashing and bumping into her right leg and knee. Her pony was coming up and he was going down, like horses on a merry-go-round, she thought.

"Get off me, you son-of-a-bitch!" she shouted as she jerked at the shank chain on the racehorse's halter. It didn't faze him a bit. He just kept right on jumping and lunging.

Maggi reached out and got a firmer hold. This time he lunged upward and outward, and his huge head came crashing down with his mouth open and his teeth exposed, hitting her kneecap.

She felt a sharp pain and saw blood oozing through her Levi's. She had no choice but to endure the pain as they continued running around the track with still a half-mile to go!

As she turned the two horses down the homestretch, several horses went galloping by them, only inciting the thoroughbred horse to try and run with them. By now, Maggi was leaning straight back in a prone position, with her feet sticking out forward in the stirrups, trying to get some leverage as she fought desperately to keep this damn horse from inching away from her.

By the time she pulled them both up on the backstretch and turned them around and walked them back to the main gap, she knew Beau was right!

Ponging a horse

28

She led the horse back to his barn, collected her dollar and headed straight for Beau's barn. She pulled up her Levis to see how bad her knee was. It made her sick when she saw the big red gash across her kneecap. It was throbbing, and the pain was getting worse!

"You still want to pony horses?" Beau remarked tauntingly.

"Well, he didn't get loose from me," she said, defending herself.

"Let's see your knee," Beau asked. "Here, put some of this salve on it," he suggested. "Don't worry. You'll live. But look, if you're going to pony, you get another horse. You're going to break your little rope horse down," he added. "I can't explain it, but you can work a horse all day punching cows, or roping. But pony ten horses on one and they will break down, especially these little quarter horse types. They just can't stand up to it," he stated.

Maggi took his advice. Since she and Beau no longer had time to rope, or the money for entry fees, she sold her rope horse for a thousand dollars, and had Beau find her a good useful horse on which to pony and walk hots for $300.

Going from barn to barn each morning she soon found out that every trainer didn't get there as early as she and Beau did, and some weren't the horseman that Beau was. She was eager to learn by watching and asking questions. While Beau was brushing off one of the horses, Maggi asked, "What does it take to be a good groom in your book, Beau?"

"To be a top groom, you should have your horse brushed and your stalls walled (the clean straw separated from the wet) before your trainer is ready to start.

"Tack the horse for the exercise boy. Lead the horse outside and leg the boy up on to the horse and lead him a few steps before turning the horse loose. This gives the boy time to tighten up his girth and check his stirrups,'' he added.

"While the horse is being galloped, you run and get your hot water, lay out your cooler, halter, and shank so they are ready when the hot horse gets back. Then you start cleaning his stall till the horse gets back. Then you bathe the horse, scrape him off, put the cooler on him, give him a drink, and hand him to the hot walker. You also check the time so the hot walker won't try to cheat on the 40 minutes —and you set up the water bucket on a bench so the horse can reach it easily so he doesn't tear the cooler ties off. Then you go back to finish the stall, adding fresh clean straw, making a deep smooth bed banking the sides so the horse won't get cast . . . ''

"What do you mean 'get cast'?'' Maggi quickly asked.

"Cast is when the horse rolls over against the stall wall, and his front feet are up in the air against it. He doesn't have sense to roll back, and there he is stuck on his back. He'll panic, thrash his head about, and skin up his legs trying to get up . . . especially at night when no one is around to help the horse up,'' he added. "Anyway—back to being a good groom—the groom then washes out the feed tubs and water bucket, hangs them back into the stall, puts in some fresh hay and fills up the water bucket. After he brings the horse in, he rubs the horse down, with a rub rag, brushes him and picks out his feet and paints his hooves with Hooflex dressing. Then he rolls up his leg bandages and does up the horse's legs, according to whatever the trainer tells him to do. When he has done up all his horses, he checks on them once more before he goes to breakfast, making sure they have water and that they are okay. He muzzles a horse that will be racing that day, this keeps the horse from filling up on his straw bedding.''

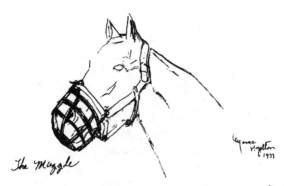

The Muzzle

Maggi had a million other questions to ask him, but she knew Beau wouldn't take the time to tell her. She would just have to wait, there was so much to learn!

By the end of the week, Maggi had learned a great deal more about ponying horses. She learned to keep the thoroughbred horse behind her right knee, thus giving her more leverage and also protecting her pony from getting cow kicked and the thoroughbred from banging his knees on her stirrup. She also learned the value of a shank chain (a 50-inch-long two-inch-wide piece of Latigo leather with a 10-inch piece of chain sewed in at one end and a swivel snap secured to the chain part). This lead strap gave the handler of the thoroughbred a great advantage in keeping the horse under control without hurting the horse or using any undue violence. Maggi found that a lead shank was a must in ponying horses. She could put it through the horse's mouth, serving like a bridle or run it up over and through the nose band on the halter. Whichever way that suited a horse best gave her control while ponying.

31

The versatile lead shank

She had just finished ponying her last horse and was putting her saddle horse up when Beau came up with a paper in his hand. "Hon, when you get a chance, fill out this stall application for the Arizona Downs meet, and I'll take it back to the office."

"How come you have to fill out a stall application? You just did before we came here," she asked.

"Because the management has to approve each horse that comes to their meet. Usually this is the racing secretary's job. He screens the horses," Beau told her.

"You mean we've got to move these horses, after getting this barn all fixed up and everything?"

"Sure. This track is allotted only so many racing days by the state racing commission. Racing's big business. Tracks all over the states are allotted a certain number of racing days, and the schedules are made up so that they try not to conflict with each other. After the Downs meet is over, I'll have to go to another track—that's if I still have the horses."

> *The secret of happiness is something to do.*
>
> *John Burroughs*

5

Arizona Downs First Time

Beau's stall application was approved for his racehorses, but he was allotted only one stall for his saddle horses. Maggi had to trailer her saddle pony back and forth from the house each day. She loved the little half-mile Arizona Downs race track and its quaint surroundings. It was all so new to her, but to Beau it brought back memories of his boyhood days when he was a jockey riding for his father. Beau wasn't one to look back and quickly pushed the thoughts from his mind and back to his training. He worked hard rubbing the bad-legged horses. He was winning a few races and placing seconds and thirds through the meet. By March, he had decided to go to Ruidoso, New Mexico for the summer. It was the only place where he could get stalls for the kind of horses he had, so he had no other choice.

That night he told Maggi of his plans, but that she couldn't go because of Steve still being in school, and also because they could not afford to rent any kind of a place in that resort town.

"We can't afford it, that's a summer mountain resort

with lakes, pine trees, mountains, and a lot of people come there for their summer vacation," he told Maggi. "And all the prices are jacked up."

"We could get the Maddoxes to look after Steve till school is out. We could live in the tack room," she pleaded.

"No women are allowed to live on the backside," Beau told her. "That's a track rule."

"I could sneak in at night."

"Yeah, but if someone saw you and reported it, I'd be in trouble with the stewards. Sorry, hon, but no dice."

Maggi was down. Everything was going wrong. She couldn't even get horses to pony with the meet almost over. She was packing their tack (saddles, bridles and medicine) when Pee Wee walked into the tack room.

"Hi Maggi," he said, as he put down a small suitcase. "I'm catching a ride with Beau to Ruidoso. He said I could stay here in the tack room till then."

"Oh sure, Pee Wee. Just put your suitcase anywhere and it'll be fine," Maggi answered, thinking, 'That's all I need is him to be chumming with Beau!'

The day before Beau was to leave, he and Maggi were busy checking the last-minute details. While they were doing that, Pee Wee went around to all the stalls of every barn, salvaging screw eyes, stall chains, buckets, brushes —or anything else someone overlooked and left behind.

"Look at that Pee Wee! He'll do anything to make a few bucks for a bottle," Beau laughed as Pee Wee came walking toward them carrying several stall chains and a bucket half full of screw eyes.

Their last night together, Beau held Maggi close to him as he spoke. "Maybe you can come up for a weekend if we get lucky and win a race." Maggi knew he was trying to comfort her and that there was no chance that she would be coming up there.

34

Ruidoso for the First Time

As Maggi watched Beau wave good-bye from his truck, she cursed the race track and its uncertainty. As she drove back toward home, she was sorry that she had let Steve go with his granddad to Prescott for the weekend. She was terribly lonesome, and Beau hadn't been gone one hour.

It was almost a month to the day after Beau left that he called late one evening. Maggi just knew something was wrong, or he would not have called. Her mouth was dry as she listened to Beau talk.

"Hon, I'm not doing any good up here with these old sore-legged bums. It's too tough here. I talked the Owenses into selling their horses, and I sold Bagger for eight hundred. I turned the others over to another trainer who is taking them on the shares. I'm leaving in the morning early and should be in tomorrow night by six, if I don't have any trouble."

"Oh Beau, I can hardly wait! I have missed you so much," she answered. As she hung up the phone, her world took on a brighter color than it had for the past four weeks. She wished Steve were here so she could tell him his Daddy was coming home.

Beau never tired of Maggi's warmth and love, and her willingness to submit to his advances only stirred him even more. He lay staring at the ceiling in the stillness of their room as he listened to her sleep, breathing deep into his shoulder as he held her close. It was good to be home, he thought.

Love, talk, laughter and a pillow fight were all on the morning agenda. During breakfast, Beau suggested, "Let's go to Prescott and get Steve and see how Daddy is doing with his horses."

"Hey, what a great idea!" Maggi squealed as she heard Beau laugh. "What's so funny?" she asked.

"You! You're always ready to go. Say 'go' and you're in the truck. With you a night at home is a night wasted," he grinned.

As Beau drove through the stable gate and into the backside of Prescott Downs, Maggi was taking in the dismal sights. Run-down barns, with the stall doors half-chewed away by nervous horses, mud holes and ruts from a recent rain . . . bridles and saddles were hanging on nails.

"Gosh, what a shabby-run-down place this is," she commented to Beau.

"Well, this has been here a long time, and they never have fixed it up," he answered. "They should tear them old barns down and put up cement ones. They're nothing but firetraps," he added.

Maggi agreed.

"Daddy's barn should be right over here in this row," Beau told her. "Oh, there's his pickup. That must be it."

"Hello, what brings you two up here?" Buck Witlow asked in a deep, husky voice. "I thought you were in Ruidoso."

"Couldn't do any good up there so I sold my mare and came home," Beau answered.

"Well, you should have brung them to me. I'd get some run out of them," Buck said kiddingly.

"You probably could have," Beau said, with a touch of sarcasm. "Where's Steve?"

"I think he is down in the tack room with Gene's boy, playing."

Maggi and Beau walked down three stalls to the tack room.

"Daddy! . . . Mommy!" Steve hollered, and came

running toward them. He jabbered about his friend Joey and showed them two cute three-month-old Australian puppies sleeping at the foot of the cot.

Maggi couldn't get over the number of items crammed into the tiny room; two cots, sacks of grain, suitcases, saddles, bridles, blankets strewn on the floor . . ; and a small table crowded into the corner, and the dirt floor covered with peanut shells.

"Don't look too hard in here. You're likely to find anything," Beau told her with a grin. "Daddy never was too tidy." Maggi just smiled back. She knew better than to say anything about one kin to the other.

"Get your things packed. You're going home with us," Beau told Steve.

"Oh, can't I stay and play with Joey for a little while longer?" he asked.

"Yeah, but pack your stuff first."

They went back to Buck's stalls where he was rubbing a horse's ankles with a leg brace, rubbing several strokes and then applying the liquid brace, and rubbing it into the horse's legs.

"Is that six points leg brace you're using?" Beau asked.

"Yep, there is nothing that will tighten down a leg better than this stuff," the old man answered. "Got everything in the world mixed into it . . . tan-bark, witch hazel, Epsom salt, vinegar .. and a few other things I can't think of right now. It's damn good stuff," he confirmed. "Been using it for fifteen years."

Maggi loved the pungent odor of the brace, yet she couldn't detect any one specific item and she noticed it stained Buck's hands. She listened to Beau and Buck talk.

"So, you didn't do any good up there?" Buck remarked.

"I just didn't have any stock, Daddy, and there wasn't any place (races) to run them," Beau told his Dad.

"Well, you can't win races when you don't have conditions and decent horses," Buck added. "You're just wasting your time. That's why I come up here with these ole sore-legged bastards. I at least win one now and again."

"Well, I guess we had better get going. It will take us four hours to get home," Beau said. "See you. Good-bye."

The next morning, Beau phoned several people who had colts to break.

"I got ten head lined up to break starting tomorrow," he told Maggi.

"Great!" she answered. "With my salary and that, we can make it."

* * * *

October came fast, with Beau leaving before daylight to avoid the heat of the day, and Maggi coming home after five. Steve had been in school over a month and so it was early to bed for all three of them. The days passed quickly.

One night, after the usual pinto beans and hamburger dinner, Beau told Maggi and Steve, "The new Turf Paradise race track is going to open this November. They will start right after Thanksgiving, I think," he added. "They say it is really nice . . . all cement barns . . . a receiving barn . . . but it's way the hell out there, at least 25 miles from here."

"God, that would be 50 miles round trip," Maggi stated. "If you came home in the mornings and went back in the afternoons, it would be 100 miles a day. That's a lot of driving.

"Yeah, it sure is," Beau agreed.

The phone rang and interrupted their talking, "Wonder who that can be?" Beau asked.

"Pick it up and find out," Maggi said, smart-ass like.

"Hello? Well, hi Doc, how are you?" Beau answered. "Sure I would. I was going to come by your place tomorrow. Funny you called. Good, I'll see you tomorrow." After he hung up, he told Maggi, "That was Doc Hardy. He wants me to take ten head of colts into the Turf Paradise track as soon as possible. They're letting horses come in starting tomorrow," he said. "He's paying me fifty a week, but I'll need you to help me, 'cause I can't gallop ten head, and get their stalls and rub them too."

"Oh, I want to," Maggi said eagerly.

"Hey, this won't be like it was with four head. We'll be all day getting done," Beau added. "We'll have to get up a lot earlier—five o'clock at least, 'cause it will take a half-hour to get there. What about Steve?"

"I'll call Maddox. I'm sure his daughter will look after him till we get home." Maggi stated.

Turf Paradise the First Time

Turf Paradise race track stood out like an oasis in the desert. There wasn't another building in sight in a hundred miles in any direction, thought Maggi as she got her first glimpse of the new track.

"Who in the hell's idea was it to build way out here?" she asked Beau.

"Bunch of guys bought this land. I don't know all their names," Beau answered. "It sure is out in the boondocks . . . they'll never get anybody to drive way the hell out here," he said.

"Well, we are!" Maggi laughed.

Beau drove his pickup past the stable gate as the gateman waved him through. As he looked for Barn C 2, he noticed there were only a few stables of horses. Maggi was looking over the rows of cement barns. "They look so drab with no paint," she thought, and the place was so deserted.

"Where are all the horses?" she asked.

"Don't worry, they'll be here as soon as the Albuquerque fair is over," he stated. "It does look depressin' with all those empty stalls, don't it?"

He parked the pickup close to the barn and unloaded the little bit of barn supplies he had; hose, shovel, rake, pick. The feed man had delivered straw, hay and grain and stacked it neatly at the end of the barn.

"Come on, Maggi, we have to get these stalls leveled and bedded down before Doc's colts get here. I'll level them, and you wet them down with the hose so they will be packed and not dusty," he told Maggi. "Then I'll put two bales of straw into each stall and you cut the wires and I'll shake out the bales."

Beau worked with ease, for he had done this so many times in the past, working the pitchfork with skill and smoothing the golden straw into a smooth, soft, deep bed.

Doc soon showed up with the stall chains and the rest of his tack. Beau unloaded them and began to snap the chains across each stall.

"Why do you use chain guards anyway?" Maggi asked.

"It keeps the stall cooler during the daytime. Letting the air circulate better through the heat of the day," he told her.

"Gosh, it looks like a horse could jump right over the chains if he wanted to," Maggi stated.

stall chains

"They could if something really scared them and they hit the guard chains hard enough, Anyway, I close the bottom doors during the night just for that reason," Beau told her.

"While Doc and Beau discussed the colts they were bringing in, Maggi swept out the tack room. When she saw spiders and scorpions, she screamed, "Oh Beau, come here —quick!""

"Oh, for Christ's sake, you can tie up a two-hundred-pound calf but are afraid of a little spider," he laughed as he grabbed the broom and began to knock the insects down.

When the room dried, Maggi inspected it carefully before she stepped back into it. Then she put away the saddles and bridles, hanging them up neatly and orderly.

* * * *

Steve was glad when they got home, hugged them both and told them about school. Maggi didn't realize how tired she was until she had to prepare dinner. It had been a long day!

*   *   *   *

Beau was nudging her, "Come one, get up! . . . Come on, get up!" he kept on.

She opened her eyes, "Gosh, it's still dark out . . . what time is it?"

"Five a.m."

"Five? . . . Why so early?" she asked, rubbing her eyes, trying to wake up.

"We have to get there before the colts come on the van," he told her, pushing her from the bed. "Come on, now. Get ready."

"Okay, okay," she said, throwing back the covers, uncovering him too.

"Hey, what are you doing?" he grumbled, pulling the covers up again.

"Why should you get to stay in bed if I can't?"

"Because it takes you forever to get ready. That's why."

By the time Maggi had coffee, the Maddox girl had arrived to get Steve off to school, and they left for the track.

6

As they approached the stable gate, a chain was hooked across the entrance, and the gateman came out from the little shed.

"Where's your sticker?" he asked Beau.

"We just got in yesterday and didn't have time to go to the office and get one," Beau told him.

"Okay, but have it tomorrow," he stated, "or I won't let you in," and he dropped the chain down so Beau could drive over it.

"Hell, the damn meet hasn't even started and that old bastard is being ridiculous . . . fussing this early," Beau ranted.

"Well, he's only following orders," Maggi replied.

"Oh, you don't know them guys. Just because they got a gun and a badge, they get carried away with all kinds of authority," he added. "They'll let some big shot just go on through and stop some little nobody like me and give me all kinds of static.

"Maybe so, but he seemed nice about it just now," Maggi said. "You should get your license and sticker today."

"Let me worry about that," he snapped.

"Okay, okay—don't jump on me," she said.

The Stable gate man!

At seven o'clock, a huge white horse van rolled in slowly, so as not to throw down any of the colts. It pulled up parallel to the barn and stopped. H-i-s-s-s went the air brakes releasing their pressure. The driver and his assistant climbed down from the high cab.

"Beau Witlow?" the driver asked.

"Yes," Beau replied.

"Just wanted to make sure we had the right barn," the driver stated, then he and his helper quickly and efficiently pulled three long panels from under the truck. They attached one to the van and added panels on each side making a ramp for the horses to come down off the van.

waiting to load the van

44

Then they swung open the huge double doors. Six horses, three abreast facing each other, began nickering and pawing.

Beau grabbed a lead shank, walked up the steep ramp, and took the pin from a bar that was across the chest of one of the colts and dropped it down. Then he snapped the lead shank chain into the halter ring, and called to one of the drivers. "Hey, grab a hold of his tail going down the ramp to steady him." Then Beau carefully led the horse down the steep ramp.

"Here, hon, you walk him a few times and let him drink only a few sips each time around. They shouldn't be too thirsty from that short trip. But I don't want them to get the colic 'cause they are hot from being so nervous," he added. Maggi took the colt and carefully watered him out before Beau put him in a stall. She was well aware that drinking too much cold water and getting the colic could be fatal to a hot horse.

As each colt was led into his stall, he began pawing, rolling, running around in circles, and kicking the stall walls. Dust was flying from inside the stalls, and the bedding was getting all churned up with dirt. Some colts even had pawed deep holes in the stall floors.

"Oh, what a mess they are making of our nice clean stalls," Maggi moaned.

"That's colts for ya," Beau grinned. "They'll be like this for a few days till they get use to all this. Hey, here comes Doc," he told her. "Doc, your timing was perfect. We just got done watering them out."

"I figured it that way," Doc laughed.

The van driver came up with a clipboard of papers attached to it for Doc to sign. As Doc signed several sheets and was still talking to Beau, Maggi quietly asked the other driver, "Why so many papers?"

"Well, we have to have a health certificate and brand inspection papers on every horse we haul. That's a state-to-state requirement," he answered. "It's to protect against theft and transporting a contagious animal."

"Oh, I see. Thanks for explaining it to me."

"Sure."

Doc and Beau talked of each colt and what time they would start walking the colts in the morning. It dawned on Maggi that Doc, not Beau, was acting as the trainer, and she didn't like that at all!

After Doc left, she started to mention it to Beau, but decided she would wait for a better time.

They walked the stud colts the next morning, and Maggi soon learned they were a pain in the ass to handle. They tried to bite her, get into the saddle with her, and were nipping at her poor pony, biting him on the neck and legs. She was constantly jerking them with the lead shank keeping them off her. They even grabbed the end of the lead shank, chewing it into a wet soggy mess before she discovered it. She was glad when the last set of colts were put up. She was grateful that Doc came out to walk a few sets, or they would never have gotten done by ten o'clock. They had cleaned the stalls and raked the shedrow (the walkway under the wide roof overhang) and the tow ring by 11 a.m., and headed for home for breakfast and a nap, before returning back at 4 p.m. to feed.

That afternoon, after running each stall (picking up piles of manure) Maggi pulled all the feed tubs out of the stalls and lined them up in front of each stall in the shedrow. She was listening to Beau tell her how to mix the bran mash as he showed her each step, using:

> a gallon of rolled oats
> ½ gallon can of sweet feed
> 2 cups of calf manna (vitamin supplement)
> 1 cup of Sho-cote (vitamin supplement)
> 1 teaspoon of mineral salt
> a pinch of buca leaves
> a pinch of baking soda
> a gallon of bran

As Beau poured a gallon can of hot water into each feed tub he told Maggi, "No, don't mix it yet, just let it steam for a few minutes. That cooks the oats a little."

While they waited he continued to tell her more. "You can mix this sloppy or dry according to what the horse's needs are. Okay, I think we can mix it up now."

As Maggi mixed each tub of feed, the aroma was pleasant to her nostrils. It smelled like hot oatmeal and brown sugar.

She could barely lift the full, heavy feed tub. As she entered the stall, the colts rooted eagerly into the bran mash, almost knocking her down, and almost turning the tub over, but she somehow managed to wave them away with one arm while she secured the tub snaps with the other.

The colts stuck their noses into the hot mash and came up with wet bran covering their muzzles, then smacked their lips together and went back for another big mouthful. They wasted a good deal with each bite as it dropped to the stall floor, but Beau told her, "Don't worry about that They'll go back and pick up every little grain later."

As the colts were eating, Doc drove up, and he and Beau began to discuss the colts in terms of which was the best bred, which had the best potential. Beau remembered some of their dams and had ridden most of them not too many years ago.

As Maggi listened she realized how far back Doc's and Beau's knowledge of horses went and how much they did know.

After Doc left, Beau and Maggi closed the stall doors and went home.

The next morning, as they approached the stable gate in the dark, Maggi spoke up.

"Oh, you didn't get your license yesterday and the gateman said yesterday morning that would be the last time he was going to let you in."

"Oh damn it, I just forgot about it," Beau stated. "I was so damn busy and with Doc being there and all."

The chain was taut. Beau stopped by the stable gate. The little gateman came out, ranting.

"You can't drive in without a sticker," he declared.

"Hey, I'm sorry, but I forgot again. I promise you I'll have it on tomorrow," Beau pleaded.

"No, you're not going in," he confirmed.

"To hell with you, you son-of-a-bitch!" Beau blurted out and drove through, knocking the chain loose.

"Oh God! Beau, you'll get into trouble for that," Maggi spouted.

"Just shut up! Shut your damn mouth!" he told her.

"No, I won't! You fill your licenses out when we get to the barn, and I'll take them over myself this morning and get that taken care of," she snapped back at him.

"All right, all right! Now just be quiet."

Maggi said no more; she had made her point, and she

knew better than to run it in the ground. She thought that in a way Beau was right. People who are given a little authority do take advantage of it and come on a bit too strong at times. Yet, Beau had been given enough chances to get his license so, in a way, they both were wrong.

She put Beau's exercise boy license aside to wait till the commission office opened at eight o'clock.

Beau told her, "Look, Doc will be here soon. Now he'll want to run things, so don't be hurt. That's his way, and his horses. You go ahead and pull all the feed tubs out and scrub them good and rinse them out and hang them up."

"Okay," she answered and began to work.

Doc arrived, saddled his huge saddle horse, and went to the race track with Beau on the first colt.

Maggi grabbed a pitchfork. She thought, "Might as well take another stab at cleaning a stall." She had been watching Beau and realized there was a special knack to it.

Muck Basket

49

She got along better this time and was doing fine till she had filled the muck basket (manure basket), a large reed basket made of two-inch fiber slats with one-inch rope handle attached. As she carried this heavy basket to the manure pile, the wet smelly urine-wet straw lay against her sleeves and shirt front. By the time she dumped it over into the manure pile, she realized she smelled like manure. "Yuk!" she said, as she tried to brush away the smell. For the next basketful, she was trying to drag it over to the pile when Beau and Doc came riding around the corner—and Beau broke out into laughter.

"What are you doing?" he chuckled.

"Trying to keep this stuff from getting all over me," she told him. He jumped off the colt and handed the reins to Doc and proceeded to pick up the basket with ease and dumped it without getting a single piece of straw on him.

Maggi just threw up her hands. "You make everything look so easy," she spoke sharply.

"Look, you go give that horse a bath, and I'll get the stall, so we can get done, okay?"

"Sure," and she walked toward Doc and the horses.

She took off the saddle and bridle from the big bay colt and put on the halter, while he was trying to bite her the whole time. Doc kept jerking him with the lead shank to keep him from it. She ran and got a bucket of water, scraper, cooler, and the soap and sponge.

Maggi reached into the soapy water and grabbed the huge sponge. It was hard to handle with all the water it held! She raised her arm up toward the colt's neck and squeezed the awkward sponge. The soapy water oozed from the sponge, down the colt's long neck, and down Maggi's arm. She felt the water run through to her sleeve, her bra, and down into her Levi's around her waist.

Bathing me

scraping off

It was cold! Again, she pulled out the sponge and squeezed it over the horse's back, and water went running down her arm again . . . and the horse wasn't half bathed yet! Beau was grinning at her as he watched her struggle with the heavy buckets, spilling and slopping water all over her boots each time.

"How in the hell do you keep from getting all wet?" she asked him. "Just look at me! I'm a mess."

About that time the colt stepped forward just enough to plant his front foot right on the edge of Maggi's toes.

"Oooh, hey—get him off my foot! Oww, my foot!" she squalled.

"Here, hold this horse," Beau laughed. "Let me finish. Christ, the way you're going, we will be here all morning."

He took the huge bucket, picked it up so easily, and proceeded to finish the bathing.

"You're too short," Doc kidded her.

About that time, the loud speaker blared out.

"Beau Witlow and Maggi Witlow, please come to the steward's office."

"What's that all about?" Doc asked

"Oh, I got into a ruckus with the stable gateman this morning and I suppose he turned me in," Beau answered.

"Oh, no! Look at me—I am a mess, I can't go over there," Maggi stated.

"You don't need to go. It's me they want to see," Beau told her. "You weren't driving. I'll tell them."

"Thank God!" she said, brushing some of the soap bubbles off her clothes.

Maggi saw Beau walking back toward the barn. He looked mad, she thought. She always knew when he was mad because he gritted his jaw off to one side, and he was doing just that. 'Yes, he is mad' she said to herself.

"What happened?" she asked anxiously

"I got fined $25 dollars, that's what happened!" he said sharply. "No, don't say another word. Just go and get the fucking license and sticker."

"Okay, don't get all over me," she answered, and left for the tack room to get their license applications. She returned from the track office and put the stable sticker on the left-hand side of the pickup windshield and thought how simple it would have been to have done it two days ago!

They all went about their barn chores, and neither said a word about the sticker again.

The next morning, on the way to Turf, Beau told Maggi, "Doc won't be here this morning. He has to go out of town, so we'll have to do all the work ourselves. You can muck out the stall while I gallop a colt, then when I get back, you can hold him while I bathe him. Then, while you cool him out, I can finish up the stall, shaking the straw and washing out the buckets and tub. Then I will saddle the next colt. By that time, you can put the first colt up and start on the next stall. That way, we can keep going and not waste any time."

By the fifth stall, Maggi had it down pat. She mucked out all the dirty wet bedding and stacked the clean straw to the wall, raked the bottom of the stall clean and sprinkled slack lime over the wet area to kill odor and discourage flies. She didn't like shaking the straw because the chaff gave her bad sinus problems and often nose bleeds. She was glad to get out of that job. She also liked the canvas mat that Beau fixed so she could just pile all the dirty straw onto it. He could later drag it to the manure pile in one trip, saving more time.

She noticed that Beau did far more than ride the two-year-olds back and forth to the race track. He took time with each colt, noting the way he came out of the stall, how well he had eaten, if he showed any signs of ailing, or if he seemed sore. She felt bad that Beau didn't have good horses of his own to train, for she knew he was a good horseman. Even sly old Doc Hardy knew he was getting a bargain at fifty a week, she mused.

While they were brushing up the colts, Bert Maddox showed up.

"Well, looks like you're making a groom out of Maggi," he kidded Beau.

"Yeah, she's doing all right. I'll probably keep her," Beau answered with a grin.

"When you get done, come over to the house tonight for dinner," he said. "We'll just keep Steve there till you come, okay?" he added.

"Fine," Maggi answered, "Sounds great!"

"Where's your dog?" he asked Maggi.

"He's in the tack room. He will be out as soon as we put

the last horse away. He has learned to stay out of the way," she grinned. "He's a smart dog."

"That he is," Bert admitted. "You have a way with horses and dogs. Teaching Rip to carry brushes and buckets. Well I got to run, see you tonight," and he walked away.

Maggi picked up one of the colt's feet, and then ran a wire brush across it to get all the sand and dirt out. She reached for the can of Hooflex dressing and pulled the paint brush from it and began to apply the dressing on the inside and outside of the hoof.

She hollered to Beau in the next stall, "Bert Maddox has been good to us, hasn't he, Beau?"

"He's a nice man all right. They are so nice to everybody, that's the kind of people they are. Come on, nice guy, let's get done. I'm starved!"

By the time the meet started, Maggi had learned to juggle her Thermos of hot coffee while driving to the track in the early morning hours. Steve went out week-ends to help and to be with them. He had become a fair little hot walker himself for an eight-year-old!

Beau had bought Maggi a good little saddle horse. She named him Sam. He was gentle and well broke, and this made it easy for her to manage the unruly colts.

Because of the lack of money, they could not afford to eat in the track kitchen every morning and drive all the way home twice a day. So Maggi improvised a hot plate, card table, and cooked breakfast in the tack room.

"Only you could have thought up this idea," Beau spoke as he wiped up his jelly with the last bit of toast. "You're something else!"

"Ya, but our blankets and jackets smell like bacon grease," she laughed.

Beau's Dad had moved in from Prescott and came by each morning leading two hots on his saddle horse to rawhide Beau a little. Maggi liked Beau's Dad even though he was set in his ways. He really never bothered anyone, she thought. He minded his own business and shame on the man that butted into his!

* * * *

One morning Doc called Beau into the tack room.

"Now listen, Beau, I don't want you to give these colts anything when we get ready to run them, understand?" he said bluntly.

"Hey don't worry about me. That's Daddy's old school stuff, giving amphetamines. Hell, it don't do the horse any good. It just makes the trainer feel better. You can't make a horse win if he isn't able or fit. This is your barn and you run it the way you want."

"I intend to," Doc answered. "Another thing, I don't want a lot of fancy vet bills, so if you want any vitamins or medicine, just let me know, and I can get them at cost," he added.

"Fine with me!" Beau agreed.

As Maggi listened to their conversation, she realized how tight Doc was, and that this accounted for the dismal barn they kept. Stall chains, cheap water buckets, and the very shabby tack, two patched coolers, the bare essentials.

So it was that Maggi rarely had reason to go to the Tack Shop on the backside (where all supplies were sold). Irma and Spike Bates ran the shop. The track actually owned the building and leased it out.

Irma was small and in her sixties, but held her age well, sporting a clear skin and blond hair. She was kind and friendly to everyone on the backside and well liked. She had acquired the grandmother image, and many came to

55

her and Spike for help, financially or spiritually, or both. She was the local grapevine but meant no harm to anyone. It was just part of her make-up.

Spike did not share Irma's affinity for chatter. He was staid, of English rearing, a tall, well-built man with a handsome face with a strong cleft chin and beautiful gray hair that was always neatly groomed. He was "all business" in the shop.

The two argued constantly over any little matter. At first Maggi swore they hated each other, but soon found this to be their way of life. And she grew to like them from the very first day she met them.

Irma was always glad to see Maggi come in and gave her a cup of coffee while she looked around the shop. Saddle shops and hardware stores had always intrigued Maggi since she was a child, and she never outgrew that fantasy.

She loved all the new halters with shiny brass buckles and bright colored plastic webbings. She thought, "Boy, I wish Beau could have all new stall guards and a stable of his own!" She knew this took money and that their only chance to have anything like this would have to be to have rich owners to train for. Someday they would, she daydreamed on her way back to their barn.

7

It was late February and the colts were ready to be okayed from the starting gate. Beau had been taking them up there the past three weeks and making them stand, backing them in and out and just walking them through. But he was too heavy to break the colts out from the gate and let them breeze down the lane. So he hustled two jockey friends to ride them up.

"Maggi, you go with the first colt, and I'll come with the other one as soon as the jock gets here," Beau told her.

"What will I have to do?" she asked.

"Nothing, just lead the colt up behind the starting gate and the gate crew will do the rest. Just don't let them whip this colt or roughhouse him around. Tell them I said so," he instructed.

"Don't worry, I won't," she assured him.

"And be sure to give the starter the colt's name," he added.

By now all of Doc's colts had been named and their Jockey Club Registration papers were in the office. Red Boy was the name of the colt Maggi was taking to the starting gate. She was nervous as she led the big bay colt down the homestretch toward the starting gate along the outside rail. "The gate seemed so far away," she mused. Red Boy kept acting up, jumping sideways, lunging and trying to wheel around and take off with the horses that kept whizzing by on the inside rail, she told the jockey, "I wish he would quiet down. I don't want him to get away from me."

"He won't. You're doing a good job, Maggi," the little rider assured her. "He's just feeling good. The work will take some of the edge off him."

The starting gate procedures have become greatly improved over the last 30 years. Horses no longer start from an open stall gate which had allowed fractious horses to bolt or break through, causing lengthy delays and uneven starts. Today's modern electric gates are opened with the push of a button from a long cord that extends from the gate to the starter's hand.

The whole starting gate structure now is completely mobile including the starter's stand and is moved to every starting point throughout the day's racing program. Each stall gate is well padded with foam rubber and covered with canvas, both in front and in back. The front door of the stalls are solid metal up to where the horse's head faces the track. Here, closely spaced rods are installed for strength and to allow the horse vision.

The official starter is a qualified man who picks his own crew of eight or more men, and is hired by track management to load and start the horses at the gate. This crew has to know and handle horses and be physically able to push reluctant horses and load them into the starting gate. A good starter prides himself on knowing each horse and its temperament. He is solely responsible for a good, even start for every horse.

The height of his platform stand gives the starter a full view of the entire gate. He can observe every horse and its jockey, giving them ample time to be ready. A microphone and speaker attached in the gate also enable him to hear each rider and talk to them. During the loading of the horses, the jockeys have plenty to say. As they pull down and adjust their goggles, take hold of the reins while a gate assistant steadies their horses by holding their heads straight, jockeys may shout and curse their impetuous mounts.

"Hold it . . . hold it . . . not ready, sir!"

"Not ready yet . . . hold it . . . Goddamn son-of-a-bitch is trying to sit down!"

These are tense, competitive moments before the gates spring open. As the horses thrash about in the stalls, mashing the jockey's legs and knees against the hard steel frame, the gate is a dangerous place. Many a two-dollar bettor lost his wager because of a horse's bad acting in the gate.

A starter has to be patient, but also demands that the jockeys get with it and forces the issue at the right time when he sees each horse standing quiet for that split moment:

"Okay, get tied on, you little bastards!" as he hits the electric button. R-i-n-n-n-g . . . as the doors swing open. They are gone!

PHOENIX, ARIZONA
STARTER'S SCHOOLING CERTIFICATE

....197......

THE HORSE.. ....
       HAS BEEN PROPERLY SCHOOLED AND MAY START
                    (WITH) (WITHOUT) BLINKERS

STARTER...

STEWARD...
                         (OVER)

59

Schooling colts at the gate

Watching the proceedings at the gate was one of the outriders whose function was to patrol the track, catching runaway horses during the morning training and at the gate when races are being run. The track hired three outriders. The outrider was on the alert to catch any horse that got away from a jockey, exercise boy, or pony girl or boy. He smiled and greeted Maggi as she came up to the gate.

By the time Maggi got up behind the gate, there was a line-up waiting. Several horses had just left the gate, and a new set was being loaded in. They were young colts seeing the gate for the first time. The ground crew just led them in quietly and made them stand for a few seconds. The colts were scared at this huge, noisy contraption. One jumped as his head hit the side of the gate. The gate-man handled him gently, talking to him in low tones till he calmed him down, plus the little jockey was petting the colt and assuring him no one was going to hurt him. After a few more seconds of this, they led him through as the front gate was opened easy. The colt's little ears were darting back and forth at all the motion. This was done again and again till it suited the starter that the colt was no longer afraid, then they let him walk through and continue on to gallop around the track so he would have no ill feelings about the gate. This would be done every day for several days till the colt was ready to stand and break from the gate with the sound of the bell ringing.

In no time, another set of horses were loaded into the gate. This time an older horse that had been acting up in the gate before his race was here to be corrected. He kept rearing up; the crew could not hold him in. Each time he reared, the jock stepped off to the side of the gate.

The starter yelled, "Let's put the tongs on him."

The gateman applied a pair of ear tongs over one ear. These tongs looked like a nutcracker. The tongs were squeezed down hard—hard, to get the horse's mind off the gate and force him to concentrate on the pinch to his ear, and he quit rearing.

Maggi heard the starter call out to her, "Okay, lead Red Boy up to the gate." Then he wrote down Red Boy's name on his list and she rode back out of the way.

Red Boy walked into the starting gate calmly enough, but once inside, started kicking like hell at the tailgate.

"You aren't going to use the tongs on him!" Maggie asked.

"No," the crew man said with a grin. "We try to avoid using the tongs on young horses as much as possible. It tends to make them head-shy. With one of these two-year-olds, if he continues to raise hell, we'll put a lead shank over his nose and give it a few slight jerks. When they're kicking, like this colt's doing, I generally use a buggy whip, and just give him a few cracks across the ankles of his hind legs. The pop of the whip scares him more than it hurts him."

EAR TONGS

He tried it, and Red Boy settled down.

Since Beau had been bringing him up to the gate for weeks and standing him and the other colts, Red Boy was ready to break with the bell. When the bell rang, the colt broke alert and ran straight out of the gate. Maggi was pleased that he did so well, and so was Beau who was approaching the gate and watched Red Boy go by.

The starter called out to Beau, "He is okayed from the gate. Pick up your slip at the office." (The slip is necessary to show the racing secretary that the colt is okayed to start in a race.) Beau nodded and told Maggi, "Go on and ride back with Red Boy." She loped off toward the finish line.

She had already bathed Red Boy and was walking him when Beau returned from the track. Doc was behind him and spoke up, "Well, I'm going to enter Red Boy next week, now that he is ready. There's an Arizona-bred maiden race next Saturday." And he left for the racing office.

"Beau, that isn't fair!" Maggi cried. "You've done all the training and now he's going to get all the credit!"

Beau whirled around testily and snapped back at her, "Just shut up about it, will you! I knew the old bastard was going to be down as the trainer. But I needed the damn job, so just shut up!"

Maggi changed the subject and told him how she liked watching them school the horses at the starting gate, but she had never realized how dangerous it was.

Maggi thought that Saturday would never arrive. She was worse than any two-dollar bettor about a race, since she had watched Red Boy from the beginning to now. He was running for the first time in his life, even though it was only a three-furlong race. Beau was nervous too, but tried to hide it with the attitude that it was just another race.

"Oh, pooh! You don't fool me . . . you're as nervous as I am," Maggi kidded.

"Hey, this colt can run . . . he has outworked everything here on the grounds. I want to bet fifty dollars on him when he runs," Beau told her.

"*Fifty dollars!*" she gasped. "Are you crazy? We don't have that kind of money to lose."

"He won't lose unless the jock falls off," Beau snapped back, "He can't, I'm betting fifty."

Maggi knew by the tone of his voice that she was defeated.

Running a horse had Maggi on a high all morning. She and Beau worked like demons to get their morning work done so they could be finished by the first race. Meanwhile, they had to eat, change into clean clothes, and have the colt in the paddock for Doc to saddle. Beau made Maggi stay out of the paddock.

"You won't need to come in, you'll just be in the way," he told her. It hurt her feelings, but she obeyed his command. At that point she hated men—but she watched every move Red Boy made as Beau held him by the bridle while Doc saddled him up.

Beau joined Maggi as soon as he led Red Boy onto the race track, and together they watched him jog off to warm up. Maggi's heart was pounding as all the babies stood in the gate. Some were jumping up and down . . . some trying to rear. She was afraid Red Boy would get to acting up too, but he was as good as gold. He broke first and took the lead instantly. He was running so fast he put five lengths between him and the other horses. Maggi was screaming and jumping up and down . . . he was going to win! Nothing could possibly catch him with that much lead. He win! (Race track jargon).

Doc put his arm around Maggi in the winner's circle as Beau held Red Boy for the win photo. As soon as the picture was taken, Beau had to take Red Boy to the test barn. He blared out to Maggi, "Oh Christ, I forgot about the halter, blankets, and buckets . . . Honey, run back to our barn and get them and meet me at the test barn. Hurry!"

Maggi took off running toward their barn and grabbed a bucket, sponge, scraper, cooler, halter and shank.

As soon as she got to the test barn, Beau took off Red Boy's bridle, slipped on the halter, and put the chain part around the colt's nose so he'd be easier to handle. The colt kept staring back at the track, breathing heavily, his nostrils distended, his flanks heaving in and out. He was difficult for Maggi to keep still because he was highly exhilarated from the race.

Beau got a bucket of hot water, poured a Lysol-type antiseptic and soap into it and bathed the colt, scraped him off, and wiped his head and eyes with the sponge to remove the excess water. After that, he gave the colt an alcohol rub, slathering it all over his body and then threw the cooler on him, tied it, and told Maggi, "Start walking him." Red Boy fought to take huge gulps from the water bucket each time it was offered to him. Maggi remembered Beau's warnings about colic as she jerked and pulled the colt's head out of the bucket when she thought he had enough.

"Here, let me finish walking him. You rest," Beau told Maggi.

Maggi went over to the test barn office and watched the procedure that was taking place. The winner from the previous race was now cooled and watered out, and they were taking him into a stall to catch his pee. The track state vet and an attendant were in charge of catching the urine sample. The attendant was called a pee catcher.

Test Barn   Pee Catcher

A horse will generally urinate as soon as he is led inside any stall, a natural reflex as part of relaxing from exercise.

When he does urinate, he stretches out his body to avoid splashing his legs. At this moment, an attendant holds a pint jar secured by a metal loop on the end of a long metal handle directly under the horse to catch the pee. The sample is then capped and sealed. The jar is labeled with the horse's name, his trainer, and the race he won. The trainer is required to sign an official card attesting to the fact that he is the legal trainer responsible for that particular horse. The urine sample is then sent to an out-of-town laboratory, and test results are generally received in three days. The tests are conducted to find if the win horse had been given any stimulants prior to the race. If the tests show that the horse had been stimulated, he is then disqualified and the purse money is given to the horse that ran second. The trainer is suspended. The length of the suspension is determined by the facts of the case.

Since drugs and stimulants are not always detectable in urine sample, a saliva and or blood test is sometimes performed. As soon as the horse arrives at the test barn, an attendant takes a syringe filled with solution and squirts this into the horse's mouth. A sterilized white enamel pan is held directly under the horse's mouth to capture the saliva. This is also poured into a sterilized jar, sealed, and labeled like the urine sample.

The state vet told Maggi that no one was allowed in the little room where the specimens were kept. When the races were over, these test jars were driven directly to the airport by the state vet. An out-of-town laboratory is used to avoid the risk of anyone intimidating a local lab technician.

By the time Beau led Red Boy back to their barn, Red Boy broke into a sweat again, he was so keyed up from his race.

"I'll walk him till he settles down," Beau told Maggi. "You get his stall ready and his bran mash."

Maggi got right to work. Taking care of a winner made the work a pleasure. She and Beau were all grins.

"Hey, didn't I tell you he was a runner? Damn, the whole race track bet on him. He didn't pay nothing, but we got back a little over a hundred," Beau smirked.

As Maggi leaned on the pitchfork watching him lead the red colt around, she sensed Beau was as high as Red Boy was, and so was she.

As soon as Red Boy settled down and began to root into his feed tub and eat his bran mash, Beau told Maggi to bring some standing bandages and cotton and leg brace to his stall. Beau sat under the big colt and began to rub his front legs with tender loving care.

"This is what makes a good race horse, honey. Lots of good ole rubbing—the most expensive medicine there is," he grinned. "This is what makes good grooms too. You can always tell when a horse gets lots of this . . . his ole hair around his ankles is kinky curly from being done up so much."

After he rubbed for almost a half hour on each leg, Beau put a cotton roll around the leg and then wrapped the standing bandage and secured it neatly with two safety pins, carefully making sure they were on the outside of his leg so when the colt lay down he wouldn't open one and it would come loose. Maggi had never caught this although she was watching Beau closely. That little trick came with experience and know-how.

Beau, Maggi and Stevie walked over to the track kitchen. They were starved and tired. It had been a long

STANDING BANDAGES

Standing Bandages

day. And the track kitchen was the place to unwind. Each day began and ended there. It was the common meeting ground for owners, trainers, grooms, and their friends. Over the predominant chatter of horsemen, a loud speaker was blaring out messages. The aroma of hot coffee mingled with that of the food on the steamtables. Maggi watched as the track kitchen cook served generous portions to them. She was so happy in this friendly group and delighted that because of Red Boy, she and Beau could celebrate.

As they scanned the steamtable, Maggi took a moment to chat with Charlie the cook, a racetracker who had devoted thirty-five years of his life to feeding the backside people.

He managed to keep a hearty menu at reasonable prices —a real feat in a world of constantly rising costs. Beau had told Maggi, "Charlie staked many a racetracker when they needed it. He didn't always get it back, but it never seemed to bother him. He always gave a free meal for an old gyp who was down on his luck and would create a kitchen job for anyone who wanted to work for his supper. The racetrackers liked him as a person and trusted him with their stomachs."

During the winter mornings when it was cold, Maggi often warmed herself by Charlie's huge kitchen stove, and invariably, he slipped her a cup of coffee and a doughnut at no charge. He knew the ones who needed help.

Stevie was badgering Beau for ten cents to play the pinball machine. Beau gave him the money, and Stevie no sooner got the money into the machine than he had an audience of six little boys around six or seven. They all had on huge cowboy hats, Levi's and bright colored Western shirts, looking like miniature cowboys huddled around the pinball machine. Maggi nudged Beau to look.

Beau chuckled. "Damn, they look cute, don't they? Reminds me when I was that age. People always say a race track is no place to raise kids, but damn it, I didn't turn out so bad. I was a Backside brat. Hell, it makes them sharper. I guarantee they know how to add and figure odds or money better than most kids their age."

Maggi agreed, for she had seen these kids work at the barn on cold mornings, never complaining, just doing what they were told to do and eager to help their parents. On weekends, the kids were not left at home, so the parents had to bring them to the track. They could hold a horse as well as an adult, and riding came second nature to most of them. Having Stevie at the track on weekends made their work easier and faster with Stevie walking hots, raking up the shedrow and tow ring, and rolling up the washed bandages.

By now four of the little boys each picked up a cue stick and began to play a game of pool. They were barely able to reach over the pool table to get a shot at the ball. All Maggi could see was four big Western hats just moving around the pool table—the little faces were hidden by the huge brims. She chuckled, trying to get Beau's attention again.

For weeks things were going smoothly, until one morning, Beau found that Red Boy had heat in his left

The Backside Brats

ankle. Beau got the vet to check it out. He said it would be best to turn the colt out for a few months' rest

"Why can't we keep him here and take care of him?" Maggi asked.

"Hon, you have to give it time. If you don't, he'll take the time by breaking down," Beau explained.

This spread gloom over their barn. Maggi burst into tears at the realization that Red Boy would have to pass up the big race in which Beau was sure he had such a good shot.

Beau wrapped his arms around Maggi, and kissing away the tears, consoled her as best he could. "You're going to have to get over letting these things bother you, or you'll drive yourself crazy," he warned. "What happens, happens. *Never look back!*"

So Red Boy was sent home and things returned to normal—until the racetrack grapevine brought in the news that Beau's Dad had claimed three good racehorses at Caliente race track, and that he had won three races with them already.

"Now, I'll have to listen to that old bastard brag all summer," Beau growled to Maggi as he was doing up one of the colts.

"You ought to be glad he is doing good. What's the matter with you, anyway?" she snapped back. "I have never seen the likes of everyone here. They're all jealous when someone gets a good horse or wins a race."

"Oh, I was just kidding. I can talk that way about him, but no one else can," Beau grinned as he pinched her on the butt. "Come on, let's get done so we can get the hell out of here."

* * * *

71

It was spring, and horses were leaving every day for other race tracks. Consequently, the track was letting a lot of gyps move in from the little Tucson track Rillito to have enough horses to finish out the race meet. This was when Maggi met a new friend, Jiggs Madders, who stabled across from their barn. She always loved old people anyway, so she took to Jiggs instantly and found him to be a shrewd old duffer. He never missed a thing! The rumors were that he was quite wealthy and yet tight as a dead heat, and that he even stole hay for his horses. Jiggs was a good-looking, healthy man for seventy -- short-legged and long-waisted. He looked like something out of an old-time Western movie. But he was a dyed-in-the-wool, bona-fide gyp and racetracker. Little did Maggi know the part he would play in her life later on. She adored the dear gentle man and had him over for coffee each morning at their barn. He seemed so lonesome, she thought.

During this morning training, Beau was taking one of the colts from the stall, and he favored his left leg.

"Oh, oh!" Beau reached down and ran his hand lightly down the front shin of the leg. The colt almost kneeled down. "Well, here's another one we'll have to turn out. He's shin bucking, of all the son-of-a-bitchin' luck."

"What the heck is shin bucking?" Maggi asked.

"It's a thin membrane tissue that runs down from his knee to his ankle. And it gets inflamed and swollen from tracking and the breezing," Beau told her. "They really start colts too young. Hell, they are hardly developed."

"Then why do they start running them so young?" she asked.

"Because of the money, dummy. Just look how sore this colt is. Hell, he wouldn't run two hundred yards and his ole shin would get to stinging and he'd just pull up."

"What can you do for it . . . anything?" Maggi asked.

"Yeah, turn him out—that's what. After he's been turned out for ten days or more, and all the heat is out of the shins, then I'll apply a blister salve over the shins. This makes for induced circulation. It's painful to the colt for a few days, because his leg will swell and crack the skin. Then I'll paint it with Reducine to keep tightening it down, and it also keeps the flies away and prevents infection. The whole procedure takes about a month in all," he told Maggi. "But it's the time that does the most good, not the medication really. Time is the best thing for any sore horse," he added.

Doc Hardy came up the shedrow and noticed Beau stroking the sore shin on the colt and spoke out in his husky voice, "What we got, another sore one?"

"Yep, his left shin," Beau answered.

"Well, I think I'll just take all these colts back to the ranch; looks like they are all going to get sore one way or another. Besides, it is getting close to the end of this meet and there's not too many places to run them. I never did believe in running two-year-olds much, anyway."

Maggi looked at Beau. She was in shock! After Doc left, she turned to Beau and said, "That means after Monday, we're out of a job."

"Yep, that's the way the cookie crumbles," Beau stated with disgust. "Don't worry about it. We'll make it," he added.

8

Maggi again began to worry about the state of their finances. What with house payments, grocery bills, and the old truck in need of repairs, they barely managed to keep their heads above water. After the colts went home, Beau kept on free-lancing breaking and riding colts. Maggi tried to get some outside horses to pony, but most of the better stables had left, so it was hardly worth hauling her pony out each morning. Besides, there was only a week left before the meet would be over. Beau told her to *never look back*. But Beau didn't want her to know how it hurt him to lose Red Boy and all the colts.

Maggi never dreamed that Doc would be the solution to their finances. Early in the month of May, he gave them a call and said that he had recommended them to another owner by the name of Les Henderson. Doc said to meet with Henderson as soon as possible.

Les Henderson was a muscular man of average height, with a red, ruddy complexion, a long flat, sloping nose, and gray hair with a yellowish cast. He twitched all the time as he talked. His ranch was similar to Doc's. It consisted of twenty-five head, mares, colts, and studs that required care and feeding. Henderson was blunt and to the point about salary and duties for both Beau and Maggi. Maggi could see he wasn't going to be easy to work for.

Beau was to start breaking and galloping two colts, Flame and Jet, on Henderson's ranch, and in October, take them to the race track. It was a good arrangement while Beau was there on the little farm. He and Maggi enjoyed the summer days doing the chores, leisurely doctoring colts, feeding, and getting Flame and Jet used to having baths. They loved the casual free lifestyle and it was close to home.

October came far too fast for Maggi. Beau took the two colts to the fairgrounds and this left her to run the little farm.

She talked to visitors about stud fees, colts available for sale, and all of the usual farm business. Maggi thought one hot afternoon that Henderson was getting a bargain in paying Beau $100 per week and her $50 to run the farm.

State Fair Meet —— Their Second Season

Fall. Beau came home from the fairgrounds one day and told Maggi, "That damn Flame is a runner! He'll win his first out. He's one of the fastest colts on the grounds. I've worked him with the top colt out there. Everyone is talking about him."

Maggi beamed as he kept on talking. It made their life a little more bearable.

Maggi was doing a good job at the farm. She had organized things and her work to where she even had time to take a break in the early afternoon. As she was browsing through a horsemens magazine in the office, Henderson stepped in.

"Well . . . since you have so much time to sit and read, you can paint the corral boards with some crankcase oil," he ordered.

Perspiration broke out on Maggi's lip. So far, she had ignored the constant added chores Henderson had ordered her to do.

"Oh no, you hired me to feed twice a day and fuss with these horses and take care of your customers. You're getting a bargain as it is . . . with Beau training your horses and me for a mere $150 a week. I'll quit first!"

"That's fine with me, I'll have your check in just a minute. And I don't want you at the track, do you hear?"

"Hey, I can go where I please! You don't own the race track," she snapped back. "Who do you think you are?"

She drove to the fairgrounds and told Beau what she had done.

"Don't worry about it," he told her.

"How will we make it?"

"We'll survive without your having to put up with him."

Maggi loved Beau with all her heart for seeing her side of it. She went home, Stevie was glad to see her home so early.

The next morning, Beau woke, "Maggi, there's something wrong with Rip. He can't move!"

Maggi bounded out of bed and ran to the dog. His gentle eyes registered bewilderment. She stroked his soft fur and spoke to him consolingly. "He's had a stroke," she sobbed.

A small grave was dug in their backyard, and Rip was laid to rest.

Rip's absence from the family left a terrible void, and the impulse was always there to call out for him when they were leaving for the track.

Two weeks had passed, Maggi glanced up one evening and saw Beau standing in the doorway. His expression was impish as he watched her washing vegetables for their supper. She noticed his jacket was bulging. As she looked again, she saw that the bulge was moving. He laughed as he unzipped the jacket, and a three-month-old black and tan shepherd pup howled in comical protest at the manner in which it was being handled.

"Oh Beau!" Maggi squealed.

"Here's something to keep you from moping around the house all day," he said.

"Oh, he's so cute!"

"He is from the Carlson litter. You remember when Rip bred their dog? This is one of the pups."

"Y-You mean . . .?"

It seemed impossible, and yet it was true. She had part of Rip once again.

It was a wonderful Christmas with the Maddoxes and Beau and Maggi celebrated their third wedding anniversary.

Turf Paradise — Their Second Season

March came, and the Henderson colts were ready to run.

Flame was in the Arizona Futurity for two-year-olds. Maggi and Beau had anticipated a possible win, but they weren't prepared to see Flame set a new world's record —51:2 for four furlongs!

While the horse was at the test barn, a sports writer came to request additional information on the colt for a story. Beau barely answered the reporter's questions. It was

Maggi who had to finish giving the information.

Two hours later, they finally left the track, and as they were driving home, Maggi cuddled Rip the 2nd in her lap and abruptly asked Beau, "What makes a futurity race different from any other race?"

He laughed, "What made you come up with that question?"

"Because I don't really understand what a futurity race is all about. I mean . . . Oh, explain it, please."

"There are all kinds of futurities. (Futurity: a race for which entries are made well in advance of the event.) First you nominate a yearling colt or a filly at any of the race tracks at the time their nomination fee dates are due. The dates and fees are determined by each track management. As a rule, by the time a colt is a two-year-old, he has paid three different fees throughout the two years. That's what makes the purse so big. The whole idea of futurities is to promote bigger purses and eliminate outside horses. The little home-bred futurity we ran in today is nothing compared to most, but it encourages Arizona breeders to try to raise better horses."

"Okay, I understand that," Maggi said. "Now, who does all this nominating—and who keeps track of the fees that have to be paid, and when they're due?"

"The track personnel sends out special pamphlets, and information is included in their condition books. Then, it's the responsibility of the trainer, breeder, or owner. All Kentucky breeders always nominate their baby colts in several futurities to help boost their selling potential."

Maggi was impressed with the long-range foresight of the horse-racing business.

"Yeah, but a lot of these colts don't ever make it to the track, Maggi. They get hurt, break down, or just can't run. This whole futurity business is just one big gamble.

"Then again, another angle comes into play when someone has a good two-year-old that wasn't nominated for a futurity race, and the trainer or owner wants to run him in that race. His owner has to supplement a stiff fee to get into the race. After these futurities are scheduled, even if only one horse shows up to run, the race has to be run. This has actually happened, and is referred to as a 'walkover' race."

"Would that be like the Kentucky Derby?"

"Well no, futurities are for two-year-olds. They're at the beginning of their racing careers. But the Derby is for three-year-olds most of whom have already proved themselves the creme de la creme of three-year-olds, so to speak.

"Owners nominate for the Kentucky Derby. They have to nominate by February fifteenth of the colt's two-year-old year—a year ahead of the Derby. The nomination is $100 at that time, then later it's $250 at the time the colt is entered for the Derby, and then $1,250 to start. Hundreds of colts are nominated at the two-year-old year but by the time their three-year-old year rolls around, only a handful are left, because a lot of them break down or just weren't good enough. So far, they have never had the race overfill their gate capacity."

"What do you mean by gate capacity?" Maggi asked.

"Well, you know our starting gate only holds twelve head. I don't know how many the Derby gate holds, but if they have more horses than the gate holds, they have to put another gate on the track. They can do that there because the track is wide enough for two gates. If they had more horses than that, then they would have to split the Derby. And having two Kentucky Derbys back-to-back would ruin the whole thing. Take all the enchantment away from the race."

"Think we'll make it to the Kentucky Derby?"

"Hell, no! There are plenty of veteran trainers who've never been close to going to the Derby!"

The sports page of the evening paper had bold headlines clear across the page!

FLAME WINS FUTURITY 51:2
NEW WORLD AND TRACK RECORD SET

It prompted Maggi to dance a silly jig. Beau broke into a sudden outpouring that left him weak with laughter. It was his first big write-up with his name mentioned several times.

Later that night, they clung to one another in the warm, soft comfort of their bed, and in the way he looked at her then and the ardent way in which she responded to him, there was no more giggling!

The next day, Les Henderson talked to Beau about enlarging his stable by claiming a few more horses, since he was doing so well. Beau was pleased and agreed to get busy right away and start studying the *Daily Racing Form* (a newspaper that is to racing what *Variety* is to show business) and scanning the horses to see if he could find some good claims.

As Mr. Henderson walked away from the shedrow, Beau told Maggi, "The tightwad is loosening up! I'll have to come to the races every day now and spend more time studying the horses," he continued as he sat down in the soft bedding by the stall door to rub one of the horse's legs. Maggi sat down beside him and began rubbing the other leg.

"Beau," she asked, "just what is a claiming race and how do you go about claiming a racehorse? Since we're going to be claiming horses, I'd like to know how it works."

"Christ, that would take all day to tell you."

"Go ahead. We're not going anywhere."

"Okay, I'll try."

"First," he began, "you have to own a racehorse, either by raising one or buying one. Now that you're in the racehorse business, you have to get a trainer so this horse can get a stall—unless, of course, you're qualified to train the horse yourself.

"After you get a trainer, you must apply for an owner's license. Now, you're a qualified owner who may claim a racehorse, if you want to.

"Once an owner or trainer decides to claim a horse, he must deposit cash money to the horsemen's office account. No checks are accepted in this case. The money has to be cash or certified check.

"A claiming race is a horse race in which horses are entered subject to claim of the right to purchase for a certain price by anyone registered for racing and starting a horse at that meet.

"The bottom claiming price here is a thousand dollars and the highest is five thousand. A horse run for that price may be claimed for that price by another trainer and/or owner.

"When I decide to claim a horse, I'll have to fill out a claim blank like the one Henderson just left with me.

"Everything written on the blank has to be absolutely accurate. If even a single mistake is make, the claim is disallowed.

"Then the claim envelope is placed in a special locked box fifteen minutes before the horses go to the post. Once the claim is in the box, there's no way to reverse it. Even if

DIVISION OF PURSES

(Unless Otherwise Specified)

PURSE	60% First	20% Second	11% Third	6% Fourth	3% Fifth
$20,000	$12,000	$4,000	$2,200	$1,200	$ 600
15,000	9,000	3,000	1,650	900	450
10,000	6,000	2,000	1,100	600	300
9,500	5,700	1,900	1,045	570	285
9,000	5,400	1,800	990	540	270
8,500	5,100	1,700	935	510	255
8,000	4,800	1,600	880	480	240
7,500	4,500	1,500	825	450	225
7,000	4,200	1,400	770	420	210
6,500	3,900	1,300	715	390	195
6,000	3,600	1,200	660	360	180
5,500	3,300	1,100	605	330	165
5,000	3,000	1,000	550	300	150
4,500	2,700	900	495	270	135
4,200	2,520	840	462	252	126
4,000	2,400	800	440	240	120

CLAIMING

All claims must be deposited in the claiming box at least ten
minutes before post time or the time fixed for the race to begin
and not later, and no official of said Association shall give any
information as to the filing of claims therein until the race has
been run. All claims shall be passed upon by the Stewards, or their
designated representatives. When a claim is filed it is irrevocable
and at the risk of the claimant.

For a period of 30 days after the claim a horse shall not start
in a claiming race for a price which is less than 25% more than
the price at which it was claimed. The day claimed shall not
count, but the following calendar day shall be the first day and
the horse shall be entitled to be entered whenever necessary so
that the horse may start on the 31st calendar day following the
claim, for any claiming price.

— 26 —

Claiming blank

the horse breaks a leg or drops dead on the track, the horse
will still be Henderson's for the money I claimed him for."

"Beau, what if the owner has second thoughts— what if
he decides that even though his horse is certain to be
claimed, he doesn't really want to lose him? Can he scratch
him out of the race before the race begins?"

"Only at scratch time, but not just before the race.
Anyway, the owner never knows that his horse has been
claimed until after the race is run."

"If the horse wins, who gets the purse?"

"The previous owner gets the purse money, and the new
claimer gets the horse."

"What if more than one person claims the same horse?"
Maggi wanted to know.

"Then they shake for it. First the track steward numbers
the unopened claim envelopes on the back, 1 -- 2 -- 3, and
so on, and then puts identically numbered little balls in a

leather bottle and shakes out a number. Say number one rolls out of the bottle first. Then number one on the envelope gets the horse."

"I see. That seems fair. What else?"

"Well, back to me claiming for Henderson. So, I claim a horse for a thousand dollars. I'll have to raise that horse twenty-five percent in his next race. This goes on for thirty days. This thirty-day period is called 'being in jail.' If someone should claim him from Henderson, that new owner would then have to raise him another twenty-five percent for another thirty days."

"Give me a for instance," Magge said, still somewhat confused.

"Okay, let's say that I claim a horse on January 2, for two thousand dollars. Now, I have to raise him twenty-five percent of that claiming price, which would be twenty-five hundred. I have to run him for that until February 2, and then he would be out of jail. After that, I can run him for any claiming price I want. *But*—if this horse is claimed from me, say on January 10, the new owner would have to raise him twenty-five percent of *that* claiming price, and he'd be in jail until February 10." ·

"Why do they have a rule like 'being in jail'?" Maggi asked then.

"It keeps trainers and owners from claiming horses continually," Beau explained. "In a way, the process protects both the horse and owner because it tends to keep the horse in about his own class, where he's more likely to win.

"But the big question in claiming any horse is always —can he stand the raise? Can he win for a higher claiming price? Is he sound enough? If there are any doubts—then *don't claim him!*"

Maggi was trying to grasp it all.

"How do you decide what horses to claim?" she asked.

"Well, a lot is luck. If you decide to buy a horse, you can have a vet check the horse for soundness, but when you claim a horse, you're buying a pig-in-a-poke. Track rules state you're not to trespass into someone else's barn or shedrow unless you're invited there by the trainer or owner. So you have to rely pretty heavily on backside hearsay and your own judgment of past performances from the *Racing Form* charts. Still, you can tell a lot about a horse's performance and capabilities by watching him come off the track after the morning workouts.

"Sometimes owners and trainers deliberately want to lose a horse. This is a risk you take.

"You might claim five good horses and the sixth horse will be a bad one. You can't always be lucky. In claiming you have to be able to stand the loss and *never look back!*"

Beau soon picked out several horses to claim. Within three weeks, he had claimed four head of horses and won two races with the new horses. Henderson was very pleased; he had never done so well as he had this winter with Beau. He became greedy.

He heard that an owner at the Caliente race track in Mexico was selling all his horses. He told Beau to go down and take a look at what he had.

"See if you can buy two or three for three to four thousand," he said.

Maggi was overjoyed at the news. She and Beau had never had a vacation since they'd been married. And driving down and spending a day would be like a holiday. But her bubble burst when she learned that Beau's father was coming also to try to buy a couple of horses for himself. And just before they were to leave, their party was increased by an old school friend of Beau's, Arni Vesquez.

He was of Mexican descent, though he had blond hair, blue eyes, and fair skin. This was Arni's first year on the race track, and he had no horse training experience at all. But his wealthy in-laws wanted to get into the racehorse business and figured that anyone could run racehorses, so Arni got the part.

Arni was clever enough to recognize Beau's attributes as a horseman and trainer. He continually picked Beau's brain. That irritated Maggi, because Beau was so willing to tell him anything he wanted to know. She cautioned Beau about giving away his trade secrets, but Beau only grumbled "What secrets?" and that she was just overly critical of his friends. Thus, at the beginning, Maggi and Arni got off to a bad start. The presence of Arni put a damper on Maggi's enthusiasm about the trip.

Beau made the necessary arrangements to have a trainer friend oversee his stable. They all left in Arni's car late that night and crossed the Mexican border at five a. m. the next morning. Training was just beginning when they arrived.

The Caliente track was set in depressing surroundings —barren dry hills dotted with hundreds of small shanty shacks and buildings. There were few trees and little brush —in contrast to the Caliente race track's beautiful Mexican architecure, tile, adobe, and lush landscaping.

"Where do these horses come from?" Maggi asked Beau, noting the Americans around the track.

"From Hollywood Park, Santa Anita, Bay Meadows, Golden Gate . . ." he answered. "It's a place for their second strings and not as tough here either. The only bad part is the Mexican government won't allow the stables to bring in any outside American grooms—only a barn foreman. The grooms have to be hired here. And that makes it tough if the foreman doesn't speak Spanish."

The were joined by a jovial man named Jose, an old

friend of Buck and Beau. He teased Beau about having put on so much weight since his racing days at Caliente. Beau introduced him to Maggi, and Jose suggested she come with him for a tour of the beautiful grandstand and track.

"Go ahead, while we look over the horses," Beau encouraged. "You'll just get tired walking around and around the barns."

Jose was right. The grandstand was beautiful, with its acres of Mexican tile in the clubhouse floors—beauty that only the Mexican culture could capture. "It seems a shame they only race on weekends," she stated. To Maggi the most unique thing of all was the portable dog track.

"After the day's horseracing is over, they roll out this dog track at night and have dog racing," Jose explained to Maggi.

"I don't believe what I see!" she marveled.

"Jeez, you know your husband Beau outran a dog with a racehorse on that little track one night just for a publicity stunt," he grinned.

"You're kidding!" she laughed. "He never told me about that . . . the rat! Who won?"

"Beau did, on the horse, of course," Jose smiled. "He was a race rider, that boy. Too bad he got too heavy."

"I would never have met him if he hadn't, so I'm glad he did. Well . . . guess we'd better get back," Maggi suggested.

As she walked toward the barn she saw Beau rubbing his hand down the ankle of a black filly. When he saw Maggi, he asked, "What do you think of her?"

"She's pretty," Maggi answered.

"She's ours. I just bought her for us."

"For us? You kidding me?"

The surprise magnified Maggi's interest in the filly a thousand fold. "What's her name?" she asked, now stroking the long sleek neck.

86

"Glad Sissy."

"How much did you pay for her?"

"Twelve hundred. Now don't pitch a fit!"

Maggi remained silent. Beau had always been partial to fillies and always managed to get the run out of them when he rode or trained them. As Maggi continued looking at the filly and petting her, Beau let her hold the lead shank. As he ran his hand admiringly over the sleek back, Maggi could sense what Beau was feeling, for she felt it too. There was not a better feeling in the world as far as she was concerned than to be around a horse—especially your own racehorse!

"I also bought two nice horses for Henderson—a four-year-old and a five-year-old. Both run for about three thousand. Got them both for five thousand. Daddy got one and Arni bought three nice colts," Beau reported.

Maggi was ashamed of her past remarks after Beau told her, "If it wasn't for Arni, I couldn't have bought this filly, because I never planned to buy a horse, and I didn't have the cash. The owner said no dice to a check, and I can't blame him. He don't know me from Adam. Good thing Arni brought ten thousand along, plus he was able to find out from the groom rubbing her that so far, she has never had any leg problems."

But still Maggi knew that Arni used the prowess of Buck and Beau in picking out his horses. Beau told Maggi to make out a check for twelve hundred and give it to Arni right away. Beau and Buck would make arrangements for the horses to be shipped to Phoenix. There was a thirty-day quarantine period at the border, and a groom would have to take care of the horses till they shipped out. Maggi instantly began to fret about the filly under a stranger's care, but Beau *never looked back*.

The purchase of Glad Sissy caused a quarrel between

Beau and Henderson. Insinuating that Beau would not concentrate on training *his* horses, Henderson stated that Beau might give extra attention to Glad Sissy. This infuriated Beau. He retaliated with rage.

"I've never cheated anyone. I've always had a racehorse all my life until now!" he shouted. "This is the only chance I can make a stake for myself. But I won't let it interfere with training your horses. But if you think it will, then you better get yourself another trainer."

In the end, Henderson insisted that he be justly reimbursed for the filly's feed and bedding. It made Beau even more livid, but he agreed to pay Henderson two dollars a day for Glad Sissy's board.

"The selfish old son-of-a-bitch!" Beau growled. "He doesn't want anyone but him to make a buck."

Les was too smart a man to let Beau go, he knew Beau was a good trainer and horseman, and he had never done so well with his horses as since he hired Beau. So he overlooked the mare even though it grated on him.

Beau let Maggi rub Glad Sissy to keep Les from thinking he was giving her more attention. Maggi soon learned that taking care of your own horse had a whole different feeling. She brushed Glad Sissy with tender, loving care, rubbing her legs as Beau had showed her. At this moment, Maggi thought, I couldn't be any happier if I were a millionaire!

Late one morning Maggi heard a loud, heated discussion coming from down the shedrow. She peeked out of Glad Sissy's stall and saw a man talking to Beau. Beau was using abusive language. She waited till the man left and then went down to the stall Beau was in. He was rubbing the horse's knees vigorously, taking his anger out in his work.

"Hey, what was that all about?" she asked.

"That old son-of-a-bitch agent wouldn't even look at me a year ago! But now that Flame has broken the world record, he's trying to come across with that long-lost buddy stuff. That's a jock's agent for you. They're the lowest around the race track. They'll lie to you, cheat you, stab you in the back, or do anything else it takes to get a good mount for their jock." He paused for a spell. "But that's what makes a good agent," Beau grumbled as he got up from the stall floor.

"What does he get out of it?" Maggi asked.

"Twenty-five percent of everything the little bastard makes. Some even get as much as half of their total earnings. You realize that a good jockey that rides six or eight a day can earn between one thousand and three thousand per week. He's got to have an agent."

"Why?" Maggi asked.

"Because the jock's busy in the morning hustling from barn to barn, galloping, breezing and working horses (to let a horse run as fast as he can for a certain distance) so that he might get to ride their horses in a race," he continued. "The agent usually will commit his jock, stating, 'Don't worry, I'll have my boy here at six a. m.' And he makes sure his jock is, if he's a good agent," Beau stated.

"If a jock had to book his own mounts, he'd never have time to work horses. Plus, jocks usually don't know all the trainers, and it's hard to try and sell yourself," Beau remarked. "But they make the money. Hell, they get $25 here for every mount they ride, plus ten percent of the purse when they light the board (finish 1, 2, 3, 4).

"Let's see, a winner here gets $45, I think," he calculated as he studied the ground. "Not to mention the stakes the owners give them."

"What do you mean stakes? Gosh, more damn things," Maggi said.

"That's up to the owner if he wants to give a jock a stake. It's like a bonus, I guess. Some give fifty, a hundred, or more, depends on the amount the horse won and how happy the owner is at that time," he laughed. "Hell, I have had lots of them promise me a hundred and then never mention it again after the champagne and good times wear off. Come on, let's get done. I have to talk to Les this morning. It's getting shipping time, you know," he said, punching her to move away from the stall door.

"Okay, don't push," she said, and headed back to Glad Sissy's stall to finish cleaning out her feet, thinking— there is so much to this racing!

Hollywood Park for the First Time

Henderson told Beau to put in for stalls at Hollywood Park. That was where he wanted to take the colts. They decided to sell the cheaper claiming horses, lose some, and turn out whatever was left for the fall meet.

Beau wasn't so fired up about going to California.

"Hey, it's tough out there. They've got some runners," he stated to Les and Maggi.

"Well, you're tough yourself," Maggi assured him. "All you need is a chance to prove it. You'd do just as good as the rest of them if you had the big money owners to back you up."

Beau laughed outright. "You're something else. I wish I had your nerve; you've got more guts than a slaughter house," he added. "If I had your drive, Maggi, I'd be president!"

After Les left, Beau said, "You know Les is crazy for

going over there. Hell, these horses would tear them up at Ruidoso, and Glad Sissy would do good there, too," he stated. "Hell, she has won three races here this winter, and it's no tougher up there than here."

"Okay," Maggi reasoned aloud. "Let's assume that you don't go. Les Henderson will get another trainer. And if Flame turns out to be a hot stake horse, why you'd poop a cupcake," she chided.

Beau howled at her quips. Maggi knew she had him now and was taking advantage of it. She had to convince this damn husband of hers that he had the ability and was a good trainer.

"You don't get a chance like this every day, you know," she persisted. "You can always go on the county fair circuit, or to Ruidoso, but not to Hollywood Park."

"Okay. I'm going. So shut up." She did.

Les Henderson agreed to pay Beau ten percent of all the winnings, plus Beau's two hundred a week salary, and added, "I'll pay all the barn expenses and feed."

Maggi was surprised, for she had never figured Henderson to be that generous. This would help keep her from digging into their savings. She had already dug into them enough this winter, since Glad Sissy had won, for a used washing machine, and for adding a living-room to the small house. With Steve getting older, they needed more room, a place where he could entertain his friends without being under Maggi's and Beau's feet.

Beau marveled at how Maggi could fix the house up with little trifles she'd make or find for such small cost. She was a good wife, he thought many times. Yet, he cautioned her about taking too much from the savings.

"I can make us some money, Maggi, if I have a little money to claim horses," he told her. And she made sure that there was enough for him to do so when the time came.

The next week they spent getting ready for Beau to ship the horses.

"Glad Sissy can't get a stall at Hollywood Park, because the bottom claiming is four thousand there. She needs a rest, so I decided to turn her out in the paddock here at home for the summer. We can get Louie down the road to look after her to make sure she has water. You call and get the stall applications and make the van arrangements, okay?" he told Maggi.

Within two days, the Hollywood Park Condition Book arrived, along with a stall application. She filled it out and sent it right back. It came back in three days, okaying the two stalls for Jet and Flame.

Maggi was reading the stall approval and remarked to Beau, "Boy, you can't plan a thing till these damn stall approvals come back, can you?"

"Nope," Beau answered. "The track management has the right to refuse anyone for stalls . . . especially if a horse's past performance isn't good, you don't have much of a chance of getting a stall at the major race tracks.

"Tracks want horses that will make up a good racing program. They don't give a damn about the trainers or the owners," he went on. "Only time they will bend over is when an owner or trainer has a top nation-wide stake horse . . . like Kelso, Miss Wiggle, My Dear Girl . . . then they'll let them bring the rest of their stable along without too much screening. The bigger, powerful stables do get those kind of favors, but they earn it, I guess."

"Say! Speaking of big trainers, you know you will have to have a couple of dress suits to wear over there," Maggi declared.

"Hey, I'm not dressing up in no damn suit," he snapped. "You can just forget that."

"Well, I can see you over there now, someone saying 'Which one is the trainer and who's the groom?' In fact, I've seen grooms here look better than you in the saddling paddock."

"Oh, is that right?" he snapped. "You go screw yourself . . ."

Maggi had hit a nerve in Beau, and she realized it was going to take some doing to get him to dress up. She just dropped the subject and went about her chores.

While she was doing the dishes, Beau came up to her, put his arms around her and said, "Hey I know you're right about the suits and all. I'm sorry for getting mad. We'll go tomorrow and pick out some things, okay?"

"Okay," she answered.

Beau's stocky frame made it hard to find the right cut and Maggi figured Western style was best suited for his stance and casual character. He looked extra slim in the tan and brown plain suits, neatly tailored, showing off his broad shoulders and narrow hips.

"Boy, do you look handsome!" she told him. This pleased Beau. The rest of the day was spent buying the shirts and shoes and he picked out two clip-on ties while Maggi giggled.

"That's something I had never learned to do was to tie a tie, " Beau told her over lunch. "I'm glad we're done with this shopping," he sighed as he settled back in the booth.

"Me too," Maggi added.

Maggi got hold of the branding inspector to make out the required hauling papers on the two colts. Contacted the vet for their health certificates. Called the van dispatcher. "We will have two colts going to Hollywood Park," she told him, "and we want to leave next week."

The dispatcher answered, "Well, I have several loads coming from there, let me call you back in a few days and give you a date when we'll be able to take you, okay?"

"Oh, yes and you are to bill Les Henderson. Here is his address," she added. "Thanks. Good-bye."

Maggi had everything done and ready, with clean clothes for Beau. She was so busy, her housework would have to wait. She figured she could catch up everything after Beau left. Then she could leave when Steve was out of school.

But Beau wrecked those plans when he told her, "There's a race for Glad Sissy the last week of the meet, so I'm leaving her at the track. You'll have to take care of her till then," he told her. "I'll have to sign a slip putting you down as assistant trainer. You'll have to take out a license."

"That means I will have to drive all the way out there twice a day," she complained.

"So?" he answered. "What's so bad about that?"

"Nothing . . ."

"You will have to take Sam too, so you can pony her every day. She don't need galloping, just pony her a slow mile," he told her.

"Okay," she answered obediently.

"Come here, I know what you need," he said with a sheepish, serious grin as he reached and turned the light out.

They were at the track just as the sun was coming over the Four Peaks mountains. Beau had taken down the stall chains and shut the bottom doors and secured them with a snap. The water buckets and feed tubs were stacked with a few other items and Beau's blue steamer trunk.

"I wish that damn van would get here," Beau said edgily.

"Well, here it comes now," Maggi said, as the big van lumbered slowly toward them. H-i-s-s-s-s-s went the air

94

brakes, and the two drivers dropped from the high cab, each working automatically fixing the doors. They were loading the two colts at the rear of the van as the front was already full with six other horses.

They loaded with no problems, Beau's trunk was thrown up into the big trunk compartment along with his buckets and tubs.

He came over to Maggi, put his arms around her, kissed her hard, and squeezed her tightly. "I've got to go, the horses will get to sweating. It's getting hot," he told her. "Be a good girl."

"I will. I love you."

"Me too."

He climbed up into the high cab, waved as the van turned, backed, and lumbered slowly out of the backside. She watched till it turned out of sight. But she could still hear the shift of gears and low moaning tones as the van was getting compression to pull its heavy load. She knew they were on the main road by now, as the noise of the diesel stacks roared till she lost the faint sound of it. She felt awful as she turned toward the barn to take care of Glad Sissy.

9

Glad Sissy was raising hell! Pawing! Nickering! since she was the only horse left in the barn. Maggi moved her to an empty stall, grabbed the pitchfork and muck sack, and began to clean her stall. Tears were rolling down her face all the while she was working. She hated this being alone. By nine o'clock she had finished training Sissy, walked her, and rubbed her down. By now it was hot . . . 113°! This routine went on for the next five days. Maggi hated the long drive out to the track morning and afternoon. Plus, it was taking tanks of gas.

When Beau called that night, she asked, "I hate leaving her out there alone. Besides, it gets too hot by eight a.m., I can't cool her out. Why can't I bring her home and train her in the back field?"

"No! You just leave her at the track. It's only for a few more days."

Maggi didn't take Beau's advice and brought Glad Sissy home anyway. She brought home the feed and several bales of straw. She bedded down the little stall they had in the hay barn. It was much cooler there under the shade trees. By seven o'clock, Maggi had Glad Sissy ponied, walked, and cleaned up. She felt very smug about the whole idea, plus she had time to get many things done around the house and to spend more time with Stevie.

Thursday night Beau called and told her to enter Sissy in the seventh race for Sunday. This had to be done Friday morning, since horses have to be entered two days ahead. Beau cautioned her that entry time closed at ten a.m. sharp, so Maggi was at the racing office early. She was nervous because she had never done this before and was aware of her lack of knowing what to do.

She stood in line at the entry booth. The entry clerk filled out the entry blank.

"Who are you entering?" he asked.

"Glad Sissy."

"What race?"

"The seventh," Maggi replied.

"How much weight does she get?" he asked.

"Uh, uh —— I think one twenty . . . but I'm not sure," she answered.

"I'll check her chart," the entry clerk said. "Let's see, she's a filly, so she gets three pounds, winner of three races she picked up four pounds . . . one hundred and twenty-two pounds she has to carry," he stated as he filled out the little corner of the entry blank.

"Who's riding her?"

"Burns," Maggi answered. Perspiration was pouring off her, she was so tense.

"Here, sign the entry blank," the clerk said.

She was done, thank God! As she walked from the office, Maggi turned and asked, "When will they draw for the races?"

"A little after ten o'clock," the clerk replied.

Maggi went to the track kitchen for coffee to wait until ten.

By ten, the racing office was jammed with horsemen. The entry clerks and racing secretary were crowded around the long counter.

"Okay, everyone. Let's have some quiet, we're ready to draw the races," the state steward announced. "We need two trainers to pull the entry blanks and shake the pills."

Two trainers stepped forward and volunteered.

Maggi watched one trainer as he stood in front of a small specially built wooden file that held the entry blanks for the first race to be drawn. The other trainer was handed a leather bottle filled with little numbered balls (called pills) and a long narrow rack in which the pills were to be set.

"Okay, okay. Let's get this show on the road," the state steward announced over the microphone, and the racing staff took over.

"This will be the first race in the book. There are eighteen entries, four will be excluded and four put on eligible. Let's have the first horse, please," he asked as he motioned to the trainer by the wooden file. The trainer pulled out one entry blank and read out, "Bold Maud."

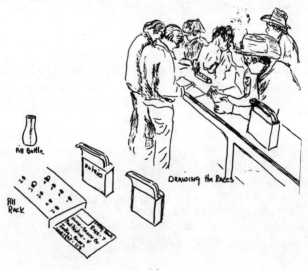

Pill Bottle

Pill Rack

DRAWING the RACES

98

"What's her position?" the clerk asked. The trainer shook out a pill. "Number 4," he answered.

The entry clerk wrote down the post position on the entry blank for the race and called, "Okay, the next horse?"

Maggi had never realized that all of this went on. The agents were jotting down all the data concerning their jocks on their Condition Books. Several trainers were cursing after the race was drawn because their horses didn't draw in (were among the four excluded), others were complaining about being on the also eligible list.

The third, fourth, fifth and sixth races were drawn and now the seventh. Maggi's mouth got dry. She was afraid Glad Sissy wouldn't get in either, as the race was overfilled.

"All right, the seventh race going for a mile for three-year-olds and up," the clerk called.

"Glad Sissy draws Number 4 post position, rider is Burns."

Maggi was relieved to hear Glad Sissy's name called first. She relaxed instantly and listened to the rest of the drawing of the race. Afterwards, she went back to the track kitchen to wait till they came out with the OVERNIGHT, which Beau demanded she bring home that night so he would know how tough the race would be.

Overnights are compiled of all the races for each day. They are typed on stencils, then mimeographed on different colored sheets of paper for each race day. The Overnight shows each race, who "drawed in," and who is on the also eligible. The track makes up the Overnight mainly for the convenience of the trainers and agents, giving them time to study it and decide if they want to scratch out from a race before the day of scratch time. In cases where a horse has drawn in too tough competition and where a trainer sees there are enough horses on the also eligible list, he knows he has a good chance of getting out of the race. The Overnight performs a valuable service since it provides all the necessary information and thus discourages constant telephone calls between the trainers and agents to the racing office.

Maggi was quite pleased that she had learned how and had entered Glad Sissy and that she had drawn in the race. It was noon and hot when she got home. She thought to herself that everything was going super . . . Until!

The next morning after she had ponied and cooled Glad Sissy out, she was leading her back to her stall. The tin roof of the stall was extremely low, and as Sissy was being led through the door, something spooked her. She lunged forward and raised her head at the same time, hitting the tin roof overhang. It shook the whole barn. Maggi knew instantly something was wrong with Sissy because she kept shaking her head and lowering it, carrying it sideways! Then Maggi saw why—her whole topknot was scalped back! Maggi was sick, and instant fear gripped her. Beau would kill her! Why hadn't she left Sissy at the track? She tried to tell herself what it was just a minor mishap, but she knew better. She called a vet, and after a novocain shot, he took fifteen stitches in Glad Sissy's foretop. After that, he gave her a tetanus shot.

Maggi told the vet that the horse had been entered in the seventh race on Sunday. He reminded her that the state vet would have to be told and that Glad Sissy would have to be scratched. No horse that had been treated with any medication forty-eight hours prior to a race could be allowed to run.

Maggi's head reeled. When Beau learned of this, he would be furious.

That night Beau phoned and Maggi found herself talking all around the subject of Glad Sissy's injury. Beau asked her did Sissy get in, what position did she draw, and Magi answered these questions as if nothing had happened. She needed more time to figure out the best way to tell him the truth. He thought the filly was still at the track. Maggi was glad to end the call. She would have to think up some kind of story to explain why she had to scratch the mare. After all, she had two days to think up something, and she was good at that.

On Saturday morning she called the office and had the vet scratch the mare . . . she had no more reason to go back to the race track.

Her major worry was Beau now, but today was Sunday—she would call him tomorrow and tell him the truth. She had planned a scouting day with Steve since she would not have to go to the races. Then the phone rang!

"Hi honey, I'm at the airport with my cousin Hank. I'll ride out to the track with him and meet you there," Beau said hastily, then "Gotta go, they're waiting for me."

Maggi felt nauseated. He was here! Going to the track, and Sissy was here at the house. She was numb. Beau would kill her for sure when he got to the track and found out the mare wasn't even in. She woke Steve and sent him to the neighbors for his scout outing without her.

While driving to the track, she had mixed emotions —wanting so much to see Beau and yet dreading it. As she drove up to the racing secretary's office, it seemed even hotter than it really was. Then she saw Beau walking toward her. The grim set of his off-set jaw told her he knew Glad Sissy was scratched out of the race.

"Why in the Hell did you scratch Glad Sissy?" he asked angrily.

" 'Cause she got hurt. It's all my fault!" she said

abjectly and told him the whole story.

He laughed aloud when she'd finished and said, "You just can't leave well enough alone, can you? Always gotta change things!"

"Oh, Beau—it seemed like such a good idea at the time! It was wrong, of course. I realize that now. I feel so bad about it!"

"No use worrying about it. Remember what I told you: you *can't look back*! What's done is done."

"Y - You mean you don't hate me for what I've done?"

"Hell, no. Now I'm taking you home."

Almost before their front door was half opened, his hot kisses were smothering her. Maggi felt the blood pulsating through her veins as his lips tingled her skin and his arms crushed her body into his. He walked her backward toward their bedroom, and they fell across the unmade bed and sank into the soft pile of the down comforter.

"Honey, I've sure missed you," he murmured.

Two hours later, they woke with a pillow fight. Maggi fixed his favorite breakfast as she listened to Beau tell her about Hollywood Park.

"I've got to go back tonight, ya know. I'm meeting Hank at the Airport Lounge."

"What does Hank do?" she asked.

"He's a trainer too. He sent two colts over here to try and break their maidens (winning a race for the first time). So he came over to check on them."

While Maggi washed up the breakfast dishes, Beau walked out to see Glad Sissy. When he returned, he commented, "Boy, she really did scalp herself, didn't she? That barn is too damn low. But it seems to be healing fast. She'll be okay in a few days. I pulled her shoes off, so she wouldn't get caught in the page wire fence in the pasture when you turn her out tomorrow. She'll be a little tender-footed for a few days till her feet toughen up." He continued to talk as Maggi finished the last of the dishes.

Steve was delighted to see his Dad, but was so tired from the scout trip that he fell asleep before Beau and Maggi left for the airport. Maggi had the neighbor girl stay with him until she got back.

They met Hank in the lounge and after the introductions they had a cocktail and began talking small talk of the hazards of flying.

Maggi spoke up. "I have been told by different pilots that the best place to sit is directly over the wings. It is a smoother ride and you don't feel the turbulence so much."

Beau asked Hank, "Where do you like to sit on a plane, Hank?"

Without looking up, Hank continued sipping his martini and said, "Inside the plane . . . " Maggi realized they had an audience in the lounge as others started laughing along with them.

All too soon, Beau's flight was announced and once again they stood at the gate, saying good-bye. It seemed to Maggi that she was continually saying good-bye to Beau when her one wish was to be with him always.

Halfway home, with tears still wet on her cheeks, Maggi recalled the love-filled morning and afternoon they had shared. She thought to herself: My husband flew six hundred miles just to make love to me! She would never forget this beautiful day!

10

When school closed for the summer, Maggi was packed, had the car ready, and the horse trailer hooked on. She was taking her saddle horse Sam to free-lance ponying horses for extra money. Louie was contacted to look after their little place just before she left.

As she turned into the entrance of Hollywood Park, she was stopped instantly by the stable gateman.

He was inside a freshly painted white cottage-type building. He asked politely who she was and the nature of her business at the track. She told him, and he let the turn bar up after he told her Beau's barn number.

"Hey, Beau!" a man hollered across from another barn, "You're gonna have to behave now. The *warden's* here!" Maggi smiled at his little joke. Beau looked up, and his face broke into a wide grin. He came over, embraced her warmly, and kissed her with total abandon. Maggi was surprised at this since he was not usually so demonstrative in front of strangers, but it made her very happy.

They unloaded Maggi's saddle horse, and Beau and Steve took him to a special barn where all saddle horses were kept.

When they returned, Beau mixed the bran mash as Maggi put the leather halters on the colts. As they fed and watered the horses, they chattered away incessantly, trying to bring one another up-to-date on everything that had happened to them both in past weeks.

The dominant thought in Maggi's mind just then was the upcoming reunion with her parents. It promised to be one of the highlights of her trip, and she soon learned that she was not to be disappointed. She, Beau and Steve were received with the warmth and affection she had long since come to expect from her family. During dinner, she gazed upon each of them, her heart full of joy. Then a warm feeling in her groin came over her as she looked fondly at Beau. She was filled with the comforting thought that tonight—she would not be alone!

Maggi got up and dressed quickly. She didn't want Beau to leave without her. On the way over to Hollywood Park, Beau spoke, "Look hon, I don't want you cleaning the stalls. It would embarrass me, 'cause no women grooms are here at all," he told her. "You can walk Flame while I get his stall . . . that will be a big help.

"Hell, they thought *I* was the groom for three days— 'cause I'm galloping my horses and cleaning their stalls and rubbing them," he laughed. "But they got the best grooms in the world here. If you want to see how horses should be taken care of, you just watch these grooms," he told her.

"They keep their stalls spotless, rub the horses till they gleam, wash out their rub rags and brushes afterward, run the stalls three or four times a day, and run the prettiest set of standing bandages you've ever seen. Of course, they are only rubbing three head, and that's all they do, so they have the time, and that's what it takes—time."

Beau parked the car outside the stable area and they headed for the barn. Maggi was impressed with the stable area. Neat, freshly painted barns. Bright-colored stable plaques hanging from each stall door, colored awnings, flower boxes and grass.

Everyone they passed was dressed beautifully, she thought. The jockeys were especially impressive—some in expensive cashmere turtleneck sweaters. . . with cardigans to match, and others in soft tailored leather jackets. They all seemed to be wearing the same french-cut riding pants, fitting their trim, athletic bodies.

"God, those jockeys look handsome!" she told Beau.

"Oh, they do?" he chided back. "Well, I can see the standard trainer's garb here is tan suede coats, tan corduroy pants, and tan corduroy caps, turtlenecks and brown field boots," he continued.

Maggi walked up to the track to watch Flame gallop. She saw Bill Shoemaker, John Longden, Harry James, Betty Grable, and Mickey Rooney . . .She noticed a mutuel grandstand right on the backside. When she got back to the barn, she asked Beau about it.

"Oh, that's just for the backside personnel—grooms, trainers, owners . . . but no women are allowed there—I think because of the language. This stand gives the grooms a chance to bet and watch the races without having to walk clear around to the grandstand. Also, the management doesn't allow any of the gate crew to go to the main grandstand or to the backside stand or to bet. If they catch them at it, they're fired."

"How come?"

"Well, I guess 'cause it just don't look right for them to be up in the muteul area. People would see them betting and think they were betting on some kind of a sure thing and think something was fishy. Anyway, it don't look good for them to be walking around among the public with horse manure all over their clothes. After all, the crew are working, and not on a holiday.''

"I never thought of it that way," Maggi agreed.

"Well, I have to go over to the office—want to walk over with me?" Beau invited.

"Sure!"

On the way to the track office, jockeys and trainers kidded Beau.

"Oh, now you will have to behave—the little wifey's here." "Hey, this ain't the gal you was with yesterday!"

Maggi loved every minute of it and nodded at the swift introductions, barely stopping.

Nine a. m. The racing office was a flurry of activity since they were preparing to close down the entry booth and proceed with the drawing. Maggi sat down on a bench to wait for Beau and picked up a Condition Book that was lying on the bench.

The Condition Book is the horsemen's Bible, Beau had told her. It contains the conditions for every race: weights assigned, distances, claiming or non-claiming, and the day each race is scheduled to run. Special conditions are taken into consideration, such as races run only for fillies or three-year-olds. It's the trainers' job to scan the book with an eye toward pointing their horses to a race that will give them the best possible shot.

Any race in the book that does not fill is substituted by an *extra* (another race) which the racing secretary hangs up the night before. Each trainer is responsible for seeing that each horse he enters is eligible for the said conditions for that particular race.

Any trainer entering an ineligible horse is subject to a fine.

The Condition Book is usually rewritten every three

weeks or so to make adjustments and changes of the races to come. This gives the racing secretary an opportunity to secure a well-rounded racing card for each race day.

All Condition Books are distributed and mailed to other race tracks, enabling trainers to decide which track offers the most appropriate races for the caliber of their stables.

Beau joined Maggi as she continued to study the Condition Book and asked her, grinning, "What race would you enter Flame in?"

Maggi pointed to the race she felt would be perfect for Flame and was embarrassed when Beau burst out laughing.

"Well, what's so funny? It's for three-year-olds, non-winners of $10,000 since April, and for five-and-a-half furlongs. It fits him to a 'T'," she said haughtily.

"Now, don't get mad. Read it again," Beau insisted.

Again she failed to see. "Okay, show me where I was wrong."

"Well, it's for FILLIES ONLY—and Flame is a colt (stud). How could you forget those big *huevos* he has?" Beau asked, as he punched her, smirking. "Look, don't feel bad," Beau continued. "Understanding how to read a Condition Book is one of the hardest things for most people to grasp. You'd be surprised how many trainers don't know how to read a Condition Book and depend on some jock's agent to put their horses where they belong. Basically, it is simple, but most people, like you just did, don't register what they are reading."

"Besides, most people run their horses over their heads, and all the horse ever gets is hot," he added. "That's why Glad Sissy had such a good shot at winning that last race. It was for three-year-olds, and upwards for fillies only that hadn't won over $2,500 since January tenth of this year.

108

NINTH DAY   WEDNESDAY, JUNE 15
(Entries will be taken Monday, June 13)

FIRST RACE   MAIDEN
Purse $8,400*. For Maiden Fillies Two-Years-Old. Bred and or
Foaled in the State of Illinois
119 lbs.
FIVE FURLONGS

SECOND RACE   CLAIMING
Purse $4,700. For Fillies and Mares Four-Years-Old and Up-
ward
122 lbs.
Non-winners of two races since May 1, allowed ... 2 lbs.
A race ... 5 lbs.
Claiming Price $5,500. (for each $250 to $5,000)
(Races when entered for $4,000 or less not considered)
SIX FURLONGS

THIRD RACE   STARTER-HANDICAP
SUSIE Q
Purse $5500. For Fillies and Mares Three-Years-Old and Up-
ward that have started for a claiming price of $5,000 or less
in 1977.
(Closes Saturday, June 11. Horses not declared by Monday 9:00 A.M.
June 13 will be considered starters)
SEVEN FURLONGS (Chute)

FOURTH RACE   CLAIMING
Purse $6,000. For Four-Year-Olds and Upward
122 lbs.
Non-winners of a race since May 8, allowed ... 2 lbs.
A race since February 6 ... 4 lbs.
A race since April 9 ... 6 lbs.
Claiming Price $7,500. (for each $250 to $7,000)
(Races when entered for $6,000 or less not considered)
SIX AND ONE-HALF FURLONGS

FIFTH RACE   CLAIMING
Purse $7,000. For Four-Year-Olds and Upward
122 lbs.
Non-winners of a race since June 6, allowed ... 2 lbs.
A race since May 9 ... 4 lbs.
A race since April 9 ... 6 lbs.
Claiming Price $12,500. (for each $1,000 to $10,500)
(Races when entered for $9,500 or less not considered)
ONE MILE (Chute)

—6—

SIXTH RACE   ALLOWANCE
Purse $8,500. For Three-Year-Olds and Upward, which have
never won two races.
Three-Year-Olds   114 lbs.   Older   122 lbs.
Non-winners of two races since May 6, all wed ... 2 lbs.
A race since April 1 ... 4 lbs.
Such a race of two ... 6 lbs.
ONE MILE AND ONE-SIXTEENTH (On the Turf)

SEVENTH RACE   ALLOWANCE
Purse $8,500. For Fillies Three and Four-Years-Old, which
have never won two races other than Maiden or Claiming.
Three-Year-Olds   113 lbs.   Four-Year-Olds   121 lbs.
Non-winners of a race other than Maiden or Claiming
since May 1, allowed ... 2 lbs.
Such a race since April 15 ... 4 lbs.
Any race since May 6 ... 6 lbs.
(Races when entered for $12,500 or less not considered)
SIX FURLONGS

EIGHTH RACE   HANDICAP
FINE THANKS
Purse $18,000*. A Handicap for Fillies and Mares Three-
Years-Old and Upward. (Bred and/or Foaled in the State of
Illinois). Nominations close Saturday, June 11. Horses not
declared by 9:00 A.M. Monday, June 13 will be considered
starters.
SIX FURLONGS

NINTH RACE   CLAIMING
Purse $9,000. For Three-Year-Olds
122 lbs.
Non-winners of a race at a mile or over since June 5, allowed ... 3 lbs.
Such a race since May 6 ... 5 lbs.
Any race since April 30 ... 8 lbs.
Claiming Price $20,000. (for each $1,000 to $18,000)
(Races when entered for $15,000 or less not considered)
ONE MILE (On the Turf)

SUBSTITUTE RACE No. 1   CLAIMING
Purse $4,500. For Four-Year-Olds and Upward, (Bred and or
Foaled in the State of Illinois)
122 lbs.
Non-winners of a race since May 5, allowed ... 4 lbs.
A race since April 9 ... 6 lbs.
Claiming Price $4,000.
SIX FURLONGS

*Purse includes an additional 20% from the
Illinois Thoroughbred Breeders Fund.

—7—

The Condition book

All the tough horses had been written out. Do you
understand?''

''Yes, it's a process of elimination actually, isn't it?''

''Yeah, kind of,'' Beau said, as though he had wasted
his time. ''Well, enough of this. Let's go. I want to pick up
a *Racing Form* at the kitchen,'' he said, pulling her up
from the bench.

''When am I going to pony some outside horses?'' she
asked as they walked over.

''I don't think they'll give you a license 'cause I don't
have ten horses in my stable. I think I will have to move
Sam off the grounds if they find out he is here,'' Beau
added. ''We'll just have to wait and see.''

''How about walking hots on him?'' Maggi asked.

''Hell, no, they'd laugh me off of the backside.''

''Why?'' Maggi asked.

'' 'Cause they consider it too risky, getting a horse
kicked, and their tow ring (space between barns) is too

109

WALKING A HOT = - . -

small for another thing . . . no room like we have at home. They hire guys just to walk hots here. Mostly winos or down-and-outers making a few quick dollars every morning. Some of the bigger stables have their exercise boys do it, and hire a few steady ones. It's not much of a job, the lowest on the totem pole," he smarted off, knowing it would touch a nerve with Maggi.

"Hey, that's what I do!" she snapped back.

He held the kitchen door open. "Oh, get in and hush!"

Maggi was impressed with the track kitchen. It was well furnished and clean, and it had the same air about it as the tracks at home. Everyone talking at once and each conversation about horses—and races.

She got a doughnut and coffee while Beau read the *Form*. Since he wasn't a coffee drinker, his impatience at having to wait for her made her gulp it down.

"Okay, I'm ready," she told Beau, brushing the crumbs from her sweater.

110

While Beau finished up with his barn work, Maggi petted and talked to the horses like a small child.

"Flame," she spoke tenderly as she petted his soft muzzle, "You're the bestest and most beautiful horse here. I bet you win the Kentucky Derby next year," she crooned to the colt as he nuzzled her collar, trying to nibble it.

Beau spoke out abruptly, "I'm glad no one heard you."

"Why?" she answered cockily.

"Well, a fat chance Flame would have winning the Derby, going a mile and a sixteenth . . when he can only run five-and-a-half furlongs, period. Damn it, he's a sprinter, dum-dum," he said, as he patted her on the fanny. "Let's go home."

Maggi loved being at Hollywood Park and made sure her father got to see the track before they left. Flame won the $25,000 Juvenile Handicap and Jet won a similar handicap in the first part of the Hollywood meet. Later, they each won another small $10,000 handicap.

"Not bad for a two-horse stable!" Maggi said proudly.

In spite of their daily routine at the track, they managed to get to the seashore a few afternoons, and Maggi tanned to a golden bronze. Far too soon, the Hollywood Park meet was over.

* * * *

Del Mar "Where The Turf Meets The Surf!"

The following Sunday after Beau was through training, they headed for Del Mar to contact a real estate agent who had advertised a house trailer for three hundred for the season. Upon inspecting it, Maggi and Beau saw that it had no bath and that they were to use the facilities in the utility room in the main house. They took it.

The Del Mar race course was located at the beach on a filled-in slew. A fresh sea breeze blew constantly, inviting seasonal vacationers along with the regular horsemen and their families. The track had been built originally by Bing Crosby and many Hollywood movie stars. In the early forties, it was well supported by members of the film world but by now had lost some of its enchantment to the new Hollywood Park and Santa Anita.

Del Mar was the total opposite of Hollywood Park —smaller, a quaint atmosphere, sparse landscaping, and windy. The barns were wooden, but well built, with the grooms' quarters on the second story of each barn.

When Flame and Jet arrived by van and were stalled, Beau and Maggi completed the routine chores and headed for their rented trailer house. But the trailer they had rented and the one they found at the location were not the same.

"Christ, I've seen better buses in a junkyard!" Beau muttered.

Maggi went inside, and when she came out, she was in tears. "If you think the outside is bad, wait until you see the inside!" and she started to cry.

They contacted the real estate man and told him there had been a mix-up and that the wrong trailer had been sent. He assured them that the mistake would be corrected at once and urged them to take a motel room for the night at his expense. The next day, the right trailer arrived. Maggi unpacked their things, bought groceries, and added a few homey touches to the interior of the trailer.

Later in the day, she drove back to the track and wandered around the barn area while Beau was feeding the horses. She saw Harry James again, talking to his trainer.

In the next instant, a long white blur swung into her field of vision, and she saw that it was a big white monkey. It swung down from the grooms' sleeping quarters on a long rope that was tied to a post.

The monkey gaped at her. Then a huge black man came out of one of the tack rooms. "Jack, ya get back up here!" he commanded. The monkey was up in one jump. Maggi hated to see these exotic pets tied and confined. They suffered so, it seemed to her.

One van, and then another van pulled in. Horses were whinnying everywhere in the barn area, and grooms were greeting old friends they had not seen all summer, exchanging gossip from other meets. Great fogs of dust swirled behind each vehicle, completely engulfing Maggi. Beau caught up with her, and they went to eat.

* * * *

The next morning Maggi, Beau and Steve walked down a narrow sandy trail that went under the railroad trestle and down to the Pacific Ocean.

"Oh, Beau!" Maggi spoke out. Exercise boys and jocks in bathing suits were swimming the horses.

"It's great therapy for horses with leg problems," Beau explained. "Saves the wear-and-tear of galloping on a track."

They watched other horses wade into the rough sea with its huge breakers coming toward them in white foamy swirls. Each horse would plunge high, trying to clear each breaker until he was far enough out to swim, bobbing up and down like a giant cork in the calm swells. Then the horses swam back and forth in the deep water until they began to tire.

swimming in the surf.

Some horses got mixed up in direction and would swim toward Catalina Island. The rider would have to slap the horse's head until he would turn back toward shore.

All the horses were swimming with halters. "That's why it's harder to turn the horses around out there," Beau explained. "If you swim the horses with bits in their mouths, you hamper their swimming style."

Maggi was intrigued by the swimming styles of the horses. Some would lunge high in the air to clear the breakers while others would crash through the waves as they met them head on. Still others floundered and let the waves knock them back. There were a few horses that could not or would not swim at all.

Maggi went every morning to watch the horses swim and visit with the sightseers. Each morning brought new surprises, one being a school of porpoises that showed up unexpectedly and swam and played around the swimming horses.

"I'm going to try to swim Flame tomorrow. He's a little sore, I think he's trying to shin buck, anyway, it won't hurt him," Beau told Maggi as he was brushing out Flame's mane.

"Well, I want to see this!" she kidded him.

The next morning, Maggi watched as Beau and the horse walked in toward the surf. Flame kept jumping the breakers as he met them head on. He attacked them viciously. Both horse and rider would disappear for brief intervals, only to reappear as they headed for another breaker.

It frightened Maggi. She knew that if Beau were knocked off Flame, and the horse rolled over on top of him, Flame's feet would be like pistons striking through the water!

Flame and Beau got beyond the breakers and Maggi relaxed. She turned her head to say something to someone, and when she turned back to watch Beau and Flame—they were gone!

She heard someone yell, "Go call the Coast Guard! Hurry!" Simultaneously, someone closer said, "Hey, Maggi . . . look! It's Beau and he can't get Flame to turn back. They're heading out to sea." She turned her head around in the direction of the voice and saw that it was Arni!

"Oh, no! Oh, no!" She kept her eyes riveted to the tiny speck so far, far away. She thought of sharks . . . of the possibility of the horse drowning and taking Beau down with him.

"Don't worry, they'll get him." "He'll be all right." "They're still close," several garbled voices were all talking to her at once.

Then she saw the Coast Guard launch moving swiftly

toward them. "Thank God!" she murmured as she watched three sailors get into a small boat and row close to Beau and Flame.

In a matter of minutes they had the lead shank, Beau was in the craft, and they were heading back to shore!

She watched the small boat come in, and when it came as close as it could, Beau got back on Flame and rode him through the breakers onto shore.

Several horsemen crowded around, patting Beau on the back and ribbing him about going to Catalina on horseback.

Maggi held back her desire to run up to Beau and hug him dearly. She knew it would embarrass him, so she just went to his side and grabbed his hand and squeezed it tight without saying a word. Beau slid down from Flame.

As they walked the horse back to the barn, Beau spoke up. "Hey, now what's the matter with you?"

"Oh, Beau!" Maggi cried out. "I just *knew* you were going to drown! I felt so helpless just standing there *watching*!"

"Well . . . I didn't drown, so quit your bawling," he told her as he reached out and put his strong arm around her shoulder. He was so wet and cold as she leaned onto him and listened while he talked.

"Tomorrow I'm taking a bat (a jockey's whip) along. I can flick it at Flame's head and keep him from cold-jawing (when a horse sets his head and can't be turned or stopped)."

The next day, Maggi saw that the bat did indeed make a difference. Beau was able to turn Flame's head easily, and he settled down and swam without fighting. Still, the incident made the trainers decide to keep a launch standing by, trolling close at hand and always ready to help.

The seawater was good therapy for the horses suffering

from soreness, but it also dried out their feet and hooves, causing them to crack. That gave Beau added problems, so he decided to quit swimming Flame.

The Del Mar meet settled down to the everyday routine and since Arni had arrived from the California fairs, he hung around Beau's barn after the morning training was done, talking with Beau.

After a while, Maggi realized he was picking Beau's brain and told Beau so.

"Oh, you're crazy! You didn't like Pee Wee, you complained about Doc, you're always finding fault with my friends. Damn it, I have known Arni for years, and I consider him my best friend. Now, just leave me alone!" and he stomped off.

Maggi never brought up Arni's name again.

Mr. Henderson came by right after Beau's outburst and asked Maggi, "Where's Beau?"

"Down in Flame's stall, I think," she told him.

"Hello, Beau. I have some vitamins and things in my car for you to give the colts. You know, I'm like Doc Hardy. I don't believe in paying those big vet bills. Anything you need, you tell me. I can get it from a doctor friend of mine. I'll go get the stuff."

"Okay," Beau answered, and as he watched him leave, he thought, "You tight old bastard. It's okay for me to stick my neck out to save you a dollar"—but having syringes and needles to give the vitamins with was frowned upon at the track—and Henderson knew it!

Maggi agreed with Beau as he spoke, but she didn't want any more outbursts today. The one over Arni was enough.

Yet Arni continued to pal around Beau morning, noon and afternoons. Maggi thought men occasionally need some time to themselves and made a point of keeping herself busy when they took off to look at a racehorse. Or even when they went to the races. Arni had a built-in deal with his rich in-laws and placed many casual bets for them. Maggi knew Beau wasn't betting like Arni was, but he was risking a few dollars now and again. Once more, Maggi rationalized that Beau needed a little relaxing fun like anyone else. This she didn't mind. It was the time he was spending with someone else rather than with her that she resented.

Beau was restless. His two-horse stable allowed him to pall. Flame was shin bucking, and was out for the rest of this meet, and there wasn't a race in the book for Jet. So Beau welcomed Arni to break the daily boredom. Yet, he wasn't aware of how much he had told Arni about horses and the way he trained them these past weeks.

Beau was painting some medicine on Flame's shins one afternoon while talking to Maggi. "I think we'll be going home soon. Flame needs to be turned out, and it wouldn't hurt Jet," he stated. "And I need to get Glad Sissy up and the few horses Les has turned out."

"Yes, and Steve's school will be starting soon," Maggi added. "Gosh, the summer sure went fast."

HOME! It sounded so good to her. But the next day they found out that Henderson had other plans. As he informed Beau, "I have decided to stay here in California and race. The purses are better and the quality of horses is better. And I want you to continue to train for me."

Beau was taken by surprise. "I thought you were going back to Arizona. This is a big surprise! Let me talk it over with Maggi, and I'll let you know tomorrow," he told Henderson as he mulled it over in his mind. Move here! California!

That night they talked for hours. It was a hard decision to make on the spur of the moment. So many things had to be considered . . . their home . . . the move . . . Steve . . . the cost. Could they afford it? And the uncertainty of it all was the big one! Beau knew it was tough racing in California, especially with a small client like Henderson.

"I just don't know if he would last if he wasn't winning any races," Beau told Maggi. "He might just decide to quit and there we'd be, stuck here without any horses."

"Do whatever you want to," Maggi said. "I'll go along with you. After all, isn't this what you wanted and worked for—a good stable?" she asked.

"Yes, but Henderson is just a tiny pebble in a pile here. Oh, I guess it's a good deal. I guess we'll take the chance, but I'm going to make him pay me a straight training fee and let me take other outside horses, if I get a chance," Beau stated.

"That's fair enough," Maggi agreed.

But when Beau told Henderson the next morning, Henderson informed him, "I have already made other arrangements. I got me a trainer who didn't have to go home and talk it over with his wife," he said flatly.

"Who?" Beau asked.

"Arni!" The sound of the name burned deep inside Beau's brain.

ARNI! he thought. The little sneaky son-of-a-bitch, behind my back . . . Maggi was right! She tried to warn me about him just using me all the time! The prick!

Beau was livid. "Good! That's fine," he snapped back, wanting to get the hell away from Henderson as soon as possible.

"Do you want to turn these colts over to him now?" Beau asked.

"Oh, no, you finish up this meet and take these colts. . .

and all my tack . . . back to Phoenix to my place. I'll settle up with you then, okay?''

"Fine," Beau snapped sharply and walked away.

Maggi had just come back from the store and was putting the groceries away when Beau came through the door, striking his head on the low frame as he had before.

"Goddamn this son-of-a-bitch fucking trailer!" he shouted, as he kicked the door open. Maggi started toward him to comfort him. He pushed her aside.

"Leave me alone!" he barked.

Maggi burst into tears and fled to the bedroom. Beau came after her, apologizing.

"It isn't your fault. I don't know why I take it out on you. It's that rotten Les Henderson. I'd like to punch that tight son-of-a-bitch right in the mouth!"

"Why?" Maggi asked, still sobbing jerkily.

"Because he hired Arni last night to take over the stable."

SHOCK!! . . . set into Beau and Maggi. They were depressed and in despair for the next few days . . . until Beau said one afternoon, "Honey, don't worry—we'll make it. We still have Glad Sissy." He laughed out loud and so did she . . . the spell was broken.

Because of the change in their plans, Beau wanted Maggi to go home earlier and pony Glad Sissy until he got there. Maggi was sorry she had brought her saddle horse. She thought she could have ridden him more, but the race tracks there were so strict about stalls for saddle horses unless a trainer had a big stable. She had been forced to put her horse out in a faraway pasture. Now she would have to go and get him, besides all the other things she still had to do before leaving—cleaning the trailer, washing all of Beau's clothes, packing and getting the car serviced. All the while she was doing these things, *that same, dull sick feeling came over her as at each time she had to leave Beau.*

YUMA! 118°! The heat was too much for her old car. The water pump went out! She and Steve, Rip, and the horse had to wait four hours for the motor to cool off so that a mechanic could work on it.

By seven o'clock, she started across the hottest part of the Arizona desert—with a six hour drive still ahead of her. Totally exhausted, she arrived home at three a.m., unloaded the tired saddle horse, fed him, got Steve off to bed, took a shower and fell into clean sheets.

"It's good to be home," she thought as she sank into a deep, fitful sleep.

11

Everyone on the backside of any race track knows that the owners are the lifeline to racing. Horse racing would not last long without the wealthy client, the flamboyant spender. These are the people who pick up the tab . . . some to support their own ego trips to the winner's circle . . . others to make the sports page headlines . . . some for sheer pleasure. They make it possible for a poor man to become a famous and rich horse trainer if he has the ability. And even a few who didn't know very much about training horses got rich because of the wealthy owners.

Beau had said many times, "As long as you got that money, there's always plenty of horses."

And he was right, for horse racing takes money to survive. It is costly and risky and can eat up a good-sized bank roll in just a few years. This was what was going on in Maggi's head on the long, lazy autumn afternoons. Somehow Beau had to get good owners. That was the name of the game!

Beau finally came home, returned all of Henderson's tack, settled up with him, and began to gallop Glad Sissy in the back field.

* * * *

State Fair Meet — Third Season

The second night Beau was at home, Bert Maddox called. He had two horses to put in training if Beau could get the stalls for them at the fairgrounds. He also mentioned two men in New Mexico, John Jacobs and Clint Roberts, who were looking for someone to train their horses. They were dissatisfied with their present trainer.

News around the race track traveled fast. Maddox had already heard about Henderson hiring Arni. He voiced his own disgust on the subject, but Beau merely glossed it over, dismissing the entire matter.

Maggi followed through on the two owners in Ruidoso, even though Beau told her, "You're just wasting your time. They probably got someone else."

"Well, Bert tells it differently," Maggi snapped back, tired of the constant battle of fighting her way past Beau's procrastination.

She called and spoke to one of the men, "Here, I'll let you talk to my husband," and she handed Beau the phone and listened to his end of the conversation.

"Well . . . I'll go to the track tomorrow and see about getting stalls," Beau said listlessly. "I can't tell you anything at this time. I'll have my wife call you tomorrow. Okey-dokey . . . good bye," he said, and hung up.

He threw Maggi sour look. "A fine stable I got . . . four broken-down bastards and Bert's horses won't be ready to run for sixty days. I'll be lucky if I get one stall."

In spite of Beau's ranting, he got four stalls and Maggi asked, "What about the other two horses?"

"I can keep them at Bob Whitey's place—"

"Who's he?" Maggi asked.

"A jock's agent. He has a little acre with some stalls in

123

his backyard. I can get them for $15 a month. It will be a pain in the ass, but if I want to keep those horses, that's the only way," he told her.

Maggi found out what he meant by pain in the ass. Splitting a stable was more work, hauling feed, rakes, saddles back and forth—to Whitey's and to the fairgrounds every day. Plus, she never realized till now how big the stalls were at the fairgrounds—15 by 15—and it took four big bales of straw to bed them down the first time. That was one thing Beau had instilled in her, " A good soft bed keeps a horse from getting body sore, and he will rest better."

The next few days Beau and Maggi worked hard, long hours getting their small stable set up. They had to borrow a lot of tack from Bert Maddox, since Beau had very little himself.

"I don't know what we would do without Bert," Beau told Maggi while he was snapping up a stall chain and putting in another screw eye.

"Speaking of the devil, here he is now," Maggi laughed.

"Hello, you two. Looks like you're about set up," Bert remarked.

"I hope so," Maggi answered. "What brings you here so early?"

"Well, a friend of mine in Hot Springs, Arkansas who sold me some dairy cows, said there was a good horse I should buy down there," he told Beau and Maggi.

"What's his name?" Beau asked instantly.

"Sir Tribal," he told Beau.

"How much they asking for him?" Beau asked again.

"$9,000," Bert replied.

"Boy! That's a lot of money for a horse you haven't even seen," he told Bert.

"I know, but I trust this guy. Here's a chart on him," he

handed Beau a slip of paper.

"Christ, he ran for $1000 claim a while back," Beau ranted. "That don't look too good. How come these people are selling him?"

"They are selling their whole stable and going out of the business," he stated. "What do you think, Beau?" Bert asked.

"Don't ask me. I hate to tell you what to do," Beau snapped back.

Maggi listened. "Why doesn't he let Bert buy the horse?" she thought.

"Well, I have to let the guy know tomorrow so I'll call you and let you know what I decided," Bert told Beau and Maggi and left—and then turned right around and came back. "Look, why don't you catch a plane and go take a look at the horse?"

"Uh, Uh—not me! I don't like to fly," Beau balked.

"Oh for Christ's sake, you flew to California and back," Maggi stated.

"Yeah, but I didn't like it one bit, and besides, this is a longer flight. Forget it," he said firmly.

* * * *

The next day, Doc Hardy was at the barn before sun-up.

"I have two colts I had sold, and these people want you to take them," he told Beau. "I can get you the stalls if you will take them."

"Sure, I'll take them—if you get the stalls."

"Consider it done," he told Beau and left.

"Hey, that will be six head here and two over at Whitey's. I'll have to get someone to help us," Beau told Maggi. "That way they can feed early, and we can take more time with the horses and do it right."

"That sounds like a good idea," Maggi agreed.

"Oh, here comes Bert. I hope he bought that horse," she told Beau.

"Well, we waited too long. Sir Tribal was sold yesterday —to a Charles Fritz from Chicago—Steve Ippolito will train the horse for him," Bert told Beau. "You know, I have a hunch about that horse. I should have bought him."

"As long as you have the money, Bert, there will always be horses," Beau told him. "He's probably a nice horse, but damn, that's a lot of money to lay down for a horse that has run for a $1000 claiming—and really hadn't shown much on his past performance," Beau added.

"Well, maybe so, but I'm going to keep track of him and see how he does," Bert said.

Bert soon dropped the subject and reverted back to his horses, inquired how they were doing, and then left.

"I wish you could have gotten Sir Tribal to train," Maggi spoke up. "He might be a good horse."

"Oh, what the hell do you know? I'm not sticking my neck out, and the bastard turn out to be no-count . . . so, just shut up about it, will you! We have enough to worry about without Sir Tribal!"

Maggi was angry, wheeled away, and went to scrubbing out a water bucket, thinking—how in the hell is he ever going to get good horses when he keeps turning them away!

Maggi liked Juan instantly. He was a small-boned man, neat and very polite. To Maggi, Juan was a luxury, for she and Beau didn't have to get up so early, with Juan feeding the five a.m. grain, plus they didn't have to go back to the track to water out the horses and shut the bottom doors and muzzle the horses that were in the next day, after they ate their bran mash. He was well worth the fifty a week!

126

In spite of Juan, her tiresome job of walking hots continued for Maggi. The cold winter mornings were miserable for her. She tried every way to keep warm, but her feet still froze. She wrapped two bulky coolers around each leg and put on two pairs of heavy socks, sweater, and a heavy mackinaw, but her fingers and feet would smart and sting from the cold frost snap. Oh, how she waited for the sun to rise and warm her cold feet and hands.

To make things worse, it rained for ten days straight, and the backside was a mess. Mud everywhere! It was so deep that the manure trucks could not get to the manure piles. They got so high it was hard to cross from one barn to another—not to mention the stench of it.

The race track itself got deeper and heavier each day. The horsemen began to complain that it was breaking horses down. But the management couldn't do anything about it; the track was too muddy to work.

But racetrackers go on . . . rain, mud, . . . whatever. Beau ran two horses opening day—Greek Boy and Shame —finishing a third and a fourth.

Maggi found it hard to believe when Beau showed her that Greek Boy's shoes had been twisted off by the suction from the deep mud.

"That's how a horse hurts himself on a track like this, 'cause his foot sticks and stays put and he pulls tendons or breaks a leg," Beau remarked.

"Then why take the chance of crippling them?" she asked.

"Because I'm stupid like everyone else. I really shouldn't run another horse, since they've had two spills today," he stated. "I look for the jockeys to call the races off."

"You mean the jocks can call off the races?"

"Yep, anytime they think a racetrack is unsafe for their

127

well-being, they can refuse to ride," he declared.

"Well, I'll be darned," she remarked. "They sure have a lot of power, don't they?"

"They sure do. When I was riding at the Caliente track one year, all the jocks felt it was unsafe to run a fourteen head field going a mile, 'cause it made it hairy going into the first turn," he told Maggi. "So, the management agreed to that request, for the safety of the jockeys and horses. After all, the jocks are the ones who are risking their necks, so they better look out for their own safety."

Maggi had never before realized just how right that was, and saw management had no choice. "After all, where are they going to get ten jockeys to replace them on the spur of the moment?" she laughed.

"Oh, don't be such a smart-ass!" Beau kidded her. "Besides, you know that most tote boards can handle only a ten-horse field- Anything over the ten-horse field is considered the 11—12—13—14 field or an entry like 1 and 1A . . ."

"Oh, I see, " Maggi answered.

"See, my eye, you don't know anything about the tote board," Beau laughed.

The rain continued, and the gloomy days and mud caused a depressed mood throughout the barn area. There was talk of the jockeys calling the races off. Beau was disgusted because he couldn't run any of his horses. Then Bert came by and made matters worse.

"Well, my hunch was right. Read this!" he told Beau as he handed him a *Racing Form*. Maggi got up and read over Beau's shoulder. The bold black print made her sick as she read the article:

SIR TRIBAL

Sir Tribal, horse racing's latest Cinderella runner, is probably one of Oklahoma's greatest contributions to the turf world. The five-year-old grey gelding is owned by Charles Fritz, a Chicago businessman, and trained by Steve Ippolito. The fleet horse is currently running at Chicago's Washington Park. Sir Tribal has boosted his lifetime earnings to $112,675, from a dismal beginning when Sir Tribal once ran in a $1,000 claiming race.

Sir Tribal has placed five firsts, three seconds, and three thirds out of his 16 starts in 1956 . . . Sir Tribal's chief victories came in the Balmoral Turf handicap and the Stars and Stripes handicap at Washington Park. Sir Tribal ran behind Maham in the Meadowland and the other in the Arch Ward Memorial when Swaps ran 7th. In the rich Arlington handicap, Sir Tribal came in third behind two of the best horses in the business: Mister Gus and Summer Tan . . . Not bad for a horse bought for $9,000, who ran for $1,000.

There was a long silence after they read the article. Then Beau spoke. "Gosh, I feel bad now, Bert—'cause you wanted to buy him."

"Oh hell, don't be silly! That's horse racing . . . win some lose some," Bert chided Beau, trying to make up for the fact that they didn't get the horse.

To make matters even worse, almost every trainer told Beau, "Hey, did you see where Sir Tribal, the horse you almost bought won the big one in Chicago? That lucky Charlie Fritz, he's getting rich with that horse!"

"Yeah, yeah—I've read it," was all Beau could say.

It was days before the talk of Sir Tribal simmered down. But not for Maggi. She thought about it for days. To be so close! Losing was not so easy for her to accept.

That Saturday, the jockeys called off the races after a bad spill in the third race.

For three days, racing was cancelled till it quit raining, and then racing continued.

Beau got lucky and won three races and two seconds in the next two weekends. Then came Armistice Day, and the big 200-mile Armistice Day Auto Race.

Horseracing was cancelled that Sunday. Saturday night they rolled the track and added a special salt chemical to pack the dirt hard for the big car race.

Monday morning regular training resumed, but the salt chemical made the track so hard that all the trainers had a special meeting with the management about it.

They agreed to dig it up and run a pulverizer on it, but luck was not on their side. Before they could restore the track it began to rain again, night and day, for the next two weeks.

The track got deeper after each race. It was almost impossible to train on it because of the gooey substances caused by the salt chemical.

Even when it finally quit raining, the race track wouldn't dry out, because the chemical held the moisture in, and the track became heavy and doughy. It was impossible for the tractors and harrows to operate on it. Management was desperate. They and the state were losing money because they kept calling off one or two races a day. Meetings were held to try to find a solution. One trainer suggested that everyone drive a car or truck around and around the track until it packed down. That didn't work. Another suggested

130

getting five hundred sheep and walking them around to pack the track down.

"Where in the hell are you going to get five hundred sheep?" everyone laughed.

Finally, management and horsemen thought of a solution that might work. "Let's try scraping the gooey mess off to one side," the spokesman said.

Four huge road graders were brought in, and they scraped down to the hard clay bottom of the race track. Pushing the loose, gummy mud down onto the inside rail of the race track resulted in a four foot wide, two foot high embankment.

When Beau saw the embankment, down on the inside rail, he shook his head. "I've seen a lot of things happen around a race track, but this is the first time I ever saw a track like this to race on. Why, horses will drop in on the rail from habit, and they'll just bog down in that deep going, you'll see."

His prediction was right. Every race two, three or more horses turning for home would drop down on the rail and hit the deep mud, and it stopped them cold! They bogged down to their flanks—exhausted!

It took twenty men each time to literally push and pull a horse out of the mud—and each time the crowd was roaring with laughter at the pitiful sight—as if the horse just sulked!

It became a hopeless effort, and finally the balance of the race meet was cancelled. Stables moved out instantly to the fairs and other meets. Only the ones who planned to race at the Turf Paradise Meet stayed on. That meet wasn't to open for another three weeks, but the Horsemen's Benevolent Protective Association talked management into letting horses come in early by agreeing to pay for the utilities till the meet opened.

This created an avalanche of stall applications at Turf. Some of the horses had to remain at the fairgrounds and be shuttled back and forth when they were to run.

Beau was one of these stables. "Me and the goddamn gyps are the only ones left at the fairgrounds," he snapped to Maggi.

"Well, look at the good side. We won't have that long drive," Maggi stated, trying to comfort his hurt ego . . . because he was turned down for stalls.

* * * *

Turf Paradise—Third Time

By the end of March, stables were shipping out daily so they let Beau move his horses into Turf.

"Now they let me have stalls—when I don't have anything left," he complained. He had only four head since he had turned out two that were getting sore. "Hell, if it weren't for Glad Sissy, I wouldn't even win a race."

Beau was down. And to add to his mood, Sir Tribal again made the headlines in the *Racing Form*.

SIR TRIBAL

Charlie Fritz's Super Horse! The sooner-bred racing star was chosen as one of 12 horses to run in the United Nations race in Balmoral late in the year. In that race only the top horses from throughout the world will complete.

SIR TRIBAL, winner of four of his 11 starts for Charles Fritz of Chicago, added $16,875 to his earnings.

Not bad for a horse that once had been entered for a $1,000 claiming race!

Beau showed the write-up to Maggí and she said, "Boy this doesn't help any, does it? That's all you need. I can't believe this horse! He just keeps getting better every time they run him."

"I guess he's the best damn horse back there right now," Beau stated. "I can just hear Bert when he sees this," he added. "He'll never let me live that down. I wish the son-of-a-bitchen horse would drop dead! Oh no, I don't really mean that either. I'm just disgusted, that's all," he retorted. "Look, you don't need to come to the track now. We can rub these four, and might even let Juan go. We really can't afford to keep him anymore, 'cause it don't look like I'm going to pick up any horses for the summer."

"Oh, something will turn up, you'll see," Maggi spoke.

"Oh, shut up! Goddamn, I'm so sick of you and your goddamn predictions! You don't know shit! What are you talking about? Just leave me alone!"

"Okay, okay—I'll leave you alone, damnit!" And she walked out of the room, thinking to herself, "What a bear! Just because Sir Tribal turned out so good, he's taking it out on me!"

Beau continued to stay in his caustic mood. Maggi got her old job back, and the days that followed were not the best.

Beau began to stay at the track longer than necessary, drinking at the local bars. This was a surprise to Maggi. She had never figured Beau as a steady drinker. She didn't like it one bit, and heated fights were the end result.

"Damn this racing business anyway. You can't depend on any security, and you're constantly moving about the country," she ranted one night when Beau came in late.

"Well, you just as well get used to it, 'cause that's all I know, and want to do!" he ranted back, going out the

133

door.

Maggi hated this part of their arguments, she never got to finish what she wanted to say. She spent most of her workday time thinking about their problems.

* * * *

It was April. Maggi came home earlier than usual. She didn't feel well and begged off the rest of the day. She found Beau stretched out on the couch.

"Well, you're home early," she said smartly, thinking maybe he was trying to behave himself.

"I got ruled off today," he said solemnly. "They're giving me till noon tomorrow to turn all of my horses over to a new trainer and to get my tack off the grounds."

"How come?" She was stunned.

"It was Henderson. He turned me in. Someone I know in the office told me."

"Ruled you off for what?" she asked again.

"For having the vitamins, syringes, and needles in my tack room. Henderson always knew where I kept all that stuff."

"Well, how long will this be for?" she asked.

"Six months—maybe a year. I don't know. I won't know till they have my hearing sometime in July. You should be happy now," he told her and turned his face away into the couch back.

"Oh Beau, what a terrible thing to say! You know I was just blowing off steam," she confronted him. "That rotten Henderson, he's the most miserable person I have ever known," she added.

"Oh, forget about it, and shut up," he told her.

The stewards were hateful to Beau. They stated that he could not put Glad Sissy in his Dad's name or in the name of any other friend who might try to run her for Beau. If anyone tried to run the horse, they too would get into trouble.

Beau told Maggi, "I got a chance to sell the mare, and get $2,500. She's running good right now. If I turn her out till I get back up, she might not come back. Besides, we might need the money."

Beau left early the next morning to get things moved and settled. When he returned home, he was sporting a black eye. It seemed he had stopped at the local bar and someone made a smart remark about him getting the ax, and the fight was on! Maggi put hot and cold compresses over his eye and tried to reassure him that things would work out, and that they would make it. After all, they always had in the past.

The next morning, the newspaper carried an ugly story pushing everything out of focus. Maggi hid the paper that morning before she left. Funny, she thought, now she and Beau were somehow closer than ever before!

12

"I'm going to see if I can find work or some colts to break," Beau said one morning as he barged out of the house.

He came back late that afternoon, grinning as he came through the door. "I've got a job at the livestock auction, pushing cattle onto the scale and loading them on the trucks," he told Maggi.

She went to greet him with a kiss.

"I'm a little rank," he said, and her nostrils verified the stench of cow manure and the odor of perspiration from Beau's body. He was exhausted. As he tried to pull off his boots, Maggi helped him peel off his sweaty shirt. "I'm getting a dollar an hour . . ."

Maggi wanted to cry. A dollar an hour! That was slave wages. She filled a hot tub, encouraged him to slide into it, and sponged the warm water over his back as he relaxed.

"I'll bet it was a hundred-and-fifty degrees in those damn alleys," he said wearily.

Maggi noticed the skin between his legs was galled from chaffing. After the bath, she put some soothing ointment over the galled area. As soon as Beau ate a hot meal, he hit the bed, and as she closed the door quietly, she thought, not many men would take such a menial job to bring home a living for his family. She loved Beau more right at that moment than she ever had.

* * * *

When Bert found out that Beau was getting only a dollar an hour, he had a fit. "Hell, you don't need that! You come and work for me, milking these cows. I'll pay you a hundred-and-fifty a week, plus all the milk you can drink."

Maggi threw her arms around Maddox.

"Hell, you kids are like my own," he said, hugging her back.

Beau was equally as good at milking cows as he was with training horses. He loved livestock and being on Bert's ranch and it showed in his disposition. Life was very pleasant for Maggi, Steve and Beau for the next few months. Until the letter from the racing commission came!

July 1958

ARIZONA RACING COMMISSION
Phoenix, Arizona

Conc:
Ruling: Beau Witlow

Dear Mr. Witlow,

The Arizona Racing Commission hereby requests your presence, for your hearing, September 20, 8:00 A.M.

Racing Commission Secretary

Maggi's first impulse was to throw the damn letter away. Things were going so well for them now.

The morning of the hearing, Maggi waited in the pickup parked outside the Commission office. It seemed like an eternity to her, yet only an hour passed since Beau went into the meeting.

She saw him walking from the building and toward her. She could tell nothing from his slow, ambling gait. His head and face were down so she couldn't read anything from them. He looked glum to her; her heart was pounding with suspense as he climbed into the truck and started the motor.

"For God's sake, say something!" she cried out "What happened?"

"I get back up September 25th," he grinned.

"Oh Beau, I'm so happy for you!" she answered, and hugged him.

"Come on, we'll celebrate. I'll buy you some Mexican food," he smiled and kissed her cheek.

That night, Bert Maddox stated, "I know you're anxious to get back to the track, but I will be losing a damn good milker!"

Turf Paradise Their Fourth Time

With men like Bert and Doc pulling for Beau, he soon had a six-horse stable put together. Beau went to Turf to check about stalls. There was no doubt he would get stalls at Turf, but how many was the problem. But with Doc's clout he got six stalls. Being away from the track for six months made Beau eager, and he plunged into training with renewed zest and vigor.

By the time the meet started, one of Bert's horses was ready to run on opening day.

Training for the Maddoxes was an experience. They were totally different people in competition—bad losers, bitchers. Bert's constant remarks when he didn't win were, "Hell, they didn't let my horse run.—That damn jock pulled him.—They knocked him down coming out of the gate."

Beau told Maggi, "Hell, they will never admit their horse just got beat. It's always someone is crooked," he added, "I hate training for people like them; if I felt like they did, I'd quit. Damned if I'd want to be a part of something I thought was crooked.

"Hey, don't get me wrong! I like ole Bert. He's a great guy, but he's got the wrong temperament for horse racing," Beau explained to Maggi.

"I understand what you are trying to say," she answered.

"Yeah, and to make it even harder to get along with him, that damn Sir Tribal has won again back in Chicago," he added.

"Oh, not again!" she answered.

"Hell, yes! He is a top grass running horse from what I heard at the track this morning. Here, read this," and he handed her the *Racing Form*.

> **SIR TRIBAL,** who once ran for a $1,000 claiming race, then was later purchased for $9,000 has amassed $55,000 this season with his eight victories under all sorts of conditions. Charlie Fritz's grey wonder will run in the STARS AND STRIPES . . . for $25,000 purse on the grass. . .

"Wow!" Maggi exclaimed. "Has he made the money for that Charlie Fritz! Bet that Steve Ippolito, his trainer, is glad he beat Bert in the purchase!"

"Oh, I don't want to hear anymore about it—I'll get enough of that static from Bert," he grumbled.

*   *   *   *

Since Beau had hired Juan back, Maggi came to the track only on weekends. It was on one of these weekends while she was brushing off one of their horses that Pee Wee came up to the door of the horse's stall.

"Well, for goodness sake, where did you come from?" Maggi asked.

"Sunland Park," he answered with a pleasant smile.

Maggi noticed he didn't look healthy, his skin was ashen white, his eyes drawn and his face puffy. "He must be drinking," she thought.

"Where's the big honcho?" he asked

"He's taking a horse to the track. Should be back soon," she answered. "What are you doing here, going to ride?"

"No, I'm too heavy. That's why I left Sunland. Couldn't get any mounts," he told her.

Right away Maggi's mind went to thinking, "Now he'll be here all winter." He was bad news as far as she was concerned.

*   *   *   *

It made no difference what she felt or thought, old friendship ties are hard to break. Beau was loyal to Pee Wee, making a job for him, letting him gallop a few horses to compensate for the few bucks he slipped to him. Maggi went along with it until it began to interfere with her and Beau, and fights resulted.

It amazed her how quickly Beau reverted to his old slovenly ways by being around Pee Wee and his crowd.

They were a casual crowd—boots, Levi's, and seldom shaven. He loved being comfortable and never was trying to impress anyone, he was just Beau—earthy and carefree. In his own mind he never thought anything was wrong with stopping at the local bar for a few drinks with the gang ... until one night he couldn't make it home.

As Beau listened to Maggi's lament, he knew he was wrong, yet he was a stubborn man. He was raised with the macho image and no damn woman was going to tell him what to do. He had been getting far too much static from the track, everyone telling him daily, "Boy that Maggi has really got you jumping!" and "You better get home, or Maggi will skin you alive. We know you can't stop by and have a drink 'cause Maggi won't let you," was the clincher, so he had to show them—and he intended to show her too.

Finally, he spoke out. "Look, if you don't like it, what are you going to do about it?" he challenged.

She was taken by surprise by this statement. "Well, if that's the way you feel, then move out."

"Okay, I will."

* * * *

Beau moved into his tack room. He felt good just to do whatever he wanted. He had all he needed; his horses and no one to bug him. Maggi tried to get him to come home, pleading almost! Pee Wee was of no help by being his constant companion and filling any void of Beau's being alone. Maggi hated him with a passion.

April and the Turf Meet were over. Bert Maddox told Maggi to come over to his house as Beau would be there to pick up his training check since Beau was leaving that week for Ruidoso. "Maybe you can patch things up," he told her.

She confronted Beau. "What's wrong?"

"It's you," he stated. "You and your goddamn smart advice and constant nagging. You always want everything to be so perfect. You don't like my friends or the way I dress. I'm sorry, but that's the way it is." And he got up and walked out the door. She was stunned by his stinging words.

Pee Wee spoke up, "Look, don't pay any attention to the S.O.B., he's just blowing off smoke. You just hang in there." She looked at him as he smiled. She thought, "I have misjudged Pee Wee; he is my friend."

Beau and Pee Wee arrived at Ruidoso. Beau missed Maggi already. It wasn't the same without her and Steve, but he pushed the thoughts quickly from his mind. He kept himself busy training the horses, spending more time than ever before rubbing their legs with tender, loving care. "After all," he thought, "time is what I have lots of."

The last three weeks were insane for Maggi. She missed Beau terribly. It was Bert who finally told her, "Go on up to Ruidoso, you and the kid. After all, he is still your husband."

She liked Ruidoso instantly. The tall pine trees and mountains that surrounded the tiny little race track—and it was so cool! She had no trouble moving Pee Wee out of the shabby house trailer he and Beau shared. He was glad to oblige.

"Okay Beau—look! Either we eat together, sleep together, and be a family, or you can just get a damn divorce!"

Beau raged out the door.

"Oh, no! Not this time," she stated, following him in

hot pursuit. When he climbed into his truck and peeled out, she got into the car and tore out after him. They were speeding down the narrow mountain road, and as they approached a sharp turn, she forced his truck off the road and down an embankment.

"You're crazy!" he shouted out the window.

"Maybe I am. But we're going to settle this now!" she shouted back.

"Okay!" he bellowed, and turned the truck around. Maggi was close behind.

"Okay," he stated as he stepped into the house trailer, "I'll get a divorce." With that, he stormed down the narrow hall of the trailer, bumping into furniture and slamming cupboard doors. Maggi just stood pat and watched him.

"If that's what you really want, fine," she said. "Nothing could be worse than the way we're living now."

She was wondering what he would do next and was surprised when he finally replied.

"Go get dressed. We'll be late for the first race."

* * * *

Reconciliation did not happen overnight. Beau was so stubborn and hard-headed, and Maggi never knew Beau could be this mean! He would cuss her out for no reason until she became the same way toward him. Then, he began to soften and change gradually. She put up with this, for now she knew he loved her, and she was sure of that more than anything else.

Maggi and Steve got their job back—walking the hots. She hated walking hots more than cleaning stalls. It was boring and timeless. "Any stupid jerk that could hold a horse could be taught to walk a hot," she thought. And it irked her that every time she would ask Beau, "How much longer does this horse have?" he would answer, "Just keep turning to the left—I'll let you know," knowing full well it ticked her off.

She decided she was going to do more important things; this was going to be her life as well as Beau's.

She soon realized all trainers were not like Beau. The biggest majority went home early after the morning training was done. Not Beau. He stayed and rubbed his horses down and spent a lot of time on their sore legs. And she had seen results in how these long hard hours paid off.

Another good therapy Beau used was to take the horses down to a small creek that ran through the middle of the stable area. An old wooden bridge reached over it to the main track, and a narrow trail led down to the stream. Almost every afternoon a few other horsemen besides Beau and Maggi would stand their horses in the cold water, letting the current swirl around their sore ankles and knees. While they talked about Sir Tribal and other things, Beau cautioned Maggi about the stream.

"Look, if any of our horses has a cut or scratch, be sure and tell me 'cause this water will sure infect it and blow up their leg as big as your head," he stated.

"I sure will," she assured him.

Beau agreed to show Maggi how to do a horse up (rub their legs with a special leg brace and run standing bandages).

He cautioned her again, "You always rub downward, never up, especially on a tendon, 'cause you will make them skin sore. And if you put a standing bandage on too tight or wrong, you can even bow a horse's tendon," he added. "That's why you've got to know what you're doing. Most people don't, and do more harm than good."

She believed him and watched him as he began to rub the

horse's leg. He poured some leg brace into the palm of his hand, then applied it to the horse's leg, rubbing it in with a downward motion, his hands moving like slow pistons as he sat, Indian style, in the deep soft bedding. She noticed the horse just stood motionless.

"See, they like this rubbing. It will put a lot of them to sleep." As he rubbed, he then told her, "Always be careful what you put on their legs, 'cause you can blister with the wrong stuff. Another thing, any time you decide to change medicine, be sure you scrub the leg down with castile soap and rinse it off good and let the leg dry thoroughly. If you put one medicine over another, you can blister the hair and skin all off." As he talked, he never stopped rubbing in the downward motion except to add more brace when the leg got dry. He rubbed for thirty minutes.

"Hand me one of those cotton rolls," he told her.

"How many sheets of cotton do you put into one of these?" she asked.

"Three or four, the thicker the better, and you fold them back and forth, making them smooth and then roll them into this size bandage. They should fit between the knee and the ankle, otherwise they will be too bulky and awkward." She watched him as he rolled the clean white cotton wraps around the horse's leg, carefully pulling it taut, and keeping it smooth.

"Now give me that flannel bandage," he asked her.

"This looks like the same stuff they shine shoes with, " she kidded him.

"It is, that's where they got it from—the track— 'cause it's soft and tough, stands a lot of Clorox and washing. You buy it in two-yard sheets and tear them into four-inch-wide bandages." She watched as he carefully tucked the end in under the cotton wrap, first securing it and then rolled the wrap around the leg, overlapping about a half inch all the way down to the ankle and back toward the knee till he got to the end. She noticed he folded back the end of the bandage.

"Why did you do that?"

"You never want to end up on the inside or back of the leg, 'cause of the pins. Always end your bandage on the outside of the leg, so when the horse lays down he don't lay on the pins and open them up," he continued. "Because, then the bandage will come off and sometimes even the pins can stick the horse."

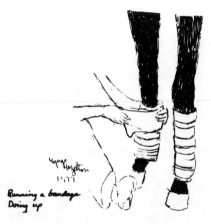

Running a bandage
Doing up

"Boy, there is more to this than a person thinks," she remarked as she watched him stick the safety pins in and secure them by criss-crossing them, so they would not come unpinned.

He let her do the other leg. She had no trouble rubbing the leg and putting the brace on. But when it came to running the bandages, she asked Beau, "How's that?"

"Well, looks like you ran them on with a pitchfork," he

laughed, and she took them off to give it another try.

But in time, she mastered the skill and began to do a horse up like a pro. After she realized how much they wasted by throwing away the cotton sheets every day or so, she improvised and bought several mattress pads, cutting them into six bandages rolls.

"Not bad!" Beau stated.

"And they can be washed over and over," she added. "It's alot cheaper than the cotton wraps."

"Hey, they're okay. We'll use them," Beau told her. She felt pleased that she had done something right for a change!

13

With only getting $5 per day per horse and the ten percent of the wins, their income wasn't much to cheer about after they paid all their bills. So, it was Maggi, Steve and Beau doing all the barn work.

Maggi and Steve got the horses ready for each race day, and there was no problem till Beau told her, "Look, this horse is so nervous—wait as long as possible before you bridle him and bring him to the paddock. But be sure to run the water hose in his mouth to rinse out all the hay and stuff. Then take the metal syringe gun, and fill it with a little glycerine and squirt some into his mouth."

"Yak! What good does that do?" she asked.

"It'll keep his mouth from getting dry," he told her. "Think you and Steve can manage?"

"Sure, I think I can do it," she affirmed.

"That's my girl."

The next day Beau wanted one of the horses that was in the fifth race to be iced that morning right after they were through training. So he sent Maggi for two bags of ice.

"He's got osselets" (where calcium forms around the ankle). "The ice will help the circulation and eases out some of the soreness," he told her.

"Well, how are you going to stand him in ice? In a bucket?"

"No, an ice boot."

"We don't have any ice boots, do we?" she asked.

"No, but I'll make some real quick," he added. He explained what ice boots look like.

"They're long cylinder-like tubes that cover the horses's legs from the ankle to just above the knee. The store-bought ones are made from heavy canvas, with leather straps sewed to the tops to run a strap over the horse's back to keep them up, and straps with buckles at the bottom to keep the ice in," Beau explained.

Ice Boots

"But you can make them easy enough," he went on. "It's an old trick." Maggi watched as he took a pair of old Levi's, cut the pants legs off, put them on the horse's front legs and tied a thin, soft cotton rope around the bottom to hold in the crushed ice. Then he took a soft, cold-water bandage and tied it at the top of the pant legs.

"There, these aren't as big as the store-bought ones, but they get the job done. Now, after you take him out of the ice, put on some cold-water bandages.'' (These are made from a knit T-shirt-like material, four inches wide and two feet long with tie strings on one end to secure the bandage in place.)

The home-made boots were filled with ice. Beau added some Choate's (freeze) to the ice, referring to this procedure as freezing a horse before a race. Maggi kept the horse in ice for four hours, thinking how uncomfortable it was to have her own feet freezing; but the horse stood quietly and patiently.

When the announcer called for the horses in the fifth race to come to the paddock, Maggi pulled off the ice boots.

Then she soaked the cold water bandages, (long-T-shirt type material bandages) in the ice water left in the boots. She wrapped them around the horse's ankle carefully so they would stay up and tied them securely with the tie string sewed in to the end of the bandage. The menthol was so pungent it nearly asphyxiated her.

She poured more of the Choate's liquid straight over the bandages. Then, she headed for the saddling paddock.

Beau saddled the horse and then removed the cold-water bandages, and handed them to Maggi. They were only put on to hold the freeze as long as possible before the horse ran. After he ran, Maggi found herself thinking—all that damn work, just for a third! But she was grateful that they lit the board.

Washing out the standing bandages is a daily job Maggi found out, and most Laundromats refused to let the horsemen bring in their horse laundry, saying it clogged up their machines with hair. So, Maggi learned to use the age-old washing machine of the backside.

The hand plunger was like a large tin funnel with a broom-like handle. She plunged it into the hot soapy

Yerbuside wool machine

bucket of water, using it like a butter churn. Its jet-type vents allowed the water to come up and run out over and over. It amazed her how clean it got things with just a little elbow grease.

"The secret to those things is to get your water hot-hot!"

"Honey, you're sure making a hand, and have the barn looking nice," he added. "I know I'm a slob, but I like it nice, too."

Prescott for the First Time

Maggi had just settled into the routine when Beau came home and told her to start packing.

"We're shipping to Prescott."

"How come?" she asked, hating to leave this beautiful place sooner than she had to.

"It's been a week since I've been able to run a horse. There just aren't any more races in the book for me." he told her. She had learned this past year that when a horse was running good, you could enter to run him back every ten days. And when you didn't get the horse in, this upset the trainer's program on the horse. It was frustrating for Beau to point his horses toward a race and not draw it, or the race wouldn't go. She realized there was more to racing than having the best horse.

"You can't win races standing in the stall," he told her. "Look, there are just two or three races left in the book —maybe they'll go and maybe not. I can't afford to just sit here and wait two or three more weeks. And this damn racing secretary ain't going to write me extras, I can see that," he added.

"I see what you mean," Maggi answered, as she thought, she had been so selfish these past weeks thinking only of her problems and enjoying the beautiful mountain resort. She quickly replied, "Okay, if we have to ship, then we'll ship. What's the first move?"

"You call for a van and get the shipping papers. You better call here before we get to the track, 'cause the races are still on and the phone booths are still locked up," he told her. (All tracks lock up all phones during the races so no one can book bets.) Then pick up all the accounts from the horsemen's bookkeeper," he continued.

"I'll get the jockey's silks from the jock's room."

"Want me to pick up the horse's papers from the office also?" she asked.

"No, I'll have to. They won't give the papers to you or to anyone but the owner or trainer."

"Oh, that's right, I forgot," she answered.

The van dispatcher told her the van would be there Tuesday night at six.

This meant they would be driving all night in order to be in Prescott when the horses arrived. Oh! She forgot to call the owners . . . to tell them they were moving to Prescott. She would do that right away.

She also found out she had to have a release slip signed from the feedman, tack man, and track kitchen before they would release the horse papers . . . to assure that they didn't go off owing anyone.

By midnight, she had the household things packed and the barn tack ready. She was exhausted when she hit the bed.

"Where are the horses' papers?" Beau asked her the next morning.

She went to get them from her suitcase, and they were not there!

"Oh, Christ, if we've lost them, we might as well go home," he snapped.

"Why?" she asked.

"Because you can't run a horse without them, that's why, and it takes weeks and tons of paper work to convince the Jockey Club in New York you lost them before they will send you a duplicate set. It's a big mess if you have lost those papers."

She turned everything over and over in the suitcase, worried sick! Then her hand felt the manila folder. "Oh, thank God, here they are," she sighed.

That morning, Beau just walked all the horses. "Shipping is just like a workout so they don't need tracking this morning; they'll be standing up all night," he told Maggi.

Maggi couldn't believe there still was so much to do. They took all the stall chain guards down, pulled out all the feed tubs, stacked them ready to load, and unscrewed all the screw eyes. Maggi could hardly lift the buckets full of chains and screw eyes.

By the time they ate a late breakfast and lunch combined, the van had arrived to load the tack first. Before Maggi could run up and shower, it was time to load the horses and leave.

Pee Wee came by to help them load the horses. When the last horse was loaded, Beau shut the tailgate of the horse trailer

Pee Wee put his arms around Maggi, kissed her, and said, "You be good to her, you miserable bastard," meaning Beau, "Hey, I'll be coming up there, after the All American Futurity is over," he told them.

"Good luck to you in the Futurity, Pee Wee. I hope you win it," Maggi said.

"Won't do any good though. You'll just blow it," Beau kidded him.

"You mean shit-head," he told Beau, grinning.

As Maggi followed Beau's truck and horse trailer, winding their way through the quaint little resort towns, the street lights were just coming on. Maggi took one last glimpse of the little house trailer tucked back into the pines, and mused, "We've had some bad times and some good times in that shoddy little place." Steve was asleep in the back seat. She wished she were with Beau in the pickup beside him, because she knew it was going to be a long, lonely trip.

They pulled into Prescott race track at 8 a.m. The van kept them humping to keep up with it. Beau was tired. He wondered how Maggi was holding up. She had worked so hard getting things packed, he mused. "I'll let her sleep in tomorrow."

He pulled in behind the van as it stopped in front of a row of portable stalls. He saw Maggi getting out of her car.

"Damn it to hell," he fumed.

"What's the matter?" she asked.

"Look at this barn—ain't that something?" he exclaimed.

She looked down the long row of shoddily built stalls put together by 1 x 12 boards . . . with a 4-inch gap between each one. An old piece of canvas was stretched over the roof and tacked down with huge nails. One part of the canvas had sagged in the middle of one of the stalls and had held rainwater from a previous rain. It was dripping down into the stall. Beau took a rake handle and pushed up the canvas forcing the water to cascade over the sides of the barn.

The barn consisted of twenty stalls. Another stable had already moved in at the west end. The same kind of stalls were directly across, leaving very little room between barns.

Portable Stalls on the fairs

"Well, I guess we just as well unload, they aren't going to get any better," he grumbled. "Look, soon as we walk and water them out, you go find us a place to stay," he told her.

"Okay," she answered.

At times like this, Steve was a blessing, helping out walking the hots and fetching hammers and screw eyes back and forth.

He had become a good little hand this summer and he really didn't like horses all that well either. Other kids in town couldn't understand. They thought he was lucky to get to ride all day!

Maggi went straight to a real estate office, and found a small summer cottage for $75 a month. It was sparsely furnished but clean and close to the track. She took it.

She put things away and showered and went back to the track, just in time to help mix the bran mash.

"Come on, let's go eat," Beau urged. "I'm starved."

"Me too!" little Stevie chimed in.

"I'll bet you are," Maggi affirmed. "You have been working like a little beaver all day."

Beau stopped to eat at the racetrackers hang-out, and they ran into Buck Witlow, who was also eating there. Maggi was always amazed at their style of greeting each other, like two Indians - Ugh and Uh-Huh was all she heard out of the two.

"C'mon Maggi, let's go," Beau said.

"What's your hurry?" Buck asked.

"Hell, we have been up all night," Beau answered. "See you in the morning."

"Why don't you let Steve stay with me tonight?" Buck asked.

"No, I need him tomorrow. I have to take everything to the track," Beau snapped back.

A torrent of rain, beating on the tin roof of the cottage, woke them up.

"That's all we need," Beau stated as he listened to the drops hitting the roof. "Rain!" They had a time getting the horses in and out, slipping in the mud, the coolers getting so soaked it was worthless putting one on.

156

As soon as a horse watered out, they put him up wet and rubbed him dry in the stall. By ten, they were through training, but still had tack to put up and horses to do up.

Maggi saw that there was one empty stall, so she improvised a tack room for the hay, grain, and straw. It had no door, so she found a few old boards behind the barn and made a makeshift door.

"What in the hell are you worrying about? Nobody's going to steal anything," Beau scolded her.

"How do you know? I agree, its not much, but it's all we've got," she answered. "Remember, they stole all the halters off the horses in Barn 4A at the fairgrounds."

"Yeah, but that wasn't racetrackers. It was someone from the fair exhibits," he stated. "Oh, let's go. I'm soaked. Boy I'm glad we aren't running anything this week, with all this rain and mud."

Between the weekends, it had stopped raining, and the track had dried out. Beau and Maggi finished up their work early so they could go home, eat, clean up, and be back by race time, for they had two horses in—running in the third and fifth races. They got to the track just about the time the horses were loading into the starting gate for the first race.

"Hey, Maggi—come on, let's go over to the rail and watch the horses run from here," Beau suggested.

"Okay," and they ran as the starting gate sprang open.

When the horses came running into the first sharp turn, it was hairy! The jockeys were screaming.

"Get over, you son-of-a-bitch!"

"Go fuck yourself!" another yelled back.

"Hey, watch it, you mother fucker!"

As they faded onto the far side of the track, Beau shook his head. "They're scared to death 'cause that turn is so

157

sharp. You know, that's just a half-mile track,'' he explained.

"Bring your horses to the paddock for the third race," came over the speaker.

"Hey, hon—let's go!'' Beau was already on the way to their barn.

Maggi had already saddled her pony and jumped on to lead Bitsize over to the grandstand to the saddling paddock. After he was saddled and the jock thrown up on him, she ponied him to the starting gate. He ran second. She picked him up as soon as he was unsaddled by the jock's valet and jogged him back to the barn. Beau washed him off, and she cooled him out until they called for the fifth race. Boom Boy ran third. Now Maggi could see why they left Ruidoso. These horses fit this meet better. Seconds and thirds were better than sitting in the barn.

* * * *

The next morning during the training hours, a Lulu McPherson moved into the one empty stall across from Maggi and Beau.

Lulu hollered out to Beau, "Hey, buddy—when did you come in?"

"A week ago,'' he yelled back, then he introduced her to Maggi. "I have known her since I first came on the race track,'' he told Maggi.

"She reminds me of the old rodeo cowgirl pictures I've seen on calendars,'' Maggi told Beau later.

"She's one of a kind,'' he grinned and headed for the race track.

Maggi was right. Lulu was of that vintage, in her big black cowboy hat, with its leather chin strap, and dyed, blue-black hair accented with a big blue scarf tied in a soft knot around her shoulders. She wore a purple satin blouse with full sleeves, a blue serge split riding skirt, and black cowboy boots with huge gold butterfly pattern. The accessories were a slick black leather vest, cuffs and belts . . . all covered with tiny bright nickel studs for trim.

She rode a big palomino gelding which made a showy contrast with the black saddle and matching bridle covered with more nickle studs.

Lulu was independent and a fair horsewoman. She owned one old class horse, Lancer, who had a bad knee and she ran him for the bottom claiming, $1,000. He was tough there and could beat those cheap horses on three legs. But like all bad-legged horses, he took a lot of leg work and ice boots to keep him sound enough to run.

To supplement her income, Lulu ponied outside horses each morning before taking care of Lancer. So Maggi offered to feed and water him till she got there. They became good friends, and Maggi spent afternoons, when she had to wait between races, visiting with Lulu and listening to her stories of the good old days.

"When I was young, like you, Maggi, I galloped my own horses, but I quit it since I got hurt at the fair grounds a few years ago."

"You got hurt? What happened?"

"Well, I was always the first one on the track in the morning. I ponied a lot of horses in those days, so I had to start early to get them all done. I was on the race track that morning before daylight. The maintenance man forgot to drag the disc off the track after he was through.

"My horse ran into it, fell down, and pinned me under him. The horse I was ponying ran over both of us. My saddle horse broke his leg and had to be put down (destroyed). I broke a leg, arm and fractured my jaw. I was seven months recuperating, and it was a year before I could ride again. It really messed me up.

"But, that's over and done with now and I'm good as new. I can still get around and ride, and that's all I care about."

Beau called out for Maggi to come to the barn. "Come on, Maggi, or we'll be late to the paddock."

"Hey, I've got to go," Maggi told Lulu. "See you later."

Regal won his race and Maggi was kept busy at the test barn for an hour. It was the fifth race before she got back to their barn.

She was hot and tired and was glad to take a breather, so she walked over to Lulu's stall to chat with her.

Maggi heard Lulu talking to someone. It was Harold, who came up regularly from Phoenix. Harold was Lulu's junior by about thirty years, but they got along famously, and had been friends for years.

Lulu and Harold were jabbering away as they sat in the corner of Lancer's stall, each sipping on a can of Coors. Lancer had a cold-water bandage tied around his left knee and was standing in a washtub full of ice cubes in which there were also cans of Coors beer floating. Just then, Lulu took a coffee can, filled it with the ice water and poured it over the cold-water bandage. Maggi could smell the Choate's freeze mixed with the ice, and the stall reeked heavily of ether and menthol fumes.

"What's going on here?" Maggi asked kiddingly.

"Well, we're killing two birds with one stone, freezing this old bastard and keeping our beer cold," Lulu kidded. "How about a beer?"

"No thanks," Maggi said, as she noticed the cans of Coors floating around the horse's leg. The old horse just stood there with his head down, dozing, not paying any attention to the cans bumping against him.

160

"I will have to get back to our barn. We have a horse in the next race," she told Lulu.

"Well, we're in the last race. He should be ready by then," Lulu laughed.

Sir Boss ran second and was claimed. By the time Maggi put her saddle horse Sam up, and she and Beau fed the horses, the last race had just run.

Maggi saw Lulu coming toward her stall. She thought Lulu had lost Lancer.

"Did someone claim him?" she asked.

"No, he win!" Lulu shouted, as she grabbed up the halter and shank, bucket, sponge, scraper, wheeled around and was gone.

Beau and Maggi decided to wait till the traffic died down before leaving.

Thirty minutes later, Lulu and Harold came leading Lancer toward the barn, laughing loudly, and jabbering a mile a minute.

"What's so funny?" Beau hollered across the tow ring (space between barns).

"We just realized we froze the wrong leg all day," and they burst out into a second gust of laughter.

"Well—be sure and freeze it again, since he win," Beau advised.

"Hey, come on over and have a beer and celebrate with us," Lulu invited as she held out a can of Coors.

Beau tore off the tab and took a sip from the cold can. "Christ . . . it tastes like Choate's freeze," he complained as he spat out a mouthful of beer.

"Well, it should. They have the beer in with the ice and freeze," Maggi explained.

"It won't hurt you, Beau, it's too far from your heart," Lulu kidded. It was very late when the four of them left the track.

Since Prescott racing was only on weekends, Maggi had time to improve their growing stable by setting up a bookkeeping system. She also checked with other trainers on their procedures and was suprised to learn the majority of them were getting $6 or more per horse a day! She confronted Beau with this fact.

"Why don't you get $6 instead of $5?"

"The owners I have won't stand still for a raise," he answered. "They are not rich people, and they just want a few horses and will stay in the business as long as they are breaking even. And that's damn hard to do here on the fair circuit with only $300 to the winner . . . seconds and thirds barely pay the jock's mount."

"I guess you're right, but we're sure not able to save a dime," she remarked back.

"I know. I hate to, but I guess I could bed in sawdust shavings," he stated. "That would save quite a lot. You know, straw is the biggest expense of any stable 'cause you use more of that than anything else. Hell, we use five bales a day at least. That would save $5 to $6 a day right there."

"But how much do the shavings cost?" she asked.

"Nothing. The saw mill lets you have it free if you haul it yourself. They're glad to get rid of it," he told her.

"Well, what in the heck are we waiting for?" she remarked.

"It's too late today. But we'll get a truck load tomorrow."

Bedding in the shavings had its good and bad points. The stalls were easier to clean, cooler, and the price was right. But the fine dust was harder to brush out of the horses' coats. Plus, they had to invest in a special ten-tined manure fork that could pick up the fine shavings and manure.

162

The last weekend Bert Maddox came up and had another clipping to show Beau that Sir Tribal had won another big race in Chicago. Again it stated that the owner, Charlie Fritz, had bought him for a mere $9,000 and that the horse had once run for $1,000 claiming . . . and now, had boosted his earnings by capturing the $57,900 Balmoral Turf Handicap at Washington Park. Charlie Fritz collected a $34,800 net purse.

Beau threw the article down, and said to Bert, "I guess that bastard will make horse of the year, before he gets through running."

"Yeah, every time I turn around, someone is calling me on the phone, telling me he had won another race back there," Bert added. "It's the truth, though. He is a damn nice horse."

"I wished we could have got him," Maggi inserted.

"Don't we all?" Beau said. "Come on, let's go eat."

Steve went to Phoenix with Buck for a load of hay that morning.

The Prescott Meet went by far too fast for Maggi and Beau. They had a good meet, winning six races and several seconds and thirds. Maggi hated the uprooting and tearing down the stable equipment when they had just got it up. FLAGSTAFF FAIR . . . next!

Maggi loved Flagstaff. The towering mountains that surrounded the little valley where the small town nestled made it hard to find enough flat ground for a race track. But the townspeople found a spot for a fairgrounds that reeked with nostalgia. The famous annual INDIAN POW WOW was held there as well as the horse races.

Maggi quickly found a cute old rustic cabin for just fifty dollars for the two weeks. But it had one drawback—a huge sawmill stood less than fifty feet away, humming its noise all day. The only relief they had from it was when it shut down for lunch and at eight o'clock at night.

"I can see why you got this place so cheap," Beau teased her one afternoon while they were trying to catch a nap. Even Steve began to hate the constant R-r-r-r of the huge saw blade as it ripped into one tree after another.

At the fairgrounds, the same old portable barns were moved in and set up. Because there was little flat space to walk a horse, everyone walked in a tiny circle around several huge pine trees. The soft pine needles and mulch were easy on the horses' legs—plus there was no dust!

The mornings were fun and pleasant, while everyone walked around the small circle, talking and joking. And there was always a story being told about experiences at long-past fairs.

It was so cool under the trees that Maggi and Beau brushed the horses there and did their legs up by the hot-walking ring. Beau wouldn't have admitted it but he was afraid he might miss some juicy gossip if he wasn't there.

On one of those cool summer mornings, he and Maggi were rubbing Bitsize's legs, Maggi on one side and Beau on the other. While they were both rubbing in the downward motion, Beau was talking to different people walking in the tow ring.

Bitsize dropped his head and began to nod till he gradually feel asleep from the rubbing.

Beau accidentally pushed his knee joint inward, the leg buckled and the horse sank down on top of Maggi and Beau, pinning them both beneath his huge bulk.

"Hey—hey! Get up you lazy old bastard!" Beau hollered at him. The soft mulch of bark and leaves had cushioned the horse's fall, but scared the hell out of Maggi.

Everyone laughed and chided them about the poor horse

being so weak he couldn't stand up.

"Hey, Beau!" somebody yelled out, "why don't you feed the poor old bastard? Then maybe he'll be able to stand up after the morning training is over."

There was no electricity and no water piped in to the temporary barn area. But the fair management brought in two water trucks for their use. After making the attempt of trying to carry two huge water buckets back and forth, Maggi stated, "You can get the water from here on out, they are too darn heavy."

"For Christ's sake, you can throw down a hundred and eighty pound calf, tie him up in 13 seconds, but can't carry a little bucket of water," he kidded her again.

"Oh, you—and what can I do—you're still carrying the buckets," she laughed.

"That's man's work, ha-ha."

"How come they set up these portable stalls so far away from the race track?" Maggi asked Beau.

"Because of the Indian Pow Wow. And there just isn't any flat space down there, I guess," he said. "It's going to be a bitch. We will have to lead the horses down there before the races start. Then tie them up to the pine trees till it's time to run them. Afterwards, hose them off, cool them out, and tie them back up to the tree till we're done, then lead them all back," he told her.

"Boy, what a runaway that will be," Maggi snapped.

"No, Daddy and I used to do that years ago when half the fairs didn't have any stalls. The horses settle down, you'll see. It's the only way, otherwise we'd never be able to make it running back and forth up that hill. Especially if I get three or four horses in one day. Besides, Steve and Daddy will be back today, and Steve can help walk the hots," he said.

The one thing Beau didn't mention to Maggi was the use

165

of the one and only water hose, and all the fights over it
with everyone wanting to use it at the same time.

In spite of its makeshift setup, Flagstaff was a lucky
meet for Beau. He picked up a new client and three more
horses to train.

Beau got nice writeups in the local paper. Maggi clipped
them out and pasted them in her first scrapbook.

The last clipping read:

BEAU WITLOW . .
LEADING TRAINER OF FLAGSTAFF
MEET AND FAIR . . WINNING 10 RACES . .
A NEW RECORD!

Next: Holbrook Fair . . and Meet

Beau laughed so hard, as Maggi packed, pushed, and
carried boxes to the truck, her hair falling down from
under her hat, her shirt-tail out . . . as she watched the
exodus of all the racetrackers heading for Holbrook.

"Honey, we're just one notch above the carnies," he
kidded.

"You got that right!" she giggled. She was silly tired,
but very happy.

After the makeshift stalls at Prescott and Flagstaff,
Holbrook's neat cinder-block barns looked like
Hollywood Park to Maggi as Beau drove up close to the
barn. He pulled out the hose and pitchforks, and he and
Maggi went to work setting up their new barn. Maggi
quickly wet down the stalls, Beau shook out the straw, and
she hung a freshly washed water bucket into each stall after
securing a screw eye to hold it. They both worked fast,
before the horses got there. Beau had just bought ten used

hay nets from an old couple who were quitting racing because of their health.

The hay nets were machine made, with cotton rope tied, similar to a fish net, in a pouch form like the old-fashoned marble bags with a drawstring at the top. Beau showed Maggi how to fill the nets and hang them in each stall.

Hay Net

"Look, hon! First you lay them on the ground and open them out, so you can cram the hay in and pack it tight like this. Then, draw the string down tight and run it through this big ring in the stall. Pull it up tight and be sure it is up high so a horse can't paw it and get his foot caught in it," he showed her. Maggi caught on instantly and began to help fill the other nets when she heard and saw—an awkward, old-vintage green school bus come lumbering in, with several buckets, ropes, barn rakes dangling from the yellow painted windows. As the bus swayed back and forth hitting potholes, Maggi saw a black horse's head sticking out from the rear escape door of the huge long bus.

"Beau, come here! You've got to see this," she called. By now, the horse was nickering as he saw other horses.

"Oh, that's old man McNulty," Beau said as he, too, watched the bizarre contraption lumber by. A shabby, whiskered man was driving, and he backed the long green bus back and forth, trying to park as close to the barn as he could. The black horse was still nickering, and stomping the floor frantically. Maggi stood in shock at the home-made getup. She was wondering how they were going to unload the horse.

The old man stepped down from the open folded door, holding a long extension cord in his hand. As he looked up, he saw Maggi. "Do you know where the plug outlet is?" he asked her.

"No, I don't," she answered.

He walked toward the shedrow and soon found an outlet. Securing the plug and hanging the extension cord over a nail, he brought it back and plugged it into an outlet in the bus. Maggi heard a fridge go on! She looked into the bus.

"Come in if you like," he invited. She was too nosey not to!

She could see the horse was closed in by two panels. He continued whinnying at the other horses as they returned his calls.

"When I unload the horse, those panels fall down for the floor, and this bed drops down, and we have our living quarters," Mr. McNulty told her. She noticed he had but three or four rotten teeth, and his speech was slurred from the spaces between them. "I also make leather belts, tooled handwork," he stated. "Do all my work right here, and Gussie helps me," he said, pointing to a shy girl.

"You're Beau's woman, aren't you?" he asked Maggi.

"Yes, I am," she replied, feeling a sense of pride within.

"You're Beau's woman" had a nice ring to it.

"Hell, I've known Beau since he was riding matches at the age of eight years. He rode and won one of the biggest match races here in Arizona when he was eleven. His Daddy had one of the best quarter horses around these parts at that time, and he beat a hot-cha horse from Oklahoma. There was $25,000 bet on that race that day," he smarted off. "I bet five thousand myself on Beau's riding. You never heard so much squalling and hollering come out of one little kid's mouth as you heard that day from the time he left the gate until it was over."

Maggi hung on his every word. She loved hearing stories about Beau.

"Well, I'd better get this old horse unloaded and set up . . . my name's McNulty," the old man broke off.

"That's quite a rig you have there," Maggi stated.

"Yeah, sure helps save room rent and utilities," he grinned, showing even fewer teeth than before. "And it gets us from one place to the other."

Maggi wondered who "us" was—his daughter or wife, when she saw the thin homely young girl step timidly down from the old worn-out bus, carrying a small kitten in her arms.

"Hello," Maggi smiled.

The shy young girl nodded with a slight hint of a smile at the corners of her mouth as she disappeared behind the bus. Maggi had noticed there were no bathroom facilities in there.

McNulty got busy unsnapping the panels and chains to unload the big black horse. Maggi thought, he sure is a good-looking race horse. As soon as McNulty opened the escape door, the horse lunged out and down from the bus, still nickering.

"Would you mind holding him till I get a water

169

bucket?'' McNulty asked her.

"No, not at all."

He came back from around the bus with a bucket and took the horse and headed for the closest water spigot.

Maggi went back to her barn still amazed at the set-up as she told Beau about the inside of the bus.

"Hell, old man McNulty has been around these fairs for years. He's had ten wives and raised 25 kids," Beau told her.

"Is that his wife?" Maggi asked.

"Yep, it's his eleventh. Ain't she homely?" he laughed. She's gotta be forty-five years his junior."

"Good God!" Maggi said.

By now she noticed McNulty was picking through a manure pile and taking a lot of the drier straw and putting it in his stall. She punched Beau to look.

"Hell, that's an old gyp trick. He'll sift through, pick

out the straw, lay it out flat on the ground till the sun dries it out, and then use it over," he grinned as he spoke. "Speaking of gyps, here comes Lil. Christ, I haven't seen her in years," Beau said as Lil walked under their shedrow.

"Lil, this is my wife, Maggi."

"Pleased to meet you," Maggi spoke, as she looked her over, thinking to herself, she sure is a pretty lady for her age—gray hair well-groomed, beautiful angular features that go with hunger, or so Maggi had always suspected. She had a figure any high school girl would settle for, accented by tight-fitting jeans and Western shirt.

Maggi loved her soft voice as she spoke, "I've heard a lot about you, Maggi—that you're quite a horsewoman."

"Lil used to be top trick rider in her day," Beau added. "How you doing, Lil?"

"No good, been to Vegas, Ruidoso, and decided to try the fairs," she said seriously. "Hell, I'm sleeping in my horse trailer to cut corners; you know how it is, buddy."

"Look, soon as we feed, come and have dinner with us," Beau offered.

"That's the best offer I've had all day; you got a deal. See you later," Lil said and left for her barn.

The Holbrook fairgrounds was busy, busy by the end of the week, and racing would start that weekend. Beau and Maggi were into heavy training and barn work! Beau was doing up one of the sore-legged horses when a small black boy asked him from the doorway of the stall, "Are you the Lone Ranger?"

"Yep, I sure am," Beau kidded him back.

"Hey, you guys, here's the Lone Ranger!" the youngster hollered, and three more little black boys showed up. Maggi heard the commotion and stuck her head from the stall and saw four youngsters who couldn't have been more than seven or eight years old.

"What are you boys doing here?" she asked.

"We want a job," one said. "Can we work for you?"

"Well, maybe they can rake the tow ring and the shedrow," Maggi said, winking at Beau.

"Oh yeah, I guess they can do that," he said , kidding them. In an hour, the barn never looked cleaner. They had raked every single blade of straw from the ground.

"Wa-l-l, we'll come back tomorrow," one boy said, showing two front teeth missing.

"Hey, what are your names?" Beau asked.

"I'm Booker T, that's LeRoy, Harold and Little Fred," the spokesman for the group answered.

Beau asked, "Why *Little* Fred?"

" 'Cause his Daddy is Big Fred!" They laughed silly giggles.

Beau gave each of them a dime and rubbed their curly little heads. "You better get home," he told them then, "before Big Fred comes looking for you."

They were there bright and early the next morning. Maggi put them to rolling standing bandages to shut them up till they could start raking. They made it obvious that they thought Steve was the luckiest kid in the world to get to ride a horse.

"You can have my job any time," Steve told them.

That afternoon, Beau took Maggi with him to look at a horse that was for sale. As Beau looked him over, he asked, "How much do you want for him?"

"Two hundred," the owner said.

"I'll take him. He's yours, Maggi," Beau told her.

"Mine?" she squealed. "My own horse! My very own horse!" and she wrapped her arms around Beau's neck, kissing him and embarrassing him to death. Then she hugged the horse's neck. "What's his name?"

"Sensation," the man told her.

He was a dark red chestnut with four white feet, a long slender neck, and a beautiful head.

"Maggi, he's not much now—a little thin—but after he is wormed and fed, he'll snap out of it. Plus, he runs down on all fours, too (runs down: when a horse's ankles are weak, the horse hits the dirt so hard it skins the hair off his heels, and raw sores form). That's what is making him stop. Those old heels get to hurting and stinging," Beau remarked. "But if you'll sit under this ole bastard and rub him, he'll win some races for you."

"He'll get the best care he ever had," Maggi assured him and started at once by giving Sensation a good hot bath, brushing him, and painting his feet with Hooflex. Then she proceeded to rub his sore old ankles.

Booker T, Harold, Little Fred and LeRoy were making good hands and showed up every morning faithfully. They were watching Maggi rubbing Sensation's leg and asked a million questions about it.

It was then that Maggi got a brainstorm. "You boys want to help?" she asked.

"Won't he kick us?" LeRoy asked.

"No. He's a real gentle horse. You know I wouldn't ask you if he wasn't," she assured them.

Maggi laughed at them. They were terrified of the horse's size, and every time he moved, they ran out the stall door!

"Now look—you're scaring him, so you've got to stop jumping up and down. Sit still and let me show you," she said soothingly. As they watched her rubbing procedure, they gradually took on a leg each and fell to rubbing softly with their tiny hands.

"What in the hell is going on here?" Beau grinned as he

came upon them suddenly.

"Miz Maggi is paying us a quarter each to rub Mr. Sensation," Little Fred said proudly.

"An' we kin git in the winner's circle when he win," they all chorused excitedly.

Maggi exchanged grins with Beau as she continued to brush the horse's mane.

"Is that right?" Beau spoke. "Well, we'll see how good a job you guys have done 'cause he is going to run next Sunday."

Maggi almost dropped the brush. "Next Sunday! Oh boy! Do you hear that, men? Better rub a little harder."

And their little hands were just flying in the downward motion.

* * * *

Sensation ran wire-to-wire and won!

After Beau led him into the winner's circle, he stood with his head erect and posed with Maggi, Beau, and four little boys crowded around him.

Another article for Maggi's scrapbook:

> Sensation wins last race of the meet at Holbrook County Fair. Trained by Beau Witlow and owned by Maggi Witlow.

St. Johns County Fair . . Next

St. Johns was more than a hundred miles from Holbrook, but Beau decided to keep his horses at Holbrook and van them over. "They don't have more than a handful of stalls at St. Johns, a few dozen corrals that are already taken by now," he explained.

Maggi was glad to hear they didn't have to pack and

move again.

As they drove into the St. Johns race track, Maggi giggled at the little grandstand. It looked lost in the vast open country that you could see a hundred miles in any direction. Beau laughed at her reaction.

"This is the bushes, all right. They don't even have a test barn here."

"What do they do?" Maggi asked.

"Oh, they hire three college boys for pee catchers and go right to your horse's stall and catch the sample. They'll do this at all the rest of the other fairs, here on out," he added.

"What keeps them from cheating, by subbing another horse's pee?" Maggi asked.

"Who in the hell gives a damn for $200.00?" was Beau's answer as he stopped the truck.

Maggi stared at the track. It looked more like a plowed field, and there was no railing on the backstretch —and a lonely cemetery was next to it.

"Look Beau, a graveyard right next to the backstretch!"

"That's the bushes for you," Beau laughed as he opened the truck door.

Lil Black walked up about that time. "Hi, you two."

"Hi, Lil," they both answered. They talked briefly and then Lil begged off saying, "I have to go and get Aristo Tex ready for the third race."

Beau offered to help her, and they walked off toward her trailer.

"I'll stay here with Rip and the horses," Maggi told Beau.

"I'll be right back," he said.

When Beau returned, he reached in his pocket and handed Maggi $2. "Here, go bet this on Lil's horse. I just heard the jocks feel sorry for her 'cause she hasn't won a

175

race all summer. So, they're going to put her horse on the lead."

"What's 'on the lead'?" Maggi asked.

"Let him win," he asserted.

"But that's supposed to be illegal, isn't it?"

"In the bushes, without any film patrol towers, the jockeys can pretty much do as they please, not that they do it all the time," he told her. "Don't let it worry you. Go get the ticket."

When she got to the mutuel window, she was surprised to find that they were tearing each ticket off by hand and wrote down the bets with pencil, and that the tote board odds were changed manually too. She thought, "Boy, this *is* the bushes!"

"Hey, Maggi!" It was Lulu McPherson.

"Are you betting on Lil's horse?" she whispered.

"News travels fast around a racetrack," Lulu said in her flamboyant way.

By now the race was about to start. Maggi took a seat next to Beau and stuffed the two-dollar ticket into her hip pocket.

The gate opened! Aristo Tex broke last. At the 3/8s pole, he was still last. When they turned for home, all the jockeys were looking back, waiting for Aristo Tex to catch up! The jocks were holding back their mounts, hoping Aristo Tex could catch up.

By the time they crossed the wire, anyone in a pair of rubber boots could have outrun the whole field and the last to the finish line was Lil's horse.

"Maggi pulled out her ticket and tore it up, giving Beau a smug look. "So, that's a fixed race!" she said and laughed.

"Come on, we've got to get ready. We're in the next race."

Bitsize and Joey both won their races, netting $400. As they drove back to Holbrook, Maggi said, "Well, that's $40 for our part. It's better than getting hit by a truck."

"You're always figuring the ten percent," Beau kidded her.

Sunday, they rode up with Buck Witlow in his big stock truck since he had the room.

As Maggi rode that day, she thought that when you had seen one St. Johns fair, you had seen them all. But the day held a surprise she had not anticipated.

At the start of the fifth race, the jockeys whipped and hustled their mounts for position as they started into the first turn. Suddenly, a startled gasp of snock and apprehension burst from the spectators as one inside horse blew the turn and bolted, taking five other horses with him and forcing them into the graveyard.

Maggi shrieked, fully expecting a bad spill, a pile-up of

St. Johns FAIR

some kind. But the jockeys kept riding, zig-zagging around the plots and gravestones, until they swung back to the far turn and onto the main track heading for home.

"Would you believe it?" Beau asked, roaring with laughter.

"*Nobody* would believe it!" Maggi answered.

They won four that day and Buck Witlow won his race. It was a happy trip back to Holbrook.

Next Fair: Safford

Maggi and Beau were getting ready to ship to Safford. Since school would be opening soon, they made arrangements to send Steve back to the Maddoxes with some other racetrackers who were returning home for the same reason. Steve was glad to get away from walking hots and "rolling those damn bandages."

Maggi and Beau arrived at Safford fairgrounds late that afternoon. The wind was blowing dust devils everywhere! Several carnie men were having a time trying to hold down the canvas covers and to tack them over the concession booths.

Maggi grimaced as she saw the shabby looking stalls . . . the doors sagging from loose hinges, chewed wood exposing holes. A run-down barn had wooden pens set up inside, and they too were chewed into uneven patterns. Beau blew his top!

"If they think I'm going to put my horses in there, they're crazy!"

"Well, go over to the racing office and see if you can get some of the better stalls," Maggi suggested.

"I am!" he said, as he headed for the main building.

When Beau came out of the racing office, he told Maggi that they would go on over to the Duncan fairgrounds and stable there.

Stalls At Safford

"We'll haul back here to run. They say the Duncan barns are new—and when their fair meet starts, we'll already be set up. It'll save another move."

"I'm for that!" Maggi declared.

Duncan was a quiet town with huge cottonwood trees along narrow roads, and a fairgrounds with whitewashed gates and small bleacher stands that held three hundred people. A rodeo arena was inside the mile race track centerfield. Long cement-block barns ran parallel to the backstretch side.

When Beau saw the van approaching, he said, "We'll put all the horses in those pens for a few hours," pointing to the corrals in the arena.

The horses pawed, rolled and kicked. They swung their heads high and sniffed at each other through the fenced partitions. They hardly took time to drink more than a few swallows of water, more interested in surveying the vast

179

countryside.

"This is what they need for a few days," Beau said. "They've been in training and shut up for so long, the sun will do them a lot of good."

Once the setting up chores were finished, Maggi found the *only motel* in town and rented a room which included an old-fashioned iron bed with coiled springs, no rug, a leaky mildewed shower, and one old dresser that had more coats of paint on it than a Main Street floozie.

The man in charge at Duncan, the man to see about anything, was Bob Lee. He was the feed man, the local constable, and the entry clerk for the races at Safford. And he owned the local saloon, the Bonnie Heather.

After he'd taken entries the next morning, Beau asked, "Where can we get an Overnight?"

"At my place after eight o'clock. The Greyhound bus drops them off from Safford," he stated.

Beau had a beer and Maggi had a Coke as he studied the Overnight.

"We're in the second, fourth, fifth and eighth races," he was telling Maggi. They finished their drinks and left.

The van arrived at eleven o'clock to pick up their four horses along with two from another stable. When the truck pulled into the Safford fairgrounds, Beau gave the driver instructions to park on top of the hill, so that the horses wouldn't hear the noise of the crowd and wash out before their race.

"We'll leave them stand right in the van," he said.

He swung open all the van doors. The horses were restless at first, in anticipation of being unloaded, but they soon settled down. Beau and Maggi sprawled out in the shade of the huge van along with some other horsemen to wait for their races to be called over the loudspeaker. The time went fast.

180

Beau heard someone shouting at him, "Hey, Beau —they're calling for the second race! The speaker's broken. In fact, the second race is coming onto the track," the man said.

Beau jumped up and climbed into the van, calling for Maggi. "Bring the bridle!"

He bridled the horse in seconds, pulled the pin holding the metal bar, vaulted up on the horse's back and rode him down the steep ramp. He broke into a high lope toward the saddling paddock.

"Just stay on him, Beau, and ride him in the race," someone said, and everyone laughed.

But he got there too late! The horse was scratched, and Beau was fined $25 for being late to the paddock. It is the trainer's responsibility to be in the paddock on time.

He reloaded the horse back onto the van and said, "Come on, we'll walk down toward the paddock, so we can hear when the races are called. I don't want the next horse scratched."

After each horse ran and was cooled out, Beau jumped them back on the van. "Hell, they are better off in there. It's cool and they have hay to munch on," he told Maggi.

When the last horse was cooled out and loaded and the van doors were shut and the big truck revved its motors, Maggi was tired, hot, and dusty from the long, hot day.

As soon as the Safford meet was over, all horses shipped into Duncan fairgrounds. The corral pens Beau and Maggi had been using were no longer available. Every stall was filled and the backside was bustling with the usual morning training and routine. Duncan Fair was the next weekend.

October is a beautiful month in Arizona and especially in Duncan, with the beautiful mountains, lush desert, and the cool nights. Working conditions were so pleasant that everyone lingered at the barns, visiting, drinking coffee for hours.

It was on one of these lazy days, that Maggi met another gyp . . . Mazie Allen . . . a widow school teacher for more than forty-five years who had retired. She was in her late seventies, but the sparkle in her clear blue eyes hid her age secret well. She looked like Katherine Hepburn to Maggi . . thin, well-bred and well-educated.

She called a small camper on a pickup truck, with four little feisty dogs—her home. She told Maggi of her adventurous life, traveling in Europe, and teaching in almost every state in the union!

"There isn't much I haven't done or seen," she stated.

"What made you want to train horses?" Maggi asked.

"I have always loved racehorses since I was a child, and my grandfather always had a racehorse for his buggy horse. Many a Sunday afternoon after church, he and I would outrun another farmer who thought he had a better horse. I loved every second of it!" she smiled, as she reminisced about her past.

When Maggi got back to her barn, she told Beau what a wonderful person she had met.

"Hell, that old bitch!" he answered.

"Why do you say that?" Maggi asked.

" 'Cause she steals hay and grain from everyone during the night. That's why she stays in the camper," he ranted on about her. "Everyone says she has money galore—teaching all those years, traveling, and yet she is tighter than a dead heat," he continued.

"I wish you hadn't told me about her, 'cause I sure enjoyed talking with her," Maggi sulked.

"Oh, she's okay, but don't let her sweet-talk fool you. She can come unglued in a second if you trip her up. She takes advantage of being an old lady," he laughed.

"Does she ever win any races?" Maggi asked.

"Yeah, once in a while her horses have all the conditions going for them, and she wins a race."

"Well, I hope I'm as spry when I'm eighty!" Maggi grinned.

"Me too!" Beau added.

Beau went to drilling the horses hard again since he had backed off the last two weeks. He was very angry one morning, and Maggi asked why.

"That damn jockey was supposed to be here to work two horses for me," he stated. "Hell, all the jocks are staying in Safford and partying. I'll be lucky to get anyone till the weekend."

"How come?" Maggi asked.

"Well, for one thing, they're too lazy, and then too, they don't even try to keep a horse from running off. It's easier to let a horse 22-it . . ." (let him bounce, run) he said. "Besides, jocks can sour a horse, 'cause they get scared and don't know horses, really. All they know is to race ride . . . most of them."

Within the next hour, when Maggi went to the track to pony one of their horses, she saw that what Beau had said was true.

A horse balked at the gap and refused to go. The jockey began to whip him, and at the same time had a tight hold on his bridle reins. The horse couldn't go forth if he wanted to. The jockey kept jerking his mouth and the little horse got to backing up, faster and faster, trying to get away from the constant jerking, and whipping. Finally, the horse wheeled and threw the boy off into the railing and ran wildly toward the barn area, falling down as he tried to make a sharp turn, and hurting his knee.

"Did you see that?" Maggi asked Beau as he came riding up on a colt.

"Yeah, you see what I mean? Now you know why I always go to the track with my horses when a boy is on them. You can't trust them at all. At least not these fair circuit jocks," he confirmed. "But there are some good ones too."

Duncan Fair the First Time

Duncan was the typical county fair, cake, jam, jellies and the quilts. Maggi loved going through each exhibit, and listening to the talk of small town people.

1 P.M. Race time! She and Beau had their work cut out for them. They had eight horses in that day. Since Steve had gone home with the Maddoxes for school, Beau hired a local boy to help Maggi at the barn.

Beau got the first horse ready, and Maggi led him over to the saddling paddock.

"Who will hold the horses while you saddle?" Maggi asked.

"A cowboy friend offered to," Beau answered.

He win!

Maggi led the second horse over, and Beau handed her the reins of the winner. By the time she was bringing up the third horse, she could see that they had won the second race. Beau grinned and remarked, "Two in a row, how about that?" as they changed horses again.

Sensation was in the sixth race. As she got him ready and kissed his soft muzzle, she whispered, "Be nice, old boy, if you could win too." As she led him over, Sam, her pony, pinned back his tiny ears. Sensation was feeling so good and bumping him around.

By the time she was leading the horses over for the seventh race, she was wild with excitement as she heard the announcement:

"The sixth race was won by Sensation, owned by Maggi Witlow and trained by Beau Witlow, making this his sixth win for the afternoon."

The roar of the small crowd was horrendous! Several horses in the barn area nearly jumped over the stall guards.

The seventh race was in the starting gate! Maggi was slipping the bridle on Dancer for the eighth and last race. As she worked, she talked to the horse, "Well, I'll get to watch *you* run." Then she listened to the call of the seventh race, "My God, he's going to win, too!" she squealed, scaring Dancer. "Whoa!" she said softly, realizing her mistake. "Come on, old man, let's see if we can sweep the card." She quickly brushed him off and led him over to the saddling paddock for the eighth race. All she could hear from the railbirds was, "I don't believe it—seven races!" "Can you imagine?"

"Who in the hell is this Beau Witlow?" someone blared out.

As Beau reached for the bridle reins of Dancer, he handed Maggi the winner of the seventh race, as systematically as though everyone won seven races in a row! Maggi went back to the barn and finished bathing the horse off and handing it to the boy to cool out.

The pee catcher remarked kiddingly, "Boy, you guys are sure making my job easy, just staying here in one barn."

Maggi heard the announcer:

"They're off"

She ran to the rail to watch the race.

Dancer broke out of the 8 hole and instantly took the lead. He was on the extreme outside. Maggi knew that if he could drop down on the rail before the turn, he would be in a good spot.

"Come on, Dancer, lay down your soul!" Maggi kept screaming.

As Dancer passed over the finish line with a two-lengths lead, Maggi squealed for joy!

"Beau win eight races!" she cried out to the crowd of railbirds.

"It's the first time I've ever heard of this," an old-timer said. "Go get your picture taken, Maggi. You've been so busy, you missed all the others. Go on!"

She got on Sam and loped him over to the winner's circle.

Beau saw Maggi coming on Sam. He mused as he watched her, "She's like a little girl every time we win a race. Bet she's got a lot to say when she gets here." He felt the same, but he kept it inside. He wished he was like her—outgoing, making friends so easily—but it was hard for him. He had always been shy and introverted. He grinned as Maggi got off her pony and ran toward him.

"Oh Beau, I'm so proud of you!" she said and kissed and hugged him. The crowd roared with approval.

While Dancer was being cooled out, Maggi heard Beau say to the pee catcher, "Aw, I was just lucky."

She thought, "Luck my foot. It took a lot of know-how and hard work! That damn modest Beau!"

Beau won it all at the Duncan Fair . . . leading trainer . . . coming away with top money of $3,000 for his owners, plus Sensation's win! Maggi had several clippings and eighteen win pictures for her new scrapbook!

By Tuesday, the better stables left for the Albuquerque

Fair, the others for Douglas. Beau had decided to go home.

"Our horses aren't good enough for Albuquerque, and Douglas is too damn far! Besides, these horses need a rest, and I have five horses to get up in Phoenix for the fall meet." he stated. "They'll need to be clipped, wormed, shod and started galloping right away. What do you say?" he asked Maggi.

"I'm ready," she answered.

They told their new friends, Lucy and Hal, the druggist from Duncan good-bye, and said they would see them next year. They also thanked them for their kindness and for the hospitality of their home during these past weeks.

They were going home!

14

Beau and Maggi found Phoenix hot compared to the cool high country they had left. Their horses had all grown a thick coat from the chilly nights in Duncan. As soon as the horses were all bedded down, and training was back to normal at the fairgrounds, Beau told Maggi, "We're going to have to clip all these horses tomorrow."

"Why?"

"Well, they get hot with that long hair, and it takes longer to cool them out," Beau explained. "And if they act up in their stalls, they get hot and sweaty and they stay damp, and when it gets chilly late at night, they catch cold easily. Besides, it's easier to keep them clean if their hair is shorter. Let's get started," he said as he plugged in the clippers and poured a coffee can full of kerosene into which he would dip the clippers.

By the time the first horse was clipped. Maggi's hands and face were covered with tiny prickly hairs mixed with oily kerosene, the result of continual dipping of the clipper blades to keep them cool and clean. Horse hair slivers got into her eyes, nose and mouth, and stubbornly stuck to her clothing.

But the horses were no more fond of the procedure than Maggi was. They were disturbed by the noise the heavy clippers made, particularly around their ears. The clippers got hot in continuous use and burned or tickled a horse's flanks or belly. Even when considerable care was taken, it was difficult to keep from gouging a horse with the clipper blades, causing the horse to spook, snort, kick or strike out with his front feet.

To avoid this and protect the one who was doing the clipping, Beau used a twitch (a chain loop that is fastened to a long wooden handle). He put the end of the horse's upper lip into the chain loop and then twisted it like a torniquet until the pressure made the horse stand still. Another method he used was to put a lead shank under the horse's upper lip, and run the chain back over through the halter rings, causing a pressure on the upper lip. If the horse fought it, more pressure was put on the chain. These methods are not cruel, but do force the horse's attention away from the clippers' noise and the tickle from the blades.

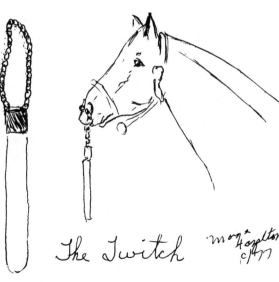

The Twitch

"How come you don't tranquilize them?" Maggi asked.

"Well, for one, it costs too much, and I can't afford it. And sometimes they still don't quiet down, and then you have all this tranquilized thousand pounds of horse flesh that can't feel anything. It would be like trying to teach a drunk to swim. Keeping the horse quiet and calm is the secret, so that he doesn't break out in a sweat. When the horse's hair gets wet or damp, the clippers gum up."

Beau was right! The clipped horses dried out quickly after their baths and they were much easier to keep clean.

With the new horses, they had fourteen horses in training. Luck was on their side when Juan showed up wanting a job. He told them he had quit another job when he heard Beau was in town. Beau and he agreed on fifty a week as wages. Maggi was glad, for this would give her some time in the afternoons to catch up on her household duties.

* * * *

State Fair Meet . . . Their Fourth Season

Beau and Maggi had a good rest and so did the horses. By the time they were set up at the track, the Albuquerque meet was over, and those horses had shipped in. Douglas was over, and the next fair meet was at Yuma. Beau planned to take two of the new horses down to get a race under their belts since they had ninety days of galloping in them already.

Things went well till Dancer bucked Beau off one morning and hurt his foot. So Beau had to hire a part-time exercise boy. Plus, he was having trouble with one of the new horses who had a bad habit of wheeling at the gap and on the track while the exercise boy was galloping him.

190

"Well, I'll have to take him with the pony for a few days and lead him around with the lead shank till he gets over that," Beau told Maggi and the boy.

So, every morning, he ponied the horse, keeping him as close to him as possible and told the exercise boy to be as still as possible on him and not to hit him with the bat at all.

Beau's soothing voice and the gentle way he handled the horse kept the horse's ears pricking and listening to his voice.

Before Torcher knew what was going on, he was half-way around the main track and was into a nice slow easy gallop.

When they came off the track and down the gap, the horse was hardly breathing, he had gone so easily, and hardly a hair was wet. He squealed and jumped, he felt so good.

Beau did this four more days, and then told Maggi, "Take the horse up and start him off easy and see how he goes."

When she got back, Beau said, "How'd he go?"

"He went like an old pro, just bowed his head and galloped nicely," she stated.

"Good!"

"Are you going to take the colts now?" she asked.

"No, I want to wait till Pete brings his colts, because I want them to have some company. Besides, the track is too busy right now. The colts get too scared their first time in company, with the other horses running by them," he added. "Besides, I have to wait for another exercise boy."

An hour-and-a-half later, Pete and his two colts came by the barn. "I'm ready when you are, Beau," he said.

"Good. We're all tacked up; just got to put the boys up on them."

191

On his way up to the track, Beau told his exercise boys, "Now keep them together, side-by-side. I want that filly on the inside because she is timid, and I don't want her bearing out," he continued. "When you turn for home let them breeze down the lane for a few hundred yards, but don't whip them. Do you hear?"

"Yes," they both answered.

When they got back and Maggi was giving one a bath, Beau said, "I just heard that Pee Wee got ruled off again."

"Oh, not again!" Maggi said, "For what?"

'They caught him with a joint."

"What in the heck is a joint."

"A battery, dummy—you've seen them," he answered disgustedly.

"Well, I never heard them called that before. And I haven't seen one either," she snapped. "Musta' been another girl."

"Hey, don't get mad," he kidded her, knowing he'd made a mistake. "Look, it's a battery about the size of a pack of gum, with electrical tape wrapped around it and two little

The Joint (Battery)
Actual Size

brass wire prongs soldered in on one end. When pressed into something, they make contact with the battery and give off a slight shock," he told her.
a slight shock," he told her.

"Doesn't that hurt the horses?"

"Hell, no. Half the horses don't pay any attention to them. Others will buck off a rider." he continued. "A minor few will run from one, usually an old cheating, lazy bastard might respond to it."

"Then why bother to use them?" she asked again.

"Because there are a few that will run from one. I don't see anything wrong with using them, no more than a whip. But the racing commission don't see it that way, 'cause they don't have any control over them. They can't tell if a jock's got one in his hand or not. They think a whip is okay, 'cause they can see it. But, hell, a jock can drop his whip so what's the difference."

"Anyway, they are illegal to use, and Pee Wee knew that," he added. "The dumb nut. He'll get a year at least. Gosh, he's wasted most of his life on the track being ruled off, for one damn thing or another.

"Oh, hell—come on, let's forget about him. I want to blow out the horse's heads before we leave this morning," he told her.

"Yaaak, I hate that job," Maggi scoffed.

She dreaded this chore which she had helped Beau do once before. Beau took an ear syringe full of Massengill douche powder and blew it up into the horse's nostril on both sides. Within a few minutes, heavy, snotty mucus started dripping from the horse's nose. "Does this really do the horse any good?" Maggi asked disgustedly.

"Sure, it clears his head and improves his breathing," Beau stated. "Daddy's done this for years, and he still does," he added.

"Well, it looks as though it sure would be painful and burn like the devil," she commented.

"Oh, it might sting for a few seconds, but it don't hurt them any more than sticking Vicks up your nose," he said. "Christ, you're always worrying about hurting the horses. You worry too much about little things. Come on, let's get the next one."

He unbuckled the halter off the horse. It was 11 a.m. by the time they did the last horse.

"Glad that's over," Maggi stated as she put away the syringe and things.

Yuma Fair

The trip to Yuma took six hours, as the road was narrow and winding. By noon it was hot! And the grounds were dusty. The constant in and out traffic had churned the desert alkali soil into a talcum powder texture. Horse trailers were parked every which way. Horses were tied to them, pawing and nickering as they looked toward the race track.

Beau unloaded and tied up the horses and said, "Come on, let's go get a Coke and watch the races. We'll be here all day, we're in the sixth and ninth races."

Both horses parked (won). It was midnight before they fed them a bran mash and 1 a.m. before they got to bed at home.

The next day was the same routine except they only had one to run in the second race. The horse ran second and they got back to the fairgrounds by 9 p.m.

The State Fair started. The governor cut the ceremonial ribbon. Carnies sold their wares. And the players came to the races.

It was fun and excitement each year for the public, but for Maggi and Beau and other horsemen, it was their livelihood.

During the meet there was talk of it being the last year they would race on the fairgrounds track, due to the big car race and the track itself being unsafe and too hard for the horses and riders.

* * * *

Weeks pass by quickly when you're getting up at 5 a.m. and going to bed at 8 p.m. Turf Paradise was opening in two weeks. Several stables had already moved into Turf. Beau hadn't heard on his stalls yet. This worried Maggi, and she thought even though Beau was second leading trainer at the State Fair meet, it didn't have any clout with the stall man. She mused that Beau almost beat the most powerful trainer on the grounds, but the older trainer had too many horses, and good ones at that, compared to Beau's little stable of cheap claimers.

"Hey, Maggi," Beau called out, breaking her thoughts. "I'm entering Sensation Friday in the sixth. There's a non-winners of $1,000 for the bottom claiming price, $1,000 that he is eligible for. So I want you to pony him in the morning," he told her, "and we'll walk him till Friday."

* * * *

Friday, Sensation was in the sixth race. Maggi had him brushed till he glistened and was wishing she had his four little black helpers here to rub his four sore old legs.

She was putting the last standing bandage on his front leg when Beau walked up.

"Well, he'd better win. You must have used a hundred

dollars worth of leg brace on the old devil," he said, as he patted the horse's head.

Maggi looked up and smiled. "He'll win . . . you'll see!"

"What's the matter with you?" Beau asked, as they were standing by the railing waiting for his race to start.

"I'm just nervous, I guess. You'd think I'd get used to the horses running, as many as we've run this summer, but when it's your own, you sure have a different feeling . . . at least I do."

"If he can beat the four horse, he can win this race, but he's a tough old campaigner," Beau replied.

"They're in the gate . . . They're off!"
"It's Ruff 'n Tuff going to the lead and Sensation is second going into the first quarter."
"It's Ruff 'n Tuff and Sensation head and head at the half."
"Turning into the far turn, it's Sensation taking command by a neck with Ruff 'n Tuff hanging on. . ."
"As they come out of the turn for home, it's Sensation and Ruff 'n Tuff, head and head, battling it out . . ."

"Ohhhhh . . . ooooo!" burst from the grandstand crowd. Sensation went down!

"Oh! He broke his leg" Beau cried out.

"Oh, no! Oh, no!" Maggi screamed.

"You stay here, Maggi. I'll go."

"No! I want to help. He's my horse."

"Okay, come on. But you're not gonna' like what you see . . ."

By the time they reached Sensation, he had gotten up again. The jockey was up and had caught hold of the dangling reins which had been thrown over his head in the spill.

Sensation was lurching in a circle around the little rider who was trying to keep him still. His left front leg was dangling loose! There was no doubt that it was *broken*.

Beau grabbed the reins from the jock and said, "Are you okay?"

"Yeah, I'm fine . . . skinned my arm, that's all. Jesus, I hate this happening to him. He was going to win . . . the game old devil."

The ambulance came to pick up the jockey and a tractor pulling a wide open horse trailer was coming down the stretch to pick up Sensation. How many times had Maggi seen it come and pick up other horses. Now, it was coming to pick up her own Sensation.

Sensation wouldn't stand still. He pricked his ears and laid his head on her shoulders. He couldn't understand what was wrong.

He was a racehorse, a runner, bred with a competitive spirit to run. That was all he knew, was to run . . . run his best . . . run his heart out.

"Oh, Sensation!" Maggi murmured, crying. "You poor thing."

The vet arrived, gave Sensation a pain shot and a tranquilizer and four men pushed him into the open trailer. He gave them no trouble . . . even on the three legs.

Maggi rode back to the barn with him, holding his head steady as he tried to brace himself on three legs.

"I'm afraid we'll have to put him down," the vet said. "He's shattered all his sesamoid bones, and no surgery can help him."

"Oh, no!" and she broke down and cried bitterly.

Beau reached over and pulled her away from Sensation.

"Come on now, honey, you go to the tack room. It's better that you don't come."

"I promise you he won't suffer," the vet said softly.

Entering the tack room, she heard the tractor start up pulling the trailer. As the tractor sound faded, she could hear Sensation nickering.

She buried her face in the pile of cooler blankets and sobbed.

Each day, it was painful for Maggi to pass Sensation's empty stall. Only Beau seemed to have the answer.

"Honey, you got to forget about him. He's gone. You *can't look back!*"

Despite Beau's robust ways and Maggi's determination to tame him, they each had great talents in their own special ways. Beau had his knowledge of thoroughbred horses and his skill in training them. Maggi had her business sense, her natural nursing ability, and a gift for make-do inventions.

One of these inventions came as a stroke of luck, coupled with the need to cut down on the use of expensive Hooflex—a five-dollar can lasted only a few days. Maggi was cleaning out their tack boxes, sorting through old medicine bottles—some with labels off, some half-filled—when she thought of a way to make use of the remnants. She threw away the bottles without labels, rather than take a chance on using something that would blister a horse's legs. She saved the mild leg braces and iodine, concocted a mixture of all of these, added them to pure lard and pine tar, and made up a very effective hoof dressing. It kept the hoof healthy and soft and penetrated deeply into the navicular part of the hoof, (nerve center of the hoof). She kept her mixture a secret and wrote down each amount of medicine that she used so the she could duplicate the product. She had no idea how good it was till Beau claimed a mare for $1,000, only to find that she had bad front feet. He assigned her to Maggi's string and within six weeks, the mare had won two races and jumped up in claiming price to $3500. Even the horse shoer remarked on the improvement.

"Hey, whatever you are painting on this mare's hooves, is doing the trick. Her feet are in the best shape since I have been shoeing her—no more corns or bruises," he stated.

"That's right," Beau answered. "Her feet don't sting anymore, thanks to Maggi's great hoof paint," he grinned.

* * * *

Seven years had passed since Beau and Maggi were married.

She thought one day, "It has been five years since we worked for Doc Hardy and had his colts right in this very barn." But the barn looked different, she thought, neat stall guards with red rubber vulcanized over the chains, freshly red-painted buckets and tubs, and twelve useful racehorses in the barn. They had come a long way in a short time.

She liked their new owner, Mr. Robson, a devout family man and strong Mormon, but he loved the racehorse business. He and Beau started out with two, then three, cheap claimers till they claimed a mare for $2,500—Ma Johns. She was like Sir Tribal, she got better with each race, and finally, she was running for allowance races.

The sportswriters from the newspapers had a field day with her Cinderella background. Beau's old friend, Nat Thorndike who worked for the *Racing Form* was the most helpful of all, by mentioning Beau in his daily column. Because Nat was a bachelor and loved to eat, Maggi made sure there was always a place for him at the table. Nat was a flamboyant fellow, full of race track anecdotes that Maggi found fascinating. He alone kept her busy pasting articles in her scrapbook, number two.

Being leading trainer and having Ma Johns helped Beau in many ways. Attracting new clients was one of the benefits.

Mr. Telly, was the next new client to join the Witlow stable. He was a retired Navy commander and was taking up racing on a small scale. He had a two-year colt that had been broke and turned out in a Manchester, Virginia farm. The colt had been nominated for the Paradise Valley Stakes at Turf Paradise to be run that spring.

Mr. Telly had a problem of getting any van to go cross-country for just one colt, unless he wanted to wait.

"Hell, that might be six months from now," he told Beau. "If you want to train the colt, you will have to go get him yourself . . . or send someone you can depend on," he added.

Beau put the trip up to Maggi.

"Don't you know anyone with a truck and trailer who could go after him, Beau?" Maggi asked pleadingly.

"Like who? Hell, if you let someone who doesn't know a damn thing about horses get him, he'd be sick or crippled by the time he got here. If you don't want to do it, then forget it. I'll just call Telly and tell him to give the horse to somebody else."

"Oh, you win. I'll go, but I want somebody to go with me."

Maggi called everyone. But everyone had a good reason why she couldn't go. Maggi had run out of names when she happened to remember Lucy, the druggist's wife in Duncan. They had become good friends and as it turned out, Lucy was enthusiastic about making the trip.

Going to Virginia meant that Maggi would not be home on Thanksgiving. It was to be their first holiday apart, and it gave her a melancholy feeling.

Rip was included, of course. Lucy didn't like him at first, but she soon recognized his value as a guard dog and a traveling companion and fell into the habit of saving him little tidbits from her dinner every evening.

They arrived at the beautiful Virginia horse farm on a cold, snowy afternoon. The next morning, they loaded up an ugly bay colt by the name of King Court and headed back for sunny Arizona.

Little did Lucy know she would become an expert in loading a horse. The first morning, when the colt refused to go into the trailer, Maggi told her, "Look, you pick up a handful of pebbles, and when I lead the colt up to the ramp and he refuses to go in, you throw a couple of pebbles at his butt." She followed orders and by the second day of their trip, the colt was broke to loading and gave them no further trouble.

"Well, I guess you know without me being along, you could have never got that colt loaded," Lucy laughed as they drove down the Shenandoah Valley. "You know Maggi, I had no idea you could do things like that with a horse," she added. "That's something."

Five days later, Maggi turned the truck and trailer into the Turf Paradise stable gate. Her thoughts were of seeing Beau. She pulled up close to their barn; Beau saw her as he was talking to a jock's agent. He came toward the truck and passed right by her!

"Why, the ungrateful bastard, he's more interested in that damn horse than he is in me," she fumed to herself.

Beau and the agent had already unsnapped King Court and were backing the colt out of the trailer.

As the long-legged, long-necked Roman-nosed bay colt stepped backward cautiously, Beau exploded.

"Christ, I wouldn't have given five hundred for this ugly son-of-a-bitch . . let alone pay five hundred to have him hauled from Virginia,'' he added. ''On top of that, he's full of girth disease.''

''What's that?'' the agent asked.

''Oh . . . '' Beau hesitated, he knew it was useless explaining, but the agent asked him again.

''It's like the mange or ringworm virus type thing,'' he told him. ''And it's hard to keep it from spreading through your stable. It gets transferred from the riding tack, boots, saddles, from the exercise boy and the jockeys; with them going from barn to barn. Even with disinfecting everything, it is still hard to keep all your horses from getting it.''

Beau watered out the gawky colt and put him up. As he looked him over, Maggi said, ''King Court doesn't know anything about a hot bran mash. He refused to touch it.''

That night, Beau held Maggi close to his body. He loved the scent of her bath powder and cologne . . . always the same familiar fresh scent he had grown so fond of. He kissed her mouth gently.

''I sure missed you, and so did Steve. He got tired of eating cornflakes for supper,'' he kidded, as he kissed her soft mouth.

15

Winter was much colder than usual. The cold frost and rain were painful to Maggi's feet and hands on the frosty, snappy mornings while she walked hots. Even though she wrapped her legs and feet in several cooler blankets, her feet still froze.

Beau kidded her, "Christ, we don't have any coolers to put on the horses, you got all of them on you."

"Well, I'm freezing cold, just sitting on this horse, walking around in a damnable circle," she pleaded.

"Oh, I never saw such a big baby," he kidded.

A groom who worked for them was from Canada and suggested, "Get some rum and put a little in your coffee in the mornings, and it will help your circulation. We do it all the time in Canada." She tried it and it worked. She felt no cold, but by 8 a.m. she was smashed. The Bacardi Rum was ruled out.

Arizona Downs Meet

March is a beautiful time in Arizona. It is spring in every sense of the word. Beau was busy these days, thinking constantly about which horses to take to Ruidoso since he had decided to go there next. Also, he mused, he would like to win the leading trainer award but knew he couldn't beat Hank Collins. Hank had too many horses and rich owners who could buy or claim any horse Hank wanted.

Beau thought, "Some friend Hank was, trying to buy King Court, just because he worked in black letter works one morning." Beau was glad Mr. Telly refused his offer of $15,000 for he felt the colt was snapping out of it now and beginning to wake up. He liked him better every time he took him to the race track.

That was Beau's reaction. Little did he know the successful effect the long-legged colt would have on his life.

King Court blossomed from the good feed, care and Beau's careful training. He had grown a good deal and since fall he had filled out well, into a sleek muscular confirmation. He was actually pretty, if it weren't for his Roman nose, but Beau even found that quality unique.

King Court not only won the two-year-old Paradise Valley Stakes, he equaled the world track record for 4½ furlongs in 51:3.

Mr. and Mrs. Telly were presented a beautiful silver tray, engraved with the colt's name, the time of the race, and Beau's name as trainer. And a check for $2,500. The Tellys were much older than Maggi and Beau, and they were non-drinkers, but they sent a bottle of champagne to them and left after the presentation.

That night, Beau and Maggi read and re-read the evening paper:

King Court . . . speed invader!
World Record Holder for 4½ furlongs
Trainer Beau Witlow

The same article appeared all over the country in the

Daily Racing Form.

"Well, I have a stake horse in my barn now," Beau bragged to Maggi, who listened to Beau boast as she clipped out all the write-ups for her scrapbook.

From that day on, King Court was treated like a stake horse. Beau walked him on foot, taking no risk of his being kicked by another horse. He was moved to the first stall by the tack room.

Every morning, admirers stopped by to see him, agents, press, jocks, owners . . . all were in awe of the big red bay colt and his Roman nose.

Ruidoso for Third Time

One evening, as Beau and Maggi were filling out their stall application for Ruidoso, a long-distance call came from Wichita, Kansas for Beau. When he hung up the phone, he told Maggi, "That was Heidi Green. She wants me to take her horses."

"Who's Heidi Green?"

"I used to ride for her at Caliente. She's got some horses at a training farm in California. They'll be coming in next Sunday on Luxart Vans. Two horses run for $5,000 and one runs for $6,500 over there, so they could be cheap allowance horses here," he stated.

"See! You're famous already. News gets around!" Maggi grinned.

"Yeah, with all your PR help, it does," he told her.

"Well, the PR part was no problem. It's getting you to have your picture taken or getting you to talk to someone for a TV interview that was the hard work," she kidded him.

"Honey, if I had your guts, I'd be President," he chuckled.

* * * *

Everyone was busy, getting ready to ship. Maggi hated not knowing where they would stay, if they could find a clean place. She thought, "Wish we had a house trailer, like everyone else had. Sure would solve the problem." Since she had mentioned it several times around the track, someone told her there was a good 24-foot second-hand trailer for sale for $1,200 — one bedroom, TV, completely furnished and metal awning.

It was a buy, and Maggi had no trouble convincing Beau, or Steve—even though he would have to sleep on the couch.

Maggi transferred her kitchen utensils and staples into the compact little galley of the trailer, filled the closets with clothes and made up the bed. A commercial hauler picked it up and pulled the trailer to Ruidoso. He would park and set it up on the track grounds, in a trailer court provided for the convenience of the racetrackers.

"Boy, sure makes it a lot nicer, having your own things and a place to live when we get there," she told Beau as the trailer left. She also talked him into leaving one car home as she didn't want to drive all by herself if she didn't have to. After she had Steve farmed out to the Maddoxes till school was out, they left late the next afternoon.

They got into Ruidoso by midnight. It was extremely cold in the high mountain altitude. Beau stopped by the barn to unload the saddle horses and to see if his two grooms had gotten there. They were huddled up in their sleeping bags freezing.

"Everything is ready. We have all the stalls bedded down," they told Beau.

Beau got into the truck. "Where is the damn trailer court?" he asked Maggi.

"Darned if I know. I think it's over on the other side of this hill. I thought I saw some trailers as we pulled in."

"Oh yes, that's where it is, all right. I remember now," he stated.

They drove through the narrow little trailer court roads. In the pitch dark, all the house trailers looked alike, and it took them a while to find theirs. Maggi dug around in her purse for the door key.

Beau unlocked the door. The temperature inside was zero. The fuse box was padlocked, so Beau couldn't turn on the power. There was no oil in the furnace.

"We'll freeze to death in here," Beau said loudly.

Maggi lit several matches, burning her fingers, trying to find her pajamas.

Beau just dropped his Levi's and dove into the cold bed. The ice-cold sheets sent him into a second tirade, and he yelled, "Maggi, come get in here and warm me up."

She couldn't find her pajamas in the dark, so she left her sweater on, slipped out of her Levi's and jumped into the bed. They clung together in a spasm of shivering laughter, and Beau methodically began to rub her legs.

"Hey, your feet—they're like ice! What's this? Christ, you have your socks on?" he laughed.

"You bet I have! You know how cold my feet get," she laughed from shivering so hard, till they finally warmed up and fell asleep.

Six a.m. The van roaring in woke Maggi and Beau, as it passed right by their house trailer. Beau was out and gone in minutes. It took Maggi a little longer. By the time she walked to their barn, Beau had the horses unloaded and the boys were getting out the tack from the van.

Heidi Green was there talking with Beau. He introduced Maggi. Heidi was a petite lady in her sixties with a lovely skin and attractive features and dressed in a very sophisticated style.

Maggi reacted enthusiastically to her warmth and open friendliness. Heidi was also outspoken and made it a habit of coming to the barn each morning, mingling with the grooms, and talking about her horses in a manner that made it obvious she knew what she was talking about. She had a disarmingly direct way about her, and stated her opinions in no uncertain terms.

"You're just what Beau needs," she told Maggi one day. "He's too easy and lets people lead him around. You're stronger than he is. He lets everyone know his business and his trade secrets. He needs someone to keep him in line. You're the stabilizer."

After the usual three days of getting set up and the horses all walked . . . the rigorous training routine began.

Maggi ponied on the main track at Ruidoso. There wasn't much room for a training track. In fact, there was hardly room for the main track. She noticed each set of horses they took up there. Beau talked and kidded around with other trainers but his keen watchful eye was on his horses as they made their little trip around the track. He never missed a thing the slightest mis-step. If one of the gallop boys would swing a horse back and forth, pulling him up, he heard about it from Beau when he got back.

"Cut that out or you'll grab a front quarter," (when a horse's gait is off balance, he has a tendency to step on himself and grab or tear the upper part of his hoof).

They couldn't tell him a thing he had not done himself.

Maggi was in awe of his ability to name all the horses that came off the track and that belonged to other stables. In just a few short weeks, his memory became uncanny. She knew this was what separated him from the others.

"Running a big stable takes lots of planning and thinking ahead each morning to get all the horses out and tracked," as Beau explained it to a new groom.

"Look, I only take one of your horses at a time, so you can get all your stall done and bathe your horse off before I take another one. Do you understand?"

"Yes, I think so," he answered. "You take one from me and one from another groom so that we have time to get our work done," the groom added.

"That's right. Now, sometimes I have to wait on a jock and hold you up, but I can't help that. So you just have to be patient," Beau continued. "Okay?" he added, hoping that the boy understood at least part of what he was trying to explain.

The meet got underway. In the opening day program, management stated it would award $500 and a trophy to the leading trainer of the meet.

"Boy, I sure want to win that!" Beau told Maggi.

"You can," she assured him with a slight grin.

Whether it was the money or the trophy that spurred Beau on was hard to say, but he was cracking, winning four races and never failing to light up the board for the first two weeks of the meet. The barn morale was good. Everyone pitched in as they all wanted Beau to win the training honors.

One cold morning during a coffee break, Pee Wee walked down the shedrow!

"Well, looks who's here!" Beau hollered out.

After coffee with Heidi and Maggi, and small talk Beau

went back to his training. Pee Wee came up to Maggi and said, "Boy, you two sure have come a long ways since the last couple of years on the fairs."

"I'll always be grateful to you, Pee Wee. You sure helped me in giving me a lot of moral support when I needed it," Maggi told him.

"Well, you two sure work good together, ya know! You're the best thing that ever happened to Beau," he said, patting her on the back.

"Well, how nice of you to say that, Pee Wee. You've made my day," Maggi told him, smiling.

Maggi liked Heidi Green better each day. She gave Beau a free rein with the horses, with the understanding that she wasn't in the business to lose money. She was the first to say, "Give him away, I'm not going to let any horse stand on my purse strings very long." She was always out early to watch her horses train but never interfered. She added an air of joy to the barn.

Heidi seemed to love everything about the profession and appreciated everyone's individual function on the backside. When her horses won, she always remembered to stake the grooms twenty dollars, and they loved her for it. In the evenings, she played poker, gin and bridge with the wealthy resort visitors, always coming out the winner! She traveled with a housekeeper-companion, a Swedish lady in her sixties.

She opened a whole new world for Beau amd Maggi, with wonderful dinners at her cabin and poker games with stakes to accommodate Beau's and Maggi's pocketbook.

Heidi had read of King Court while in California and when she saw him, she said: "My, Beau, he's a much bigger colt than I imagined." Beau led him out for her approval. "He's a good-looking animal. I hope he wins the

Futurity. It would be a feather in your cap,'' she kidded Beau.

"The hell with the feather. I'll take the money," Beau laughed.

Because Heidi's horses had been in training, they were ready to run as soon as they got over the trip. Jo-Jo was running the second week of the meet.

"I want you to come sit with me Saturday," Heidi told Maggi.

Maggi, Beau and Heidi were her cheering section for Jo-Jo who was in the third race. He broke beautifully and was well in front with a two-length lead. Then he began dropping back — a length at a time — until he was dead last.

"Must of broke down!" Beau said curtly, getting up and heading down to the finish line, where he stood waiting for the horse to be picked up by his groom.

Blood was oozing from Jo-Jo's nostrils as they led him back to their barn. Maggi caught up with Beau and the groom.

"What happened?" she asked.

"He bled. That's why he quit running. It's the altitude. I didn't know he was a bleeder. Go get the vet, Maggi."

The veterinarian administered a shot that would have a quick clotting effect on the animal's blood. "He should stop bleeding in a few minutes," he said reassuringly. "Put a sponge soaked with cold water under his halter over his ears . . . This is the fourth bleeder I've treated today. This humid, heavy air pressure doesn't help these old bleeders any."

"Well, there isn't any use in trying to run him here anymore," Beau said after the vet left. "I'll wait till we get to Albuquerque. Damn the rotten luck! I wanted to do some good for Heidi," Beau stated. "I guess that's why they ran him so cheap in California."

"Why do some horses bleed and others don't?" Maggi wanted to know.

"Lots of different reasons. It's a weakness— generally a run-down condition of the horse. Humid weather or altitude don't help, or sometimes its too much Vitamin B-12. My Dad always bragged he could hold any damn bleeder with coagulant shots and by tying a piece of wire around the root of the horse's tail before he ran. He swore by it! I've never had the best luck holding a bleeder the way he did," Beau said despondently.

"Well, if he gets used to this altitude, Beau — couldn't you run him again?"

"Damn it, just let me run this barn. If he bleeds here one more time, they'll rule him off for the rest of the meet — and Albuquerque too. They are strict about bleeders because if they choke and go down, they can cause a bad spill and get someone hurt or killed."

"I only meant —"

"You don't know what you're talking about!" he said, and stormed off as if the whole thing were her fault.

* * * *

Mr. Telly flew in alone for the Futurity trials. He was a very fidgety, nervous man and he drove Beau nuts. Beau made it a point of avoiding him as much as possible.

"Let Maggi show you where Heidi's box is," he would say, or "Maggi, take Mr. Telly over to the track kitchen for some coffee."

Mr. Telly was a good owner for he knew racing and never pestered Beau with senseless questions and made most visits to the barn in the early mornings so that calls were not so frequent . . . Beau really appreciated that in him, if only he were not such a nervous man.

The Futurity trials consisted of four divisions of races. King Court drew in in the toughest division, with all the better colts. The pressure mounted as each trial was run, and their times were recorded. Maggi's heart was pounding as she watched Beau pony King Court to the starting gate himself. He wasn't taking any chances on the way the horse was being handled. Furthermore, he would rather be doing that than sitting in the clubhouse with fidgety Mr. Telly.

King Court won his division, and his race was the best time of all, four heats. After the presentation in the winner's circle, they all went over the the test barn. Mr. Telly was ecstatic with joy.

"I never thought I'd have a horse this good!" he said, over and over. "I just hope I can stand the pressure of this business. I'm already worried about all the things that might happen to him."

Maggi and Beau laughed at his anxieties, although they could readily understand his feelings. A good racehorse can cause emotional traumas, there is no denying that.

Beau examined King closely for any leg problems the next morning.

"No signs of heat or swelling," he told Maggi and Heidi.

"I think you have a good shot of winning the Futurity if he doesn't get into any trouble," Heidi said confidently.

"Oh, Heidi, I sure hope you're right," Maggi answered. Everyone was all smiles.

Pee Wee dropped by to offer his congratulations on King Court's win and to announce he was getting married.

Beau wanted to know, "Who would be so dumb as to marry you?"

"The cute little redhead that worked at the fifty dollar

window," Pee Wee replied. "I'm having a reception at the Hi-Ho Bar. The owner's paying for the whole bash!" he said smugly.

"How come?" Maggi asked.

"Oh, 'cause I tout him on lots of winners, and he loves to bet," Pee Wee laughed.

"You know, Pee Wee, you're like a cat — you always land on you feet," Maggi said in amazement.

After Pee Wee walked away, Beau remarked, "A fat chance of that marriage lasting. Hell, she drinks more than he does."

"Oh, no!" Maggi moaned. She felt that maybe this would be Pee Wee's chance, and now even she had her doubts. With that kind of foundation to start on, there was nothing to build on.

*　　*　　*　　*

Once in a while things ran smoothly at the barn. And this was such a week. No one got mad, no one quit, no horse got loose or broke down, Things were going so well, it actually got boring. UNTIL!

One morning Beau and Maggi got into an argument about the vet Beau was using. Maggi disagreed about the vet's ability, and felt he should use the other vet, Dr. Ord, who was the better vet and most in demand on the grounds.

"Goddamn it, Maggi — he's too hard to get! What the fuck do you know about it, anyway? Let me run this goddamn barn! Dr. Brown is okay, so shut up about it!"

Before she could say another word, Beau walked away. She was livid. She hated Dr. Brown; he was too indecisive in his diagnoses and lacked race track knowledge. Why wouldn't Beau listen to her?

After their sudden outburst, things quieted down again. Everyone was busy with the steady routine — and Maggi was still turning to the left! She was waiting for the day she wouldn't have to walk these damn hots!

* * * *

Three days before the Futurity. Tension began to pick up around the barn. Maggi felt it. Beau was edgy, and she steered clear of any encounter with him. Dr. Brown was at the barn that morning doing whatever was necessary with all the horses. Beau stopped him just as he was about to leave.

"Hey, Doc! I want to give King Court some vitamin supplement — you know, iron, vitamins, and so forth."

"Sure," the vet said, and walked to the back of his truck to get the supplies. He withdrew several vitamins and blood-builder supplements into a large ten cc needle and gave King Court the full ten cc in the main jugular, then wiped the spot with a piece of cotton soaked with alcohol.

"That should do it," he said and left.

Maggi finished folding all the coolers and put all the tack away. Beau came back from the racing office.

"Come on, let's go home. I'm hungrier than a bitch wolf with seven pups." He grabbed her by the belt loops on her Levi's, twirled her around, and they walked toward their truck, arm in arm.

An hour later, the groom came to the door. "King Court very seeeek — come queeek!"

Beau jumped up from the couch, grabbed his hat, rushed out the door and drove off with the groom. Maggi ran out and followed them in Beau's truck, carrying her boots.

When they arrived, King Court was lying down, trying

215

to roll over. He was wet with sweat.

"Quick, go find a vet! Go get Dr. Ord!" Beau ordered as he made the horse get to his feet. "Tell him that King has the colic real bad!"

She jumped into the pickup and drove to where the vet lived. The creek made it impossible to drive right up to his cabin from the track. She either had to drive fifteen miles around to reach his cabin or walk up the mountain path. She parked by the vet's car at the bridge, jumped out of the truck, and ran across the bridge and up the steep hill. Her legs felt as heavy as lead as she struggled onward. As she got closer, she saw the rustic cabin framed against the pine trees and saw that smoke was rolling out of the chimney.

" Doc!" she cried frantically. "Doc — Doc, it's Maggi Witlow. Please come quick!"

He was out on the porch by the time she reached the last turn in the path.

"What's wrong, Maggi? What's the trouble?"

"It's King Court, Doc. He's so sick! Oh, please come quickly!"

Dr. Ord nodded. "I'll be right there," he said, as he started down the steep path toward his vet truck.

When he reached the barn, King Court was still up, but making repeated attempts to lie down. Beau managed to keep him walking. The vet took the horse's temperature. It was one hundred and five!

"That's a mighty sick animal," he told Beau. "What'd Doc Brown give him?"

"I don't know exactly. Just a jug of vitamins, I think. Juan's gone to look for him. He should be here any minute."

Dr. Brown arrived, they consulted briefly, and Dr. Brown said authoritatively, "We'll give him strychnine and mineral oil to knock out this colic."

"Let me point out," Dr. Ord intervened politely, "that this colt's in the big Futurity on Saturday. He'll have to be scratched if you give him any strychnine now."

"Yeah, that's right. Let's try just the oil. If it doesn't help, we'll have to go ahead with the other. Okay? Now keep on walking him until he passes the oil. Don't let him lie down. We don't want a twisted gut on top of all this."

"Go saddle the pony, Maggi," Beau ordered. In a few minutes, she was walking King around with three coolers over him to keep him from cramping.

Half an hour later, the oil passed, but the colic had taken its toll. King was fatigued.

"By rights I should scratch him," Beau remarked. "Any other race and I wouldn't give it another thought. But damn it, this is a big purse. I don't know what to do."

*　*　*　*

Later, in his stall, King nibbled at the hay.

"Look, Beau — he's eating now."

"Come on, Maggi. Get away from his stall. Let him alone."

On their way home, Maggi broke down and cried.

"Maggi, that's horseracing. It's just a bad break, that's all. Nobody's fault."

The decision was made to run King Court in the Futurity, although Beau was honest with Telly concerning what had happened to the colt, and the possible effects this might have on his performance.

"Hell, I'm willing to take the chance," Telly said, "if you think he's all right. You know I trust your judgment, Beau."

"Well, it all depends on how much the colic and oil have taken out of him," Beau explained. "One thing's for sure

217

though. I won't let the jockey punish him."

On the day of the Futurity, King Court looked every inch the capable contender. Beau saddled the horse up and gave explicit instructions to the jockey.

King Court broke out of the gate on top. He was holding the lead by three lengths as he turned for home, and then, began dropping back.

"He's getting tired," Beau said, as he watched the jockey closely to make sure he did not abuse the horse. The jockey sat still and King finished a bad third.

While the colt was being bathed, Beau walked up and down, cursing his own stupidity. "I should have my head examined for letting him run! I've probably knocked him out for the rest of the summer now!"

Not winning the Futurity depressed them all, although Mr. Telly took it in the most sportsmanlike manner. "Hell, don't feel bad, Beau. I'm tickled we got third." He bid everyone good-bye and left early.

Maggi coaxed Beau to a Saturday night dance to lift his spirits.

The summer slipped by quickly, the Ruidoso meet would soon be over, and Beau began making shipping arrangements for the Albuquerque State Fair. One evening, a sheriff's deputy came to their door. He asked for Pee Wee Foy.

"He's not here," Beau said. "What's he done?"

"You friends of his?"

"Yes. Why?"

"He just tried to ram his trailer house off the side of a mountain with his wife in it. When the manager of the trailer park showed up, he took off. We thought he might have come here."

"No. We haven't seen him all day," Beau replied

honestly.

"Sorry to have bothered you," the officer said, and went on his way.

"That crazy son-of-a-bitch!" Beau roared. "He's plumb nuts, I tell you!"

"Let's go and see if Trudy's okay," Maggi said.

When they arrived, a crowd of people had gathered around the trailer . . as it hung with one end jutting over the steep cliff. The axle had caught against two boulders and kept it from plummeting over the side. The front of the trailer was badly damaged where the car had battered it with repeated rammings.

"Christ, will you look at that!" Beau said. "That guy's nuts — absolutely nuts!"

They found Trudy huddled on a small couch. A pressure cooker of beans had been left on the stove during the fracas. It had exploded, and now there were beans on the ceiling, walls, and all over the furniture and the floor.

When Trudy finally lifted her head to tell her version of the story, Maggi saw that her face was swollen and one eye had an ugly black bruise. In that moment, Maggi hated Pee Wee.

By the following morning, the whole backside was gossiping about Pee Wee, who had since been found and thrown in jail. The best place for him, everyone agreed.

But the night he was arrested, Pee Wee jumped out of the patrol car, landing on his back and moaning that his spine was broken. The officers did not dare move him, so an ambulance was called. But X-rays soon revealed that he had not sustained any back injuries. Pee Wee was then taken to jail, to court, and sentenced to two months at the county farm.

All the racetrackers agreed that this would be a good thing for Pee Wee. He had always gotten away with his antics in the past. Now, he would have some time to get his head on straight.

*   *   *   *

Coming from the local Laundromat one afternoon, Maggi could hear someone calling out her name. As she heard it again, rather faintly, as if from a great distance, she looked about curiously, and then the voice became more insistent.

"Maggi! Hey, Maggi. Over here! Hey, Maggi — it's me."

Then she saw it was Pee Wee, dressed in a clean khaki suit and a jaunty Stetson, riding in the patrol car beside the warden.

"I'll see ya at the track," he called to her as the traffic light changed to green.

Later at the grandstand, Maggi asked him, "How did you manage this number?"

"Well . . . I got in good with the warden because I fixed their windmill — pulled a sucker rod — no one else knew how to fix it. After that, the warden took a liking to me. He even dropped me off at the trailer so that I could see Trudy before coming here."

Maggi laughed outright. "I can't think of anyone else who could get away with what you do."

"Hey, Beau!" Pee Wee yelled. "Come over here, you ole rascal and say hello to me."

Beau walked slowly out of the saddling paddock and over to where they were standing. "That must be some jail to let the likes of *you* out," was all he said.

Pee Wee got himself on "good behavior" and managed to be back riding on the race track before the meet was over. But with everyone shipping out, he had a hard time getting mounts. He was going to Albuquerque as soon as Trudy finished her work at the mutuel window.

Albuquerque for the First Time

Heidi went home to Wichita, promising Beau and Maggi that she would see them in Phoenix in the fall.

The Maddoxes came up for a weekend and took Steve home to stay with them until Beau and Maggi arrived home. Maggi had their trailer hauled to a trailer court close to the Albuquerque fairgrounds.

Albuquerque was cold, dusty and windy. As they tried to set up their barn, the wind fought them viciously, blasting sand into Maggi's face and hair. There was no way to avoid it as sand engulfed her in strong, angry swirls. The fairgrounds were spread over four hundred acres. Long barns were set side by side, in rows, which created a channel for the wind to howl through. There were exhibit buildings everywhere and Indian camps below the Sangre de Cristo mountains beyond the Albuquerque Fairgrounds.

Beau stated the next day, "It's too damn cold and windy to give the horses a bath outside, so we will use one of these empty stalls. And after the fifth race, just rub them down with a towel. I don't want them catching cold," he told all the grooms.

It was sheer hell, the whole fourteen days, cold, dirty, windy. But it was well worth the misery for they won seven races and claimed three useful horses for Mr. Robson. Then the horses were running out of conditions.

"It's too damn hot in Phoenix right now, and I can't run anything here now, so let's go to Duncan and catch the tail of the meet. It'll pay the owners' expenses," Beau proposed.

"Oh, fine! I'll get to see Lucy and Hal," Maggi enthused. "And she will get to see King Court. Bet she won't even know him now. And we can park our house trailer right at the end of the barn under that cottonwood tree," she added.

"You're crazy!" Beau kidded her. "Come on, let's go eat so we can start packing and get a van."

Living right by the barn with the racehorses was convenient. Lucy and her husband came over often. On cold mornings, Maggi served doughnuts and hot coffee as they all sat about and talked of past and present happenings. Maggi thoroughly enjoyed company as well as the opportunity to be a hostess.

King Court was out of place at the little Duncan fair, and Beau had to take a lot of kidding about it. He was accused of trying to hog all the purses with a horse that was obviously overqualified for that track.

He did not want to send King Court home in the heat and sunning in the corrals was good for him, especially after Albuquerque. Still, the small space to which King was confined did not allow him the exercise he required. Beau was worried that he might hurt himself frisking about the stall.

"I'm going to have to gallop him tomorrow," Beau told Maggi. "He's too high."

"Why don't you run him in the allowance race here?" Maggi wanted to know.

"Because no would enter against him. And if they did, the racing secretary would put a hundred and forty-five pounds of weight on him to handicap him. Besides, it's too risky."

Mr. Telly was helpful to Beau here, he had an uncanny ability to scan a good horse from the charts in the *Racing Form* and bring it to Beau's attention. Beau would check him out for soundness, and many a good claim was made from this partnership.

The Duncan meet passed quickly, and it didn't take Maggi long to button down the trailer and send it on its way. Maggi and Beau loaded up the two saddle horses and pulled out of the Duncan fairgrounds, not realizing then that they would never return.

16

Arizona Downs — Third Time

At the Arizona State Fairgrounds, nothing had changed. The track was worse than ever before so it was agreed by the State Racing Commission that the Fair Meet days be moved to Turf Paradise race track.

Again, the long drives faced Beau and Maggi, and she began to think seriously about their building a home nearby.

While they were at Del Mar, they had purchased an acre of land a half-mile from the track for a mere $1,000 — $30 per month.

"How in the hell could we build a house? We don't have that kind of money," was all the help she got from Beau. But Maggi was a determined gal. It took her a month to get the utilities brought in, and so the little dream house she had pictured in her mind would have to just wait.

A new owner by the name of Ted Byron, who had seven maiden three-year-olds and one unbroke yearling colt, came to Beau.

Ted Byron came with a conservative approach (for himself). He agreed to pay a minimum of three dollars per day per head to Beau. He would pay the shipping, shoeing, and vet bill, and whatever they won, he and Beau would split down the middle. Beau took the deal because he needed the horses.

As he told Maggi, "This is not a good deal if these damn colts can't run a lick. I'd lose my ass. But three-year-olds are good property on the race track, and unless they're just bums, we should make out all right on them."

Ted was a handsome man, a middle-aged bachelor with a distinguished touch of gray at the temples, six-foot-four, and not fat. His manners were of a gentleman, and he loved the ladies, and they him.

Beau and Maggi liked him instantly, the three became good friends, having dinners together often. He was like one of the family by the time the winter was over. And Beau had done well with the three-year-olds.

Ted spent his summers in Seattle, Washington, hunting and fishing. His income came from owning a city block in downtown Seattle, and he clipped coupons from that tidy little investment.

Ted was a smart man and never interfered with Beau's training method and respected his advice and ability as a horseman. They got along well in this regard and up until the present, had never had a harsh word.

Ted was a flamboyant dresser when he came to the races. But during the morning training he looked no better than a working groom mucking out his stalls. Ted was one person who never looked good in Levis, rugged boots and heavy jackets . . . He looked out of place . . . But he loved pulling his old sloppy hat down over his head and taking in the morning training with all the backside and was well liked by every one kidding and talking about horses . . . He was a hooked victim . . . addicted to the backside . . .

Beau favored Ted's colt Searcher, but felt he was too big

225

for his age. "We'll have a problem trying to keep him racing sound," he predicted.

Ted was an early visitor to the barn each morning. When Heidi came in from Wichita, they immediately became fast friends.

"You're getting a nice clientele built up with people like Ted Byron," Heidi told Beau. "He's a real gentleman."

Maggi had overheard the remark and was overcome with a sudden warm feeling of gratitude for the presence of people like Byron and Heidi in their lives.

King Court Goes to Santa Anita

One morning as Maggi was holding Searcher so that Beau could bathe him, he told her that Telly wanted to run King Court in a $20,000 claiming race in Santa Anita.

"That's all he's really worth, and he can't beat those better allowance horses there," Beau told her. "Besides, they'll put too much weight on him here. I wish I had the money to buy him."

While Maggi was trying to digest all this, Beau told her that she would have to go to California.

"Oh, Beau, no!"

"Yes, goddamit! Now don't start that again. I've got to stay here and run this stable. You know that as well as I do. You can visit with your Dad while you're there. I'll give you a call every night and let you know what to do with King. I've got to ship him out this weekend, and he'll be stabled in Hank's barn. I've already phoned him. Hank will be down as the trainer."

"Then why do I have to go?"

"You know how Hank is around horses. I want you to keep an eye on things and make sure the colt isn't abused."

Maggi hated the whole idea of the trip but could see no

way to avoid it. Before she had much time to think about it, she was already underway, and soon found herself in Santa Anita, driving toward Hank's barn.

She had mixed emotions about the eighth race in which King Court was entered. She wanted him to win, but she dreaded the thought of losing him. She tried to feel businesslike.

She watched King Court take the race easily by six lengths, and yes, he was claimed. As she saw King Court being led from the saddling paddock by a total stranger, she had a dismal feeling in the pit of her stomach. She stared after King Court for as long as she could keep him in view.

Hank handed her a copy of the claiming slip and said, "Hell, Maggi, what're you so upset about? You got twenty thousand for him! I'd say that was something to cheer about."

"I know, but he was our best horse, Hank. There'll never be another like him."

"Sure, sure—I understand," Hank said, although Maggi knew that he didn't give a damn.

When she spoke with Beau on the phone, she detected emotion in his conversation. After eight years of marriage, she knew him well, and the long silences told her that Beau was as sick at the loss of King Court as she was.

"Well, Telly will be glad to hear that," Beau concluded. The horse had been making a nervous wreck out of Telly and his wife. They constantly worried that King would get hurt or die. They much preferred having the money.

When Maggi returned home, Beau was nowhere to be found. The cold numbness spread through her body at the thought of what coming home to an empty house had meant in the past. Then, she heard his truck outside, and ran out into the drive to meet him with open arms. He hugged her tightly and did not criticize her tears at the loss of King Court. For once, he did not remind her that this was "only a business." When she glanced up, she saw that his eyes were also moist, and that his jaw had been stubbornly set against the risk of showing any emotion. He could not trust himself to say anything, and Maggi was overcome with a new feeling of compassion for him. She clung to him and said nothing, for clearly, there was nothing to say.

* * * *

In the days that followed, they resumed their regular routine, and on one of her trips to the track kitchen, Maggi made the acquaintance of a newspaper man who seemed extremely interested in their stable. Maggi encouraged his inquiries — and obtained some good coverage in the paper for her trouble. She knew that any kind of publicity was better than none at all, and before long, new owners would be influenced by what they read about Beau, and he was more and more frequently approached to train their horses.

Beau had a maddening habit of turning all prospects away by saying he was not sure he could get the stalls for their horses. Maggi openly criticized him for this.

"You never know," she cautioned him. "The one you don't take could be the very horse you've been waiting for."

"Oh, hell! Nobody's going to give me a Kelso to train around here. You can get that out of your head right now," Beau would insist.

But Maggi was relentless in her quest for more good publicity, even though it was difficult to get Beau to cooperate with the track management on publicity shots.

During one such photographing session, Beau and Maggi met Michael Hansen, a young, slender blonde-haired fellow who handled publicity stints for the track and was responsible for organizing the pictures to be used in the newspaper. Mike quickly learned that it was Maggi he could look to for cooperation.

He took time to show Maggi the many different jobs on the backside. One of the major important jobs was the film patrol man. He had the job of photographing each race from beginning to end. With a stand at the main stretch and backside stretch he had to climb the high tower pole each race and man his cameras with the aid of a good helper and process the film after each race in case that the stewards needed to look at it in case of an objection called either by a rider, trainer, or the officials . . . It was the film patrol man's job to have these films ready.

He had to be at the track every morning around ten o'clock so that the trainers and riders could also view the films to check where their horses went wrong if so, or to see if he had any interference from another horse . . . Beau made it a ritual each morning to view the films that his horse ran in . . . Maggi often thought what other business is so monitored and watched so carefully.

Mike was born into horseracing. His father was president of the Downs meet but did not favor Michael with any impressive positions. So, during the four-day race meet, Mike was saddled with different jobs: clerk of scales, publicity man, entry clerk. As clerk of scales, he had to check every jockey's weight before and after each race. If the jockey's weight after the race was two or three pounds more than what had been printed in the program, this announcement had to be made to the public. It was Mike's job to warn the jockeys to watch their weight since more than a three-pound weight gain meant that the rider would be taken off of all his mounts that day.

Mike had grown accustomed to attempted bribes on the part of jockeys who were overweight but hoped to get away with a few extra pounds. Mike would complain about the pressure that was being placed on him, but always adhered to the rules.

If a jockey and his tack weighed less after a race due to the accidental loss of one of his pads, the horse he rode was automatically disqualified. Michael enforced all rules according to the book.

Mike was fun to be with, and he, Beau and Maggi quickly became close friends. Maggi was pleased to see Beau in the company of someone who talked intelligently and had long-range ambitions for his life. Mike was good for Beau and Maggi. He boosted their morale.

"Hell, Beau — you rank right up on top of the list with the best trainers!" Michael would say. "This meet's just started, and you're already leading trainer."

Beau, Maggi and Michael became good friends, . . . telling all the good and bad that had happened in their lives. Beau even told him how close he came to getting Sir Tribal to train for Bert Maddox. Michael expressed his sadness that Beau didn't get him.

It was a few weeks later in the winter that Michael came to the barn with an article on Sir Tribal.

"Here's a column on that horse, thought you might like to see it," Michael stated.

"Not really," Beau said, but grabbed the paper from his hand and began to read the column:

SIR TRIBAL RETIRED
FROM PLATER TO TURF HERO

Gallant old Sir Tribal has run his last race. The colorful "Gray Ghost" has broken down at the age of 8 and will be retired to a life of ease.

His owner, Charlie Fritz, says Chicagoans never will forget this hard-hitting thoroughbred. Once a $1,000 plater in Ohio, he emerged as the terror of the turf here. For sheer gameness, Sir Tribal was in a class by himself. He had a tremendous heart. He feared no rival. Horses that challenged his lead usually did it in vain. He cost $9,000.

Sir Tribal was purchased by trainer, Steve Ippolito for Chicagoan, Charlie Fritz at a cost of $9,000. Competing in the toughest competion he won $260,000 with 19 victories.

As Beau set the *Form* down, he looked up at Michael and Maggi. "Well, I won't have to be reading about him anymore, thank God. You don't know how many times this horse has haunted me and Bert," he told Michael "Now the old bastard broke down. I bet if he were a stud, that Fritz guy would have gotten a million or more for him," he stated.

"I thought you would like to see it," Michael added. "It's a Chicago *Racing Form*. I got it from the office."

"Can I keep it to show Bert?" Beau asked.

"Sure. Look, I have to get back to the office. See you later," he said and then left.

Turf Paradise — Sixth Season

Beau had lost several of the Ruidoso horses and had claimed some new ones — already thinking ahead for the summer racing. Within a few weeks of the Turf Paradise Meet, he was leading trainer.

Maggi had to have the little toe on her right foot amputated from severe frostbite during the winter. It put her on crutches for the next two months. But soon she managed to ride and walk those damn hots again! She took a lot of razzing from the racetrackers.

"Hey, what some people won't do to get out of walking hots!" and "Boy, that Beau, he's a real slave driver!"

Hot walking was one thing, but the insurmountable bookwork was Maggi's next hate. With the increase of grooms in their barn and an exercise boy, it seemed to Maggi she was at the desk continually.

One warm, beautiful morning during training hours, Ted Bryon came from the track after watching Searcher work out of the gate. He blared out to Maggi with a smile, "Searcher worked five-eights in one minute flat! He's a runner! And I almost forgot to pay the final installment for the Ruidoso Thoroughbred Futurity. I think Searcher can win it!" he beamed.

"Hey!" Beau cautioned him. "He's a nice horse, but he hasn't done anything to get that excited about. He's waking up and showing some speed, but hell, I'll be glad if he just breaks his maiden."

Ted and Maggi knew that Beau was being realistic, and they all laughed at their tendency to over-react to a fast work.

The Turf Paradise meet was coming to an end. Heidi had already left for Wichita, a little earlier than usual. She hadn't felt too well all winter but promised to meet them in

Ruidoso when the weather warmed up. Ted made plans to come to Ruidoso, but went home to Washington to tend to business first.

But the best news Beau and Maggi heard was that Mike had managed to get the clerk of scales job along with a racing office position in Ruidoso. Maggi was elated to hear they would be spending the summer together.

It was official: Beau had won the leading trainer's award for the first time at Turf Paradise — with twenty-five wins.

"Not bad for a cowboy from Buckeye, Arizona," Maggi said proudly and was joined in a toast by Ted and Mike lifting their glasses to Beau.

Detour to Sunland Park

After their little party was over and they were driving home, Beau seemed preoccupied.

"What's up?" Maggi asked. "You're too quiet."

"I've got to go to Sunland Park with Mr. Beely's six head," he told her. "You'll have to go on to Ruidoso alone. Beely wants me to run his horses in Sunland Park until Ruidoso starts up. If I don't do it, he'll just give them to someone else. And Ruidoso won't start for three weeks yet."

"Oh, God, I hate it when we have to split the stable!" Maggi replied angrily. "You just can't win in this damned business!"

"You can handle it!" Beau continued. "I'll take the two new grooms, Juan and the others can go with you. Steve can stay with the Maddoxes until school is out."

Thirty-six head of horses to ship, and Maggi had it all to do. She dreaded the separation and suddenly remembered that Pee Wee was riding at Sunland. This thought left her a little apprehensive as always.

233

Knowing that men are sensitive about taking orders from any woman, Maggi carefully told the grooms, "This was what Beau wanted done." They worked well for her.

Ruidoso for the Fourth Time

Although she didn't show it, Maggi was scared to death. Could she handle running this big stable of horses?

The van arrived at the Ruidoso track. Fifteen head were new horses that she didn't know too well; so she matched up their descriptions with their registration papers. The job took all morning and meant switching horses from one stall to another so that each groom had his own string all together. The wind and cold didn't make the job any easier for all of them.

Maggi had a surprise for Beau. Several weeks before, she had ordered twenty-five red and white new plastic

New plastic webbings

webbing stall guards to replace the old stall chains. A big red *W* was set in the middle of each guard. The webbings looked so elegant after the grooms had snapped them into place that Maggi could hardly wait to see Beau's face. She was tired, but she felt good as she mused that it was just two years since she first came here. How much things had changed for the good!

Maggi was still daydreaming when suddenly a jockey walked up and introduced himself.

"I'm Robert Black," he said with a Texas drawl. "Beau is giving me first call here." (First call: when a jockey rides for only that stable.)

Robert was stockier than Pee Wee, and taller. He had just turned nineteen and was recovering from a broken collar bone from a spill at Sunland Park two months before.

"I'm heavy from the layoff," he admitted, "but I'll lose it in the hot box."

Maggi watched as he strutted while talking. She found his cocky arrogant manner disturbing.

"Show me Searcher," he demanded. "Beau's bragged on that colt all week. Says he's got a shot in the Ruidoso Thoroughbred Futurity for two-year-olds."

He followed Maggi to Searcher's stall, stepped back and took a long, appraising look, and burst into harsh laughter.

"You mean that's *him?* He looks like a plow horse — a big fat Percheron! How can Beau be so high on the moose? He's awkward as hell."

"He'll win the Futurity too!" Maggi exploded at him.

"If he does, I'll eat him!" Robert retorted and walked away with his hands jammed into his hip pockets. He stopped suddenly and twirling around on his heel, added: "Oh, by the way — what time you want me here tomorrow morning?"

"Six o'clock sharp!" Maggi said flatly.

"Yawl better come wake me up. I'm in trailer space ten here on the grounds."

"I'm not going to come to wake you!" Maggi told him sharply. "If you can't get yourself up, you can't be much of a man."

"Hey . . . you're hard on a guy!" he drawled.

"I have enough to do with worrying about the likes of you."

"Okay, I'll be here," he said, as he turned away again and continued looking at the horses on his way down the shedrow.

Maggi was still fuming at his impudence when one of her grooms walked up and said, "They say he's ornery to get along with, but a good bug boy (apprentice rider). He was leading rider at Sunland all last winter before he got hurt."

Maggi knew that a *bug boy* was an apprentice rider who had not yet won fifty races in his career. To get started, he was usually assigned to a trainer — such as Beau — and worked under a contract that stipulated he would ride exclusively for this one trainer.

"Having the bug" as it was called, meant that the bug boy could deduct five pounds from whatever weight the racing secretary had assigned to the horse. The five pounds off helped to compensate for his lack of experience against more skilled riders. It also gave the trainer a mild advantage in return for taking the risk of a "green" rider. He might lose a race now and again because of the boy's lack of riding ability, or the boy's poor judgment could even result in injury to the horse. But once the jockey became a good little race rider and got "hot," everyone would want to ride him and get the five-pound deduction off the weight their horses must carry. The weight factor varied from state to state — as much as seven to ten pounds.

Beau liked using bug boys who were capable because the weight allowance was a real advantage on small, frail fillies and young colts.

But not all bug riders ended up as jockeys. Some never managed to win fifty races in their entire career. Before a bug boy could apply for a license, he had to work for a reputable stable for two years — mucking out stalls, polishing tack, and galloping horses. Some bug boys got tired of waiting for the chance to ride and would quit. When a trainer decided the bug boy was ready to ride, he would accompany him to the racing official's office and give his recommendation. The officials would then personally witness the jockey's ride from the starting gate during early morning training, and arrive at their own decision concerning the boy's competence. With the stewards' approval, the boy would be issued his apprentice license.

Robert Black had already been through this procedure a year earlier with another trainer. He was making good money in a hurry and that accounted for his cockiness.

A jockey's constant battle to keep his weight down also contributes to his temperamental disposition. While Maggi could sympathize with this somewhat, she nonetheless found it extremely difficult to tolerate Robert's habit of arriving late each morning. Improving her relationship with Robert Black was a long, tedious process, but Maggi knew the importance of getting along with everyone, particularly with Beau away. Having full responsibility for the horses and grooms made her appreciate Beau's pressures, and it helped her to justify some of his moodiness and temper flare-ups.

Two weeks had gone by. It was still cold. Maggi was

walking the last two hots when a jock came up to her and said, "Hi, I'm Sherman. I'm going down to Sunland this weekend to ride. Beau said for me to bring you down when I go."

"That's the best news I've heard all day!" Maggi screamed.

When they drove into the backside at Sunland, all Maggi could see was the outline of the grandstand. The wind was blowing viciously across the flat sandy area blotting out everything in a cloud of gritty dust. They had difficulty finding Beau's barn, but finally they heard Beau calling out loud. Maggi jumped from the car and ran to his tack room.

He slammed the tack room door behind them, grabbed her and kissed her, leaving her lightheaded.

"I guess you've missed me," she said with a sly grin.

"You *know* it!" he said, pressing his body against hers.

"B-Beau!" she protested weakly.

"Okay," he said, with a flirtatious wink.

Maggi could see that Beau had everything packed and ready to go. As soon as he ran the two horses that day, the van would come by to load them up.

Maggi was pleased to hear that Pee Wee had won several stakes and was leading jock at Sunland. She was hoping this would strengthen his resolve to stop drinking.

* * * *

"Riders up!" the paddock judge yelled as Beau lifted Pee Wee on his mount. He ran third and second that day, ending their stay at Sunland.

Maggi fell asleep holding Beau's hand as the truck started on its way to Ruidoso.

The next morning, Beau told her to sleep in. Maggi felt

238

guilty about it, but she didn't argue. The warm, soft bed felt too good! She fell back to sleep, reminiscing about the night before.

* * * *

Ruidoso was a summertime town, and with the races about to start, it began to pick up a faster pulse! Families were coming in for holiday weekends and the races. Heidi and Ted were the first of the owners to arrive and the only owners who stayed for the summer. The other clients would come only when their horses would be running.

Beau's barn was filled with talk and laughter over good hot coffee with Heidi and Ted. Heidi remarked as she watched one of her horses gallop, "You can sure pick out Beau's horses on the track; they're all so fat, slick, and well groomed . . " Ted agreed with her one hundred percent.

Michael had arrived also. The racing office was open, taking entries and getting the racing program lined up. After the daily routine was over, they all met at the local bar for a few beers and jokes. Michael confessed he had a girl he was in love with and intended to marry in the fall.

"Congratulations!" came with a kiss from Maggi, and a lot of kidding from Beau.

Heidi insisted that Maggi join her and Ted in her box during the races. "And make Beau come too," she urged.

"I'll try," Maggi replied, "but you know how he hates to dress up and all."

"Well, you can make him if anyone can," Heidi laughed. "He'd still be on the Prescott fairs if it weren't for you."

Ted laughed. "He is so damn earthy . . . that guy . . but

239

I love him."

"Yes, but that has nothing to do with this business." Heidi interrupted. "He should take pride, as Maggi says, and try to took better than just a roustabout."

Maggi and Beau were happy to see Steve arrive. He was growing, and they could see a change in him just the two months since they had last seen him.

Maggi grinned. "Now I have some hot walking help."

"Ohhhh, Mom—do I have to?"

"Hey, you like having a new bike and nice things, don't you? Well, you can work like the rest of us," was Beau's sharp answer to Steve's wailing.

On the tow ring, Steve was turning to the left with Maggi the next morning.

Michael surprised Beau and Maggi when he left after the races one Sunday, chartered a private plane, flew it himself to Phoenix, and flew his girl back with him. Jill was young, tall, blond, and pleasant—the Lauren Bacall type—and very much in love with Michael. She stayed a week, and on the last night when they took her to the airport in El Paso, Michael slipped a ring into her champagne glass. It was inscribed, *Marry Me*. It was a gay night in El Paso as the four awaited her flight for Phoenix and back to her job.

* * * *

The meet was going well for Beau Witlow. With thirty races won, he almost had a cinch on the leading trainer award. He won races for all of his clients and many more for Heidi and Ted. His only problem was with Robert, who whined about everything: missing his girl in El Paso getting up early . . having to gallop too many horses . . being tired. Beau had to have Maggi wake him up every morning.

Her only device was, "I'll turn the hose on you if you don't get up." Robert took her seriously.

The longer Maggi was around Robert, the more she realized how hard it was for a jockey to live and keep his weight down. Because Robert was large-boned and bigger than most riders his age, he gained weight just looking at food. He was always in the hot box, after morning training, especially on race days. He was in a constant battle trying to avoid food and liquids — often weakening and then having to flip (vomit) it up. This flipping made Maggi almost lose her dinner.

Beau explained to her one night, "The constant flipping, dieting, water pills, and the hot box dehydrate him and then he has a terrible desire for any kind of liquids. And water will put weight on a jock faster than anything. Just one glass will add three to five pounds to most jocks' weight."

Robert showed the strain, too; his face was drawn tight over his high cheekbones, and his eyes were set deep into the eye sockets. Plus, he was so damn fidgety and restless that he drove everyone nuts just to be around him for any length of time.

"That's why he likes to go to El Paso to see his girl — balling her keeps him from eating and thinking about food," Beau laughed.

But dieting wasn't the only problem that Robert had. The frequent rains at Ruidoso created a dangerous track, and sometimes it rained so hard it limited visibility. Many times Maggi had seen Robert come back after a race on a muddy track, with five pairs of goggles hanging down from his neck. The first time she asked Beau, "Why?"

"Well, when a jock leaves the gate he will have at least five pair of goggles stacked on his head. Then as he's riding the race and horses in front throw mud on his goggles, he pulls the dirty pair down so he has clear vision. He continues pulling another pair and another pair until the race is over!"

Beau, having been a jockey in his early years, knew how senseless it was for a trainer or owner to give a jockey too many instructions before the race. There was no guarantee what would or could happen when the gates flew open. And a jock was on his own. Like anyone driving down a freeway and someone cuts in front, the driver has to use his quickest and best judgment to try to avoid a wreck. The same problems occur inriding a horse race.

Beau was very precise on explaining the horses' problems or habits and told the jocks:

"Look, this horse likes to come from behind."

"Wait on this horse, if you can. And try to move him at the 3/8s pole."

"He don't like to come on the inside rail—he gets scared. Try to keep him on the outside, if you can."

"This horse don't like too much stick, or he'll sulk."

Don't let this horse take the lead too soon, or he will just hang it up.' (Won't try to win)

But most of the time Maggi only heard him tell the jockeys, "Well, you're on your own. Try and win, and good luck." And the jocks liked him for having confidence in them to use good judgment.

"Jocks have to be able to take advantage of the breaks," Beau told the owners. "That's what wins races. When you're trying to guide a thousand pounds of horse flesh, and you're all bunched up in a tight spot, you're trying to keep from clipping another horse's heels to keep from going down. You're not thinking of winning a race at

242

that time, if you got any brains.

"The worst thing out there race riding is the apprentice boys who are all in there trying to make a hot name for themselves, taking risky chances. I know, 'cause I was one of them once," he said, laughing as he stated this fact. "Hell, most of them do the best they can."

Maggi gradually developed a different attitude toward all riders. She thought, pound for pound, they were the mightiest of men and earned every dollar that they made. It was a dangerous, hazardous profession.

"Robert is a good race rider," Maggi was the first to say. He and Beau's stable were a winning combination throughout the Ruidoso meet. Thus far, they could do no wrong.

* * * *

The big Futurity trials. It had rained all night and the track was a muddy, sloppy mess.

"Hey, don't worry about the mud. Searcher can handle the going," Beau told Maggi.

In spite of two grooms quitting that morning, and things being in a hectic state, Maggi and Beau managed to be back in the paddock, dressed in their best and looking very impressive. Maggi had bought a fresh spring dress with bright colored unique trim against her black thick curly hair. She looked beautiful.

"Boy, don't we look pretty?" was Ted's sincere comment as they waited for Searcher to come into the paddock.

The big gray colt walked into the paddock, calm and unconcerned as the groom turned him around in the saddling stall. The valet came with Robert's tack, and he and Beau soon had Searcher saddled up. Robert came strutting out of the jock's room with an air of arrogant confidence.

"Don't be so damn cocksure," Beau warned. "That number three horse has got plenty of gas too. Try to get Searcher out of the gate fast and go the lead. That's our best shot — coming around outside. The rail is heavy from all that rain."

He legged Robert up on Searcher, and they all headed for the grandstand. Beau disappeared into the crowd. Maggi joined Ted and Heidi.

"They're off!"

Maggi heard the announcer's call and watched as Searcher took the lead by two lengths.

"And coming down the backstretch, it's Searcher in front by three lengths! They're heading into the far turn. It's Searcher now being challenged by Miss Prince! They're turning for home, Searcher is out in front by a length! Oh! Oh! Searcher's bolted to the outside rail and taken Miss Prince with him!
And it's Searcher coming back! He's gaining now and back in the lead! It's Miss Prince and Searcher! It's Searcher by a neck, ladies and gentlemen!"

"We win! We qualified for the Futurity! Oh, Heidi, Ted — we win!" Maggi squealed over and over. They all hugged one another, and Ted was ecstatic.

"I can't believe it myself!" he said.

Beau met them in the winner's circle. As Maggi began to prattle away, he waved her into silence. "We're going to get our number taken down. The objection sign is up on the tote board," he told her.

"Oh, no!" she moaned.

They watched in silence for five minutes. Searcher's number was taken down and placed third.

"What the hell happened?" Ted asked Beau

"It involved only the first three horses, and Searcher bolted coming down the lane," he stated, "Hell, we're lucky they didn't put us last."

Maggi was so let down, she tried to fight back the tears as she looked at Beau.

"Hey, hon—he's still eligible for the futurity," Beau assured her, "He's qualified."

"Oh God, I thought we lost it all!" Maggi said, and felt somewhat relieved.

"What in the hell made him bolt?" Ted asked Beau.

Probably his right shin's bothering him a little. I told you he was trying to shin buck. I'm going over to the test barn and see if he pulled up okay."

"Why is he at the test barn? He didn't win," Ted said.

"In races as big as this one, they always take the first four horses to the test barn," Beau explained. Heidi stopped by after the races were over to see how things were.

"He pulled up good, Heidi," Beau assured her.

"He would have won by six lengths if he hadn't bolted," Heidi told Ted.

"I'm just glad he came back in one piece," Ted said.

"C'mon, I'm buying steaks tonight. After all, I did win third money."

"Just a minute, I want to tell his groom what to do," Beau told Ted. "I want to leave him open tonight. (No bandages or medicine) I want to see if there's any heat in his ankle, while it's cool in the morning," Beau told the boy.

"What do the bandages have to do with it?" Ted asked Maggi.

"Well, if you bandage the horse tonight, his leg will have a little heat from the friction and the medicine, and you can't tell if it's from that or from an ailment." she tried to explain. "This way the leg is either cold or has some heat."

That night at dinner, Beau told Ted, "I'll work Searcher with a special prong bit that will keep him from running out on the turns. He might not win the Futurity but I guarantee he won't blow any more turns."

"How does this prong bit stop him from doing that?" Ted asked.

"It's just like it sounds, prong bit. There are four prongs on the outside of the bit, and when enough pressure is applied from the reins by the jockey, the prongs press inward toward his lip on the outside, making him uncomfortable enough that he will avoid it by running straight. It don't hurt a horse one bit, 'cause the prongs are similar to light plugs, only thicker," Beau confirmed. "I'll

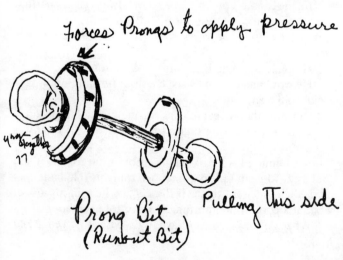

Forces Prongs to apply pressure

Prong Bit
(Runout Bit)

Pulling This side

show you tomorrow."

"Good I'd like to see one just to know how they work," Ted answered.

And the evening turned to their next hope—the Futurity in two weeks.

Futurity Day!

The sun was shining, the track was dry—a perfect Futurity day. Robert broke Searcher out fast and dropped down on the rail with a two-length lead. Searcher was hugging the rail. Robert had a tight hold on him. Searcher began pulling away from the field. Miss Prince made a bid to catch him, but he shook her off at the 3/8s pole. Turning for home, Robert took his stick to Searcher. He wasn't about to let the big colt quit on him now, and he hit him every time he touched the ground.

"It's Searcher, all by himself—by eight lengths!" the announcer blared.

"All by himself!" Maggi echoed as Searcher crossed the finish line. "We win! We win!"

"A beautiful race!" Heidi said, with genuine admiration. "Just beautiful!"

Beau was already on the race track waiting for Searcher to gallop back. Ted and Maggi hurried down as the official sign flashed Searcher's number on the tote board.

"And now!" the announcer said, *"Entering the winner's circle, the winner of the Ruidoso Thoroughbred Futurity Race for two-year-olds—Searcher, ridden by Robert Black, trained by Beau Witlow, and owned by Ted Byron."*

A deafening roar came up from the crowd as Searcher stood for his picture—next to a huge silver trophy.

As they all stood by in the test barn watching Searcher cool out, everyone came by to offer congratulations. Searcher pulled up sound from the race. Ted treated them all to a wonderful dinner. Maggi and Beau talked of the bountiful purse they would split.

"Our first big break," Maggi remarked. "Ten thousand dollars!"

"Yeah, you realize a lot of people work all their life to save that much money, and we made it in a minute," Beau said. "That's horseracing for you . . ."

* * * *

The next morning Searcher was so lame that Maggi had to actually whip him with the leather shank to get him out of his stall so they could clean it. He had shin-bucked in both front legs!

"I'm glad he waited until now to do it," Beau said. "He's got the money now and can have a long rest."

Shin-bucking affects the thin membranes of tissue that run down the front of the shin bones on the front legs of a horse, between the knee ankle. The tissue becomes inflamed and sore from the strenuous training and running, and it generally happens only to two-year-olds. Occasionally, a three year old will shin-buck, particularly if it had not suffered with this malady during the previous year. Althought a colt will sometimes shin-buck more than once, racetrackers are in general agreement that if they "shin-bucked good" the first time, they would probably not have a recurrence. Shin-bucking is common in young thoroughbreds, and impossible to prevent. As treatment, *firing* is one way to encourage circulation or remove inflammation, but it still is no guarantee that the horse would never shin-buck again.

"We'll fire Searcher as soon as his legs cool out," Beau told Maggi. She hated this unpleasant procedure.

Beau made a pole corral at the end of his barn and put Searcher there during the sunny days . . waiting till his legs cooled out before he could be fired.

When the legs were cooled out, Dr. Ord came to fire his shins. He heated an electric pin similar to a wood-burning tool, and punctured Searcher's shins, punching tiny holes into his shins about a quarter-inch deep and apart, making a pattern similar to a four-row cribbage board.

He then painted the shins with strong iodine solution and wrapped them in thick, thick cotton bandages to absorb all the blood and iodine solution.

"Now Maggi, this will be your job for the next two weeks," he told her.

"Yaaak! I always get the fun jobs," she grimaced, knowing what a mess it would be.

During the two-week period, Searcher's legs swelled and cracked open, and pus oozed fron the holes and bled. The odor was sickening.

During this time Searcher had to wear a specially made neck cradle which prevented him from gnawing at the bandages and legs when they began to sting and itch.

"Make sure you have the cradle on," Beau told her. "I've seen horses gnaw their legs down to the bone by morning just because the cradle came off."

When the eighteen days has passed, Maggi had to paint Searcher's legs with Reducine. In another three weeks, Searcher's legs once again began to look normal. As Maggi took off the last bit of scurf, she said, "Thank God that's over!"

The Cradle

Forty-five days later, Searcher was back in training, his dappled chestnut coat gleaming in the sun.

"He's the fastest horse I've ever trained," Beau told Ted. "I'm planning to run him in an allowance sprint race next week." There was lots of talk that Searcher wouldn't be fit after the long lay-off.

Searcher won the race by four lengths.

"Hey, Beau, looks like you got a racehorse on your hands!" a trainer called down to him as he stood in the winner's circle. Beau grinned with satisfaction, for he knew it was so.

Racetrack news travels faster than the speed of light, and Searcher became an instant celebrity, having won the Futurity, set a track record, and now, winning the allowance race. His best year was still ahead of him, and Beau told Ted that he intended to lay Searcher up for few months when they got home to let his bones get stronger.

"You're the boss," Ted said in immediate agreement.

250

Beau won the trophy and $500 cash for leading trainer. That evening, while they were celebrating the leading trainer award, Heidi congratulated Beau and then said, "Beau, you should move on to better race tracks. You're too good a trainer to waste your talents here in the bushes. You two should go back East where the big money owners are and the purses are bigger."

After they got home that night, Maggi said, "Heidi's got a good idea, don't you think?"

"What the hell are you talking about!" he said. "I couldn't get stalls back there. I don't have those kind of horses to win back East. You and Heidi are full of pipe dreams."

Maggi went ahead anyway and wrote letters to every eastern track asking for their Condition Books and emphasizing the fact that Beau was thinking about coming there to race next summer.

As she twirled another sheet of paper into her typewriter, she had little idea of what chain of events she was setting in motion!

17

Albuquerque — Second Time

By the time they reached the Albuquerque Fair, Maggi had received ten Condition Books and personal letters from various race tracks in Michigan, Ohio, and Kentucky. Beau studied them closely, to find some to fit the caliber of his horses. He became interested in the Detroit Race Course and Hazel Park meets, which began in April and ran through October. Hazel Park was also in the Detroit area. The minimum purses were $4,000 for the bottom claiming races of $2,500. In addition, Beau knew the Hazel Park racing secretary, Tom McDaniels.

"God, I've known him for years!" he said out loud.

"Good, call him!" Maggi urged, already dialing long distance, even as Beau insisted that McDaniels would never remember him.

On the other end of the line, it soon became obvious that McDaniels remembered Beau very well. Also, he had read in the *Racing Form* about King Court and Searcher and was enthused about having Beau's stable come to Hazel Park.

Hazel Park, the Experiment

Beau was very impressed that McDaniels remembered him. And from the conversation on her end, Maggi could tell it was good, When he hung up, he turned and said, "Damn it, Maggi, why are you always right about these things?" and slapped her on the buttocks when he saw the smug look on her face. "I told him we might come next year."

"Yes, I heard."

*   *   *   *

Albuquerque was the same fourteen-day razzle-dazzle madhouse as always, with wind, dust, horse racing, rodeos, Indian dances and thousands of people filtering through the fairgrounds. Many racetrackers came just for the above, but the majority came because the purses were so good and they could claim some useful horses. Everyone dropped their horses down in claim to win the big money. The halters were flying every day as six to eight horses were claimed.

Beau won eleven races and this pushed him to the top of the trainer standings. He lost three horses by claim on opening day, but claimed four new horses, one for himself.

Little Paul was a nine-year-old route horse that could run in the mud. He was a big horse, weighing well over 1,200 pounds (big for a thoroughbred, the majority weighing around a thousand). Little Paul also had big feet, the size of dishpans.

"I guess that's why he can handle the mud," Maggi commented as she looked over their new horse.

"They say he is web-footed, he can handle the mud so well," Beau laughed. "I've been looking through the

Hazel Park Condition Book, and there is a race for him, the Waterland Series going a mile and 1/16th. The purse is $8,000. Sure be worth hauling him back there. And it would be a good way to find out just how tough it is there, and what kind of horses fit," he added.

"That sounds like a great idea. When are we leaving?" Maggi asked.

"Oh, hell, I can't go. I have too many horses to get up and at the track. You know we can't just go off and leave the barn to the grooms. Christ, every horse would be broke down by the time I got back.

"Look, you and Robert can go. He knows the horse and can ride him, plus he can help you drive and take care of the horse," Beau said.

"Robert!" she sputtered. "I'd be spending half the mornings getting him up. And as far as his helping to drive, I wouldn't drive to the store with that crazy loon."

"Well then, just forget about it. I just thought it would be a good way to see if we would like it back East. And maybe win part of the race," Beau snapped.

"Oh, there you go with the martyr stuff again. Okay! I'll haul the son-of-a-bitch back there, but you better be there for the race."

"I promise I will, and ride back with you, okay?"

"Okay," she answered, thinking that she wasn't looking forward to the 1,600-mile ride with Robert. It would take three days, at least — allowing for stops each night so Little Paul wouldn't be worn out from the hauling.

The next day as the sun was coming up, Maggi and Robert left the Albuquerque fairgrounds, loaded down with hay and grain on one side and Little Paul on the other side of the horse trailer.

They made one out-of-their-way stop in Wichita, Kansas

to visit Heidi and spend the night at her ranch. Robert was a perfect little ass and bore the whole trip, ate like a man out of work, and mooned over being separated from his girl in El Paso. He held Maggi up for twenty minutes at each gas station with his long distance calls to his sweetie. Maggi was ready to kill him by the time they reached the Detroit area and Hazel Park.

Hazel Park was squeezed into a factory area, a dismal and depressing setting. The barn area was cramped and the track was a 5/8s mile course, with sharp turns. The clubhouse sat right next to the outside rail, to save space.

Black grooms were the majority at the track, and Robert made a stupid remark while they unloaded Little Paul, "I don't like this place already. I am not mixing with any damn niggers."

"Shut your damn mouth — you'll get us both killed," Maggi ordered.

She left Robert sulking in the car, and went to put the registration papers in the office and get their license forms to fill out. She was told by the state steward that they would have to have two leading trainers sign the licenses recommending them.

"Jesus," Robert lamented. "Who in the hell knows us around here?"

"I'll get someone," Maggi assured him.

As Robert read the signatures of Marion Van Berg and Tennessee Wright, he exploded! "Hey, they are the two top trainers of the state. How in the hell did you get them to sign?"

"I just asked them, that's all," she kidded.

They found a motel close by and Robert barricaded himself in his room — on a *fast!* He had gained twenty pounds in the three-and-a-half days.

Maggi entered Little Paul for the first leg of the series.

The first race was a prep race. The big race would be next week. It rained bucketfuls the afternoon before the race, and Maggi told Robert, "Well, Beau said all you had to do was to throw water in his face and he win. Okay, he's got mud today."

Maggi fretted in the paddock. Beau was nowhere in sight. It was almost time for the horses to be saddled when Beau came walking across the path.

"Thank God you got here!" she said, relieved.

"Little Paul ran a good third." Beau said, "He got a little tired at the finish. He'll run better next week."

But the next morning the horse had heat in his left ankle. As Beau felt both legs, he said, "Well, that's that! We might as well go home. He won't get anything. That's why he eased up yesterday," he added.

"Oh, no! He doesn't walk lame," Maggi said hopefully.

"Well, he is sore, and we're going home," Beau snapped. "I'll go get his papers, and you start packing the stuff."

Tom McDaniels, the racing secretary was glad to see Beau. "You'll come back next spring, won't you? You'll do good here, and we have damn good purses and so does the Detroit Race Course," he added. "We alternate each year, you know. DRC will be the first meet next spring . . . Look, here are the dates."

DRC starts APRIL 25 through JULY 8
HAZEL PARK JULY 9 through OCTOBER 30.

"Will you give me stalls?" Beau kidded.

"All you want," McDaniels promised.

This made Beau feel good; the trip was worthwhile after all.

256

They headed for Arizona, and Robert immediately began complaining, "I want to fly home. I don't want to drive three more days. I got to see my sweetie." He didn't let up one second.

Finally, Beau had had enough of him "Okay, goddamn you, I'll drop you off at the Topeka airport, now shut up," he snapped.

Robert went into the most bizarre antics of joy that Maggi had ever seen any adult perform.

"You're nuts!" she told him.

Beau and Maggi drove away from the terminal entrance, leaving little Robert standing with his little sasual bag, with his riding whip sticking out from one end.

"He's so full of bennies and pills to lose weight, he's half crazy," Beau said.

"Well, I'm glad you see what I put up with the last five days," Maggi answered. "God, it's so peaceful already."

The trip was fine from then until they stopped for gas and Beau checked Little Paul in the trailer. He called to Maggi, "Come here. Look at that floor, He's stomped the damn bottom out of it. Just one little sliver is holding his foot from going through. We will have to switch him over to the other side."

Maggi held Little Paul while Beau moved the hay and grain. Then they reloaded the horse and got on their way.

"It's a good thing you noticed that. He would have ground off his whole hoof by the time we got to Santa Fe," Maggi said.

"God, I guess so," Beau answered, and then they became quiet, each deep into their own thoughts.

Maggi mused: four thousand miles . . . Robert . . . not running in the race . . . crazy! Then she dozed off.

Turf Paradise — Seventh Season

November. The Turf Meet got underway after Thanksgiving.

Maggi was bored and took the escalator up to the roof of the grandstand, where the press box and announcer stand were located. . . Nat, the *Racing Form* caller also was located here. He had to familiarize himself with the horses running in each race and he had a helper who sat beside him while he called the race beginning from the gate, stating how they broke. Next he gave the positions at the quarter pole, the half-mile pole, the three-quarter pole, the stretch and the final finish position of the entire field of horses. The helper would write down this information on a chart then teletype it direct to the Los Angles *Daily Racing Form* offices and they would print up the racing charts and have this information out on the streets by morning, Maggi said a brief "hello" to him as she passed through and he nodded back. The constant 'tapocka tapocka tapocka ta' of the two teletypes going made the room very noisy, as she stepped into the soundproof room of the announcer's booth.

It sat higher on the corner of the roof. The view was vast. She could see every part of the track and as the horses came by for the post parade, they looked funny as she stared down on their backs.

"Hey, this is neat up here. Boy you can see everything," she remarked.

"You sure can," Ralph said.

"Hey, I'm not in the way here, am I?"

"No, be right with you."

Maggi waited as she watched him rewind his tapes getting ready for the next race . . . she thought about him. .

258

He finally got a break, the local announcer had a better offer in New York and Ralph was hired to take his place. The old announcer trained Ralph until he felt he was able to do it on his own.

Ralph spent countless hours of hard work going to a special school for announcers in the evening. During the race day, he stood side by side with the announcer as they studied each race, familiarizing themselves with each horse and their colors. The names of each horse had to be pronounced accurately and clearly.

This was done 10 times during the race day program each and every race day. Ralph spent long hours at the racing office familiarizing himself with all the horses' and jockeys' names.

He practiced making tapes over and over calling races off of a program by himself night after night to get it right. By end of that winter he was calling most of the races with the old announcer standing by in case something went wrong.

But there was no chance of that now. He was infallible and loved his work too much to screw up. He sounded good over the PA system and had developed a unique style of his very own.

"Hey, I've been hired as the steady announcer, I've got to be the happiest guy in the whole world."

"Well you worked hard and deserve it . . . " she answered. "Thanks Maggi, you have been my best supporter," he stated and swung around turning on the PA system . . . *"They're going to the gate"* . . " Maggi motioned goodby and left and walked down through the stewards' stand. The three stewards were getting their binoculars up to their eyes to watch for any foul play. It was their job to push the objection button at this control booth after the race was over and view the patrol film. It was their job to decide if any fouls or interference were by intent or bad racing luck, and to disqualify a horse in the case of the former. Maggi waved a quick hello to them for she knew they had no time to visit and quietly slipped down the back stairs and catwalk off the grandstand roof . . . She heard Ralph *"They're off . . . . . . "* and grinned.

Heidi and Ted owned the majority of horses in Beau's stable. Beau had a new owner from Phoenix who planned to bring his horses in from California when it was time to ship. Beau was getting a good, sound stable for the East. He had a good meet at Turf Paradise and was leading trainer again, Maggi was on scrapbook number four.

Searcher was the horse to beat these days at this track. After he won two of the allowance spring races, and set a new world record, the horsemen wanted no part of him. Also, the racing secretary was forced to put far too much weight on Searcher to make him equal to his rivals. Beau backed off Searcher after his last win. He'd wait until they went back East.

Detroit and DRC for the First Time

Maggi packed the house trailer and had it sent on its way. Just when she thought everything was under control, Beau informed her she would have to go to Omaha with Searcher. There was a sprint handicap that he had a good shot of winning, and with Beau going to Detroit, someone had to go with Searcher. Who else but Maggi!

"Okay, I'll go, if I can get Maddoxes to look after Steve. But you will have to have a van haul him. I'm tired of hauling a horse trailer every time I go anywhere," she complained. "It's bad enough going by myself."

"Well, Ted will follow you there," Beau stated, trying to encourage her. He knew it was a lot to ask of her and gave her no argument about the van.

First, they had to organize shipping to Detroit. In April, everyone else was wanting to leave too, and vans were at their busiest. Maggi had a problem trying to find enough vans to haul their thirty-six horses to Detroit. She finally called a California trainer about shipping by railway express cars.

"Hell, Maggi, it's the only way to go, when you're shipping that far," he confirmed.

Maggi did some checking before she presented the idea to Beau. The REA dispatcher had informed her, "We have to know the date you want to ship and how many horses."

"April nineteenth and thirty-six head," she told him.

"You'll need two express cars. The cost is five thousand per car," he told her over the phone.

It took much arguing and talk to convince Beau, especially when he heard the cost was five thousand dollars per car, and that they would need two cars.

"Hell, Heidi and Ted and the other owners won't stand for that kind of expense!" he ranted.

Maggi talked a good stick. "Look, it isn't much more in shipping cost than the three moves we made last summer, and this is one move till we come home."

"Okay, okay—go ahead and order the express cars," Beau agreed.

The time came too soon, and the cars arrived. A dispatcher called and wanted Beau to come down and let him know how to set up the partitions in each car. There were three sliding doors on each side of the car. Small high sliding windows lined both sides, and there was a water tank at each door with a hose attached. A toilet and sink were in each car.

"Partition positioning is up to you," said the dispatcher. "We can set them up to give a horse room enough to lie down or just to stand."

Beau told how he wanted to set it up. He gave more room to the better horses and less to the saddle horses. Beau noticed the heavy grates for urine drainage. It was an advantage over van shipping where horses have to stand in their own excrement.

The shipment was to take three-and-a-half days and nights with no unloading. The dispatcher asked them to bring straw to the loading dock the day before departure so his yard crew could put some in each partition. The dispatcher wanted Beau to start loading at eleven a.m. on loading day because the train would pull out at four p.m. sharp.

Maggi borrowed a big flat-bed hay truck, and she and the boys hauled all the tack down to the cars the day before they were to ship out. She and the crew packed it in, tied it down, and padlocked the car doors.

On shipping day, their vet, Dr. Trotter, tranquilized all the horses by nine o'clock. Maggi went on ahead to the loading dock to make up Beau's bed. She rolled out his sleeping bag on a spring cot she had just bought at a second-hand store.

All of the horsemen came down to watch them load, for not many stables from Phoenix shipped by rail.

As soon as the first horse walked into the car, Maggi discovered they had nothing to tie the horses with. Chains were standard equipment in vans, but apparently not on trains. Panic! Then she remembered she had a nylon lasso in one of the tack trunks and dug it out. A kind horseman helped her cut it up into three-foot lengths, and they unraveled it so they had enough pieces to cross-tie each horse.

They had six head loaded in the first section. Because it was a small loading dock, they had to spot (moving horse car into position) the next door to the ramp, and it slowed the loading. To go back into the other section of the car, they had to jump two feet from the dock to the car.

Maggi worried they would never get loaded in time. The engine to pull them to the main train was backing in slowly and made her even more nervous. Tempers were getting frayed, and everyone was getting tired. They'd all been going since five a.m. Even Dr. Trotter was still busy fixing a box of medicine and things for Beau in case he had to doctor a sick horse. Still, everything was going well until Beau blurted out, "Damn, I counted wrong! I've got one more horse coming and he's late!" Beau moved the saddle horses closer together to make the extra room.

Loading on the train

The last was a flurry of loading all the grooms' folding beds, cots, grain, suitcases, boxes of food, a dog. The horses were pulling the hay from their hay sacks, and immediately the fragments began falling on the grooms' cots.

The two express cars were joined up in order that Beau could walk from one to the other and make periodic inspections while the train was moving. But there wasn't any walking room available on the sides of the express cars so Beau and the grooms had to climb overhead on the partitions in order to crawl from one end of the car to the other. The dispatcher filled the water tanks in each car and an ice container for the men to keep their food cold and from spoiling.

"Okay, let's pull the ramp back," the dispatcher yelled. "The engine is ready to go."

Beau came and kissed Maggi good-bye as she hugged him extra hard before jumping back onto the loading dock as the train started to pull away. The steel gray cars marked **Horses** rocked back and forth toward the main depot and were coupled onto the passenger train and pulled out at four p.m. by the dispatcher's watch.

Venture to Omaha

Maggi packed late into the night. She forgot the payroll and had to get it in the mail so that it would arrive in Detroit on Monday. Then she fell into an exhausted sleep that kept her from moping about the absence of Beau.

Just before the Turf Paradise meet ended, Heidi had been stricken with cancer. Maggi and Ted decided to stop by on their way through Kansas and visit her. They stayed at Heidi's house the second night en route and went to the hospital to visit her. With her customary enthusiasm, Heidi expressed excitment at the news that Maggi, Beau and Ted were going back East to big-time racing.

"It's the only place for you and Beau," Heidi told Maggi. "I'll be joining you in a few weeks. Find a nice place for me to rent."

Maggi and Ted glanced at one another and said they would.

"And be sure to send me all the newpapers so I'll know what's going on," Heidi added with her authoritative air.

Maggi and Ted promised, fighting tears. They knew they would never see Heidi again.

They arrived in Omaha the next afternoon, Searcher had already arrived from Phoenix and was stabled in Barn A in the capable care of a trainer friend of Beau's.

Robert was there too, having turned over another "new leaf." He promised to be by the first thing in the morning to work Searcher five-eighths of a mile.

The Ak-Sar-Ben track was owned by the City of Omaha. It was Nebraska spelled backwards. All proceeds from the track were farmed back into municipal improvements and as a result, the Omahans wholeheartedly supported horse racing, and the public was free to visit the backside at any time. Maggi learned that the Board of Directors was changed yearly, which cut down on any opportunity for power-play manipulations. Maggi felt that this was the way all tracks should operate for it made a good marriage between racetrackers and the City of Omaha. This was not the case in most other cities, where racing was a private enterprise.

The next morning, Robert worked Searcher 5/8s as Beau had requested. The horse pulled up sound and frisky after the work. Robert disappeared for the balance of the day. Ted went to his hotel until the race.

Back at her motel, Maggi busied herself with the

payment of monthly bills and payroll. It was nearly midnight. When she heard the phone ring, she glanced at the time. She quickly recognized the voice of Heidi's brother, Karl.

"She's gone," he said in sorrow. "We've lost her, Maggi."

"Oh, God, Karl—I don't know what to say! We all loved her so. I'm so glad you called. Please let us know if there is anything we can do."

When she had hung up the phone, she stared fixedly at a small spot in the carpet until the spot became distorted through her tears. She felt Rip's head as it came to rest in her lap. She marveled at the dog's perception. He could always sense when something was wrong. She patted his soft head and said, "Oh, Rip, we're going to miss her so much!"

Rip whined and curled up close to her feet.

* * * *

Searcher drew the number four post position, and when all the entries had been drawn, Maggi and Ted went over to the track kitchen for a cup of coffee. They spotted Robert sitting playing gin rummy.

"Hey, Maggi!" he called out amiably. "They dug up the race track last night and that rail sure is a heavy mother. Searcher ain't going to like it a little bit!"

"Well, there's nothing we can do about it now," Maggi replied as she sat down to the steaming coffee Ted brought. Robert shrugged indifferently and turned back to his game.

The heat and humidity of Omaha made Maggi perspire as she struggled to saddle Searcher in the paddock. Her head had begun to throb dully. She gave Beau's last-minute instructions to Robert, who seemed indifferent to what she had to say. Perhaps he resented her advice, or simply didn't care—there wasn't any time left to think about it. She legged Robert onto Searcher and she and Ted wished him good luck. Then they walked toward the huge grandstand to watch the race. Among forty thousand people in this heat, Maggi thought.

"Searcher goes to the lead!" was the first call.

Maggi craned her neck to get a better view. She saw Searcher drop down on the rail and watched him run some fast fractions as the tote board clicked them off—21 seconds for the quarter. At one point, he was flying as his big stride pulled the earth under him. Maggi and Ted had no idea who was in the second or third position as their eyes remained riveted on Searcher. It was then that they saw Robert take to his whip, and instinctively Maggi cried out, "No, Robert, not now! Wait!" She turned anxiously toward Ted. "He's moving too soon, can you see?"

Robert whipped Searcher like a wildman, hitting him hard, as if he could *force* him to win. Searcher responded and increased his lead by four lengths. As he rounded the turn for home, the crowd was roaring and the announcer could barely be heard. But it was then that Maggi's eye caught sight of the black horse moving up fast from behind. The black horse was not moving as swiftly as she thought. Searcher was tiring, dropping back fast and Robert continued to whip him relentlessly. She saw Searcher drift out from the rail as a tired horse will. Momentarily, he was in second place, and then, in one jump across the wire, another horse nipped him, and he finished third.

The welts that covered Searcher's flank told the story Maggi knew that Robert had used bad judgment, that he had known that the track was heavy, and never gave Searcher a breather throughout the whole race. Robert made himself scarce, and Maggi was glad of that. She had nothing to say to him, for she knew it would only be a wasted effort.

But Ted was more vocal. "That goddamn Robert! Why the hell didn't he give the horse a chance? Jesus, he pushed him the whole five furlongs!"

After he had calmed down, Ted left for home, saying he would see them in Detroit the following month.

Maggi was sorry that she did not bring their own horse trailer. After countless trips to the track kitchen in search of a van driver, someone introduced her to a local trainer by the name of Jack Van Dyke, who owned his own van and did his own hauling, as his father had a large stable of horses. He told Maggi that he would haul Searcher to Chicago for her but could not guarantee the trip to Detroit, because his father had his own ideas on how his horses travel best and sometimes preferred to give one horse two stalls. He also advised her against mentioning to anyone that he intended to haul Searcher since he wanted to avoid problems with the ICC trucking regulations. Maggi assured him that she appreciated his assistance beyond words and would certainly not jeopardize her chance to ship Searcher to Sportman's Park in Cicero, Illinois.

While Maggi was trying to get Searcher shipped to Detroit, Beau was on his last day of the train ride to Detroit. He and his crew had learned to throw open the car doors each time the train stopped for passengers or mail. It got very hot in the express car, with all the body heat from all the horses, even though it was almost zero outside. Beau saw huge hunks of ice floating down the many rivers they had passed.

He had to admit that Maggi was right! Shipping by rail was the best way to go this far. The horses had all the hay they wanted and water to drink. Each afternoon Beau and his grooms mixed them all a gallon can of plain bran with no grain. This kept their bowels loose; there was less danger of impaction and colic. Even though they had to stand up for the three-day journey, the horses were relaxed in their small quarters. They even dozed when the train ran a long smooth run between towns.

Beau felt sorry for his grooms because their beds were directly under the horses' heads, the hay nets dripped loose hay all over them. There was no way they could keep their beds clean. As for Beau, he chuckled the first night and day he tried to sleep on the spring cot Maggi had fixed for him. It joggled him up and down each time the train hit a cross tie . . . rump to rump ti rump ti . . . and during the day when he tried to read, his paperback book went up and down. It wasn't until he figured out that by taking his mattress and sleeping bag and putting them on the wooden floor of the car, he could stop the joggling and the up and down motion as he read. In Detroit as they unloaded the horses from the express cars the horses kicked and bucked as they came down the loading ramp . . . they felt so good! And none the worse for wear-and-tear, after traveling three-and-a-half days and nineteen hundred miles!

For Maggi, it was a long, lonely drive to Sportsman's Park, and as she drove through the depressing factory district to the track backside, the sky had a gray cast to it. The gateman stood in a dingy white shack and would not make a move to come out and greet her. She got out of the car, and he finally told her in a gruff voice that Van Dyke was in Barn H. The gray brick barns were so close together that there was hardly enough room to park her car in between. She noticed a huge billow of smoke gushing from a high stack — the city dump burning trash.

The Van Dyke foreman told her their van wouldn't be in until late that night. She was tired, felt dirty in the dismal surroundings, and left to find a place to stay at a motel that someone recommended to her. It was a depressing, shabby motel that catered to quickies, and throughout the night, she was continually awakened by the car doors slamming and engines starting.

In the morning, Maggi found that luck was still on her side. Mr. Van Dyke, Sr. had room for Searcher on his van, so Searcher was loaded and on his way to Detroit.

Maggi arrived at the Detroit Race Course while the races were still underway. When she found Barn 20 all the grooms greeted her warmly. She told Searcher's groom when he would arrive. The trip had left her feeling grimy. She was hoping Beau would be at the barn, for she felt too crummy to go up to the grandstand, especially if the new clients were there. About that time, Beau came around the barn. She hugged and kissed him — he was happy to see her!

"Hey, I just heard the good news about getting Rucker's horses to train," she blurted out in joy. "He has some real good horses!"

"Yeah. I was surprised, too, when he called me, and McDaniels was so good about giving me the extra stalls . . Hey, that's why I came down," he changed the subject. "I had an idea you'd be coming in. The Ruckers want to take us out to eat after the races."

"Oh, then I better get going. I need to shower and change. I'll meet you at the house trailer," and she called to Rip to get back into the car.

"I'll have one of the grooms show you where the trailer park is," Beau said as he told one to get in his car.

Maggi almost fainted as she entered their once-clean house trailer. The rug was dirty with dried mud, ash trays were filled with butts, and the sink was full of cans and dirty dishes. Good old Beau, she thought, he has had some of the grooms stay with him. She quickly threw the dishes under the sink and closed the door, ran the vacuum, and threw every loose shirt and pair of pants into a closet. Then she showered, changed, and just in time! The Ruckers and Beau drove up . . .

During dinner, Maggi studied Willis Rucker, a medium-sized man, with a reddish pale skin, a face framed with sandy hair, and small, beady eyes. He wore a well-tailored plain brown suit, with tie and shirt to match. Dody, his wife, was a beautiful lady — petite, thick brown hair, soft hazel eyes, and a smooth, silky skin. She was dressed expensively and in good taste, and spoke in a very soft sweet tone. She looked far younger than her fifty years. Maggi liked them instantly. They were just nice solid people, she thought. And they were charmed with Maggi's wit and laughed at her encounters in Omaha and Chicago. The Ruckers were staying the entire week and had planned a trip to Niagara Falls, insisting Beau and Maggi join them. Maggi was all for it.

After dropping the Ruckers off at the Ambassador Hotel, Beau began to tell Maggi about the train ride and the great reception he got when he arrived at the track.

"It's been fifteen years since anybody's shipped in here by rail, and it really stirred 'em up. They had to rebuild their old loading ramp so we could unload.

"It was wild, Maggi! The first day I walked the horses, every trainer and groom came over to watch us walk our hots on horseback. They thought we were cowboys and nuts. Wait till you see the write-ups I got for coming in by rail! You'll have lots of clippings for your scrapbook now!"

"Oh, great!" she coaxed. "Tell me more. How did the horses behave on the train?"

"Good. They just dozed most of the time. Only my saddle horse got sick, but I caught him early and gave him a shot of medicine. Every horse came off that train bucking and kicking. I only walked them one day because they shipped so good. I'm convinced that shipping by rail is the only way. The loading is a hell of a lot of work, but believe me, it's worth it in the long run!"

unloading in Detroit!

18

Her amorous reunion with Beau had obviously drained
the last of her physical reserves, for when Maggi woke, it
was ten o'clock. Even Rip was still sleeping close by. She
stretched luxuriously and thought about making coffee.
She finally managed to tumble out of bed to get her day
started.

"Glad to see you finally came to life!" Beau said as he
walked in. "Howzabout some breakfast? We've got to be
back at the track by two o'clock. I'm in the second race
and the Ruckers want us there for lunch. Their horse is in
the ninth."

Beau brought out the clippings:

> Arizona Invader Who Took Detroit
> by Storm
> . . . the leading trainer and his
> winning jockey, Robert Black, to
> ride his powerful stable

"Beau, what I'd give to have Heidi see all of this!"
Maggi said.

"I know, hon. It's a shame she had to die. C'mon now. We've got to rattle our hocks or we're going to be late."

Maggi was pleasantly surprised to see Beau emerge in a tie, jacket, and pair of new field boots. He looked extremely handsome and she told him so.

The Ruckers were at the clubhouse table. Their afternoon together began pleasantly enough, until Beau returned from the barn with a grim look and spoke out:

"Lyn, my old groom, gave Worn & Torn some phenylbutazone and figured the forty-eight-hour period wrong," he said. "So, if the horse wins, and the tests come back bad, I will get ruled off."

The words "ruled off" burned deep into Maggi as she recalled the past. Surely it wouldn't happen again, just when things were going well for them.

"Why didn't you scratch him when you found out about this?" Maggi asked Beau, obviously upset with Lyn's stupid mistake.

"Because the racing secretary wouldn't let me out. It's too short a field. I'll just tell Robert not to let the horse win."

When Beau returned from the paddock, he assured them that Robert understood what had to be done.

"It's almost a comedy, trying *not* to win a race!" Maggi said, with lightheartedness, but quickly shut up when she saw the cutting glance Beau gave her.

In the ninth race, Worn & Torn was laying fifth as the field came out of the clubhouse turn heading for home.

"We're in good shape," Beau remarked with a sigh of relief. "Just stay there, Robert." But tension came back into his face when Worn & Torn began to pass one horse and then another. Robert's head was buried deep into the horse's mane.

"Jesus, Robert! Hold him back! Pull! Pull!" Beau

274

screamed as if Robert could hear him. Another horse challenged Worn & Torn, head and head, neck and neck down the stretch, across the finish line.

"Worn & Torn wins!"

Numbly, Maggi, Beau and the Ruckers all looked at one another. Maggi managed to say the right words to the Ruckers, even as her mind raced ahead to all the possible consequences of this situation. How could Beau have been so careless as to depend upon a forgetful old man like Lyn? Why hadn't he managed to get the horse scratched? Why? Why? *Why??*

They went to the barn and discussed the possible test results with the vet.

"It's close — just a few hours short of the forty-eight hour ruling, so there's always the possibility that the test will come back okay on Monday," the vet said encouragingly.

"Yeah, and now, we'll have three days to sweat it out," Beau said morosely.

Willis Rucker and Dody were taking it very well and giving moral support to Beau and Maggi.

"Look, we might as well go on to Niagara Falls. It will help pass the weekend faster. You'll sit around here and worry yourself sick," Mr. Rucker told Beau.

They all tried to be cheerful, even kidded about the possibilities of it happening, trying to laugh it off. But the stigma was still there, in spite of the beautiful falls, beautiful flowers, and the Canadian countryside. As they drove back toward Detroit on Monday morning, they stopped for breakfast. Beau called Robert to see if the test came back bad. When Maggi saw him smiling as he returned, she knew everything was all right.

"Thank God!" she whispered deep inside.

"Good!" Mr. Rucker shouted. "Now, let's celebrate. After all, we won a race," and they all burst into healthy laughter.

After the races Monday, the Ruckers flew back to Phoenix. Mr. Rucker was an astute businessman, and never believed in staying away from the store too long. He trusted no one. Beau and Maggi enjoyed the Ruckers' visit, but it was good to get back to their normal barn routine.

Rucker was the most frugal of all their clients. He took every saving advantage. He calculated all his trips to Detroit and Chicago with the auto dealers, so that he could write off the total trip. He never ordered a win photo, he wasn't impressed with the folderol of the press or fanfare . . . just the money! . . . He was the only owner who complained bitterly each time they raised the training fee. He always was discussing deals with Beau, each time having to badger with Maggi . . "You don't give any deals at your agency, neither do we," was her answer . . Though he didn't appreciate any women telling him what to do . . . He was from the old school . . men were the only ones allowed to voice any opinion . . .

He confused Maggi as he was a joy and spent money freely when he took them dining, and wagered more than any client they trained for. Maggi often studied his ruddy complexion and his "ferret" ways, darting, twisting in his chair calculating his next move . . . and catching his game!
. . .

The one thing she disliked him the most for was that he had no sense of humor and was not a man to be kidded . . And she saw to it she minded her manners well in his presence.

Rucker made his phone calls brief and to the point,

Mountain Bell wasn't going to get any extra from him . . . As always Maggi or Beau reversed all charges to their owners. Rucker was the last one to worry about a long conversation. This pleased Beau.

Tuesday morning Beau was *hot* at the exercise boys because they had gone on a binge the night before and were late and hung-over.

"Come on, goddamn it, you guys, the track will be closing in twenty minutes," he yelled at the boys. As they all rode toward the race track, he told them what he wanted them to do.

"Merv, you take a good hold on that horse and don't let him gallop out fast, make the son-of-a-bitch arch his neck, and pull on the bit, damn it!" he snapped.

"Jim, you get on the outside of Merv, and don't let his horse drift out, make him stay down on the rail, you hear?"

Tony, was an ex-jock who never made it. Beau liked him because he could gallop a horse and yet was light enough to breeze or work a horse just the way Beau liked one to go.

"Tony, you gallop around the 3/8s pole and let him bounce pretty good down the lane and then let him gallop on out around to the 5/8s pole," he told him.

Beau rode over toward the winner's circle in front of the huge grandstand to watch his horses perform. He watched each one as they broke off into a nice slow gallop, tucking their heads down to their chests. He always made the boys bring the horses up a ways on the track and let them stand for a few seconds and relax and look about before they started off galloping.

Tony was the last to break off, as the horse galloped steady toward the 3/8s pole.

Beau pulled out his stainless steel stopwatch that was inscribed on the back:

Leading Trainer
Turf Paradise
1961

He pressed down on the stem to clear the second hands. He waited till Tony approached the 3/8s pole, then clicked the stopwatch.

He thought, "The colt's running easy," as he looked at his watch . . . first quarter in 22 seconds flat. "Not bad," he mused. As the horse came down and passed over the finish line, Beau clicked the watch again: 34:1. He was satisfied as he watched the horse run on out and clicked the watch again at the 5/8s pole. "Not bad for his first work," he thought as he rode over toward the horses to pick them up.

Maggi was rolling washed bandages when Mr. Ascot, the track identifier, stopped by, told who he was, and said, "I have to identify all your horses and need to take pictures."

"We've already had all of our horses tattooed this spring in Arizona, just before we shipped," she stated.

"I understand, but we don't identify by tattoo number here," the official explained. "I take photos of each horse from all four sides full view. Then I take a separate picture of each night-eye on the inside of the horse's leg."

"Well, I'll be darned. I never heard of that before," Maggi replied.

"Well, it's the most foolproof identification there is. No one can change the night-eyes. They are just like finger prints," he continued. "Tattoo numbers under the lip can be duplicated on a ringer (another horse)," Ascot stated. "And you know they get blurred sometimes and are hard to read correctly. Plus, after a few years the tattoo ink tends to fade some.''

"I see," Maggi said. "Well, this is all new to me. When do you want to take these pictures?"

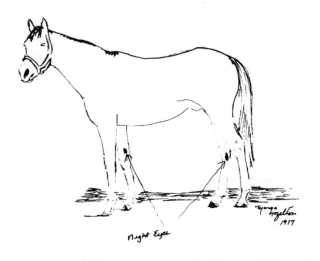

Night Eyes

"I'd like to get started right now, and get as many as I can today," he replied.

Maggi watched him set up his Polaroid camera and the horse's registration certificates which he had obtained from the racing office.

"You mean all thirty-five head have to be photographed?"

"They sure do. If you'll bring each horse for me and hold him, we'll get started."

Maggi led each horse out into the sunlight, held him still and curiously examined the little callous spot on the inside of the horse's leg. She saw that the patterns were indeed different. "Why do they call them night eyes?" she asked

"Don't really know, ma'am. That's the common name,

but the technical name is chestnut, or sometimes castor."

By noon, the sun had faded behind the clouds, and Mr Ascot put his camera away. "It looks like rain," he said. "I'll have to come back tomorrow and finish up."

The next morning he returned and invited Maggi to see the pictures he had taken the previous day and how he had set them up. Turning the cover of a looseleaf notebook, he showed her eight-by-ten full-view shots of each horse's four sides: directly below were four small photos of each horse's four inside legs, illustrating each of the night-eyes.

Maggi tried to explain the procedure to Beau but he wasn't interested.

"I've got better things to do than stand around and look at those pictures," he said.

As Beau walked away, Robert came to tell them that he was getting married the following week. They never knew when to take him seriously, so Maggi and Beau reacted with general indifference. But Robert spent days trying to find a place to live close to the track, and the discouraging search made him more cantankerous than ever. He kept threatening to go home to El Paso to be with his "sweetie." Beau was getting tired of his threats. He was depending on Robert to ride, and the constant uncertainty concerning Robert's plans frustrated him.

Finally, Beau could stand it no longer. "Go ahead and leave, you son-of-a-bitch! I'm sick of all your threats. So, do whatever you want. You're passing up the best opportunity you've ever had — you dumb bastard!"

Incredibly, this outburst improved things for a time. Beau and Robert were a winning team — the leading trainer and the rider of the meet. The public adored them both. They knew they could bet on Beau's stable of consistent runners.

* * * *

On the day of Heidi's death, her stable began to run under her estate. The administrator of her will and property advised Maggi that the bank would pay all bills from then on. All of the horses' winnings as well as any monies from horses that were claimed were to be issued to the bank. This procedure would continue until all the horses had been disposed of. Maggi informed the horsemen's bookkeeper of these requests and told him to mail everything directly to the bank.

Heidi's green and white silks were worn for the final time when her last horse was claimed. Maggi cried when she heard the announcement. A great lady was lost from racing.

The Detroit Race Course treated Beau well. Whatever he needed for his barn was provided immediately.

"I'm getting better treatment here than I do at home," he confessed to Maggi. "That makes the two thousand miles of shipping worthwhile!"

Maggi was pleased to see that Beau no longer seemed so intimidated. He was the leading trainer at DRC with forty-eight wins to his credit — not bad for a cowboy from Arizona, she thought.

Hazel Park for the First Time

You wake up in the morning, and lo!
Your purse is magically filled
with twenty-four hours — the
most precious of possessions

Hazel Park track was just outside Detroit in Hazel Park. Still, a move is a move, and everything had to come down, only to go back up again. Beau asked the racing secretary for some sand to fill in the mud holes in front of his barn, and the sand arrived at once.

Vic Conners, the track president, was a master at welcoming people, particularly the backside crew. He kept his office open to all trainers, owners, agents and jockeys. He had two refrigerators stocked with cold cuts, rolls, bagels, soft drinks, beer and milk. It was more like a delicatessen than a chief executive's office.

When there was no table available in the clubhouse close to the finish line, Conners gave Maggi and Beau his private table for six, so they could entertain their owners in grand style. Everyone spoke well of Vic Conners, and it was easy to see why. His many attributes included his obvious regard for the public in such things as barber shops, a warm enclosed grandstand, and good food served at fair prices. Even the announcer's closing message at the end of each day's racing program was aimed at the public's well-being.

"Drive carefully, folks, and thanks a million!"

Robert flew to El Paso to get married, returning with his bride and pulling a U-Haul trailer which contained all the fancy wedding presents, still in their boxes. As Rose Marie unloaded them all, they quickly filled the small kitchenette apartment Robert had found in a local motel. Rose Marie prepared her first meal for Beau and Maggi with great difficulty, trying to work in the cramped space with little idea of how to go about things. It was quite a ritual. She had creamed tuna on toast; no one complained.

Rosie was a beautiful girl with a flawless peaches-and-cream complexion, plus huge blue eyes and naturally curly brown hair. She was one year older and five inches taller than Robert, and outweighed him by forty pounds. Robert spoke of his bride proudly, "Ah sur got me a beautiful wife, ah do!" he said in his Texas drawl. And everyone agreed.

Rosie was a happy addition to the Witlow stable, and the four of them spent many cheerful Sundays picnicking — with Robert overeating. Robert and Rosie soon found a house trailer in the same court where Maggi and Beau lived. Its condition was less than a new bride might have hoped for, but "At least this trailer has a bathroom," Maggi commented, referring to her experience at Del Mar.

"This trailer isn't much," Maggi continued. We're parked by the incinerator, and the foul odor of burning trash is not easy to get used to. And poor Rip has no place to run, the ground is so damp."

"You all make me feel at home," Rosie told Maggi and Beau. Maggi knew it was hard for Rosie to set up housekeeping the way she wanted to and that she was having a hard time adjusting. Maggi convinced her that it would be best to send all of their nice gifts back to her mother until she and Robert managed to get a place of their own. Rosie was simply a young girl in love with an egotistical jockey, so Maggi counseled her about saving money.

"Robert's job is an extremely risky one. He can get hurt or killed, so if you have something to fall back on, it helps. Begin right now to make a habit of saving as much money as you can."

Rosie wisely took Maggi's advice, and soon began to save Robert's earnings. Under her surface prettiness, the girl had lots of drive.

* * * *

283

Late September. The Hazel Park meet was over, and the Detroit weather had turned bitter cold, with daily temperatures below freezing. Beau's horses didn't have many conditions left. Robert was five to ten pounds overweight and was in a slump. Beau was forced to use other riders, and this made Robert even more restless and determined to go home.

"Rosie's never been away from home this long, and she misses her family," Robert explained.

Beau and Maggi were glad to see them go. Robert's silly, childish behavior had begun to grate on their nerves.

Since the horses would have nearly a month to rest before the Phoenix meets started, Beau decided to ship them in three vans to save money.

Vic Conners came by their barn to say his good-byes.

"We want you back next spring," he told Beau in his friendly way. "You're good for racing, and the public sure likes you and your stable."

"Don't worry," Beau replied. "We'll be back all right. You run a great meet here — one of the best. We appreciate the way you've treated us."

Maggi was quick to echo Beau's comments.

To cap off a perfect summer, the papers ran feature stories with bold headlines that proclaimed:

Invader from West Wins
Leading Trainer Honors

Maggi quickly collected the write-ups for her scrapbook.

As they began their drive West, Maggi settled back and let herself drift off into the old daydream of building a home of their own one day.

* * * *

Their little old house looked mighty good when they arrived, but the demanding routine of getting the horses settled again left little time for socializing with their friends. Steve looked fit after spending the past months with his grandfather, but Maggi could tell that he had missed them, and worried about how they would arrange his schedules for next spring.

A few days before the Fall meet at Arizona Downs was scheduled to start, Maggi looked out of the tack room and saw Robert walking down the shedrow toward her.

"Hi!" he said jauntily. "Ah come up from Sunland Park for a few days to see about maybe riding here. How is everything?"

"Everything's fine," Maggi told him. "Where's Rosie?"

"She didn't want to spend the money for another plane ticket."

"So . . . what brings you up here?" Beau asked, with an edge of sarcasm in his voice.

"Don't try to pretend you aren't glad to see me. You know you are," Robert retorted smugly. "Ah been thinking about coming up here to ride. Ain't doing no good in Sunland Park."

"You're nuts!" Beau snapped. "You had the best chance in Detroit. You should have stayed there with all those big stables. Hell, that's where all the money is. Even I'm nuts for coming back here. But I have to on account of my owners, and it's home . . . and I don't have good enough horses to go to New York or Florida."

"But I don't like it back there," Robert insisted. "The people and the living conditions are rotten."

"You're stupid," Beau grumbled. "Hey, I heard Pee Wee got ruled off."

"Yeah, he did," Robert confirmed Beau's question.

"What for?" Beau asked, stepping into the stall of one of his horses to check him over.

"Oh, he took a bribe from some two-bit trainer who wanted him to pull his horse . . . I think. The trainer was brought on the carpet to the stewards, and he told the whole story and ratted on Pee Wee," Robert continued. "The bad thing was the damn horse couldn't run to start with . . but you know Pee Wee. He'd rather make a crooked dollar than an honest thousand . . . But, wait till you hear this! Pee Wee had been ruled off about two months and last Sunday at the races my mother-in-law was standing by the paddock. A little old lady came along and stood by her. After a few minutes, the little lady turned and said, 'You don't know me, do you, Mrs. Clemens?' My mother-in-law turned and stepped back for a better look. 'No, I'm afraid I don't remember you . . .' The little old lady began to laugh and nudged my mother-in-law. 'I'm Pee Wee, Mrs. Clemens. I'm Pee Wee!' Well, my mother-in-law just about cracked up. She said he looked just like any hundred other little old ladies, standing around with a leather bag, thick stockings on, and the damndest hat and gray wig. He even had a pencil with a flower on the end of it, Mom said, to mark his program. Hell, he stayed there all day and no one ever knew it was him but Mom," Robert chuckled.

"Why, that little shit-head! He'll figure out a way if there is one," Beau laughed. "They can't keep him away from the track . . . no way! Is that all he does?"

"No, He's driving the hay truck across the street for the feed man . . . but still touting someone when he gets the chance," Robert grinned. "You know that little son-of-a-gun. Never a dull moment around him."

"Tell him hello for us," Maggi said as Robert sauntered

off in the direction of the stalls.

When Robert did not find Searcher, he came back and asked Beau about him. "I turned him out for a rest and because his ankle was acting up again," Robert was told.

"Well, take care of him," Robert said. "Ah want to win that speed handicap back in Detroit next year."

"You just worry about riding, and I'll do the training," Beau retorted curtly and turned in the opposite direction as he recognized Michael walking toward them.

"We sure missed you guys at Ruidoso this year," Michael told Maggi and Beau. "It wasn't the same without you two."

"How's your girl Jill?" Maggi asked.

"Would you believe that I'm getting married next month?"

Robert went back to El Paso and Sunland Park for two more weeks and then came back to Turf Paradise to ride for the winter. It was impossible to depend on his coming out in the mornings. Even his agent gave up on him. Rosie and he fought bitterly about his laziness.

"How long does he expect people to put up with his antics?" Maggi asked Beau one morning.

"Who knows? All jocks are the same though," Beau muttered indifferently. "No point in getting upset about it.

"You let a jock bother you, and he will have you talking to yourself. They are so damn dumb. Left school after the sixth grade, to ride some damn match race . . . Hell, I ought to know. I did the same thing.

"You know, we work our asses off to train these horses and get one of 'em up to a race. Then you turn the son-of-a-bitch over to one of these little bastards. All of your months of training and the owner's money are in the hands of the jockey you picked to ride. And they are too damn lazy to get out in the mornings and breeze a horse for you,'' Beau spewed out.

"Come on, I'll buy you some breakfast," Michael laughed, and they all left for the track kitchen, still chattering.

"Wonder who was listening?" Maggi mused.

Michael and Jill's wedding was quite different from Beau's and Maggi's. It had a country club atmosphere, catered food, sparkling champagne, and a honeymoon in Hawaii. Maggi teased Beau that she'd be satisfied with two weeks in Eloy, Arizona.

Turf Paradise — Their Eighth Time

At Maggi's encouragement, Beau continued to dress as he had in Detroit — coat, tie and so forth. It wasn't long before other trainers followed his example. Nat was giving Beau beautiful write-ups in the newspapers and from the publicity came more new clients.

Jack Bullington, a Chicago millionaire, sent word that he wanted Beau to train some horses for him. Beau would not get in touch with the man. He knew Bullington had a good string of horses in Chicago and a very reputable trainer.

"Hell, all he wants to claim here is a bunch of cheap claimers," Beau muttered. "He don't intend to take horses back East. Why in hell would he want me anyway?"

Maggi reminded him, "Bullington wants you because you're *good!*"

"Why in the hell would he want me to train a couple of cheap claimers here when he has a big powerful stable in Chicago? His trainer's the leading trainer back there," Beau argued.

"He must want to run horses here or he wouldn't be

trying to get in touch with you. At least talk to the man, Beau.''

"Okay, okay. We'll see him at the clubhouse tomorrow," Beau said, mainly to put an end to the discussion.

Jack Bullington was a large, round man, extremely overweight, but he had learned to carry himself well, considering his bulk. He wore generously cut Pucci-tailored suits. His voice sounded raspy and hoarse, and he spoke breathlessly as if the air were literally being forced from his lungs.

"I want to buy some horses for you to train," he told Beau. "I live here in the winter, and *I want some action!* How about it?"

Bullington was the worst of all their owners about calling daily and asking the same questions over and over. Beau was always patient yet irritated from the constant instant replay of his own answers. "Yes I will call you when I know what post position he gets." "Yes I will let you know if he gets in . . '' "No I don't know if I can get Shoemaker . . .'' "No he is not sick, just 'cause he stands over in the corner of his stall . . .'' Maggi could sense the strain each time she overheard these conversations and yet she knew this was the business . . pacifying the clients.

* * * *

Late January. Ted and Willis Rucker suprised Maggi and Beau with their twinge of jealousy over Bullington and his monoply of wins in Beau's stable. Ted badgered Beau until Searcher was finally brought back into training. He settled down after Searcher won two sprint allowance races and set a track record on his first two outs (races) of the meet.

A problem arose that Maggi hadn't counted on. With several owners now engaged in their stable . . each in their own right deserved due consideration from Beau. But when three horses each of different owners were to run in the same allowance race . . Maggi was tested for her best performance and tact, to keep the owners all happy and to show no sign of favor, not to mention Beau's tact in selecting jocks so that they all felt they had a good rider. A very touchy situation and Maggi was glad this did not happen too often . . .

Willis Rucker wasn't spending his money buying or claiming. He preferred to raise his own horses, so he didn't have too many horses in training until toward spring. Then Beau began to bring all his laid-up horses in. Ground looked better than ever. Rucker was very pleased with his first win toward the end of February at the beginning of the Turf Paradise Meet.

"Now, everyone's happy," Maggi laughed, after Rucker was presented a bronze plaque in the winner's circle.

"We've got a good shot with Worn & Torn in tomorrow's race too," Beau answered.

The next morning, Maggi was glad she was walking the last set of hots. It was almost ten o'clock, and she wanted to get her work done so she and Beau could leave for home. The Ruckers were meeting them for lunch. She was looking forward to that and to the feature race that Worn & Torn was in. She had already mentally picked out what she was going to wear.

She had just put up her saddle pony and was hanging up all the bridles. "Hey, Maggi, come here," Beau called out.

"What do you want?" she answered.

"I want to blister this mare's knee before we leave," he said.

"Okay, but remember we were going home so we could get cleaned up," she reminded him.

"Yes, I know," he said smugly.

Beau got a halter and shank—and put the halter on the mare Clara's Devil. Maggi got the blister ointment and the twitch (a long wooden handle with a chain loop on one end of it).

"Here's the twitch," she said as she handed it to Beau. He put the chain loop over the end of Clara's muzzle and twisted it tight like a tourniquet.

"Okay, I've got her, now paint that stuff on her left knee," he told Maggi.

"You just want it on the front part of her knee?" she asked.

"Yes."

Maggi knelt down beside the mare's leg and began to apply the ointment blister.

"Hey, you're letting that get on her tendon," Beau snapped.

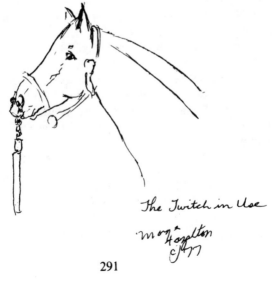

The Twitch in Use

Morg Hazelton
c 1977

291

"No, I'm not," she insisted.

"The hell you're not!"

"I am not," Maggi assured him and at the same time stuck her head around the mare's leg to make sure she was not getting any of the strong blister ointment on the tendon. As she peeked around the horses's knee, a sudden hard jolt hit her just above the left eye! A hot burning sensation came over her! Maggi grabbed her face and went toward the stall wall.

"Ohhh — oooooo! What happened?" she asked.

"The goddamn mare had thrown a fit and jerked loose from me . . . and plowed her knee into your eye . . . Jesus!" Beau gasped, as he came into the stall toward her.

Maggi felt the blood spurting through her fingers and running down her arm. The pain was unbearable!

"Let me see how bad it is," Beau said, taking her hands away from her face.

"Oh, Christ! She's knocked your eye out," he stated emotionally.

"Oh, no! Oh, no!" Maggi said, crying in terror and from pain. "It burns so bad! Get Dr. Trotter!"

"I'll be right back," Beau said and left running.

He was back in seconds. "Come on, honey. I have the truck right here. Doc said don't waste any time. Get to the hospital and take the blister ointment with us."

Because it was Sunday, the traffic was nil, and Beau broke all speed records to the hospital, even wishing a cop had been around to escort them.

St. Joseph's Hospital is run by nuns, and they took over the minute Maggi came into the emergency door!

An eye surgeon was on call and was brought down instantly. In a few seconds, Maggi's eyes were irrigated and washed out, and the doctor was sewing 26 stitches over Maggi's left eye.

"There, you should feel better now," he told her.

"Am I going to lose my eye?" she asked him.

"No, you're not going to lose your eye," he told her. "You'll be fine. But you were a lucky gal. If that ointment had been liquid, you might have lost your sight. You come and see me next Monday," the doctor told her and left.

As soon as they got home, Maggi crawled into bed. Beau showered, shaved, dressed and left for the races.

Maggi lay in the darkness of the room with a pounding headache, thinking, "I'm going to miss the luncheon and this fun day!" Then she drifted off into a half-sleep, too exhausted to even turn on the radio and hear that Worn & Torn won the race.

Searcher won the Cactus Wren Stakes for three-year-olds bred in Arizona. Ted praised Beau for the way he kept up the big gray stud. "It's because of your care and handling of the colt," he said.

It wasn't two days after Nat and the press had spread the news of Searcher's winning and setting a new track record for five furlongs that a Tulsa quarter horse breeding farm called Ted to buy the horse for stud prospect.

"I told them we weren't ready to retire him yet," Ted reported. "What do you think, Beau?"

"Hell, he should make twenty-five thousand this summer, if not more, if he don't break down," Beau commented. "He's in his prime. Christ! He's just a four-year old."

"Look, I'll call them back and tell them when you're ready to retire him. I'll let them know if they're still interested," Ted said.

* * * *

April. With the Turf Paradise Meet coming to a close, it was time for everyone to make plans for shipping. Beau was still shipping to Detroit. Hazel Park was the first meet. For openers, three grooms gave notice they were not going back East. It was too cold, and the living conditions on the backside were hard on them. Maggi and Beau had to agree it was all true.

"I'll have to raise the wages as soon as we get to Detroit, or I won't get anybody to go back or stay," Beau stated.

Maggi agreed, but said that he would also have to raise his training fee to fifteen dollars a day as soon as the horses got to Michigan. She was ready for Beau's outburst and before he could speak, she continued, "The purses are good back there and the owners can afford it. If they can't, then they had better get out of the business. You know we're not in this for our health," she said firmly.

"Oh, that's all you can say! What a fucking good trainer I am, and they can afford it . . . you keep raising the training fee, and you'll see," he snapped back.

"Well, then I guess we'll just take money out of our savings all summer so that we can keep our *owners* . . . because that's what we'll have to do, if we don't raise the training fee."

"Okay — okay, goddamn it!" And Beau stomped out of the room, cursing till his voice faded.

Shipping time brings out the worst in everyone! It was one fight after another with Beau and Maggi over shipping dates. How many horses going? And still trying to run horses — owners wanting to have last-minute dinners.

Maggi felt that she had had it. Then she heard that because of a disagreement between Michael and the Turf Paradise management, Michael was leaving to work at the California tracks for good. Maggi and Beau were just sick that Michael and Jill would not be in Arizona in the fall.

Then another problem came up when an agent for the Internal Revenue Service came to discuss matters concerning the Witlow payroll.

"It's been brought to our attention that you have not been deducting Social Security taxes from your employee's salaries," The IRS agent said. "Is that correct?"

"Yes," Maggi said. "But you see, we worked only one groom for a long time." She hadn't realized that they had grown from a small one-man payroll to eight people who were paid a straight salary without deductions. That was the common method of payment on the backside.

Maggi was stunned when the IRS man told her, "you owe three thousand dollars in back Social Security taxes and penalties."

She couldn't believe she had been so dumb! Yet everyone paid in the same way on the race track. No one took out or withheld anything from the grooms' wages.

"How come you're just catching up with us?" she asked.

"Well, to tell you the truth, someone turned you in," he stated. "You sure don't have very good friends . . . but I got a job to do."

"I know," Maggi replied. "How soon do I have to have the money?"

"The longer you wait, the more penalties," he said. She realized she would just have to draw it out of their savings, that was all. She assured the agent it would be taken care of the next morning.

Beau jumped all over her for being "so dumb, so stupid," until he found that ninety percent of the backside had not withheld a dime thus far.

"They'll be next, is what the tax man said . . . the government is clamping down on all race tracks," Maggi informed him.

Maggi quickly engaged a part-time CPA to help her with the new, sophisticated bookkeeping and payroll. She set up a special set of horse-keeping records to fit their needs, with the approval of the CPA. She mused that for a gal who wasn't good at math in school, she had come a long ways!

Just when she thought that things were again going smoothly, she realized she had to stay home until school was out, Steve was fifteen. His sports required much after-school time, driving him back and forth. And she knew he was at an age where he needed support and guidance. It was more than she could ask of the Maddoxes. Six weeks before she could join Beau!

One day, when Maggi was at the track, she ran into Jiggs Madders in the track kitchen.

"What are you going to do this summer, Jiggs?" she asked.

"Well, I think I'll have a shot at Detroit too," he answered, much to Maggi's surprise. "Can't let Beau get all those fat purses," he laughed.

Hazel Park — Second Time

The express cars arrived. Everything was ready to load.

The vet had his hands full, getting all the horses wormed and their teeth floated. Many young colts had caps on baby teeth that had to be knocked off. Front milk teeth had to be pulled to let the new ones come through.

Some of the older horses needed back molars filed. Constant grinding of hay mixed with dirt caused the molars to become very sharp on one side and cut into the sides of their mouths as they chewed. A horse with sharp molars ate less and so slowly that he often would not get the required amount of food.

Race horses are the best tended and cared for animals in the world. Between Beau and Maggi, their horses never wanted for a thing.

It took all morning to load tack, unload it, and drag it into the railway car. It was stacked and packed and tied tightly so when the train started rolling back and forth, the tack wouldn't shuffle around.

On the last day of the meet, Michael and Jill came to their barn to say good-bye to Maggi and Beau. Michael had to be in Golden Gate the next day to start as clerk of scales there. Maggi and Beau hugged them dearly and tears filled all of their eyes.

"We're sure going to miss you guys . . . good-bye!" Maggi and Beau waved as Michael and Jill drove away slowly in their old car, towing Michael's little black Renault, which was crammed with all of their belongings.

With Michael and Jill leaving and having to face another separation from Beau, Maggi's depression increased, and Beau's attempts to make light of the separation did not console her. When his train and horse cars pulled out, she went back to the barn to pick up loose ends. She rushed through her chores that night as if hurrying would somehow shorten the time.

In the end, the six weeks passed rather quickly. Steve became more communicative about school and brought friends home. One of the friends had attended a military academy in Missouri the previous year and enthused about his experiences there. This aroused Steve's interest, and before long, he was talking to Maggi about whether he could go to that school.

"How do you think Dad would feel about my going there?" he asked.

"I don't really know, Steve. You'll have to talk to him about it."

"Could we send away for a catalog?"

"Sure, I'll take care of it," Maggi promised.

When she and Steve arrived in Hazel Park, Maggi immediately drove to the trailer court. The location was better than the one they had had the previous year, and there was room for Rip to run. Steve decided to stay behind and watch TV while Maggi went to the track to meet Beau.

It was four-thirty in the afternoon, and the races were still underway. She found Beau at the barn, talking with a slim, dapper young man. When Maggi ran up to him, Beau greeted her, but coolly. Maggi chalked it up to his shyness about showing affection in public and thought no more about it. He introduced Erik Goldberg to her. After some small talk, Erik left.

Later, Maggi asked Beau, "Who's he?"

"Oh, he's a real nice guy. He's taken me to some real nice places to eat. He's born and raised here in Detroit."

"What does he do for a living?"

"He's a bookie. Bets on ball games, hockey, and the horses," Beau said defensively.

"What does he want with you?" Maggi demanded.

"Nothing! Can't I just know the guy without all this third degree from you?"

"You know the racing rules on your license application. It clearly states that you are not to be affiliated with any betting organization. You're such an easy mark for a guy like that! And how come he singles you out instead of hanging out with the old-timer trainers here, since he's lived here so long?"

"Oh, God, Maggi — lay off, will you?" Beau shouted in a sudden explosion of temper, and left.

It was not the meeting Maggi had pictured, driving the

last three days. She felt tired and shut out. Later, when she slipped into bed beside him, cuddled close to his warm, strong body, it seemed an eternity before he finally turned to embrace her. As her arms slipped around his neck, she tenderly kissed his face. Whatever thoughts she had just a few minutes ago had disappeared. She was with her husband now!

The following morning, Rosie was the first to welcome Maggi back.

"We sure missed you!" she said exuberantly. "I told Beau we'd have fun now that you're here. Actually, we haven't seen Beau that much 'cause Robert's trying to keep his weight down so he hates to go out to eat. We've been sticking close to home."

"Well, we can do other things besides eat," Maggi laughed. "We can take small trips to Canada on Sundays, play gin, and go to the movies."

Robert got tired of the constant dieting and gained several pounds. He began to lose mounts because of his overweight and was impossible to be around. He kept talking about leaving again for Ruidoso.

"You're nuts!" Beau told him. "If you'd just tend to business, quit drinking so much Scotch, you wouldn't be overweight. You're never satisfied, wherever you are . . . oh, to hell with you. Go on, leave, you dumb bastard. Go to Ruidoso. That's where you belong."

Robert and Rosie left that night.

The hot and cold relationship between Robert and Beau was hard on everyone. Maggi was glad he was gone; he was so damn silly, she thought many times, just plain silly.

Beau had no problem getting the better jockeys to ride for him and kept on winning his share of races. The only advantage with Robert was that Beau could trust him not

299

to tout his horses to other trainers who might want to claim off of Beau. Just as Robert touted Beau several times onto some good sound horses he had ridden for other stables. It was dog-eat-dog in this business, Maggi mused.

Maggi asked Beau one morning about what happened to Jiggs.

"Oh, he went back home. Hell, he was silly to come clear back here with just two head of horses. It's too chancy," he continued. "Look, he came when we did — it cost him six hundred to ship them here. Then the one horse got virus right away, and this knocked him out for thirty days or better before he will be able to run. And his other horse grabbed a quarter his last race and tore off half of his heel; it will be two months before he can run him. So, he went on home to wait for the Turf Paradise meet to start this fall. That's all he could do, unless he claimed a few more horses . . . and he does well just to take care of two."

Maggi understood what Beau was saying. "I understand now. I never thought of it that way before. Even some of our horses break down after we get here, and get colds. Our stable dwindles down to thirty we can actually run. Gosh, we would be out of horses if we didn't bring sixty at least."

"That's right," Beau confirmed. "The little guy gets the worst of it. He's bucking too many disadvantages. Hell, remember how hard it was for us, on the fairs, even trying to get a jockey to ride for us. They will always cater to the big stable, and you can't blame them. Well, let's get to work. I'm starved!" he told her, and mounted his pony to take another set to the race track.

Beau's stable was winning races. Headlines daily favored the rosy-cheeked cowboy from Arizona, linked with names of all his clients and the Chicago tycoon, Jack

Bullington. Beau won ten races for him alone. Mr. and Mrs. Bullington were ecstatic. Each time, they flew in from Chicago for the races. And Maggi was kept busy picking them up at the airport and taking them back after the races were over. Bullington was always in a dead rush to make his flight. Beau would have no part of the catering to the owners. "Let the ole son-of-a-bitch hire a cab," was his reply.

"He is the kind of an owner trainers dream about," Maggi snapped. "He's got the money to buy good horses. So, if it pleases him to have me cater to him, I will. Hell, I'd kiss his butt in the winner's circle if I had to. That's part of this business you don't understand," Maggi stated.

"Oh, I know you're right — but that's your job. I'll train the horses, you train the owners," he chuckled.

And she did. During one of her trips taking the Bullingtons to the Detroit airport, she persuaded Mr. Bullington to claim more horses and so increase his stable to fourteen head.

"Only you could talk the old man into claiming more horses," Beau commented. She beamed. "no one else would have the guts," he laughed.

Race track gossip of Beau's ability as a trainer and horseman spread rapidly from track to track. Mr. Bullington was aware of it and happily boasted, "They say our best trainer is here in Detroit."

Beau knew to whom his remarks were pointed and warned Maggi against making any comments about Bullington's other horses and trainer in Chicago. Even though Maggi would have liked Beau to have Bullington's first string of horses, she was proud of his ethics toward other trainers and would not disobey his command.

The more she was around Beau at the barn, the more she

knew how good he really was. Every morning, seven days a week, no matter how busy he was, Beau always took the time after all the horses had been tracked and walked, to walk around the whole barn, looking in each stall and carefully scanning each horse. His keen eyes never missed a thing. He could tell immediately if a stall wasn't mucked down to the bottom and if lazy grooms were trying to cheat by leaving foul, soggy bedding hidden under nice clean straw.

Beau would often slip under the webbings and check to see if the horses' feet had been picked out, scrubbed with the wire brush, and painted with foot dressing. Shame on the groom if he had passed over these duties.

Many times Maggi heard him yell at a groom in the next stall, "Hey, what in the hell! Why haven't you cleaned this horse up?" or "Why in the hell didn't you pick out his feet? or "Hey, come back here. This horse has no water."

No matter how tired he was he went through his ritual morning and evening. He could tell at a glance when a horse wasn't right just by the way he stood in his stall.

Always in the mornings before he took a horse to the track, he checked its ankles and knees — and especially the ones he had worked the day before — for heat or a sign of a problem starting. He was always ready to quit if the case warranted it. Beau would not train a sore going horse.

"I'm turning this horse out. No use trying to run him," he would say. "If I don't give him time, he'll take the time later on, by breaking down (pulling a suspensory muscle — by the *hoof*), cracking a sesamoid bone (by the hoof), or bowing (a tendon). Beau had tons of patience when it came to horses. Maggi often wished he had the same with her.

One morning Beau was holding and looking over a horse while the groom gave him a bath. He snapped at the groom "For Christ's sake, when was the last time you washed out this horse's sheath (case over the penis)?''

"I don't remember," the groom answered.

"Well, look at the crud. His sheath is caked full of dirt and wax," Beau pointed out. "That will make him sorer than hell and hamper his running. You wash it out as soon as he is ready to be put up," he commanded. "Have you got plenty of castile soap?"

"Yes," the groom replied.

"Okay, get Pete to help you, so you don't get kicked. It's a touchy area and they don't like it anyway," he added. "And be sure you rub some Vaseline over his penis and sheath after you have rinsed it out good, so he don't get irritated from the soap."

The six-day-a-week racing increased the daily grind in every way, and their larger stable brought more complications. Maggi was keeping the books, walking hots, plus socializing with the owners. She confronted Beau, "Why don't we hire a barn foreman?"

"What in the hell for?" he wanted to know.

Maggi snapped back, "Well, it would sure help take some of the responsibility off me. After you are through training, you go the office, and I pick up around the barn, rush home, cook, wash, hurry back to the races; it seems we never get caught up. You need someone at the barn in the afternoons to get your horses bridled and make sure the grooms aren't late, instead of you running back and forth. Also to take care of little things — like seeing that all the bridles get picked up and put away. The last two bridles the grooms lost at the test barn cost us four hundred bucks. That's just carelessness, Beau. Hell, the damn grooms don't care where they throw the stuff down."

"Oh, big deal," Beau mumbled, but Maggi knew she had made her point. "Who in the hell would you hire?"

"How about Roy Sanborn, our exercise boy?" she prodded. "He's been with us a year — he's conscientious, a good worker, and he knows the way you want things done."

"He's pretty young," Beau reminded her. "What would the old guys think?"

"I don't think that would be a problem because everybody likes him. And after all, you're still the boss."

Roy was sincerely flattered and took on his new responsibilities. He would have Beau's and Maggi's horses saddled by five a.m. After the morning training was done, he made sure every bridle and cooler were put back neatly in the tack room as he had seen Maggi do every day. He was the first back to the barn in the afternoons to make sure the grooms were getting their horses ready for their races and that they had the right bridles, tongue ties, and the like that the horses were to run in. He'd come to the paddock for further orders from Beau for the next race coming up. In less than three weeks, not a bridle was stolen or lost.

"Making Roy Sanborn our barn foreman has already saved us fifty a week in lost bridles," Maggi smarted off.

When a trainer is winning, he finds that his horses become claiming targets. Especially in Detroit. The majority of stables there didn't believe in laying up their horses during the winter as Beau did. This created a great demand in the East for fresh horses. So far the other trainers had left Beau alone. Until they realized he had good, fresh horses. Within a week, eight of his horses were claimed. Beau had to let a groom go. Bullington told him to claim one off of them.

"Hell, I'm not going to," Beau decided. "Christ, they're all so damn sore. That's the trouble; they can pick me clean, and I can't replace the ones I lose."

The other trainers also found out that Beau ran his horses where they belonged, and they weren't so sound either. The other trainers never got the run out of them that Beau did.

"I don't know how he got any run out of that ole sore bastard; I can't get him to run at all," was the constant remark about Beau's ability. The trainers soon cooled off on their claiming.

Beau would never take a horse back. Once he lost one, he let him go. That was his policy, in spite of having horses, claimed from him. You have to claim or buy horses, or you'll be out of beer. Beau bought two nice useful horses from a small stable that was leaving.

One of the horses turned out to be a stall walker. As the horse walked around and around and around in the small space, Beau tried different tricks to stop him. He even cut a hole in the wall so the stall walker could see the horse in the next stall. It didn't work.

"Well, I guess I'll have to try a goat. I hate a damn stall walker worse than anything," Beau said.

The goat did the trick. The horse immediately adopted him as a companion and quickly settled down. He won three races in a row for Beau before he was claimed.

The day he was claimed, Maggi said it was no wonder the poor thing was a stall walker. "He hardly gets settled before someone else whisks him off to strange surroundings again."

"Don't let it bother you," Beau cautioned. "I hated to lose him too, so just put it out of you mind. Now, we've got this damn goat bleating his brains out for him."

"Why don't we take him over to the guy who claimed the horse?" Maggi suggested.

"Because he'd tell me to go to hell," Beau retorted.

305

"He'd take it to mean that I was trying to help him run his business. I'll just take the goat back to the guy I got him from."

Detroit Race Course—Second Time

Hazel Park was another banner season for Beau, the leading trainer again. Detroit Race Course capitalized on his success by using Beau Witlow's name and his horses in press publicity write ups:

Arizona Trainer Here
With Top Stable

Maggi eagerly went to work clipping these items out to put in her scrapbook, number four.

When they moved to DRC they realized that the house trailer had suddenly become an inconvenience. It was hard to find a trailer court close to the track.

"It isn't worth the trouble to haul it around," Beau said. "We'd be better off renting a house with what it costs having the trailer hauled back and forth." Maggi whole-heartedly agreed.

The DRC meet started with three wins on opening day. Ted Byron arrived and stayed on for the meet. Searcher won every sprint race they wrote, and his winnings soared up to three hundred thousand dollars for his life's earnings. Ted's other colts were performing well, too, plus he lost six by claiming. He had done well financially with his stable. He was very fond of Maggi and Beau. They ate dinner together every night and spent Sundays at a movie. Ted had become family.

The Ruckers flew in on two different occasions, which were nice breaks for Maggi and Beau and kept them from getting homesick.

19

Home to Turf Paradise

Now it was fall again, and the shipping details began to gnaw at Maggi and Beau. They discussed the upcoming school term for Steve and the best way to handle it. Steve mentioned the military school in Missouri to Beau.

"He's at an age where he needs good discipline; and this might just be our answer—if it doesn't cost an arm and a leg," Beau suggested.

Maggi took care of everything, and Steve was on his way. They would not see him until the holidays.

"I never thought I'd be sending my kid to a private school," Beau remarked.

"Well, I hope we did the right thing . . . and I hope he likes it," Maggi answered. "Besides, I'm glad I don't have to go home early for school, and it will be kind of fun, being alone for a change," she smiled happily.

* * * *

Erik, the bookie, kept hanging around their barn, and it irritated Maggi. He was so pushy . . . so know-it-all. And he certainly didn't consider her a part of Beau's life. This was what made her dislike him the most. Always wanting Beau to traipse off somewhere without her. She resented it very much and told Beau so. They smoothed the issue out, and peace was made for the time being.

* * * *

Poor Maggi, just when her life was in fair order, and the barn was running smoothly, Beau began to suggest she go home, get a builder, and start building their new home by the race track.

"No," was her first answer. "Why can't we wait until we can both go?"

"Because I know you. You can have it started by the time I get home. It'll sure be handy to live that close to the track. Beats that driving eighty miles every day."

She could not argue. The thought of a new home was too much to resist.

In two weeks, the bank loan went through, a fair-circuit owner touted her an honest contractor, and the new house was underway. Maggi parked their trailer house on the site and began living in their new location.

Beau called in October to tell her the horses were on their way by van and that he was coming with the vans. She could expect him in two days.

She hired a boy to get their barn and stalls bedded down, washed clothes, and fixed her hair. She wanted everything letter-perfect for Beau. It was late when she heard a rap on the trailer house door. It was Beau!

"How did you get here so soon? I just talked to you this morning!" she said as she wrapped her arms around his neck and squeezed him tightly.

"I just decided at the last second to fly home, so I grabbed up everything." Then he began to laugh, sheepishly. "Guess what? I forgot the alarm clock, so I put it into a paper sack, grabbed my cowboy hat, and took off. About twenty minutes before flight time, I felt everyone was staring at my big hat, so I stuck it in the sack with the alarm clock and put it up on the rack over my seat in the plane. Then I heard the damn clock—tick, tick, tick, ticking. I was sure everyone would think it was a bomb. So, I got out of my seat, grabbed the sack and got off the plane, found a wastebasket and tossed the bag into it."

"You threw away that good alarm clock and your hat?" Maggi asked in amazement. "Why didn't you just tell the stewardess what was in the bag?"

"I don't know. I guess I didn't think about it."

She burst into a roar of laughter. "Oh, Beau, nobody but you would do anything that crazy!" As she hugged him and kissed his mouth, "I love you," she said.

"The contractor promised faithfully we can move in by Christmas," Maggi explained to Beau as he walked around the block walls that were going up for their house.

"I knew you would have this going. Man! You can get more done in just a short time," he chuckled as he walked toward the car. "Come on, I want to go over to the track and check out the stalls."

"Oh, Robert and Rosie are here," Maggi reported. "They're renting a house about a half-mile from us. They like our place. And Michael and Jill are coming over for a visit next weekend."

The fall was special, with the new house and friends coming daily. Maggi invited the Maddoxes for their first official dinner in their new home. "You sure have it homey looking," Maddox exclaimed.

And Christmas, with Steve seeing his new room for the first time filled Maggi and Beau with special pleasure.

Arizona Downs—Fifth Time

Robert and Rosie filled some of the emptiness left by Michael and Jill, but it wasn't the same. Ted, too, missed Michael and spent much time with Maggi and Beau. He came to eat with them or to take them out nearly every evening. Everything was coming up roses. Ted had six colts in training, and according to Beau, they were all good useful prospects. Maggi bloomed with happiness. Racing had been good to them, and she was so proud of Beau. He had come a long way, overcoming some of his shyness. The Bullingtons sent a wood-inlaid serving tray for their new home. Bullington's horses ran so well for him all winter that he was talking about buying some good colts in Kentucky.

And before Maggi could line her cupboards, it was April and time to ship to Detroit Race Course for the third time! Then another surprise she wasn't counting on changed her plans.

Sportsman's Park for the First Time

"I'm going to take fifteen of the better horses to Sportsman's Park in Cicero, Illinois—near Chicago," Beau told her. "I'll take Roy with me."

Maggi thought of splitting the stable again and listened without comment.

Beau continued, "Four to five thousand to the winner there. Hell, you can run a cheap twenty-five hundred claimer and win more than he's worth!" Finally Beau asked, "What are you so quiet about?"

"What about the other thirty-six head?" Maggi asked.

"Why, you can train them and get them loaded on the train. You'll have Doc Trotter to help you."

"Oh, great—fine, Beau! Why am I always the one who has to stay behind? You know how much I hate it!"

"Well, I can't keep these horses standing in the barn either," Beau retorted hotly. "I have to take them where they have a shot making some money. We've got to consider the damn owners too, you know. They don't much care how you or I feel."

"Okay. Just drop it!" she cried out. "You made your point!"

* * * *

The whole barn was busy getting everything packed ready to ship. Van arrangements were made. Beau remarked after figuring how many horses he would have, "Look, we will have at least ten more horses this year, so I will need more stall guards. I'd like to get those new metal

NEW STALL SCREENS

screens instead, they are a lot cheaper than the plastic webbing, and they don't rot or break," he stated. "Think we can afford that many?"

"I think we can manage," Maggi answered.

Maggi got busy and with the help of a groom painted the screens a bright fire-engine red to match the rest of the barn tack. She had to agree with Beau. "I think the screens look great. Sure wish we could get enough for the whole barn," she stated. "But at $25 per screen, that is not likely right now."

"There is one thing bad about them," Beau told her.

"What's that?" she asked.

"You can't duck under them so easy like the stall guards, and the damn grooms will be leaving them unsnapped from time to time, letting a horse get out. So, we will have to caution them about that. It's easy to do; I have done it myself lots of times," he added.

The van compartment was loaded down with tack. Then the horses were walked into their stall partitions. The van doors were swung shut, Beau threw his metal trunk up into the cab. He came to Maggi to kiss her good-bye.

"Hey, now—don't cry! You make me feel so bad when you act like this."

"Okay. I just hate being separated from you, that's all."

"Well, I gotta' go, the horses are going to get hot if we don't get moving," and he climbed up into the high cab of the truck.

He waved to Maggi. He knew she was crying. It made him feel bad having to leave her, but just then a horse was raising hell in the van and his thoughts turned to take care of that matter. As the van rolled slowly out of the backside area, when he turned back to wave again, Maggi was out of sight.

DRC for the Third Time

Maggi began to organize the shipping to Detroit. She had been opposed to shipping that far by vans, but Beau had said hotly, "No, we are not shipping by rail. It's too damn much money, since they've raised their rates . . . and it's too goddamn much trouble, loading them here on the van, unloading them at the railway dock, then loading them on the train. Christ, they can be four hours down the highway by then." So, they shipped by van.

Shipping day, three vans were parked close to the barn. The grooms began to load all the tack, buckets, tubs, and their own gear. The drivers offered little help and disappeared to the track kitchen to coffee up. Maggi had her hands full because there were so many stud horses and colts.

She appealed to Doc Trotter, who had given the last horse his tranquilizer shot. "It doesn't make any difference how I figure it, Doc, we still end up with a stud next to a mare or a filly," she stated.

"Well, let's see if we can switch the saddle pony over here," Doc suggested. They switched the horses back and forth till they had them where the stud colts were next to a gelding or another colt.

"Boy, that was a lot of figuring, with all those damn stud colts," Doc laughed.

She waved the grooms good-bye and shouted above the loud diesel engines, "See you boys in Detroit Monday!"

20

Five days later, Maggi drove into the Detroit Race Course in sleeting weather. Their barn looked deserted. Every bottom and top door of every stall were closed. She honked the horn, and a groom stuck his head out of their tack room door.

"We're in here, Mrs. Witlow," he said against the biting cold.

She quickly ran toward him and closed the door fast. All the grooms were huddled around a tiny little electric heater that was struggling its best to warm the cold tack room.

"One of the horses died in Albuquerque," a groom told her. "Pneumonia, He burst a lung."

"Oh, how terrible!" Maggi said. "Which horse was it?"

"Rocket. We couldn't get a hold of you or Mr. Witlow so we didn't know what to do. The vet where we stayed that night signed and filled out a slip stating the cause of death. I have it in my suitcase. You want it?"

"Not now," Maggi said. "It can wait until later."

She knew she would have to contact the horse's owner and the insurance company as soon as possible. Too much time had elapsed already.

She found that she would have to wait two days before she could move into the house they had rented. She checked into a motel close by. At the barn, she told the grooms to walk the horses only long enough to clean their stalls and then to put them right back.

"It's too darn cold to try and train them," she explained.

"Come on, all of you guys. I'll buy the dinner," and she drove them to a warm restaurant and made sure that they had all they could eat and all the hot coffee and pie they wanted.

As soon as she had moved into the house, she had a phone installed and put in a call to Beau. He told her that he would be coming in the next night with a jockey who was riding for him. He also told her that he had lost one of their clients, Brad Bradford, and that she could expect a van the next day to pick up his horses.

"Why did he decide to quit?" Maggi asked anxiously.

"Okay, I'll tell you—but don't give me any I-told-you-sos," he said grudgingly.

"What happened?"

"Well, you know me and my not calling. I didn't call Bradford after one of his horses ran and won. He just got mad. That's all."

"I see."

"Okay, okay—I don't want to hear it." he retorted. She shut up. But it hung in her mind all night—the money they'd lose, losing the good horses . . . and it was all so *uncalled for!*

* * * *

She was glad to have Beau back running the barn. She had begun to hate all the responsibility and the fronting for him. Dealing with men was a touchy spot for a girl.

Moreover, she had gotten so far behind in her bookwork, she hadn't even had time to unpack anything. But everything soon fell into place. Beau had to let one of the exercise boys go, but the boy was glad to leave. He hated the cold weather and Detroit.

On opening day, Beau won four races.

"What a way to start the meet," Roy, the barn foreman grinned because he and the rest of the crew all got five dollars for every win for their stakes—as was customary in all stables.

Jack Sidburn was doing most of the riding for Beau at DRC until Robert and Rosie came in from New Orleans and shot poor old Jack out of the saddle.

Maggi tried to ease the hurt. "I'm sorry about the way Beau has acted."

"That's okay. I know he and Robert are good friends and have been for years. I understand," Jack said.

"Robert has changed. He looks older, more drawn and very pale," Maggi told Beau.

"Hell, he should. He's been on bennies, pep pills, hitting the hot box, flipping, and drinking too damn much. And besides, he is getting older, and it's harder for him to keep his weight down."

Beau was right. Maggi couldn't have a bottle of liquor on hand for entertaining that Robert didn't drink it up before the night was over. Rosie was at her wit's end, and they were fighting constantly over his drinking . . . until Ted came from Seattle.

Ted had a nice way of talking, and he gave Robert a good lecture. He made it clear that Robert was wasting his chances of making good money by being so lazy and not watching his weight. Robert shaped up. With help from Rosie, he was up and at the track by six, working and galloping horses for different stables. He hired a good agent and began to ride four or five horses a day. Even Maggi could tolerate Robert those days.

Victory at River Downs

Searcher didn't like the DRC track; it was too heavy and cupped (the horse can't get a hold) out on him. So Beau gave up running him there at all. In the *Racing Form*, he spotted two races for Searcher at the small River Downs track in Ohio. The races were $25,000 speed handicaps. Poor Maggi! She had no choice but to trailer Searcher down there.

Winning both handicaps made it at least bearable for Maggi in the humid sultry afternoons along the Ohio river, where River Downs was built.

These $25,000 handicaps pushed Searcher's life earnings well over three hundred thousand. His name and track records were known throughout the racing world and breeding farms. Ted was being approached daily by people who wanted to buy Searcher. He discussed the offers with Beau and Maggi and they all decided they would talk about Searcher's future when they got back to Arizona.

"I know one thing, Beau," Ted remarked after their long talk. "Searcher wouldn't have made this much money if you hadn't picked his races and hauled him all over this damn country - - er - - I mean, Maggi hauled him," he laughed. "Plus you sure have kept him sound all the time."

Beau grinned, "It's been my policy to keep my horses in the worst of company, and myself in the best."

Beau was smart in running his horses. He knew what they were worth, and he never got too high on any of them. As he told Ted, "Hell, Searcher isn't a stake horse. But he can outrun most of the bush league kind of horse. And

317

that's why we've been taking him off to those little bush tracks like River Downs. None of the trainers from Aqueduct or Hollywood Park are going to bother sending a horse down there when they have purses like that every day where they are!''

''Well, I have never done better with my colts since I have been racing than I have since I met you,'' Ted said firmly. ''And Jack Bullington's horses here have made more money than his big stable in Chicago . . . thanks to you,'' he quipped. ''I hear rumors that his Chicago trainer has really been screwing him,'' Ted added, ''with a lot of under-the-table deals in buying horses for him.''

As Maggi listened, she thought that it seemed that every owner Beau got had been burned by someone—either by bad training, a trainer not knowing what he was doing, or being dishonest. She thought how nice it would be if Beau could be an owner's first trainer and his first experience with racing. She wished for someone who would give Beau a trusting, free hand to buy, claim, sell, without being afraid because of past experiences.

Maggi had heard that horse breeders would offer a bribe to trainers or agents who bought horses for their wealthy clients, even though some trainers were already getting ten percent from the owner for acting as his agent in the purchase.

Some trainers cheat their clients in other ways, too—in buying horses for them and jacking up the price from what it really is, not caring that the horse they are buying is a good quality or potential runner. Some trainers count strictly on the training fee and will lie about the horse if it is sound or not. These trainers last only temporarily, because the Racing Commission steps in and puts a stop to such practices, but in the meanwhile, many good clients are soured on racing. And that's a shame, thought Maggi, for many of these owners could have had a good relationship with an honest, qualified horseman, even though they may not have made a big profit. In racing, one is lucky to break even—it's a rich man's hobby. But it can be a fair game, Maggi concluded.

Hazel Park Meet—for the Third Time

On the last day of the DRC meet, Beau was presented a five-hundred-dollar stopwatch for his leading trainer achievement. He was clocking his horses with it the first morning at Hazel Park, when Vic Conners came by to welcome him back and remarked, "You should let your wife wear that. She's the one who does all the work," he chuckled.

Robert overheard the remark and chimed in, "Yeah, if it wasn't for her, he'd still be at little ole Prescott, Arizona . . an . . . " Robert stopped as he saw the look on Beau's face, a tight set jaw showing that he did not appreciate that kind of humor.

"Hell, we're just teasing you," Vic Conners said. "Don't get mad!"

Beau just grinned and rode on back to the barn. Little did Maggi know that those remarks were going to change her life!

That year, Jack Bullington asked Beau to go to the Keeneland sales in Kentucky in July to buy two yearling colts.

"Oh, Beau!" Maggi said excitedly. "Just think —Kentucky-bred colts!"

"Christ, he won't be spending more than twenty thou!" Beau said. "Last year his Chicago trainer bought *one* for a hundred thousand! He lets that damn crook talk him into buying the horse and then beats him out of half of it. That's what everyone around here is saying. And the horse wasn't any good to start with."

Maggi said, "So what? You'll do good with these two and before long, he'll buy more."

"I don't know anything of the kind, and neither do you. There are no guarantees in this business, so pipe down. Besides, there'll be a hundred millionaires there buying the best-looking, best-bred colts. I read the *Racing Form* where they averaged sixty thousand per horse last year. Fat chance of me getting much for twenty thousand."

His perpetual pessimism annoyed Maggi beyond the limits of control. "Stop being such an ungrateful bastard!" she snapped at him. "I can remember when we had horses like Sensation and Flame, and were damn glad to have them."

"Nobody's arguing that," he said, "But the best trainers in the business will be there. They'll think I'm some clod from Arizona."

Keeneland Annual Yearling Sale—New Opportunity

They were going! Everything was set. Roy Sanborn could take care of the horses. Beau made out a training chart for him to follow. Maggi was plagued with leaving their barn to such a young man. But she wanted to go! So she had no choice, even when Beau told her Erik was going to oversee their barn while they were gone. She thought Beau must be out of his mind, letting a complete stranger nose around his barn—and a bookie on top of it. But she wanted to go to Keeneland so she kept her mouth shut.

Keeneland, Kentucky—nostalgic, old, beautiful—with miles of white fences separating one horse farm from another. The Keeneland sale was held at Keeneland track where they raced yearly. It was a fairyland of wealth and beautiful horses. Maggi walked into the sale building over hand-made brick, laid on a dirt floor where the damp, humid moisture encouraged moss to grow between the bricks. The air was pungent with the odor of mustiness. Pine wood chairs, each fitted with a bright, canvas-covered cushion, were set in theater order on the brick floor.

An immaculate sale ring was guarded by potted plants and encircled with thick white rope tied to old iron post rings. The auctioneer and his four bid catchers wore bright red jackets during the afternoon sales and black tuxedo coats for the evening sessions. The yearling colts glistened under the bright lights as they were led in for the bidding. A huge totalizer board flashed the hip number of the colt and the amount of the last bid each time the price was increased.

Maggi felt that Beau must be intent upon walking them to death as he went from barn to barn, inspecting each colt he had picked out of the sale catalog. Each farm had its attendants bring out each yearling for inspection and walk him in a small neat circle for the buyer to look over.

Beau told Maggi, "These poor colts get so tired being taken in and out so many times, they even get sore footed on this gravel ring."

Many trainers and owners had brought their own veterinarians to check out the soundness of the colts they wished to purchase. Beau had to rely upon his own keen eye.

At noon, Beau and Maggi walked to the Keeneland clubhouse where they met the Bullingtons. For the lunch break, an elegant buffet of fresh shrimp, salmon platters, cold meats, hot corned beef, roast beef, salads, egg dishes, compotes, fresh fruits and pastries was spread out.

Attendants in starched white coats with regal manners carried the diners' selections to their tables and came around with pitchers of cold milk and silver pots of hot coffee and tea. They suggested all the elegance and grace of the eighteenth century.

Jack Bullington was well-known and captured the immediate attention of the black maitre d', an old-timer who had his own gift for welcoming those who were prominent. Bullington obviously relished the opportunity to introduce Beau and Maggi to people who were important names and faces in the *Daily Racing Form* and sports pages. When the night sale was closed at eleven o'clock, Bullington's chauffeur drove them all to the Campbell House where Bullington had reserved suites.

Beau was not a flyer, and because the flight down was very rough, he insisted they go back by train. Twelve hours later, they arrived in Detroit. Erik was there to pick them up and also to pick Beau's brain. As Maggi listened to his questions and Beau's answers—"I bought two nice first crop colts out of Bagdad. Everything else was so damned high!"—she was wishing that he would not be free with his information.

When the yearlings arrived in Detroit, Beau had the exercise boys start breaking them right away. By the last day of the Hazel Park meet, the colts were broke to a saddle and had learned to rein well. Then Beau turned them out on a nearby farm until he was ready to ship back to Arizona.

"A rest will be good for them after this and all the handling from the sale," he said.

Maggi began to fantasize them a super-runners that would make Beau look really good as a yearling buyer.

Being the leading trainer at DRC and at Hazel Park didn't spell the kind of money for Beau that trainers earned in New York or California. But it helped to build up his reputation, and the honor was not to be dismissed lightly, in Maggi's eyes.

At the first sign of snow flurries, Beau and Maggi were ready to ship out to home . . . to their new house and their friends. They drove the four-day trip as though the sheriff's posse were chasing them!

Arizona Downs for the Sixth Time

Home never looked so good! Beautiful, warm Arizona weather and their little house looked like mansion. Beau turned out Searcher and the Bullington colts in the new paddocks they had set up during the summer. It was then that they missed Jill and Michael the most. Beau and Maggi could hardly wait for all of them to get together at Christmas.

Robert and Rosie went on to New Orleans with a big stable. With no company of close friends, Beau became restless and began to take up with the slackers, playing cards and coming home late far too often.

Maggi was glad when Turf Paradise started. Then Beau didn't have time for the carefree slackers. Michael and Jill came at the holidays, with all the California track news.

"That's all we heard, was Searcher, and how good he was running," Michael told Beau and Maggi. "Heard you bought two colts for Bullington!"

"Yeah, he named them Hole-in-One and Driving Range, 'cause he likes golf so well," Beau answered, and took Michael and Jill out to see the horses.

"What do you mean, he named them? I thought you got

to do that, Beau."

"Oh, no, that's one of the owner's pleasures—naming his own horses," Beau grinned.

Maggi spoke up and said, "Mr. Bullington not only named the two new colts, but he also found out that he could reserve names for future colts."

"What do you mean 'reserve'?" Jill asked.

"To save time, because you don't always get your first choice. Look, it's like this," Maggi went on, "One, you can send in four choices in order of your preference, for names. The New York Jockey Club checks its records to make sure that the name chosen has not been spoken for before. You're allowed only sixteen characters in each name, isn't that right, Beau?"

"Oh, yeah. Also, if you buy a horse and you don't like his name, you can rename him if he hasn't started yet—but it will cost you $50 to do this."

* * * *

Driving Range won his first race and looked like a promising colt for the summer.

"Another sprinter," was the talk around the track. "That's all Beau can train is speed horses!" Venom was pouring from a few lips. "They're just jealous," others told Beau.

"Hell, don't tell me about racetrackers. They are the first to put you down—and the first to put their hand out to help you up!" Beau replied.

There were winners—for Bullington, Ted, the Ruckers, and the one-horse owners during the winter meet.

Maggi loved her part in having cocktail parties and dinners for each occasion. Their daily routine hadn't changed, there was only more of it! Up at five, train, walk

324

hots, eat, move horses in and out, race—that was their life. Eating out with different clients and racing four days and they loved every second of it.

*   *   *   *

Searcher turned six, and Beau and Ted finally agreed it was time to retire him to stud. There were new, younger colts coming up, and Ted and Beau wanted to quit while Searcher was still on top. When the decision was made, Maggi took over. She advertised the horse through full-page color photos in the pages of national quarter-horse magazines.

Within one month, they had an answer from a Tulsa, Oklahoma quarter-horse ranch. They bargained with Ted to lease the colt with the option to buy him later if he proved to be a good sire.

As soon as word of Searcher's retirement was out, Michael's father, in his capacity as president of the track, planned a special farewell ceremony for him. Robert and Rosie flew in for the event and one of the largest crowds that Maggi had ever seen at Turf Paradise pushed toward the saddling paddock to get a last close look at their favorite horse! As he pranced and danced about, he looked regal. Beau legged Robert up, and Robert rode Searcher onto the race track in front of the cheering grandstand.

"Ladies and gentlemen," the announcer said in a nostalgic tone, *"it's Searcher on the main track. Winner of three hundred thousand dollars throughout his racing career. Holder of two world records. He will now gallop around the mile course one final time, bidding his faithful fans adieu, before being retired to stud. Let's give him a*

325

well-earned round of applause, in tribute to a magnificent career, and in fond farewell.''

As Searcher galloped slowly, with his huge neck arched and his head tucked close to his chest, he pricked his ears at the noise that rolled toward him from the grandstand and swept majestically along the railing and down the backstretch.

Tears welled up in Maggi's eyes as she sat at the clubhouse table watching this beautiful horse who had earned the money that built their new house and who had made Beau's name renowned in racing. She knew that Beau, wherever he was in the crowd, must be experiencing similar thoughts at this moment.

Ted decided to take Searcher to his own little breeding farm and breed some of his mares to him first.

"I want to breed to him before he leaves Arizona," he said firmly.

Beau was pleased at the decision, for he loved the old horse and looked forward to having him around so he could see him now and again.

Bullington's colts gradually began to fill the void left by Searcher. Driving Range was the strong contender for the upcoming Phoenix Gold Cup and Hole-in-One was improving every out. Beau had already gained a strong lead for the trainer standings.

Maggi was into scrapebook number fourteen.

21

One night the sound of the telephone ringing sometime past midnight woke Maggi. It was Pee Wee.

"Listen, I got to have five hundred real quick for bail!" he said.

"Pee Wee, listen—can I call you back?" Maggi mumbled, not totally awake or alert.

"Okay, okay. Got something to write on? Okay, I'll tell you where to get in touch with me."

Maggi wrote down the address and number, not thinking to ask any questions. She fell back into bed. In the morning, she called him back and then told Beau the story.

"Wire him the money," Beau told her.

"But—"

"Don't argue. We've been friends all our lives, me and Pee Wee. Hell, we have been broke, rich, hungry, parlayed our gals, been in jail a few times too. The little bastard!"

Maggi wired the money. They heard no more from Pee Wee until a van driver told Beau he was galloping horses on a horse farm in Virginia.

Detroit for the Fourth Time

"Fifty-five head, how in the hell will I get them all back there?" was Beau's concern.

"By rail," Maggi asserted. "It's the only way."

"Hell, I don't want to ride on that damn train again, three times is enough for me," Beau ranted back.

"Well, I have already asked Dr.Trotter if he would ride back on the train," Maggi stated. "He said yes, and I figured each owner could pay him fifteen per horse. Good insurance for them and good for the doctor."

"Six express cars? Boy, you guys have really come a long ways," the dispatcher said over the phone. "Oh, you'll be glad to hear we have a new long-loading dock. A whole train of cars can be spotted at once. No more moving ramps back and forth."

"Hey, that's great!" Maggi answered. "Okay, April nineteenth is the date set," she confirmed. "See you then. Good-bye."

Shipping day everyone worked like pros, and they had plenty of help. Maggi had set up coffee and doughnuts for everyone present, grooms, vets, Ted, Bullingtons, Rucker, and several friends who came as sightseers. Doc put his cot and bed roll on board, and all the supplies he contemplated he would need for the trip. He kissed his family good-bye and boarded the long train.

Beau and he exchanged some last-minute details. The dispatcher motioned the engine in and with a clunk of the huge buckling, the iron hitch snapped shut, and the six express cars moved away, slowly at first, picking up momentum in a few short seconds as they chugged over to the train depot.

Thank God for Vic Conners, Maggi thought. He *made* Hazel Park pleasant for everyone, for there was nothing nice about the dismal factory area and the cramped living quarters in the adjoining neighborhood.

Beau won four races opening day and was well in the

lead of the trainer standings by the time Robert and Rosie arrived, sporting a new Corvette. Robert had been racing in Omaha, and as always, got sour and left. He knew he could always ride a few for Beau, especially when he read in the *Racing Form* how well Beau was doing at Hazel Park.

At first their reunion was fun, then Robert began the old card game and drinking bit until it got completely out of hand, and Maggi had her say. The drinking and games broke up, but deep inside, Robert began a resentment toward Maggi and the power she had over Beau. He was determined to conquer that!

But Robert continued to aggravate Beau too. He was never on time at the barn when Beau needed him to work a horse. On one such morning, Beau was about to get another jock when Robert came running up the shedrow.

"It's a good thing you got here. I was going to let Pincay ride him," he snapped at Robert.

Robert just made a silly remark and got on Driving Range and fixed his pedals (stirrups). Beau told him what he wanted him to do.

"Look, this colt is sitting on the tailgate and getting left at the start. I want you to jack him up (whip his ass) before putting him in the gate. Then make him stand up close and keep him from sitting down on the gate," he added. "I'll have the gateman hit him with the buggy whip when they ring the bell."

Beau watched the colt being loaded. He was shaken up from the cracks of the whip on his rump. Robert held him steady, and the gateman had hold of his bit, keeping him from rearing up. The starter spoke. "Okay, Robert—I'm hitting the button." R-i-n-n-n-g . . . and Driving Range shot out like a bullet.

"That's more like it," the starter told Beau.

"Good. Then I don't have to bring him back?" Beau asked.

"No."

Racing six days a week was still new for Beau and Maggi. They were used to the casual four days in Arizona and the weekends on the fair circuit. At first it was new and exciting, and fun for Maggi. And Beau loved the continuous action, until his horses began to run out of conditions. Then there were days when there wasn't anything in the barn running.

Maggi found no pleasure in just going to the races and sitting when Beau wasn't running a horse. It was Beau's concern to go every day to watch and keep an eye out for possible good claims. On those days, Maggi used to shop and do other things because she actually found racing boring. She wasn't one to bet on the horses, so what else was there to do, but sit and watch. . .

D R C Meet

The nasty rumors of Bullington's Chicago trainer were still prevalent around the backside. One evening after the meet at DRC had started, Mr. Bulllington called from Chicago.

"Hello, Maggi. Look, you get Beau to come over to Chicago, and he can pick out several of these horses that are not doing any good here."

"Okay, Mr. Bullington, I'll tell Beau as soon as he gets home."

"Hell, no, I don't want to butt in on another trainer's business," Beau said flatly. "That old man is crazy to even ask me to do that."

"He said that it was all right with Jim Winedot. In fact,

330

he was the one who suggested it," Maggi stated. "I can't see anything wrong in going over there. I think you should go," she pleaded with him.

They took the night train to Chicago. Bullington's chauffeur met them at the station and drove them to the Drake Hotel, close to Bullington's high-rise apartment on Lake Shore Drive. Later, the Bullingtons and Beau and Maggi drove out to Arlington Park.

It didn't take Beau long to see why Winedot wanted to get rid of seven horses. Beau's keen eye saw all he needed to know.

"This horse is bowed and not worth training at all. The others all have ankle problems. One has a hot knee. I just want you to know this before I take over any of them," he told Bullington. "I don't want to be blamed for breaking them down," he added.

"Well, Beau, this is the first time I had any idea that any of these horses had problems," Bullington replied, then snapped at Jim Winedot, "How come you never said this horse was bowed before?" Beau turned away and walked far down the shedrow to look at one of the horses again. He didn't want to hear Winedot's answer. He felt embarrassed for the man and knew he was in a touchy situation.

Before they left, it was understood that all seven horses would be shipped to Detroit except one outstanding stake horse, Tally, that Jim Winedot wanted to keep—naturally. In fact, Tally was running in the feature race that afternoon.

Bullington and his wife insisted that Beau and Maggi come to the races and have lunch with them in the Post and Paddock Club, a very posh club for members only. It was done in red velvet chairs, white flocked walls; plush thick

331

red carpets adorned the terraced table area.

Jim Winedot joined them. It made Beau most uncomfortable and he moved about restlessly in the soft velvet chair. To make matters worse, Jim Winedot kept boasting about how many lengths the horse would win by. Maggi mused that she had never heard Beau once state a fact like that about any horse he had running.

Tally was last by ten lengths. Beau felt awkward for Winedot but remained silent.

Mr. Bullington raged, "What the hell went wrong?"

"I think the saddle must have slipped back," Winedot offered as the reason.

Beau nudged Maggi, and they got up and said, "We're going to make a bet." When Beau saw Winedot finally leave they returned to the table.

"Well, I settled it with Jim, I'm sending Tally along with the rest of the horses. You do whatever you see fit to do with them, Beau," he stated "I'm through with Winedot. My wife has been telling me for the last two years he was a crook, and I wouldn't listen to her," he ranted.

Maggi was ecstatic! Beau had Tally!

Beau made his position clear to the other trainer.

"Look, Winedot, I just want you to know that I didn't have anything to do with this decision of Bullington's. I was told you wanted me to come back here to weed out the culls and get them off your hands."

Maggi sensed how painful this was for Beau and admired his openness and direct manner. And while Jim Winedot might have been all the things the rumors suggested, he was extremely cordial about the shift, and very meticulous about shipping the horses.

After the horses arrived in Detroit, Beau culled them out, selling the two studs to a small breeding farm in Kentucky. Three were claimed and Beau ended up with three decent horses. Tally was a stake horse and won the two biggest stakes in DRC. The news soon traveled nationwide, along with the fact that Beau had taken over Bullington's first string.

"Nothing is permanent, only temporary," Maggi reminded Beau when Bullington wanted him to race in Chicago.

"I don't have good enough horses to go to Chicago. Hell, I'd be lucky to win four races," Beau grumbled to Maggi. "What about Ted and my other clients?" Beau wanted to know. "I can't just dump them."

But Bullington still argued.

"Okay," Beau said finally. "I'll give it a try. We're not running much here, anyway. So, we'll go on to Chicago for the last few weeks, if you can get stalls and a place for me and Maggi to live."

"Don't worry about the stalls, and I will see that Mrs. Webber finds you a place to live," he promised.

Introduction to Arlington Park

Arlington was gigantic when compared to small Hazel Park and DRC. It sprawled over hundreds of acres.

The Webbers, who owned and ran the track, hardly acknowledged that the Witlows were on the grounds. Through Jack Bullington's insistence, they had a mobile home for Beau and Maggi to rent on the track. Three hundred dollars for two weeks. It wasn't much better inside than the one they had rented in Del Mar. Maggi made sure it was clean and let the rest go.

Beau was very insecure at the Arlington Park track. He wouldn't let Maggi do a thing without barking at her. He complained every day.

"Just look at the Condition Book. Not one goddamn race I can run in. I must have been plumb crazy to let the ole man talk me into coming here," he ranted on. "Hell, I'm shipping to Albuquerque, I at least might win a race or two, and pick up a few horses for winter.."

Albuquerque Revisited

They vanned to Albuquerque. Maggi told Beau he was making a mistake, and when they drove into the dirty, windy barn area, Beau knew it. Maggi didn't bother to unpack their car. Levi's and boots were all they would need. Eleven days later, after winning six races and claiming four horses the Witlows were driving home. One month early.

Ten Years at Turf Paradise

In December, Beau was installed in the Hall of Fame, a highly coveted honor bestowed by the track management for that person making exceptional contributions to horseracing in Arizona.

Maggi brimmed with happy tears when she heard the announcer:

"Ladies and gentlemen, for outstanding racing achievements and stable during the past ten years . . . Let's welcome Beau Witlow into the Turf Paradise Hall of Fame!"

Maggi had a party following the ceremony. All their friends and the barn crew were there. It was late, and many had gone home when Maggi missed Beau!

Everyone had gone, and it was two a.m. when she heard his truck. She opened the door. The truck Beau was driving was not his. The front fender was bashed in, and the bumper hung by a piece of wire. The hood gaped open, and the windshield was cracked.

"Where's your truck?" she asked, as Beau crawled out from behind the wheel.

"Whataya mean . . . ? It's mine. I've got the keys, don't I?" He stood before her in drunken defiance.

Maggi grabbed the keys from him, got under the wheel and saw that the truck had one of those crazy switches that started when it was turned.

"Where did you go?" she barked at him.

"Ta the track," he mumbled sloppily. "Ta check the horses. Ya gotta check on horses, ya know."

"Yes, I know! But you've got someone else's truck, you dumb bastard!"

"It's my truck—dammit!" Beau insisted. "The keys work!"

Maggi watched him teetering where he stood and decided against arguing further. She started the truck, drove back to the parking lot, and spotted Beau's truck.

She made a quick switch, fearing that the long arm of the law would reach out and grab her at any minute.

Driving home, she could not help but laugh at Beau and the mixup with the truck and the keys.

Notwithstanding such incidents, it was certainly good to be home again. There were many things around the house that required her attention, which was always the case when they returned to a place that had been closed down so long.

Maggi used the time wisely, decorating a little, doing

bookwork, painting the barn and feed tubs, and visiting. Beau did the same, jostling horses in and out, breaking yearlings, and mostly visiting. He heard Robert was doing well in New Orleans and Atlantic City. Michael and Jill were coming back.

As Beau came in late one afternoon, he said to Maggi, "Hey, do you realize Searcher is eight years old? He'll have some colts running this year."

"It doesn't seem possible," Maggi answered. "It seems like yesterday he won the Futurity."

"Yeah, funny you brought that up, because I saw Ted today and he seems cool and hasn't said much about me taking his new colts," Beau remarked. "I bet he's got another trainer. You know, owners are like horses, they change trainers all the time," Beau said hatefully.

Maggi listened, but remained silent.

Arizona Downs for the Seventh Year

The Downs meet started. Beau and Maggi were working so hard, neither of them realized their lives were changing. Beau was a celebrity, and everyone wanted to buy the leading trainer a drink. Beau could never stop at just *one* drink. Late hours followed, and tempers flared, for Maggi was hot-headed.

After each encounter, Beau yelled, *"Just leave me alone, goddamnit!"*

Unconsciously, Maggi became a little depressed each time, even though she kept right on making all the shipping arrangements for the coming summer. She was so confused—summers and winters were running together. Was it fall or spring?

Maggi and Beau were homebodies at heart, but they

never spoke of this to each other, keeping the despair of uprooting and shipping to themselves. Beau knew deep inside that he would have to race in Chicago if he wanted to keep Bullington. Many trainers would jump at the chance to have his stable of horses. Bullington had clout in Chicago. If a horse were eligible, he could get the stalls. Maggi hated the thought of not going back to their secure Detroit. Vic Conners and DRC were so good to them. Just when things were going so well, she thought, why did they have to uproot and go somewhere else? But owners and the horses decide where you're to race, she realized.

Ted and Beau decided that Ted would turn all his horses out during the summer and Beau would pick up the new yearlings in the fall and race them in Phoenix. Beau thought it strange at the time, but was not one to push anyone and let it alone. Rucker was overjoyed that Beau was to race in Chicago. He loved the purses! After days of shuffling and claiming, Beau had forty head going to Chicago—by rail. Doctor Trotter agreed to be on hand for the three-day trip.

Arlington Park for the Second Time

Arlington Park was cold the day they arrived. Beau was six stalls short!

"I told you it would be like this!" Beau raged to Maggi. "They don't give a fuck about me and my two-bit stable. Christ, when they can have Buckpasser and Forward Pass, why in the hell would they want to bother with me?"

"You go talk to the racing secretary," he told her. "You're a good talker. See if you can't get those six stalls back."

All Beau needed to do was ask, and Maggi was ready to

move heaven and earth for him. But over the phone, the racing secretary adopted a rather caustic attitude and made a point of reminding her that "Beau was lucky to get the stalls that he had."

"Thank you very much," Maggi retorted stiffly. "I'll attend to this right away."

"If you've got any ideas about going over my head, you can forget it. Won't do you any good," the racing secretary told her flatly.

"No! I wouldn't do anything like that. I'm just going to order four vans and ship to Hazel Park. They treat us like people there," she snapped and added, "Thank you very much—and good-bye."

"Well, did you get him to let me have the stalls?" Beau asked eagerly as she came down the shedrow.

Maggi plunged into an explanation of what she had done. She feared Beau would be furious, but he surprised her.

"Good for you!" he said. "The sons-of-bitches."

"Well, I'm just sick and tired of us being pushed around," Maggi flared. "We've had years of that, and I hate this whole business of kissy-facing all the time. We've worked hard. We are well liked in Detroit."

Beau instructed the grooms to stop unpacking, that they would be going to Detroit as soon as they could get some vans.

Within half-an-hour, Mr. Webber himself drove up to their barn in his big Lincoln. He apologized concerning the stall situation, insisting that there had been some sort of unfortunate misunderstanding.

"There was a mixup with the stall man," was his alibi. He stated he didn't want Beau leaving. "Jack Bullington is a long-time friend, this was his home town, and he would be highly offended if he couldn't race here."

After he left, Beau grabbed Maggi and swung her around in a circle. "Honey, you're the greatest! I knew you'd get those stalls. I love you!" He kissed her enthusiastically and squeezed her so hard that she could hardly breathe.

Arlington Park was first-class racing—there was no question about it—with big stables and wealthy owners. If there were a horse for sale, he was sold by evening. Most of the stables had been coming to Arlington Park for years and were established. Beau was the lowest rung on the ladder—a bitter pill to swallow since he had been doing so well in Detroit and now was forced to climb back up again. It hardly seemed fair, but in such a cut-throat business, nothing was fair, Maggi thought.

The trainers and owners of the higher echelon stables were wined and dined by the Webbers, every Saturday night in their home called the Inn, a huge white building next to the grandstand. Maggi heard that well-known movie stars, prominent personalities of all kinds, and even Mayor Daley himself were often guests at the Inn. Maggi had seen many beautiful homes, but this was a mansion of forty bedrooms.

Maggi spent many afternoons with the Bullingtons at their clubhouse table, observing the luxurious Inn where the rich owners stayed. She was curious about what it looked like inside.

Another feature back East and at Arlington Park that was new to Beau was the Turf Course (grass) races. Up to the time he shipped back to Detroit, he had never run a horse on the grass. Santa Anita was the only track on the west coast that had a turf course. They were unheard of in Arizona.

At Arlington Park, the grass course was inside the main track. Maggi puzzled about what made a horse run better on the grass than he could run on the dirt. She asked many questions but got no feasible answers. Even the best trainers couldn't explain why some horses did well on turf.

She herself couldn't see why a horse could run faster on the lumpy, bumpy, spongy course, but they did nevertheless.

Beau tried the turf course for several horses that didn't run too well on the dirt. One horse, Max, became a super grass horse. He moved up from a $3,500 claimer to an allowance grass horse. Grass was his cup of tea.

But the turf races had their drawbacks for training. First, the trainer had to get permission from the office to gallop any horse on the grass. And the horse had to be entered in a grass race before he would be allowed on the course for training. This was to prevent overabuse of the course and prevent tear-out of the divits.

Even after the trainer was permitted to work his horse, he had to wait till after ten a.m. when the main track was closed down. This was to avoid any wrecks since horses had to cross the main dirt track to get onto the turf.

There was no sneaking onto the grass course, for two to three attendants were in charge of this operation and would not allow anyone to enter without presenting the pink approval slip from the racing office.

Maggi went with Beau one morning to watch one of their horses work for the first time on the grass. He was a new horse they had just claimed, and Beau thought he might like the turf.

Beau said, "Look, you lead him up the lane a few feet and let the jockey have him then. I want to clock him from here."

"Okay," she answered.

The "dogs" (sawhorses) were set up close to the rail.

The track did this to save the grass for the major race (keep the horses off the rail). Maggi worried that the horse might duck down inside and run into one of them. She never did like it when they put up the dogs on a main track after it had rained. All those sawhorses sticking out away from the rail were dangerous during morning training.

As the horse jogged, she liked the wisping sound of the tall grass hitting his legs . . . S-w-w-w-shhh. . . as she pointed him up the lane and stopped. She let the horse take a good look at the center field. He knew he was going to work, his eyes became alert, his whole body became on the muscle.

Beau watched the horse as Maggi ponied him up the lane of the turf course. He noticed the horse to be a little sore on his left leg. He watched him carefully to see if he would warm out of it.

By the time Maggi had ponied him up to the turn of the course, he seemed to be going a little more smoothly.

As she stopped and let the horses settle down for a few seconds Beau got out his stopwatch and had it ready as he kept his eye on the horse, waiting for Maggi to let him go.

"Okay, are you all set?" Maggi asked the rider.

"All set."

She let go of the bridle and the big bay horse sprang to gallop freely . . . S-w-wissshhh . . .

Two other horses were working on the grass, and went whizzing past him. He lunged forward and broke into a nice free gallop.

Beau could see the boy taking a good cross (setting his reins for leverage) on the horse and getting down low on him as he approached the finish line. He was to work a full mile.

Click! Beau got him at the half. Click—again as the

horse came over the line. He looked down at the time. Not good, he thought. He must be sore. As he rode toward the horse and rider, he decided he might turn the horse out. He would wait and see how his leg felt in the morning.

Maggi came riding up. "Well how did he do?" she asked.

"Well, I think he's a little sore but I think he's going to handle the grass fine."

Beau was making a strong bid for the leading trainer title. The Webbers began to take another look at the cowboy trainer from Arizona! The racing secretary started to crawl under his desk the first time Maggi went into his office.

"I thought you might throw something at me, after the way I ran your barn down," he grinned. "And your old man is beating the socks off everyone . . . Do I have egg on my face!"

Maggi grinned back, shook his hand, and they became friends from that day on. Beau finished up second leading trainer, winning thirty-three races. The eastern trainers too began talking about the cowboy from Arizona.

Sportsman's Park for the Second Time
Keeneland for the Third Time

It was a thirty-mile move southwest of Chicago to Sportsman's Park in Cicero. Maggi remembered the dismal area well and was glad when the Keeneland sale time came up. Bullington had promoted another wealthy client for Beau and he, too, bought three colts at the sale. When they got back, Maggi clipped write-ups from the sports pages:

Bullington Pays
Two Hundred Thousand
For Six Yearlings at Keeneland Sale

She placed these in scrapbook number twenty.

Bullington often stopped by the barn after the races just to see his horses, driving up in his big chauffeur-driven limo. Maggi made every effort to make the visits pleasant but Beau always ducked around the barn to the other side to avoid the deluge of questions. Maggi understood Mr. Bullington wasn't the only owner, and the constant repetition of questions were tiring to Beau, and even to her at times. Yet she was fully aware that these people made it possible for her and Beau to have the material things they now had, and she was grateful.

Success didn't spoil Beau Witlow. He still got up at five a.m. It was nine o'clock one morning, and he still Had several sets to go to the track. He thought, "I'll have Maggi go with the last two sets." He glanced at his watch. He needed to hurry over to the racing office to enter as they would be closing soon. As he waited for the boys to get the horses tacked up, he mused that he couldn't just leave the exercise boys on their own. "They'll do as they damn well please if no one goes with them," he told Maggi. "Now be sure and go up with them, or the lazy little bastards will let the horses '22' it (run faster than necessary) around the track.

"Hey, come on you bastards, let's hurry it up!" he shouted toward the stalls.

When he got back, Robert and Rosie were at the barn waiting to see him and Maggi. "What brings you two here?'' he asked.

"I've got a mount in the Hundred Thousand, Saturday," Robert stated.

Maggi also was surprised to see them. "Hey, we heard through the race track grapevine you had done nothing but good back in New Orleans and Omaha, and even Atlantic City."

"Hell, he's rich," Beau smarted off. "He's made more damn money these past years than he ever thought possible."

"Yes, and I'm stashing it away for a rainy day," Rosie remarked.

"Well, we owe it to you, Beau. If you hadn't brought me back here and got me started, I would still be riding quarter horses at Sunland Park and not have a dime," Robert stated.

"Well, we're really happy for both of you," Maggi said.

When you're hot, you're hot! And Robert was hot! He won the Hundred Thousand. And having a wife as beautiful as Rosie didn't hurt either. The men flocked around this beautiful girl with the porcelain skin and beautifully coiffed brown hair. Life was good to Robert and Rosie, Maggi mused, as she watched all the fanfare. After the celebration was over, there was a sad farewell at the airport among the four. Even though Maggi had her reservations about Robert, she loved the little shit, and he was one of the best race riders around as far as she was concerned. She knew they could always depend on Robert for an honest ride.

This year, Steve enrolled in Michigan State for his further business education.

Hawthorne Park for the First Time

Sportsman's Park and Hawthorne were back-to-back—two huge racing plants side by side, one in one county and the other in another, right on the line. Maggi had heard many tales of the old days of Al Capone running Sportsman's Park while the "Purple Gang" ran Hawthorne Park. The good part of the two race tracks being side by side was that horsemen did not have to move. The tracks cooperated, each letting the other use its barns. So, all Beau had to do was ride over to the other track to train and run.

Beau finished third in trainer standings at Sportsman's. He was bucking one of the largest stables in the East. Van Dyke, Maggi's friend from Ak-Sar-Ben, who vanned Searcher, was one. He had a stable of a hundred head of horses and was commuting back and forth from Omaha, New Orleans, and Atlantic City.

After the long summer, several of Beau's horses were sore, some were claimed, and some he turned out, dwindling his stable down to eighteen head, and they were running out of racing conditions.

"This is the problem with a small stable," he told Maggi. "After a horse has won two or three races, it's hard to find 'Winners of three races' for the right claiming price where he can run. Races are either too tough or too short, or the horse has made too much money. Christ, I could have run Driving Range in the cheap allowance race: 'Non-winners of $10,000 since June' — but he was one dollar over and it wrote him out," Beau spewed.

Maggi began to understand racing more and more as Beau explained, and she saw the frustrating parts for the trainer — the owner pushing, wanting his horse to run and a trainer trying his best to run the horse where he belongs,

345

where he has a chance to win. Beau badgered the racing secretary daily to write him a special race for his horses that the Condition Book didn't have. Many a morning Beau came home cursing, "The son-of-a-bitch could have let the race go with five head, but he called it off, 'cause he wanted three more head in the race."

"Why?" Maggi asked.

"He says it's not a good betting race for the track. You should know that by now," he snapped back.

"Oh, I forgot," Maggi was sorry she asked when he was in this kind of a mood.

In spite of all the hassle, Beau won several more races before Hawthorne was almost over. As soon as it began to snow, he was ready to ship home. By rail.

Beau was realistic when it came time to leave for home and told all his owners, "Let's try and lose the cheaper horses and the ones that have problems . . . no use you paying a shipping bill on them 'cause we'll probably lose them in Phoenix anyway, and you get more for a second here than you do a win at home."

The owners agreed that made good business sense. When it came time to ship home, only three express cars were ordered. Doctor Trotter flew in and rode back on the train. He didn't know he would be greeted in Phoenix by the TV press. Beau was a celebrity in Arizona now and so was Bullington's Driving Range!

22

Arizona Downs for the Eighth Season

"You know, I'm crazy for coming back to Arizona," Beau remarked as he drove their newly purchased white Cadillac on a highway between Missouri and Kansas. "The big purses are back there. Look at Robert. Christ, he made more money last year than I have the last five years. Hell, we lose money every year racing in Phoenix, you know that?"

"Yeah, that's okay for a jockey. But you can't keep racing horses six days a week, year in and year out. That's what's wrong with most of the horses back East. They're worn out," Maggi answered. "No wonder they claim so many horses off you. You come back East with nice fat, fresh horses, with all kinds of conditions."

In spite of her lengthy spiel on the subject, Maggi knew Beau was right. They were always in the red at Turf Paradise by shipping time. She always had to dip into their savings for payrolls and so forth.

Beau's success in the East had everyone fighting to take him and Maggi out to fine restaurants when they came back to Arizona.

"Where in the hell were they when we could have used a good steak ten years ago?" Maggi kidded as she and Beau laughed about the days they ate beans seven days a week.

Turf Paradise for the Twelfth Time

Turf Paradise officials saw a change in Beau. He was easy to talk to without his getting hostile. The officials bent over backwards to cooperate with him and showed they had great respect for him as a horseman. "We're so proud of you and Maggi on your wonderful success in Chicago," they told them both.

No matter how lucky—or what—you are around the race track, the training still has to go on seven days a week. Maggi was still walking those hots. Both she and Beau were getting up every morning at five. They were trying to keep good help and facing the everyday problems, such as soreness, shin-bucking, office contacts, and racing conditions. But a new problem emerged one day as Beau came back from the racing office.

"Something's up with Ted. He isn't as friendly. I bet he's going to give his horses to another trainer next winter," Beau said.

"Oh, you're kidding," Maggi answered. "Not Ted."

"Well, you don't know a damn thing about Ted," Beau snapped back. "He's like everyone else—looking for a deal. I told him I had to have more money for training those colts back East. Hell, it was costing me money to have his horses, ever since I've been getting eighteen a day and I raised the grooms' pay . . . well, I'll be glad if he does get someone else," Beau spewed.

Maggi knew better than that. He did care, or he wouldn't have brought it up. But after she called Ted and invited him to come for dinner and he answered, "Sorry, Maggi, I have other plans," she, too, felt that something was up. But she didn't have time to worry about it then—it was shipping time.

Arlington Park for the Third Time

"Eight thousand dollars per express car!" Beau ranted. *"Fuck it! We'll go by van!"*

"Do you realize it would take ten vans to haul seventy head and all the tack?" Maggi asked.

"Yeah, but where are you coming up with forty-eight thousand dollars?" he answered.

"I'll pro-rate the forty-eight thousand into the number of horses going and bill the owners right away so we can have it by shipping time," she explained. "Why do I have to argue with you every year about shipping?" she pleaded. "Damn you, anyway. You're so damn hard-headed. If the owners can't stand the shipping price, then let them get out of the business, is what I say," she spit out and slammed the door.

Seven express cars were ordered. Maggi made her point, especially when she brought up losing Rocket on the van.

"You know he got hot and sweaty standing in the van while the driver stopped and had something to eat and gassed up—and didn't bother to open the van doors. Then, when he started up and the cold air whipped through the vents and hit Rocket's wet body, he got chilled and developed pneumonia."

It was then that Beau threw up his hands, "Order the damn cars!"

Beau came to Arlington Park with a much better grade of horses this year. The yearling colts of Bullington's were four-year-olds now and had become good allowance horses and won most of the bigger races. By the second month of the meet in July, he was leading trainer by thirty races. Mr. and Mrs. Webber were in awe of his abiltiy, for Beau was now second in the national trainer standings in the world!

One afternoon while the races were still running, Mrs. Webber came to Beau's and Maggi's clubhouse table. "I want you and Maggi to come to the Inn tonight for dinner," she said to Beau.

"Nope, we can't tonight," Beau stated flatly. Maggi's heart sank as she thought, "Why did he refuse?"

"Can't you cancel whatever it is?" Mrs. Webber insisted.

"Nope," Beau state firmly.

"Well, then—you come next Saturday night."

"Okay," Beau mumbled, not having a chance to find another excuse.

"Good. We'll see you then. Come in the Post and Paddock entrance—the red side door. Just ring the bell and our houseboy will let you in."

Maggi realized that Beau was trying to squirm out of it again so she spoke up as soon as Mrs. Webber left. "This is what we've been working our heads off for, Beau—to move up in racing! You'll never get anywhere by backing out of things all the time," she declared.

"Okay, we'll go if it means that much to you," he said indifferently. "Now, let's watch this race."

Maggi's adrenaline was pumping. They were actually going next Saturday night, she thought as she turned her head toward the Inn. It looked like a mansion at the far end of the grandstand—white, with red awnings, and elegant window boxes, each filled with red geraniums to match the red tile roof. She let her eyes follow down the wide curved driveway where Cadillacs, Lincoln Continentals, and Rolls Royces were parked one behind the other—some with their chauffeurs standing by. Maggi could hardly wait to see what the inside was like. What would she wear? Her head was swimming.

"Hey, hey, come on," Beau was nudging her, breaking

her daydreaming. "Let's go, the races are over."

"I'm coming," she answered.

* * * *

Saturday night. Maggi had changed four times to be sure she had the right dress on. Beau looked like a banker in his black suit. As she pushed the polished brass door bell, the huge red door opened, and they were greeted by a very personable Cuban houseboy in a red jacket. He invited them in. As they stepped into the vast room, Maggi was awestruck at the beautiful white floor of expensive tile. Bright-colored chairs, couches and love seats were arranged around several mahogany coffee tables, where men and beautifully dressed women sat, with gleaming jewelry on! On the other side of the room were fifty round dining tables, each set for six with elegant Lenox dishes, sterling silverware, and lavish flower arrangements of mixed blossoms in the center.

The houseboy asked their choice of beverage and soon returned with their vodka and tonics. As Maggi raised her glass to draw a sip, her eyes saw the huge crystal chandelier that hung from the high ceiling, its prisms sparkling in the brilliant lighting. A curving bar trimmed in polished brass and black leather in impeccable taste set off the farthest corner of the room. Each wall was adorned with paintings easy on the beholders' eyes. Maggi looked at each for a moment as she and Beau stood alone.

The buzzing of conversation was low key as each little group made its own small talk.

"Let's go," were Beau's first words. "I told you we wouldn't know anyone here."

Maggi felt so cheated, because she knew he would leave. And then! "Hello there! I'm Ada Rice, why don't you come over here and sit with me?" she invited.

Maggi could have kissed this lovely kind lady, even though she had never met her before.

"How nice of you to ask us," Maggi answered and looked toward Beau for approval. Mrs. Rice spoke as though she sensed their discomfort, "Come on, I want you to meet a few friends of mine . . . Bill Shoemaker and his wife Babs, this is Maggi and Beau Witlow," she purred.

"Pleased to meet you," Beau shyly answered and reached out and shook hands with Shoemaker. Maggi was entranced by Babs. Her skin was a perfect white and flawless, beautiful short curly soft black hair framed her perfect face, nose and eyes. But the part Maggi liked best was that she was so warm and friendly to Beau and her.

"Hey, you bum, why don't you ride me on some of your horses?" Bill asked Beau.

Beau reddened. "With all the big stables and horses you have to choose from, I was afraid I would have insulted you to ask you to ride my horses," he replied and everyone laughed.

"Well, ask me any time. I like to ride for a trainer who gets a lot of run out of his horses," Shoemaker continued.

"Okay, I will," Beau agreed.

The little houseboy was hitting the gong. Gong! Gong! Everyone took a place in the line toward the long buffet table. Dinner was being served—with steamed celery, baby carrots, rib eye roast, creamed new potatoes with tiny pearl onions, and aspic salad filled with artichoke hearts, topped off with cherries jubilee and coffee later. The Rices and Shoemakers joined Maggi and Beau at one of the tables.

For once in her life, Maggi listened as Mrs. Rice filled her in on the great Inn. It originally was the exclusive Post and Paddock Club, for members only. Mr. and Mrs. Webber's home burned, so Mrs. Webber converted the clubhouse into their home. It was considered a great honor to be invited to the Inn. Mrs. Webber was very careful in picking her guests. She had two of the finest cooks—Miss Lillian and Mrs. Betty, sisters—who were racehorse fans and loved to bet, and had a good sense of humor.

Mrs. Rice also told Maggi that right after the dinner was over, the staff would quickly clean up, offer coffee and after-dinner liqueurs to those who wanted to stay and play gin, or bridge, or visit. But the main concern of Mrs. Webber was to see that a poker game was set up for a few of her cherished friends who loved playing poker. The stakes were high. Ada said she and Babs were two of the eight who were included in the game. She also told Maggi of the beautiful guest rooms at the Inn, each with its own cedar-lined walk-in closet and huge bathrooms. Each room overlooked the race track. Guests could stay in bed and watch the horses galloping in the early morning training sessions. Maggi's mind was absorbing each detail.

Beau nudged her and whispered, "Hey, you know who Mrs. Rice is?"

"No. . ."

"*She owns Lucky Debonair,* the Kentucky Derby winner last year, and Shoe rode him," he grinned.

"Ohooooo—and to think we're sitting here with all of them! I think Mrs. Rice is the nicest person to make us feel welcome," Maggi replied.

"Well, let's go soon," Beau replied. "I don't want to stay very long."

"Sure," Maggi smiled. She didn't want to push Beau too far.

As soon as the big poker game got underway, only a few of the house guests remained playing cards in sets of four. Beau and Maggi thanked their host and hostess and slipped quietly out the red door.

The next morning at the barn, Maggi heard more scuttlebutt about Mrs. Webber from the other horsemen and trainers and their owners.

"She runs this track." "She caters to the rich only." "She has no use for a loser." "You had better not cross her." "Shoemaker is her fair-haired boy. She think's he's the greatest jockey in the world." "She likes Hartack, too, but he is too independent, and she can't control him," were the stories Maggi heard all morning as soon as the backside had learned that she and Beau had been Mrs. Webber's guests the night before.

Beau remarked later, "I heard she had run off all the big eastern stables with her iron hand . . . That's probably the only reason I ever got stalls here. She needs the horses."

"I'm glad you had a good time last night," Beau told Maggi. "You don't let anything bother you. The people sure liked you — you're so full of bull-shit. I can't talk to people like that," he stated.

"Oh, Beau, you're every bit as good as anyone at that party, and everyone liked you. And I love you." Beau reached and grabbed her hand and held it during the short drive home.

Steve flew in the next day and Beau put him to work galloping horses. It was good to be a family again, Beau mused as he watched Steve working that morning.

Maggi soon found out Mrs. Webber was not only an excellent hostess, but also a demanding person. She insisted they come the next Saturday, and the next. She realized Maggi was a warm, outgoing friendly person. And everyone liked her wit and sense of humor, and Beau's shy modesty was certainly a welcome change. They had become a popular pair at the Inn.

The Bullingtons were invited many times also, but declined due to other functions. Plus, Mrs. Bullington was not overly fond of Mrs. Webber and her dynasty! Mrs. Bullington catered to no one. "With $40 million, who cares?" Maggi thought.

Bullington was the first millionaire that Maggi had ever been on close personal terms with, such as dining out with him and his wife. She often wondered how they lived different from them. What did he do with his time? She could hardly wait, as she and Beau were to meet him in his office this morning on Michigan Avenue for a business talk, and lunch at his private club.

The office was everything she imagined, beautiful wood paneling and desks, thick carpets, rich chairs of selected fabrics and ash trays of the finest. It was the numbered paintings lying on the card tables that caught her eye, she asked, "Who paints?"

"I do," Mr. Bullington answered. "Gives me something to do since I have retired."

"Well you do nice work," she replied as she looked at several he had completed.

During the luxurious lunch she mused to herself, 'I wonder if all the executives on the famous Michigan Avenue are chauffeur driven to their plush offices each day and sit at their desks and paint numbered oil paintings.'

She looked across the table at the man who was worth 40 million dollars. He was just like any one else, he had to keep busy. She marveled at his zest for life.

The Inn functions were like anything new; fun, exciting and an adventure for a while, but soon Maggi began to feel trapped and so did Beau. At long last when the Ruckers arrived, Maggi thought they had an understandable reason to decline the invitation. Not so! Mrs. Webber just included the Ruckers.

After the Ruckers had left, Beau put his foot down. "Look, I don't want to go there every damn Saturday night. I'd like to play cards with our friends, or go to a show, or just stay home! Besides, we don't have anything in common with those people other than the races. Hell, they spend more money in one day than I can make in a year," he ranted.

"Well then, what do you want to do?" Maggi asked.

"Just tell her no, we can't come — won't come!"

"They say she gets mad when she doesn't get her way, and you have to admit she has sure been nice to both of us. She has even tried to steer several new clients toward you, boasting that you're the best trainer on the grounds. But I'll leave it up to you from here on out. I'm not going to fight you every Saturday night over that," she added, and dropped the matter.

Beau was too easy, and Mrs. Webber was a pro when it came to having her way, so the Saturday nights at the Inn continued. But Mrs. Webber went too far with Beau one night when she insisted, "Look, Beau, we have one empty chair at the poker table. Will you sit in?"

"No," was his instant reply. "I am out of my league in that game — with Mrs. Shoemaker, Mr. Marsh, president of the Santa Fe Railroad, and others like that. Hell, I never ever owned an electric train let alone play poker with the head of a railroad," he kidded her. "No way. Sorry."

"Look, you play and I'll pick up the tab," she insisted.

"Uh-Uh," Beau snapped. "Look, I like to row my own canoe. If I can't afford to play, then I won't play," and he turned away and went to the bar.

Mrs. Webber was surprised. She had seen another side of Beau Witlow and she admired him for his honesty!

The last Saturday night of the Arlington Park Meet, Mr.

Webber made a small toast to Beau. "Here's to the best trainer and horseman that I ever saw!" he stated. "If someone had bet me a year ago that Beau Witlow from Arizona would be leading trainer at Arlington Park, they could have broke me. We're glad to have you here, Beau, and we want you to come back next year," he added.

Everyone raised their glasses and toasted him. Beau felt warm and embarrassed. He wanted to get out of the room. He felt that everyone was looking straight at him. He thought, "Where's Maggi?" He wanted to leave!

Maggi beamed as she watched the boyish smile come across Beau's face. She knew he was embarrassed, but pleased at the same time. She liked this shy and endearing quality in him. As she made her way over toward him, she knew he needed her!

Hawthorne Park — Second Time

Tearing down a large stable and putting it up again twenty miles across town is the same as going two thousand miles. It still has to be done. By the time the shipping was over, it was Keeneland yearling sale time. Their fourth time!

Two days later, the *Daily Racing Form* sported in big black print:

BEAU WITLOW BUYS
SIX YEARLINGS
For Jack Bullington and Shoe Tycoon, Samuel Floger—
Spends total of $385,000
for his clients . . .
Picking six yearlings of quality blood lines . . . .

As Maggi put that into the scrapbook, number twenty-seven, she thought, "You've come a long way, Beau Witlow."

Beau had the six yearlings sent direct to a breaking farm in Colorado. "It's cool there and I know the man who does all the breaking, and he is good with colts. By the time we get home in October, they will be broke and ready to come to the track."

Maggi spoke up. "It seems we stay longer every year. Gosh, we will hardly get home and it will be time to leave," she stated.

"Well, they keep adding more dates to these meets back here, that's why," he answered. "Like I told you, we are crazy to go home at all. There is no money to be made at Turf. The only reason we go home is 'cause it's home, and our friends are there," he added.

"Yes, and you and I would freeze to death here in the cold winter," Maggi laughed. "Besides, money isn't everything."

"Well, I'm getting tired of this motel room myself. We'll be going home soon," he told her. "Right now, I have to go over to the barn. Be right back. You go get the *Racing Form* when it comes in at the office."

Maggi picked up a *Form* and tore open the unclipped edges. A small squib caught her eye and she read it with shock!

> CHARLES (Pee Wee) FOY was
> killed by a truck in El Paso, Texas,
> Saturday . . . Well-known jockey
> won the All-American Futurity . . .
> 1954 . . . .

"Oh, no!" she cried out. "How awful!" She read the

358

small block again. She heard Beau open the door.

"Honey, I just read that Pee Wee was killed," she said sadly.

"Yeah, I just heard it, too. His old agent came over to the barn and just told me," Beau answered. "He said he heard Pee Wee was drunk, it was late at night, and he just stepped off the curb and a truck hit him. He was killed instantly."

"Are you going to the funeral?" she asked Beau.

"Hell, no. It will be over by the time I could get there," he stated. "You send some flowers to his Mom and the funeral service," he told her. "There is nothing I can do for him now."

Two weeks later, the Chicago weather changed to snow and cold winds. Chilling mornings made it impossible for trainers to get their horses to and from the race track.

Beau's help threatened to leave! The bleak, gray overcast spread gloom over the factory area, and everyone became depressed.

"Order the cars. We're going home!" Beau told Maggi.

"Hurray, we're finally going home!" she squealed, and put her arms around Rip. "Do you hear that, old boy? Home! Your own trees . . . a yard . . . no more pounding the pavement." She was ecstatic.

"You're nuts!" Beau laughed at her childish ways, but he also loved her for them.

They had a last minute dinner at the Bullingtons' plush high-rise apartment, overlooking Lake Shore Drive and Lake Michigan. Maggi could never get used to this style of living. It was so foreign to her to think that anyone actually lived like this. No land, no yard, just space, elevators, doormen . . . .

"So distilled," she thought.

359

Arizona Downs for the Ninth Time

Home was the place to be for any holidays. Michael and Jill were constant companions. They ate, got smashed, sang till wee hours of the morning, enjoying each other's friendship. They called Robert and Rosie often during the fun nights, and they all shared good times and laughter, and prompted Robert and Rosie to come for short visits.

Maggi wasn't sure where it started, but Beau began to come home late after the races were over. He had begun drinking again. For a while she thought it was because of Pee Wee, so she made no remarks at first. But it got worse. Drinking brought out the worst in Beau, and he snapped at Maggi for no reason, wanting to start an argument just so that he would have an excuse to leave the house. Maggi tried everything, humor, wit, patience, and nothing seemed to work. It was as though the devil had possessed him these days. She didn't know this Beau at all! Even Steve began to question why Beau was never at home when he called.

Maggi was planning a small dinner party at home and was worried that Beau would not show up for it, when Nat Thorndike knocked on the door.

"Oh, am I glad to see you!" she said and hugged him dearly.

"Well, I have been working at Aqueduct, for the *Racing Form*. I thought you knew that," he stated.

"No, I didn't," she answered. "Well, come on in and I'll make some coffee."

Over coffee, she filled Nat in on all their latest news and about Chicago.

"Yes, I had read how well Beau had done," he answered.

"Are you going to work here at Turf this winter?" she asked.

"Yes, they finally got that old man, Murphy, to retire, and I requested the job and got it," he laughed. "Where in the hell is Beau?"

"He should be home soon," she answered, but inside, she knew that she lied! She wasn't sure where Beau was! "Look, I'm having a few friends over. You stay and eat with us."

"That's the best offer I've had, unless I get a better one," he said, making Maggi laugh.

Maggi made a few calls to see where Beau might be but had no luck. She quickly called Michael and Jill and told them that Nat was here. They said they'd be right over!

The dinner was a success, and Beau came home! Maggi was happy with the total evening, and Michael goaded Nat, "Come on, tell us one of your funny stories."

"Oh, my goodness!" Nat laughed. "I didn't know anyone would want to hear about my old hard-luck times," he kidded. "Well . . . okay!

"This one goes back to when I had just quit working as the telegraph operator for the New York Central railway. I got me a job with the *Daily Racing Form* as a chart caller. (A chart caller is one who calls out the positions of each horse during the race, from the 1/4 pole, 1/2 mile pole, 3/8 s, and the finish. These are teletyped to the main office and put in the *Form*. They are called charts or cuts on each horse.)

"Well, I had just finished working at a small bush track in Canada. I didn't have a car, so I decided to ride with Benny Poller, the jockey. Benny had done real good up there, he musta won fifty races. So the day we took off in his worn-out old car, he handed me a thick envelope.

'Here, keep this for me,' he said. 'I might get drunk and spend it or lose it.'

"I knew he had some cash in the envelope, so I just stuck it inside my coat pocket," Nat said.

"We had been traveling for three days, and his old beat-up car just up and died one afternoon between God and no place.

"We sat in that old car for hours, waiting for someone to come along. I finally told little Benny, 'Look, we're not going to run into anyone on this old deserted road. We'd better start walking because it's going to start snowing.' Now Benny had all his clothes, dirty socks, shirts, shorts, piled in the back seat of his car.

"We found an old box inside of an old barn and stuffed all of his things in it and tied it up with some old wire.

"I had an old worn-out coat that someone had given me, and I put it on. It was getting colder than hell. The sleeves were frayed, and one pocket was torn half off, but I didn't care. At least it was warm. Poor little Benny only had a light jacket and four sweaters to keep warm. By the time we got to Chagrin Falls, we were both frozen stiff," Nat laughed.

"The town wasn't much, but Benny found a car dealer. 'I don't have a decent car that would make it all the way to Arizona,' he told us. 'But I will drive you to the next town, where you can catch the train,' he offered. 'But it will cost you $50.'

"I said anything was better than just sitting out in this wilderness and freezing.

"He dropped us off at the little depot building. Benny pulled out fifty bucks, paid him, and that was the last time I ever saw that man.

"The depot was closed. No one was in sight, and it was two a.m., and snowing like hell," Nat continued. The whole group was sitting on the edge of their seats by now, listening intently.

"I looked up on the bulletin board for the train schedules. It showed a train was due in thirty minutes.

"So, we waited, huddled up close to the side of the depot building, knowing that in just a little while, we would be on the warm train, heading for Phoenix.

"I could hear the train whistle far off in the distance. I said to Benny, 'Well, it won't be long now.' We saw the flashing strong light swinging in a circular motion, breaking through the sleeting snow. That damn train came whistling by at ninety miles an hour, and passed the depot . . . and us . . . never even slowing down a slight bit!

"As I watched the red light flashing back and forth from the rear car, I turned and looked down at poor little Benny and asked, 'Benny, how much you got in this here envelope?'

" '$20,000,' he answered.

"I broke out into loud laughter and so did he. Here we were freezing to death; no car, no train, him with that old box of dirty clothes and me and my six suitcases, with twenty grand in my pocket!"

Before he could finish, someone asked, "Well, what happened? How did you get home?"

"Oh, hell, I knew I wasn't going to just sit and stand out there on the dock all night. So, we broke the window, got into the depot, turned up the furnace, and slept on the floor until morning.

"When the telegraph man came in, we paid for the window, bought tickets to Wichita and then home.

"How about another piece of apple pie?" he asked Maggi. "I think I have earned it!" he grinned.

One of the guests who had never met Nat remarked, "Boy, he is funny. I could listen to him tell stories all night!"

Maggi answered, "Yes, he is never without a smart answer. He even makes jokes about his big head — says his mother rolled over on him, or that he was the result of a dry birth.

"He is a true racetracker in every sense of the word. He wouldn't want to do anything else. I think he would work for nothing, if he had to," Maggi added. "I really like him, and he's been good to us."

On December 4, Bullington's colt, Zap, set a new world record of 1.07.2 for 6 1/2 furlongs. It was telegraphed and telephoned all around the world — a day Beau and Maggi would long remember. Mr. Bullington was at the height of his glory over the colt turning out to be a runner.

"That lucky old bastard," Beau remarked to Maggi. "Every year since we have been buying colts at the

Keeneland sale he has come up with a pretty nice horse, better than average. No Kelsos or Buckpassers, but good useful allowance horses. I don't think it's occurred to Bullington what a lucky son-of-a-bitch he is,'' Beau concluded.

Maggi spoke up. "It's not all luck. After all, he has a damn good trainer who picks out those colts in the first place."

"Oh, get off that trainer shit, I don't want to hear it," he retorted.

It threw Maggi every time he reacted this way. He was always so defensive and yet she knew that deep down inside, he had to know he was good!

Maggi wasn't the only one to praise Beau. Other horsemen and his barn help were equally as proud. Near the end of the meet, Maggi had a party for all their grooms to show their appreciation.

"Without you, Beau couldn't have been leading trainer. It's you taking such good care of your horses and your loyalty to Beau that make it possible," she said.

After the evening was over, while Maggi was putting things away, Beau commented, "They really appreciated the party. It was nice of you think of it," he smiled. "I know I'm an ornery bastard at times, but I do love you."

Chicago Again

Maggi was advised that the railway companies were thinking about cutting out runs that were no longer worth their while. And the run from Phoenix to Chicago was one of them.

The railway express office informed her there was no

shot of getting seven cars shipped to Phoenix. "Too costly . . . have to send an extra engine."

She asked Mr. Bullington if he had any clout in Chicago, and clout he had! "They better send seven cars, or I will stop shipping millions of dollars worth of sporting equipment each year," he bellowed. Seven of the best cars in the whole Chicago train yards arrived two weeks earlier than necessary!

Maggi marveled at the clubhouse table, how little Mr. Bullington would actually wager on any horse including his own. He truly was a sportsman not a gambler. As she had watched him this day peel through crisp 100 dollar bills and pull out a 5 or a 10 and say, "I'm going to bet $5 and that's all," and strut off toward the window. . .

* * * *

Just knowing that they were welcomed in Chicago made leaving home a bit easier. Maggi thought that with no more worries about getting enough stalls, a place to live, and things of that sort — all the anxieties should be gone. But the problems of horse racing still prevailed. This time it was the barn help; the grooms didn't want to go back to Chicago. They didn't like the cold weather and living conditions . . . too many blacks on the backside. It took several weeks to be sure of the ones who were going and the ones who were not.

Steve was still at school and wanted to know if he wouldn't have to work that summer. Beau make it clear. "Look, you are not going to just sit around all summer and do nothing. Besides, I can use you back there. Help is hard to find!"

* * * *

When Beau and Maggi got to Arlington Park, Doc Trotter and the crew had the barn completely set up. Maggi appreciated that she didn't have the job to do anymore . . . and she thanked Dr. Trotter for seeing that it got done just before he left on the plane going home.

Beau and Maggi had hardly dozed off into a deep sleep when the phone rang . . . first it was Mr. Bullington, thirty minutes later Mr. Rucker called, then Harry, then Mr. Kelly . . . Each asking the similar question . . . none thinking of the time factor that it was two hours later here in Chicago . . .

* * * *

Zap won three races by August and had boosted his income up to $150,000. He was one of the best horses in Beau's barn. Beau had put together the best stable he ever had, and each horse was paying his way. Winning races daily boosted everyone's morale — the crew's — everyone's!

The Junior Derby

Maggi had not planned on this trip at all! She was delegated to take charge of saddling The Kid at Miles Park in Louisville, Kentucky for the Junior Derby.

Beau sent his groom and exercise boy and Maggi's saddle pony along. He wanted someone around the colt all the time. He was taking no chances of the colt getting sick or cast in the stall, without someone around to pull him away from the wall. He had seen too many horses cripple themselves fighting trying to get up. After all, The Kid had just won the $20,000 Joliet Stakes. He could afford to send two boys down with him.

Maggi took good old Rip along for company. By now he had become a veteran traveler. She was thinking while driving, "I hope Beau had sent enough bottled water for The Kid," (A precaution so that he wouldn't go off his feed and change his habits before the race.) She found everything in order when she got to the barn in Miles Park. She checked the stall to be sure it was bedded deep, and that the sides were banked to prevent the horse from getting cast. She checked the hay net to see that it was tied high enough so The Kid wouldn't get to pawing in it and get a foot into it.

She mused as she checked these things out that no matter how hard you try to avoid accidents, horses still get hurt. These horses are so accident-prone—just a simple nail sticking out can cause a horse to lose an eye.

She made it as pleasant as possible for the two boys to stick around the barn, bringing them snacks and a rented TV.

She picked up a Condition Book that Eddie had given her and read the track rules. At each meet the rules are different. As she read the rules she thought of Beau, and of all the things a trainer has to remember. . . she had no idea! as she read the small print. . .

TRACK RULES

ENTRIES:

Entries close at 8:15 a.m., Scratch time, 7:00 a.m., unless otherwise specified. Jockeys to be named at time of entry, if not then, at time entries are called. Trainers must have an apprentice engaged before claiming the apprentice allowance.

After horses have been registered with the Racing Secretary listing their owners, no horse will be transferred (unless claimed at this meeting) without permission of the Stewards who will require a notarized bill of sale from the registered owner.

CHANGE OF EQUIPMENT

Permission to change equipment must be secured at the time of entry. The Paddock Judge will be on duty at the Racing Secretary's office for this purpose until close of entries each day.

IMPORTANT ADDED RACING OFFICE INFORMATION

No entry shall be received of any horse not stabled on the grounds of the association, unless its stabling elsewhere has been approved by the Horse Racing Board.

The starters for a race shall be determined by lot in the presence of bonafide horsemen and the post positions shall be in order in which they are drawn. The same method shall be employed in determining the starters and post positions in the races that are divided.

In all overnight races with more than eight entries, trainers may declare out to that number by the specified scratch time, such practice to be determined by lot if necessary. Declarations below eight may be made only by permission of the Stewards.

No entry shall be accepted from any stable not properly licensed.

A horse shall be entered in no more than one race on any one racing day, sweepstakes included.

Any horse listed on the "also eligible" that is declared, will receive no preference regardless of any scratches in the race itself, but this horse shall not be considered an "in today" horse.

All owners must be licensed and insured before entries of their horses may be made. If in doubt please check at the office of the Horse Racing Board. Owners already licensed who have made change of trainer are requested to see that the insurance is properly adjusted in view of such change.

Trainers are requested to check and amend their list of all stable help in order that their 1975 license cards may be validated by the Horse Racing Board for admission to the Fair Grounds.

The stewards reserve the right to withdraw or scratch any horse which, in their opinion, will not qualify for the race in which it has been entered.

All horses placed on the Stewards' List, Veterinarians' List or Schooling List, will be posted on the bulletin board outside the Racing Secretary's office and will not be permitted to enter until they have been taken off, and approved to start.

All horses which have never started must have approval from the Starter before entry will be accepted.

No horse which has not raced recently will be permitted to start until satisfactory works have been recorded.

ELIGIBILITY AND ALLOWANCES

Starter races, plater purses, combination races and optional claiming races shall be considered a claiming race of equivalent value.

Back at the motel, she put in a long-distance call to Beau. No answer. She made two more tries and finally dozed off. At five a.m., her phone rang and startled her awake.

She recognized Beau's voice and immediately asked, "Where were you last night?"

"I was here! Where in the hell do you think I was?"

"I tried to call six times—until ten o'clock. There was

never any answer. I let the phone ring for almost a half hour. Nobody could sleep through that!"

"Look, dammit, I was here! Now, shut up. How did the horse ship?"

Maggi brought him up-to-date as quickly as possible and promised to call him when she knew what post positions they had drawn.

"When you work The Kid tomorrow," Beau told her, "be sure and pony him around to the 3/8s pole so he don't run off with the exercise boy."

Maggi assured him she would and hung up the phone. At that moment, she hated Beau and his damn ways. Damn it, she was doing the best she knew. And for him too! She reached over and hugged old Rip . . . she felt so alone.

She quickly dressed and headed for Miles Park. She appreciated no traffic at this hour, especially in a strange town. She regretted that she had made arrangements with the newspaper press. They wanted to do a story on The Kid, as he was the hot invader and also—on her, as the first woman to ever saddle a horse in the Junior Derby! Now she would have to wait until eight o'clock for the photographer before working The Kid that morning.

It had rained during the night, and the track was a deep muddy mess. By the time she and The Kid came back to the barn, it was hardly a glamorous picture. Both of them were covered with mud. Eddie, his groom took the hose to The Kid to wash most of the loose mud off. Then he sponged him off with hot soapy water.

Maggi put her saddle pony away and while waiting for the racing office to open she took a look around the barn area.

She could see Miles Park was very old from the structure of the barns. Wood did not age like that overnight. Even the dark olive green paint had chipped away from the dried-out lumber. A black groom who had been raised near-by told her, "This track was built in the eighteen hundreds." Miles Park reeked with nostalgia. Old magnolia trees stood in front of each barn, showing their age in gnarled, twisted limbs. The more Maggi looked down through the rows of barns, the more she thought of fire! These barns would go up so fast! Everything was in their favor to burn. Dry! High pitched roofs with their attics opened at each end for cool ventilation in the hot, humid climate. She shuddered, thinking of a fire and quickly dismissed it from her mind.

Even the racing office building was of ante-bellum architecture—wood floors, high metal square ceilings. She filled out her trainer's license first. Then she entered The Kid and sat down to wait until they would draw for the race an hour later.

She heard that the Junior Derby was overfilling, and there was talk of having to split the race. All because the leading trainer at Miles Park had six colts that were nominated—and four of them were maidens.

The racing secretary tried to talk him out of keeping those colts in the race as they surely did not have a shot of winning anything. The trainer knew it, but was just being a poor sport. He figured if the race split, he'd get part of it, especially if he should draw in the easy end of the race.

There was lots of bitter talk in the secretary's office, while Maggi and other horsemen waited for the outcome. Maggi listened as one trainer spoke up.

"You know, they had this same problem when Caneraro won the Kentucky Derby. Remember, they ran twenty-seven head in that race," he stated. "They were thinking of splitting the Derby, but they decided it would take all the enchantment from the race. And so, they went ahead and ran it with twenty-seven head."

Another trainer spoke up. "Oh, yes, I remember that, and after the race was over, the officials had a meeting about changing the rules for the next year to avoid that happening again. First they decided that all three-year-olds had to have made a certain amount of money to be eligible. But that made it look like discrimination against other three-year-olds. Plus, it would spoil the nostalgia and the tradition of the Kentucky Derby that started in 1875."

"Only an ass would put a horse in the Kentucky Derby that didn't figure in the race," another trainer kidded. "Same with this stubborn bastard here. He's just spoiling the Junior Derby race for the track and the horsemen if it ends up splitting."

Drawing was delayed until three in the afternoon, in hopes that the trainer would change his mind. No shot! They were splitting the race, and the track had to put up an additional twenty thousand for the other race. It took much of the enchantment out of the race instantly. Just as though there were two Kentucky Derbys. Maggi thought admiringly that Beau would never be like this trainer. Beau would never run a horse in a race he didn't figure in. He wouldn't embarrass himself or his horse just for the sake of running in a particular race.

The Kid drew the number four post position in the easy half of the split. The two tough horses drew in the other. This made The Kid look like a cinch.

Maggi called Beau to tell him the news. He picked up the phone on the first ring. She told him how fast the colt worked. Beau seemed to think it was a good performance in view of the muddy conditions.

"Eddie Burns will fly in tomorrow morning," he told her. "You pick him up, okay?"

"Sure."

He gave her the flight details. She went on to tell him about the press interview. Beau did not seem at all interested in this phase of the conversation, and after a while, Maggi asked him if something were wrong. Before she knew it, they were quarreling about his attitude. He hung up.

She turned and spoke to Rip, "What in the hell is the matter with him, anyway? I've got to be crazy to come down here and take all that shit from him!" she blurted out to the bewildered dog.

In a moment, the phone rang. Maggi answered, "Hello."

"Honey, look, I'm sorry I hung up. Hey, I love you. Its just that you make me so damn mad at times—but I love you."

"I—I love you, sweetheart," she said.

"Good luck tomorrow."

"Bye," Maggi said softly and stared at the phone a long time after hanging up the receiver.

It had begun to rain again . . . harder and harder . . . it was a monsoon outside! Maggi worried about what the condition of the track would be like tomorrow.

On race day she met Eddie Burns at the airport, and took him straight to the jock's room so he could hit the sweat box. She was glad Eddie remembered to bring Rucker's green and gold racing silks with him. She knew how important it was to the owners to see their colors in a race.

Race time. Maggi was invited to the special VIP Room on top of the grandstand. It was very small but impressively decorated. And the handful of people there, she was sure, represented some of the wealth in Louisville. After a beautiful buffet lunch, she began to *stall walk*. She worried about everything possible—would the groom be there on time? Was The Kid okay? And that damn mud! Eddie Burns—would he be afraid and not try to win because of those sharp turns? He was an older jock and had had his share of spills. He was too wise to jeopardize his life for the sake of any race.

She waited in the beautiful little paddock, under the tree that had a big black number 4 nailed to its trunk. Eddie, the groom was leading The Kid toward her. The Kid looked so good, she thought—fit! He was a pretty horse—black and well-proportioned. The valets came from the jocks' room, carrying all their jocks' tack.

Burns' valet stopped by The Kid, laid the tiny saddle on the ground.

Maggi wet her two forefingers with spit, and wet Kid's withers, only because she had seen Beau do this.

The valet threw a clean saddle towel over first, and smoothed it out.

Then came a soft sponge pad.

Then came the numbered 4 saddle cloth.They smoothed it out and folded it in front.

Then the tiny saddle.

Maggi pulled the leather girth up tight!

The valet threw the elastic overgirth over the top of the tiny saddle.

Maggi stretched it out and down under The Kid's belly, ran it through the buckle, and handed the end to the valet. He secured the end. (Overgirth is an extra protection in case the regular girth should break or come loose.)

Maggi checked and pulled the webbing straps from the stirrups, tucked them under the elastic girth, and pulled the stirrups down. She slipped the reins over The Kid's head. The valet secured the number 4 on his bridle. Maggi tightened up his nose band. Then she pulled The Kid's front legs forward from the cinch to ease any pinching.

The jockeys walked into the saddling circle.

Burns knew The Kid, so she had nothing to tell him that he didn't know. "Just try to get out, and make the lead, Beau told me last night," she said.

"Riders up!" the saddling paddock judge commanded.

The Kid shot out the gate like a bullet! He had speed. Lots of speed. The mud wasn't fazing him one bit. He was eating up the five furlongs. At the three-eighths pole, he was fifteen lengths ahead of the field! The only way he could lose now was for Eddie to fall or to fall himself, Maggi thought. But no way was he going to lose this race. He came down the lane, pricking his little pointed ears at the crowd's roar as he crossed the finish line—fifteen lengths the victor!

Two men carried Maggi across the muddy race track for the winner's presentation. She giggled about the whole muddy mess and said, "This reminds me of Sir Walter Raleigh."

Eddie, the groom, was the first to greet her. He was ecstatic, for he loved the little horse as though it were his own. Within seconds, a beautiful blanket of pink baby roses was draped over the puffing Kid's neck, He was puffing hard, his nostrils flared out, showing the pink membranes inside. "The mud made him tired," Eddie Burns remarked. Maggi nodded in agreement.

Utter chaos. Television cameras were busy catching every angle. A television announcer put a mike in front of Maggi's face.

"How does it feel to be the first lady to saddle a Junior Derby winner?"

"Wonderful! I'm so happy he ran so well, with the mud and all. I only wish my husband Beau could have been here, too," she smiled. "And, of course, Eddie, our jockey gave the colt a good ride," she stated, turning around and shaking his hand and encouraging the announcer to talk to him.

"When you have a good horse like The Kid to ride, it makes a jock look good," Burns stated, and the crowd applauded—even though The Kid paid only twenty cents on the dollar.

After a quick champagne toast in the VIP Room, Maggi rushed Eddie Burns to the airport as he had to be at Arlington for the tenth race that day.

She went back to the barn to make sure The Kid pulled up sound. Everything was fine. "Here's twenty bucks, Eddie, go buy yourself a steak dinner. But don't stay too long," she added.

Maggi was very let-down when she couldn't get Beau on the phone. She left word at the desk that she would be in the main dining-room with a couple she had met at the VIP Room. She was glad they invited her to join them for dinner; she didn't want to be alone tonight. She also had a call in to the Ruckers to tell them the good news.

"*Mrs. Witlow, please come to the main desk,*" came the voice over the intercom in the dining room. She hurried, eager to tell Beau everything.

She was disappointed to hear Rucker's voice on the other end of the line. He was very pleased with the good news, but reminded her of the cost of the long-distance call and shortly hung up.

She rejoined her dinner companions. By nine, they left. As Maggi got ready for bed, after letting Rip out for a romp, she was deeply depressed. Beau had not called back.

When Maggi drove into the backside at Arlington Park

the next day, she had the blanket of baby roses draped over the front seat of the car with the big silver trophy beside it. The grooms rushed out to the car as soon as it came to a stop and greeted her with an excited round of congratulations.

Beau walked up to her and she kissed and hugged him hard, telling him of all the fanfare. He interrupted her sharply and told her to calm down.

Maggi bit her lower lip and fell into dead silence as the grooms continued laughing and talking. What had she done? The Kid had won! She'd done everything the way she was told, hadn't she? The thought occurred to her: Could Beau be resentful or jealous of her?

The wind picked up. Maggi felt chilled and walked toward the tack room, continuing to talk with the grooms, describing every detail of the race as she remembered it.

"Eees thees your trophy to keeep?" one of the grooms asked.

"No, Juan," Maggi explained. "It has to go to Mr. Rucker."

Later that night at home, Beau asked, "What in the hell is the matter with you?"

"Nothing, I'm okay," Maggi answered curtly

"Don't give me that, I know you like a book. Hey if I hurt your feelings, I'm sorry about that. I'm really glad you had a good time. I know how much you like all that kind of stuff. You really eat it up. That lucky goddamn Rucker has raised more good colts on that run-down, germ-infested farm and comes up with more runners than anyone. Oh, The Kid's a nice colt, but no Buckpasser either."

Maggi listened without comment. She loved Beau and tried to understand him but at times it was hard. Beau had hurt her deeply and yet, he wasn't even aware of it.

Maggi was hurt, but she wasn't a sulker. She was back into the swim of things the next day. The fun-filled days at the barn and winning races made their work seem less demanding. And the visits and dinners with the Bullingtons and Ruckers and other clients broke up their long weeks of dull racing.

Arlington Park — Year Four

Mrs. Webber came down to their barn one morning and said, "I want the Ruckers to be my guests on their next visit here."

When Maggi told the Ruckers the news, they were very flattered and accepted the invitation.

For the first time, Maggi drove her car up the winding driveway. Parked behind a Rolls, Mr. Rucker unloaded her car and carried their bags to the main door of the Inn and rang.

A housemaid opened the door and showed them to their quarters—a beautiful room done in gold-flocked wallpaper. A bright gold, and the room was enormous for just being a bedroom. Beautiful covered chairs and a card table sat at one end. Two huge double beds were covered with heavy tapestry spreads. Draw curtains to match the spreads would keep the room dark for later sleepers.

As Maggi hung up Mrs. Rucker's coat she gasped at the size of the cedar-lined closet. It was almost as big as her bedroom at home. A two-sink bath adjoined it, tiled in marble with gold appointments. Mrs. Rice had told it right; they were beautiful rooms.

But the best part as far as Maggi was concerned, was that it was right on the race track. She never heard of a house being on the race track.

"Isn't this neat?" she told the Ruckers. "You don't even have to go to the races. Just sit here and watch them from your room. You have to admit this is different!"

The next morning Maggi begged off walking a set of hots long enough to go have coffee with the Ruckers. She wanted to sit and watch the track from the Inn, just once, and she figured this was the only chance she would have. She didn't want to miss it.

"Go on!" Beau laughed. "I don't see what's so great about that." She loped her horse up to the driveway, tied him securly to a post and walked toward the Inn.

The Kid won the race the Ruckers had come to see. It always made Maggi feel good when the owners' horse won when they came for that reason. It didn't always work out like that, but even if the horse was second or third, it was better than running out of the money.

Then came the end of the meet.

"Ladies and gentlemen . . . Your attention, please. The leading trainer of the Arlington Park Meet, Beau Witlow, is being presented a gold watch by managing director, Jack Bloom. Would you give a nice round of applause to Mr. Witlow."

Sportsman's Park—Fourth Year

It was so hot and humid at the Keeneland sale that year that Maggi was glad to get back to Chicago, even to the motel in Cicero and to Sportsman's Park. Beau was pleased with the yearlings he bought for Bullington and Floger. Other than the usual nitty problems of barn help and hot walkers not showing up, life was being good to them . . .UNTIL!

Beau came into the motel room, "Well, I got ruled off this morning," he told Maggi.

"You WHAT?" she gasped, as she turned from doing her bookwork on the desk.

"Yep . . . they found two gallons of DMSO (dimethylsulfoxide) in my tack room."

At first, Maggi started to say, "Why in hell did you keep it in there to begin with," but caught herself in time. "Who found it?" she asked eagerly.

"The state vet," Beau answered. "I know why, 'cause I asked him to take Boom off the vet's list and he wouldn't, just for meanness, so I called him a prick."

"Do you think he did it on purpose?" Maggi asked.

"Yes, I do . . . 'cause everyone else is using it too, so why just me?"

Maggi never did like his using DMSO, mixed with leg brace or straight. It was a wood-treating agent used for a penetrating preservative. It was the belief of all horsemen and some vets that DMSO would make any leg brace penetrate better, but it had its side effects. It was damaging to the kidneys and liver in time, if used excessively. The horses were given additional blood building shots to supplement or to avoid any aftereffects. But Beau was the boss in this case; Maggi wasn't one to push her disbeliefs. You can't knock success. Although Beau had a high regard for Maggi's opinion, that was one of her problems—she was usually right.

Beau turned all of his horses over to a local trainer he believed he could trust. Maggi called Mrs. Webber right away for any help she could give in persuading the racing commission to be easy on Beau. Mrs. Webber went to bat for Beau!

That evening, the Bullingtons invited Beau and Maggi for dinner, specifically to clarify some questions in

Bullington's mind. He said, "I don't want to be involved in crooked racing."

"Oh, everybody's always saying racing's crooked. That's just another myth about racing. Oh sure, you always read all this stuff they use on horses—in the newspapers. There are some sons-of-bitches who think they are trainers and that hop is the only way to make a horse run. Just keep track and you'll see that those kind don't last long.

"I've seen 'em come and go through the years. But I've done nothing wrong, and there is no official ruling about DMSO. Hell, every trainer here has been using it all winter," Beau told him.

"Then why in the hell did they suspend you?" Bullington asked.

"Because the Food and Drug Administration says that DMSO contains a harmful penetration agent. Not so! All trainers mix it with leg brace so that the brace penetrates better. Hell, some people are using it for their arthritis," he added. "Look, if you feel this suspension is going to jeopardize your good name, then maybe you should get another trainer."

"Now, Beau," Bullington countered, "I didn't mean that. I know you're honest and a good trainer. I've never doubted that for a second. I intend to stick by you and wait this thing out," he declared. "But don't let it happen again."

"Don't worry about that," Beau said, with his shy, boyish grin. "I'm not enjoying this embarrassment any more than you, and I'm real sorry it happened."

"Okay, let's forget it now, and go have a real nice dinner," the old man proposed.

Nevertheless, while eating dinner, Bullington brought it

381

up again.

"Listen, Beau," he began, "I don't like the idea of my horses getting stimulants or anything like that. I have a good name, and I just don't like that sort of thing, or this business of getting ruled off. It's embarrassing for me and my wife. . . ''

Maggi saw Beau's face turned red, his teeth clenched, a look she recognized only too well. He was angry!

"Look, Mr. Bullington," Beau said flatly, "I have never given a horse a damn thing but good feed and care. The vet gives them blood-building vitamin shots, once a week. Just like you take. These are modern times. Everyone takes vitamins. I give them to keep the horses' blood count up. Christ, they've been doing it for years. And let me set you straight on one other issue. You can't make a horse run that can't run. There just ain't no hop in the world that *can make a horse win*. All that stuff a few stupid trainers give a horse don't move him up at all. In most cases the horse would win without any junk if only the damn trainer realized it.

"I have been in the racing business for over twenty years, and I could never make a horse win if he wasn't fit and able—by using some damn stimulant," he stated. "Do you believe me now?"

Mr. Bullington was sorry he had brought up the matter and said, "Yes, I believe you. Now, let's forget it."

Beau had his hearing the next day, and he was suspended for eighteen days. He turned his horses over to a trainer friend during that time because he and Maggi were denied the privileges of the grounds until his eighteen days were over.

23

*There is always another chance
...This thing that we call
"Failure" is not the falling
down, but the staying down.*

Mary Pickford

To make the suspension time pass more quickly, Maggi talked Beau into going to New York. They climbed the Statue of Liberty, strolled down Park Avenue, ate in Chinatown, saw the Russian Circus at Madison Square Garden, and visited Radio City Music Hall and the Rockettes. They also rode a horse-drawn carriage through Central Park, saw Broadway shows and had lovely dinners in the Edwardian Room at the Plaza Hotel where they stayed.

On the last morning, Beau went down to settle their bill. When he returned to the room, he tossed a little white box on the bed.

"For you!" he said to Maggi. "For sticking by me."

She tore open the wrapping; a gold lion brooch, with diamond eyes and a ruby nose.

"Oh, Beau!" she said excitedly. "He's beautiful! I think I'll name him Yorky, because we had such a wonderful time here."

The diamonds sparkled from Yorky's eyes each time a light caught them as Maggi looked at Yorky pinned to her coat lying on the chair in the Broadway Limited while it sped toward Chicago late into the night. She heard Beau snoring in the upper berth and soon fell asleep with diamonds in her own eyes.

Beau was reinstated two weeks before shipping time.

"It's been a long summer, hasn't it?" Beau said, as he steered the big Cadillac westward.

"It sure has!" Maggi answered, not taking her eyes off the road toward—HOME!

Turf Paradise for the Fourteenth Time

When the horses arrived by rail, Roy Sanborn, their foreman, told Beau he was moving to California to get married and quit racing. Lonnie, their exercise boy who had been with them for two years, was very capable and able and eager to take over the barn foreman's job. He was a good deal smarter than Roy so Maggi put more and more responsibility on him. It took him a few months to learn how to get along with the help without antagonizing them but in time, the barn ran more smoothly than before.

As soon as everything was unpacked from shipping back to Phoenix and in its place again, the same boring routine set in.

One morning, Maggi was coming back from taking some colts to the gate to be schooled when she saw a horse coming down the stretch, running away with his rider. The boy had blown a pedal (lost a stirrup) and it was impossible for him to get any leverage. He was getting very close to the rail, and suddenly, the horse swerved and threw the exercise boy over his head.

"Let go!"

"Let go of them reins!"

"Let go!"

All the trainers were screaming to him but the boy hung on to the bridle reins, determinded to keep the horse from getting away. The outrider was coming, but he had been on the far side of the track.

The horse whipped the boy under the rail and he hit the

384

goose-necked pole with a terrible jolt, jerking the bridle right off the horse's head.

The boy lay motionless. An ambulance was called and soon left the grounds, screaming its way to the nearest hospital.

"He's a friend of mine, damnit! I sure hope he isn't hurt bad," someone spoke out to Maggi. "That's that damn free lancing (gallop for any stable on a daily basis) for you. All the stables give you the hard-to-gallop horses no one else wants . . . or some outlaw that has crazy habits. A guy is taking his life in his hands, 'cause he never knows, and they damn sure won't tell you," he ranted on. Maggi just looked as he ran off the head. She felt sorry for the boy and knew that what his friend said was true. She remembered when Beau rode many of them himself. An hour later, one of the agents came by Beau's barn with information on the injured boy's condition.

"It don't look good for Bernard. They say he's severed his fourth or fifth vertebra. He could be permanently paralyzed."

"The poor little bastard never really got a shot at being a race rider either, but that's racing," Beau said as he walked to the office.

The incident upset Maggi. She wished she could be more like Beau at times—just turn away and *never look back*.

Santa Anita Revisited

December. Beau announced that he was going to ship Lonnie over to Santa Anita with ten of their better horses.

"Ain't no place to run 'em here," he said.

"Here we go again, splitting the stable," Maggi spat out. "God, how I hate it when we do this!"

385

Beau retaliated angrily, "Every time I have to do something with the horses or the barn, I have to argue with you about it. Goddamn it to hell, either let me run the son-of-a-bitch or run it yourself!"

Maggi knew that when he got this angry, she was better off keeping her mouth shut. And he was right: The better horses wouldn't get to run more than once at Turf Paradise or Arizona Downs. There just weren't that many of that caliber to fill a race. And even if they filled a race, Beau's better horses would have to pack one hundred and twenty-nine pounds or more. She knew they were in this business to make money and win races. Feelings had no part in racing. Nevertheless, splitting a stable was a great hardship on everyone, plus the cost to the trainer of extra phone calls, extra tack, and a certain amount of waste unless you had a good foreman to look after your supplies.

Maggi got busy and set up another payroll horse book for Lonnie, since she would have to rely on him to keep accounts at Santa Anita.They would communicate by phone the Friday before payday. It was her worry to make sure all the tack and little picky things were done. She often wondered if Beau had any idea how many little details went into shipping and splitting the stable? He always just said, "You can take care of everything."

Santa Anita Park race track lies at the foot of San Gabriel Mountains, in the small town of Arcadia, California. It was built in the early thirties in a Spanish style. Age had only made it more picturesque, with the gnarled and twisted branches of its huge old pepper trees spreading out over the beautifully maintained grounds. A full-size bronze statue of the great Seabiscuit stands below the huge grandstand in a bed of assorted flowers. It seemed like a hundred years ago to Maggi since she was here with

King Court.

The barn they gave Beau was the last barn at the far end of the stable area. Ten stalls were all he could get. He told Maggi he was intimidated already. She felt that he was uncomfortable—a reaction she hated to see in him. But Lonnie loved it at Santa Anita.

"Hey, this is first-class racing," he stated. "Everything is so clean and well kept," he said as he pointed at the smooth, wet-down granite roads shaded by the old pepper trees.

"To hell with the damn trees," Beau grumbled. "It's going to take all morning to train. Hell, we're a mile from the goddamn track. But I guess I'm lucky to get stalls," he conceded.

"Oh, they've heard of your good horses—Searcher, The Kid, Driving Range," Maggi said in a joking way.

"What the hell are you talking about? They run horses like them every day here for ten thousand, claiming," he laughed back. "There is so much damn money here, these owners can't spend it fast enough. They think nothing of claiming a horse here for twenty-five thousand every day. That's why I might be able to claim a few good horses for five or six thousand. Six and five thousand are the bottom here, like fifteen hundred is the bottom at Turf Paradise. Sure they have problems like any claiming horse does."

Maggi and Beau drove over each time it was necessary or when Beau was running a horse. Beau still refused to fly. By February, he had claimed six nice, useful horses for five and six thousand apiece. Two could run a route of ground, four ran six or seven furlongs. Beau had them vanned home and turned out. The lay-up was good for them, and by the time he was ready to ship back to Chicago, their thirty days would be up and they would be out of jail.

This was great for Beau and his owners. They got nice,

fresh, good, useful horses. But the racing secretary at Santa Anita didn't like it—an outsider coming in and claiming horses and taking them away from his meet. This caused him a shortage and made for short racing fields. Little did Beau realize the secretary was conspiring a rule that would put an end to this.

Arizona Downs — Tenth Year

By March it was hardly worth Beau's time and money to keep the horses at Santa Anita any longer. There just weren't that many races left in the Condition Book. Beau shipped back to Phoenix.

Before Maggi knew of it, Rucker and Beau went into a horse partnership. Each put in twelve hundred. They bought their first filly for twenty-five hundred. And later they claimed a few more with the winnings the filly made. Maggi told Beau, "It's a good deal, all right, good deal for Rucker. You're sharing all the expenses and you're not getting your trainer's ten percent of all the wins (first, second, third and fourth). You're getting cheated. No wonder he was willing to go partners." she stated.

"Let me run the goddamn barn and shut your damn mouth. I know what I'm doing!" Beau stormed.

Maggi saw no way to make her point with him when he got so angry. He was so stubborn. But what Maggi didn't know was that Beau didn't realize Rucker's advantage until she pointed it out.

How? How could he have overlooked the ten percent? Why was she so damn smart to catch it! Maggi was livid. Rucker could buy and sell them a hundredfold. The ten percent Beau got was the money they could save. The training fee barely paid all the bills and fed them. Rucker knew this, but the more Maggi and Beau got to know him, the more they found he was very tight with his money. It was just the way he ran his small horse farm—poor fences, bad help, the cheapest hay he could buy. Until Beau came along and got onto him, he wasn't feeding his mares and colts a well-balanced diet. Maggi liked Rucker and his wife, they were very kind and often invited Beau and Maggi to their beautiful home for dinner. And Rucker spared no expense when treating his guests to fine wines and food. But when it came to the horses, he cut every corner. And sometimes more than the corner. He was the only owner to complain each time the training fee was raised. And each time Maggi stood her ground with him, not getting any support from Beau.

"Well, we can't stay in business if we don't raise the fee," was always her answer. "I'm sure you wouldn't continue to sell your cars if you were losing money," she told him.

"Well, you can't blame me for trying," was his reply with a grin. He admired Maggi's tenacity—a quality he was very familiar with.

Beau made it loud and clear. "It's too late to bring it up now, and don't you go and say anything to Rucker, do you hear?"

"Yes," she murmured.

Rucker and Beau did make a good team. Everything they bought or claimed made them money. Their twelve hundred dollars parlayed into twenty thousand. Rucker loved his horse business and loved to gamble . . . on a sensible scale. As he stated once, "I don't bet a lot, but when I win, it really makes me feel great! Hell, I usually just spend the money for fun things like eating out. I can't explain it! I've made a thousand on a car deal many times, think nothing of it . . . but if I win a thousand at the races, it seems like ten.''

Maggi knew he wasn't a gambler in the true sense of the word. He wouldn't bet his last dime, and he did enjoy watching his horses win and the sportsmanship of it all. He wanted good horses—the kind everyone else on the race track dreams of. And the best way to get a shot at having a good race horse is to buy the best-bred yearlings you can afford, as Bullington and Floger did every year at the Keeneland sale.

But Rucker wouldn't spend that kind of inflated money. The Kentucky-bred colts were inflated, there was no doubt about that. But the supply and demand caused that situation.

The California Thoroughbred Breeders Association sale at Pomona was more Rucker's style. It fit his pocketbook better. The California sale was to be held at the end of March. Rucker didn't want to take the time to drive over. He approached Beau to fly.

"Nope," Beau said, "No way."

"You're being silly," Rucker argued back. "Flying is the safest way to travel."

Maggi listened, she was very much for Beau flying—and for putting an end to the countless hours they spent driving to Keeneland each year, back and forth to California, to Ohio, everywhere! She knew she couldn't say a word. Beau wouldn't fly if he thought it was her idea. She continued to listen, hoping Rucker could persuade him. Rucker was a car salesman. He hadn't spent thirty years at it not to have learned something about people. He had a way with Beau, a good way, and Beau began to weaken.

"Okay, I'll fly, but I'll have to have a couple of drinks before," he kidded Rucker and winked at Maggi.

* * * *

Beau (Lindy) Witlow returned by plane with Rucker, after spending ten thousand dollars for two yearlings. For an hour, Maggi listened to Beau as he enthused, "There was nothing to it. These new jets fly smooth as glass," he explained. "And the airplane stewardesses aren't bad either," he said, grinning and winking at Rucker.

"Oh, oh, there won't be any more of that, 'cause I'll be going the next time, Mr. Lindy!" Maggi snapped.

As soon as the California yearlings arrived, Beau started breaking them. He had much to do, and it was already April. Three weeks to get sixty head of horses ready to ship. Everyone was hopping to it those lazy spring afternoons. Grooms were clipping one, two or three horses every day, getting all of them shod.

Beau didn't like the way the horseshoers shod horses back East. So he tried to have all his horses shod with new shoes before he shipped out. Nick Dowell at Turf Paradise was the best plater (horseshoer) in the world, as far as Beau was concerned. Nick could keep a horse from hitting (scalping the inside of his hind legs with his own feet) or correct a heel so that it took pressure off a sore ankle. And he was fast! He could skim around the four feet of a thoroughbred racehorse and make it look easy, plus do a good job.

Nick was shoeing Maggi's pony one afternoon when he asked her, "Hey, isn't that Bernard?"

"Yes," Maggi told him. "You know, he's paralyzed from the waist down."

"I heard that," Nick answered, tacking the last shoe on her pony. "Wonder what in the hell he'll do for a living now?"

391

"I guess insurance compensation," she added, as she watched Bernard struggle with the wheel chair in the heavy-going dirt. Her eyes filled with tears, as she recalled the story Nat had written about Bernard.

> A Life-Long Dream
> To Be a Jockey
> Snuffed Out in One Minute . . .

When Maggi began to line up shipping arrangements, she was told this would be the last year for the train. The runs were to be canceled.

"Too slow, everybody is flying now," the dispatcher told her.

She knew this would be a problem coming home in the fall. What would they do? She would worry about that when the time came.

Arlington — Hawthorne — Sportsman's Park

Arlington Park was the first meet, Hawthorne next, then Sportsman's Park.

Mrs. Webber had begun a twenty-million-dollar hotel during the winter. It was almost finished when Beau and Maggi arrived. As Mr. Webber told them, "It's a good thing it's nearly done — she just about ran out of contractors." She was so intent on getting the hotel opened, hardly anyone saw much of her during the meet.

But the meet went on. And it was a good meet for Beau and his clients. Until it started to rain . . . and rain . . . and rain . . . for fourteen days! The small creek that ran through the barn area could not handle the runoff. During the eighth race, the water rose to two feet in the saddling paddock and grandstand. It was raining so hard, the horses were saddled under the huge tunnel that led through the grandstand onto the race track. Everyone was sure the race would be called off, but they didn't know Mrs. Webber; not the feature race! In spite of the downpour she managed to persuade the jockeys to ride.

"Hell," everyone commented, "they're afraid *not* to, for fear she wouldn't let them come back next year."

The track was sloppy, sloppy, but not deep. It was raining so hard Maggi could barely see the horses running down the backstretch. The wind swirled sheets of rain in every possible direction as the horses passed the finish line.

"Those poor jocks! They're earning every dime they make today," Maggi told Beau.

"She's crazy to run this race in this weather," he added. "Come on, let's go. They called off the last two races."

When they got down to the main floor, water was rushing through the grandstand. Maggi pulled off her shoes and hose and hiked up her skirt. Beau did the same and rolled up his pant legs, and they headed for their car. It was on dry land.

"Boy, we are lucky it's up here," Beau remarked.

As they drove toward their barn, they saw hundreds of cars in the low end of the huge parking lot under four feet of water where the lot ran parallel to the creek. In some cases only the car radio antennas were showing.

"Christ, I bet our barn is flooded," Beau worried, and water *was* running a foot deep through the shedrow in and out of their stalls. Every bit of bedding was wet.

"Jesus, what a mess!" Beau yelled. "Hey, you guys, bring shovels and make a bank to turn the water away from the barn. Come on!"

Maggi started to get out of the car. "Stay there, damn it, you'll spoil your dress," Beau commanded.

He and the crew worked like mad until they had a small

berm built in front of the barn, and it turned the water away. The water inside was going down already.

Robert's old agent came by and remarked, "If you think this is bad, you should see Millionaire Row! The water is already up to the horses' withers. Kelly is moving all of his horses over to Washington Park. He's already sent one van out. It'll be a week before the water stops running through his barn, right by the creek."

"Oh, no!" Maggi exclaimed, and he left to tell Beau, who was running a hose through the drainage pipe to flush out the clogged straw and mud. The water flowed through freely and began to recede in the stalls.

"As soon as the water goes down, throw out all the wet bedding and put three new bales in every stall or we'll have a barnful of sick horses," Beau ordered.

Beau told the crew that he would be back later and waded back to the car. He drove over to the Millionaire Row barns. The huge two-ton metal manure bins were floating around everywhere like tiny barges. The angry, muddy water swirled at the tops of the stall doors and then out again, carrying straw, leaves, twigs with it. Some straw clung to the horses' backs as they nickered in fear, churning about in the deep water.

A trainer walked up to their car and said disgustedly, "Ain't this the biggest damn mess! I have three colts in there, and I just fired their shins. Don't you know the goddamn legs will be blown up with infection from all this mud!" He laughed ironically and then added "You know, I came here for years and always envied the stables on Millionaire Row. I thought if I could ever get stabled here I'd really be somebody. Well, this year I finally made it!" He started to shake his head, and slowly walked off toward an approaching van that had come to pick up another load of his horses.

"I guess we're lucky, Beau," Maggi said. "Look over there, those two cars are ruined." The cars were totally submerged. More than half of the barns close to the creek were flooded. All the horses had to be taken out and stabled over at Balmoral, Crete, Illinois. It would be weeks before the creek would subside. The flood was caused by one of man's great engineering feats — by putting in a freeway and cloverleaf, the engineers made a natural dam behind the stables area. It would take weeks for all that water to run through the flumes, down the creek, through the barn area, and out toward the rivers.

Sunday morning. It stopped raining, giving the Webbers time to get the plant cleaned up. Two trucks with cable winches pulled cars out of the deep water all day long, letting them drain on the high hill by the Inn. Beau's barn was a mess. The grooms had all their bedding and tack strung everywhere to dry out. Stalls were still muddy and more new straw had to be put down. So much to do, Beau walked all the horses in the morning. Maggi hosed out the muddy tack room. It was late in the afternoon before everything dried out and was put back. Maggi had tons of coolers and bandages to take to the Laundromat. It was after eight p.m. before the barn looked normal and orderly. Maggi came back with several buckets of Kentucky Fried Chicken and a case of beer. They all sat inside the tack room and talked of the flood, as they heard heavy equipment in the background still working to restore some control over the flooding stream.

Monday, despite the mud and the creek running full tilt, racing continued. The backside talk was, "Mrs. Webber wasn't about to let a little rain stop the races, even if she had to lead the horses up herself in a row boat." It was a mess! Hardly anyone wanted to run the last few days. So no one was a threat to Beau's training standings and he won the honors easily. When the meet closed, everyone was eager to get out of Arlington Park and move over to Hawthorne Park . . . and dry land!

Maggi counted the days till that meet was over. She ordered the horse cars. It was then that she was notified that this would be the last time they could ship by railway express — Bullington or no Bullington!

Arizona Downs — Eleventh Year

Fall, winter, spring, Arlington Park . . . Hawthorne . . . Sportsman's Park — horses and racing were their way of life.

"Did you have a good summer?"

"How many races did you win?"

"Heard about Zap?"

"Hey, Rucker has a nice colt, The Kid."

"How's Driving Range?"

"Heard you won the big one back East!"

The same old chatter at the start of a new meet. But a new feature had been introduced this winter — a mechanical hot walker — creating a great deal of controversial discussion among the hard-heads.

The hot walker machine was contrived of a simple turning gear made from a rear axle box of a car, with a metal pipe welded into it, and four metal extending arms attached. Tie ropes extended from the arms . . . with swivel snaps attached to secure the horses to the ropes. The entire contraption was powered by a small washing machine motor, making it turn to the left slowly in a small circle.

The hot walker

The horsemen were not ready for this yet. As they watched it being used, they commented:

"Give me a good hot walker any day."

"Hell, a horse can get hurt on this thing."

"Fifteen hundred dollars — for that?"

"The damn thing's too bulky to move and haul around."

"Where in the hell are you going to put it?"

There were four of them installed on the grounds already. Several horses had managed to break loose from them, which didn't help the sales of the new machine.

On the other hand, a trainer who had bought one reported prophetically: "Maybe they're not foolproof — but one thing's for sure. That damn machine will be there in the morning. That's still better than being short a hot walker all the time."

397

A good point, Maggi thought, since she was the one who had to be there every morning. Beau was against them and stated, "Hell, there's always someone coming up with a gimmick. They won't last."

"Beau, aren't there more women on the backside this winter?" Maggi asked, noting another change at the track.

"Yep. The good old grooms have died off, and the few good ones left are in New York or California — where the money is. That opens up a job for the gals who like being around horses. They're making damn good grooms and they're hard workers."

"Like me?" Maggi asked coyly, fishing for a compliment.

"Yeah, like you," Beau said. "Anybody who likes horses makes good barn help. These small purses have a lot to do with it, too. That's why wives're helping out now, because good help is getting hard to find."

Maggi went to the track the next morning. "Help, my foot!" she thought. The wives were doing all the work while their husbands just rode their fat saddle horses back and forth to the race track, kibitzing with other trainers, jocks and jockettes. The wives were doing it all, she noticed — the leg work, cleaning up, serving coffee, running and fetching whenever they heard the husband command:

"Get me the shank!"

"Go get me the clippers!"

"I need the scraper!"

Maggi thought that morning about another new matter the track had approved. Girl jockeys and exercise girls were now allowed to hold licenses. She wondered if that wasn't the real reason the wives were coming out in the mornings. And rightly so, she thought, for the girls were pretty, capable, and well-built.

Turf Paradise — Fifteenth Year

About the first of February, Harry Obrien came to Beau
to train some horses for him. Beau brought him to their
home for breakfast. Harry was a handsome man, gray-
haired, tall, and with nice features, and dressed in the
finest of threads. He spoke of his wife Hilly and was eager
for Beau and Maggi to meet her. Maggi liked him
instantly.

Harry told Beau, "I'd like to claim three or four more
horses, for five thousand or so. I have always done well in
the past."

Beau knew Harry understood racing and would be no
problem. He would let Beau run his horses where they
belonged—a factor that Beau almost insisted upon.

They met Hilly the next day, and the four of them, and
Michael and Jill, became very close friends before the Turf
Paradise meet was over.

Maggi liked Harry and soon found out he had a thing
for new cars and homes. In just the short while they had
started to train for him he had built three homes, moved in
and out of each of them and was about to take house
number four. Plus he had just traded in car number four
for a new Cad . . . Seems he didn't like the color of the last
Lincoln Mark IV . . .

Chicago Again

April . . . came far too fast for Maggi. She hardly had
her pantry stocked when it was time to cut back. Shipping
by rail was out. Beau and Maggi argued and discussed the
shipping problem for weeks.

"Let's fly them like the big stables do every year when they come back to Chicago," Maggi suggested.

"That costs too much money," Beau answered.

"Well, I'm going to call Charlie Wittingham and see just how much," Maggi said.

Twenty thousand dollars to fly thirty-nine head to Chicago on a DC8 (often called a stretch eight), one of the fastest commercial planes in the air. Maggi fought Beau on all the advantages she heard from Wittingham.

"He said it's so easy on them you can run them the next day," she told Beau. "Three-and-a-half hours from Phoenix to Chicago. That's saving a lot of wear-and-tear on everyone."

After three more days of talking it out, Beau made his decision. "Okay, I'll fly the thirty-nine best horses and van the other twenty-seven head."

The wheels were set in motion. While Beau trained and ran the stable, Maggi took charge of shipping. By that time she had it all down pat. She made a list of each owner, his address, and his horses — Xeroxed it and gave one to the vet, Dr. Trotter, one to the van drivers, and one for herself, and one for the Murty Brothers' foreman who took care of all the flying arrangements. Murty Brothers handled it from there as soon as Beau gave them the date: April fifteenth, loading time eleven p.m.

To Maggi's surprise, the Murty Brothers took care of ordering the vans, a service included in the plane price. She was grateful for one less job to do. Two grooms were sent on three days ahead to get the stalls ready at Arlington Park. Other grooms would fly with the thirty-nine head. The twenty-seven head and the other grooms would go by van after the Turf Paradise meet was over.

The plane flew in early the next morning. All the tack was hauled down and packed into the belly compartment of the huge plane. Lonnie and the crew worked all day getting it done.

"My God, every year we have more and more tack," Beau spieled when another truck load left for the airport.

The Murty foreman worked loyally setting up the portable partitions in the long hulk of the cargo plane. He told Maggi, "You know, we have to do this two and three times a week. You see, the FAA stipulates we have to pull these panels out after each flight and wash down the plane inside before the urine has a chance to eat into the wiring and so forth."

"You have to take out everything . . . the floor mat, too?" Maggi asked.

"Everything," he stated. "That's for safety precautions. Besides, we never know if we'll get the same plane each time."

Maggi watched the foreman. He knew what he was doing, she thought, as he directed his crew of three men about the plane, carefully bolting down each partition.

"This has been a lot of work, shipping from Phoenix," he told Maggi. "I even had to haul in our loading ramp from California because Phoenix Cargo here doesn't have one. They said they never have shipped a horse out of here before." Maggi just shook her head.

Doctor Trotter informed Beau, "I will not fly with the horses." It wasn't necessary for that short time, anyway, but Beau and Maggi had to laugh at Doc's earnest protest.

Shipping by air was a little different from shipping by rail or vans. All the procedures were much the same except the time factor, plus the plane would not leave until Beau was ready.

Flying was old-hat to the Murty dispatcher, but not to Maggi and Beau. They were worried how the horses would react and load. So was Doctor Trotter. He wasn't sure, so he had two of his colleagues come down, just in case.

They were all amazed at how coolly the horses loaded. Each quietly walked up the narrow steep loading ramp, turned into the long tube of the DC8 and walked down to its place. Even the ones that were on the sides didn't seem to mind as their ears brushed the top and sides of the curved panel. They stood very still as each panel was shut from behind and bolted tight — each horse in his own little crate. Beau had the grooms stand in front of each section. Three abreast was all the plane could allow.

Nat, Michael, Harry, Hilly, Rucker, everyone came to the airport to watch the loading. Finally, the last horse was backed into the tail end of the plane and secured in. As Beau, Maggi, and Doctor Trotter looked down that long slender hulk of airplane, it looked more like three hundred head of horses than thirty-nine. The tension for everyone worrying about the loading was over. The plane was almost ready to take off. Last minute things were being done. Box lunches were furnished by Murty, even an overlooked goat was lifted up by a giant lift platform with several grooms. The Murty dispatcher checked: Nothing loose could be aboard the plane, no buckets, no forks. Everything had to be put into the cargo compartments below.

The steep loading ramp was pulled away, the air-conditioner was turned on, their crew waved good-bye, the two huge hatch doors were lowered shut. Michael and Beau were the last to climb down the ladder by the cockpit. The powerful jet engines whined, then started up into a roar, causing wind currents and blowing everything in its path upward into the black night air.

Everyone felt so small as the long plane taxied down to the runway. R-o-oooarrr — as it took off over their heads, lifting upward and turning its silver wings toward the east. Not until only a tiny speck faded from sight did anyone move. In twenty minutes, van, vets, cars, people — and Beau and Maggi were gone. The airport was dark.

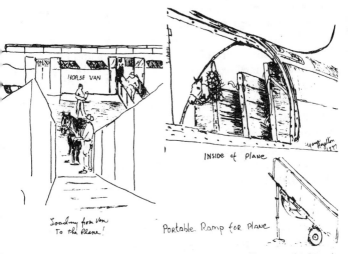

HORSE VAN

INSIDE of plane

Loading from Van To the Plane!

Portable Ramp for plane

By the time they all had a bite to eat and Beau and Maggi were home in their bed, the phone rang. It was seven a.m. It was Lonnie. "Well, we made it okay and the horses are all bedded down in their stalls here at Arlington Park," he laughed aloud. "Ain't that something? Three-and-a-half hours beats the train all to hell."

"Thanks for calling," Beau said. "See you in two days."

Since Beau would fly, he and Maggi decided to fly to save time. Beau trusted Lonnie, but he still liked to check on his horses himself. Maggi had had one of the exercise boys leave two days before to drive their car back. She got a crate for Rip. Steve had called from college to say he had a job at a resort hotel for the summer and would see them in August. The only worry Maggi still had was about Rip, being in the crate and locked in the dark cargo hold of the plane.

Lonnie had the barn in top shape when they arrived. He had a local vet check all the horses, making sure none had a temperature or was coming down sick. It was bitter cold still.

"The horses seem to thrive on it, kicking and bucking in their stalls, Hell, they don't even know they've been moved," Beau laughed.

Lonnie flew back to Phoenix to take care of the balance of their stable and to come back with those horses on the vans in two weeks.

Arlington Park Meet for the Sixth Time

Harry had just moved into home number seven, beautifully decorated and furnished. "This is the last move we'll make," he stated.

"For about a year," Maggi grinned.

Beau had entered seven head. They all finished in the money: three wins, second, third, second, second.

That night, Beau and Maggi were the last to arrive at the Inn. The houseboy Jose had their drinks almost before they had a chance to say hello to anyone. Maggi winked at Beau on the treatment they were getting.

"P-ssst!" It was Mr. Webber motioning them to come to the kitchen. As they entered the huge, stainless-steel, restaurant-type kitchen, they saw a keg set in a tub of ice.

"Look at this, will you?" Mr. Webber laughed a jovial chuckle. "One of Maizie's friends had this sent to her, she is so crazy about caviar."

Maggi could not believe it—a whole keg of Russian caviar!

"They flew it in today," Mr. Webber added. "Here—try some," as he pulled back the wet sack covering the black eggs, and dipped a spoon into the black mass.

"Not for me!" Beau rebelled. "I don't like it."

"I do," Maggi said, "I love it!" As she nibbled the spoon of caviar, she asked, "Where is Maizie?"

"Hell, you know where she is—at the damn hotel," he grinned. "That's all she does from morning to night. She's obsessed with that place, but she should be here soon."

As they walked back to the recreation room, Maggi stopped. "Oh, Beau, look! It's Jimmy Durante and Desi Arnaz over there."

She was delighted when Mr. Webber introduced them to her and Beau. She loved Durante. He was nice to comment on Beau's ability as a horseman. She thought Desi Arnaz was much better looking than he appeared on television.

After the wonderful dinner of fried soft-shell crab, rice, steamed celery, Lillian's delicious lace cookies and home-made ice cream was over, Maggi caught Beau's eye. It was time for them to leave. Since Maizie Webber had disappeared as soon as dinner was over, they said their thanks to Mr. Webber and left as they heard the poker chips rattling.

Between racing six day a week, the Webbers, and the Bullingtons, Beau and Maggi had very little leisure time. Maggi enjoyed their evenings at the Bullingtons' luxurious apartment in the Lake Point Towers on the Gold Coast strip. Nothing was spared. Everywhere she looked was pure money—paintings, ivory carvings, antiques. The Bullingtons had the entire sixty-fourth floor, overlooking all of Chicago and Lake Michigan.

And to cap off the evenings, Mr. Bullington always sent his chauffeur to pick them up and bring them home, because Beau would always say, "I don't want to drive through all that traffic."

*   *   *   *

Just when life seemed to take a good turn for Maggi and Beau, Beau again fell into his old habits of coming in late.

"If you don't stop this, and the drinking and worrying me sick, you're going to lose your good clients," Maggi burst out at him. "They keep calling wanting to talk to you about how their horses are doing. After all, you owe them that, to keep them informed what is going on. That's part of the business. After all they are paying the bills."

"Fuck the clients," was his drunken answer. "They don't own me—and neither do you.

"They don't know what the hell they are talking about when they call. All they want you to do is run their horse on a certain day because their friends are coming to the races that day and they want to see the horse run. Don't matter how many times you try to explain to them that you point toward certain races that fit each horse, and he is eligible for. I can't believe people who are so rich and supposed to be so smart in the business world, can be so dumb about racing."

The fights continued and grew worse when Robert and Rosie shipped in, planning to stay the balance of the meet. Robert was just another excuse for Beau to drift off. Maggi could hardly stand Robert, and now she found him actually stupid and silly. Beau was as bad—they were like a Laurel and Hardy movie over and over.

The more Maggi fought Beau about Robert, the more he went to his defense. She was making heself sick over the matter. After the four of them had been together, Beau would always have a few cutting remarks.

"You don't see Rosie making a big damn fuss over Robert drinking, do you?"

"Well, why should she?" Maggi snapped. "You're picking up the tab, and Robert doesn't make an ass of himself the way you do. Rosie's conning you so that Robert can ride your horses. For that matter, he's conning you as much as she is, and you're just too damn stupid to see it!"

Nevertheless, the four of them did spend many fun evenings together. After all, they had all started out with no money back in Detroit, and reminiscing about those days brought back many memories and rounds of laughter when they remembered the things they had been forced to endure.

Sportsman's Park for the Sixth Year

Shipping time around the track, even across town, brought the worst out in everyone! Beau, Maggi, and the grooms were all affected.

Maggi had her hands full with paper work and setting up the tack room. Beau had his hands full putting certain horses with certain grooms . . . and when he had to listen to all the other inevitable complaints, his temper became short.

"I want that tack room!"

"No! I have dibs on it! I put my bedroll in it, so it's mine!"

"Hey, Beau! I don't know why he should have first choice over the tack rooms . . . "

"Okay, you guys—knock it off, all of you! What the

407

fuck do you care where you stay as long as you have a place. Now come on, and cut out this goddamn arguing and get this tack put up!''

The grumbling continued.

"Hey! Where's my rake?''

"Who got my good brushes?''

"Beau! Someone stole my suitcase!''

"Hey! Who stole my good shank out of my tackbox?''

"Beau! I want to put my icebox in *that* tack room, but Manuel said I couldn't 'cause his bed wouldn't fit with it!''

"Beau, Juan broke the leg on my table on purpose! He just jerked it off the van! He better buy me a new one!''

"Beau! Phillipe got mad and quit. Got on the van and left. Said it's too cold for him here!''

"Hey! Who took my good pitchfork, the one with the 'J' carved on it? I'd know it anywhere. I've had it for three years now and can't work without it. Beau!''

"Beau! You said I could rub that horse, and Juan says you're gonna give it to him . . .''

"Hey! I told you guys to knock it off!'' Beau yelled, but he mused, 'They are okay,' he knew they had been working hard and steadily. In spite of their bitching, their horses always came first, to be bedded down and watered without wasting any time.

Robert hated Sportsman's Park. He was never relaxed at that track. Maggi never could understand why, because he did so well there. Rosie wasn't crazy about the place either, but she would put up with anything for the love of money—as long as she had her eye shadow and eye liner along, Maggi surmised.

Robert hit a riding slump, wasn't getting many mounts and was making it hell for everyone around him. He drove Beau crazy with continuous threats of leaving.

408

Maggi could hardly tolerate his childish drinking antics. Always the clown, she thought. She knew Robert would pack up his tack as soon as Beau's stable dwindled down to a precious few.

Despite all the years Robert still was not predictable or dependable when it came to being at the barn in the early morning. It was on one of those mornings, as cold and gloomy as only Chicago weather can be, that Robert didn't show up.

Beau was furious! He wanted to work Driving Range 3/8s for a little sharpening up before the big race Saturday. Out of rage, he grabbed the first jockey who came by, and put him on the horse, and went to the race track with him. Driving Range was a tough horse to pull up and Beau warned the jockey, "I'll pick you up so don't try to pull him 'cause he gets to swinging back and forth." But the jockey didn't wait for Beau to ride up to the horse as he pulled him up. Driving Range began to swing back and forth, weaving until Beau finally rode up to the horse's side and grabbed the bridle and eased the horse to a slow jog.

"Goddamn it, why didn't you wait till I grabbed him?" he snapped at the rider.

"I didn't think you'd get there."

"Oh, the fuck you did!" Beau snapped again, "Well you fixed the son-of-a-bitch for the race!" he barked—as he looked down at the horse's left front foot. "He has grabbed his quarter."

Beau got the vet who gave Driving Range a tetanus shot and said, "That's all I can do till you get the shoer to cut off all that part of the quarter and part of his hoof. Then I will bandage it," he added. "Let me know when the shoer will be here."

Beau turned to Maggi. "Go find Sam and tell him to get

409

here soon as he can.''

After the hoof was cut away, the vet cleaned the area with disinfectant and bandaged the hoof.

"That goddamn lazy little Robert," Beau burst out, "I should have my head examined for messing with him! We can just forget the $50,000 race Saturday . . . that was our only chance of making anything the rest of this meet," he told Maggi in disgust.

Late October. The dismal Turf motel and Cicero surroundings didn't help the depressed mood that hung over Beau and Maggi.

Robert and Rosie had shipped out without saying a word. They just left during the night. But this wasn't anything new with Robert, so Beau and Maggi were not too upset. If anything, they were glad for their peace of mind.

Sundays in the motel were the worst. Thank God for the Bullingtons' hospitality, and for movies, Maggi thought. Beau was compelled to stick around till the last of the Sportsman's Park Meet. There were some races in the book for the few horses he had left. But during the waiting period, he was lucky to run a horse one or two days a week. These were dull, boring days at the races for him and for Maggi.

Beau mostly just sat and scanned the *Racing Form* for any exciting news . . . or a possible horse to claim. But it was late and all the good horses had been picked over. Nothing but bums were left this late in the meet, he mused.

Maggi couldn't sit through the long afternoons like that. She was too restless. She walked the grandstand over and over. . . studying the tote board. Often she bought herself a soft ice cream cone and brought one to Beau—anything to pass the time. She often thought, "It's like being in prison. You can't leave, yet there is nothing to do—just sitting and waiting for a race."

From one of her trips around the grandstand, she came back to the box where Beau was sitting, handed him a cone, and said, "Hey, I just heard of a good horse you might want to claim. Everyone in the grandstand talks about him after every race."

"What horse is that?" Beau turned and asked.

"That Mother Fucker!" she laughed glibly.

"You smart-ass!" Beau said with a laugh.

"Well, it's true. After every race, in the clubhouse or downstairs, everyone keeps saying that 'If it weren't for that Mother Fucker, I could have won' . . . or 'They won't beat that Mother Fucker today!' " she laughed.

24

Harry was building his tenth home, it was perfection in every way. "We went for broke this time, the last one," he stated.

"Are you trying to convince me or yourself?" was Maggi's answer.

The last four years had passed so fast and with little change except that Beau had won his share of the larger races—$50,000 and $100,000. Even the small futurities had grown into big purses and were getting bigger each year. Horses were in greater demand than ever, and the prices soared at the Keeneland sales, getting more ridiculous each year. One yearling colt out of a top mare by Buckpasser sold for $500,000 to a Japanese conglomerate. Racing was on a fast-changing trend these days! Training fees were up to $23 a day.

Harry cut back his stable and Rucker made sure that most of his horses were in partnership with Beau. Everyone was feeling the change. Grooms demanded $175 a week. Exercise boys that were tops got $200 easy. Hay and grain prices also increased.

As more tracks opened and more dates were allotted, demand increased for more and better horses. No longer did a trainer take the time to turn out a horse and give him a rest. Everyone was too greedy, so many horses broke down. Horses were a commodity, something to turn over and make money.

Many good owners were getting shafted by the Johnny come lately trainers. They talk a good line but when it comes to the training and taking care of their horses they cut every corner possible. Not bedding the horses well and feeding them the cheapest hay and grain. And not training them daily so that they were properly fit for a race, causing horses to break down. They only lasted as long as the owner could afford to pay, but it seems there is another one born every minute . . . as Barnum and Bailey stated years ago.

Maggi was surprised that more and more trainers were being given licenses, who didn't know a damn thing about a horse, let alone a race horse. It was sickening to her to see such people filtering into the racing business. And how they took care of their horses, because the cost of having a horse in training now was costly:

30 days in training	$23 per day	$690.00
Shoeing		29.00
Vet		50.00
Plus 10% of wins		

She began to figure in her head that it cost an owner close to $900.00 or more for a month per horse to keep him in training . . . it was a rich man's sport! she mused. Not possible for a small man to last.

* * * *

At the start of the seventies, Maggi was amazed at their monthly overhead:

413

```
Hay and grain ......................... $10,000
Payroll .............................. $25,000
Tack and Supplies..................... $2,500
Phone ................................ $600
```

It seemed to her that they had more money left a few years before than they did now after paying all the nut. If it weren't for Beau's ten percent and what his own horses made, they wouldn't be able to save much. She wondered how the smaller stables made it.

Turf Paradise — Sixteenth Season

There was more than expenses on Maggi's mind these days, and her thoughts drifted off to those problems. Beau was drinking again. He came home late too often! Maggi felt so left out and alone and tried desperately not to let herself drop into despair. Beau had changed. He wasn't easy to get along with. His temper was short. And he hated his commitments to his owners—having to phone them to let them know if and when their horses were running and where the horses finished in the races. Maggi and he fought bitterly over these encounters, with Beau grabbing his hat each time and rushing for the door.

* * * *

By fall Harry showed up in a Rolls Royce, his twentieth car since he joined the Witlow stable . . .

Things were smoother at the holidays and their Christmas together was the best one ever. Maggi spent whatever she wanted to on gifts for her family and friends.

For the first time, Christmas shopping was fun, and the holiday season sparkled with festive parties, good times, and special racing events.

By January, regular hot walkers had become unreliable, and Maggi had so much to do, she wanted to quit walking hots. Beau was forced to use the hot walking machines like everyone else. Then another problem came up. The leather halters couldn't stand the strain and pull from the horses. The tack repair man was kept busy trying to keep them sewed up. Then a nylon halter was invented especially for use on the hot-walker machines, and it quickly replaced the old conventional leather halters.

Everyone used the nylon halters, for they didn't have to be soaped, were not affected by dampness, were cheaper, and came in all sorts of bright stable colors. The fact that they would not break created a hazard!

Beau and Maggi told the grooms, "All of you be sure to take those damn halters off as soon as the horse is off the hot walker. Tom Savage's horse broke his neck last night. He got his foot caught in his halter and couldn't break loose. They found him dead this morning.

Arizona Downs — Meet Twelve

April. At about this time, backside gossip was that Ted had sold Searcher for two hundred thousand dollars.

"If it's true, why didn't Ted tell us?" Maggi asked Beau.

"Because he didn't want to give me my ten percent of the sale," Beau snapped.

"Oh, Ted wouldn't do a thing like that," Maggi insisted.

"Yeah? Well, you don't know people when it comes to

big money. They sure change."

"Well, why don't you ask him?"

"To hell with him," Beau said. "I told you a year ago he had something up his sleeve . . . the S.O.B.!"

"Well, I'll ask him if you won't," Maggi said. "After all, that was the deal he agreed to when he retired Searcher."

Maggi called Ted's ranch every day, but had no luck finding him in. She wanted to ask him if the rumor were true.

It was on a race day that Maggi saw Ted in the clubhouse. He saw her and tried to avoid their meeting face-to-face by turning the other way. Maggi was too cunning; she headed him off at the stairs. The track announcer was blaring over the speakers right above their heads.

"Post time in three minutes!"

"Hey, Ted—wait up."

He stopped. "Hello, Maggi, how are you?"

Maggi didn't want to bandy around. She hadn't come to socialize. "I'm fine, Ted. Hey, did you sell Searcher or not? We have heard so many stories all spring. And that you got two hundred thousand dollars for him. That true?"

"Yes . . . I did . . . "

"How come you never called us and told us?" As she was talking, she could see that Ted was uneasy and actually embarrassed.

"What do you mean?" he remarked, hedging.

"You know what I mean! Beau's ten percent of the sale. That was the understanding from the day Beau took him to train. We would split half, and when you sold Searcher,

Beau would get ten percent. I even set up the ads and did all the advertising to get him sold . . . you know that." As she watched him, he could not look her in the eye.

"Well, you know we never put anything in writing," he said very curtly.

"You mean you have no intentions of giving Beau his ten percent?"

"Yes."

"What about your word?"

"Oh, hell—lots of people say things and change their minds later," he stated with firmness.

This was a different Ted—not the sweet, kind gentleman she had known all the past ten years. But Maggi still argued. "After all the hard efforts Beau put into making the horse . . . and having me trailer him all over the Ohio and Kentucky counties to special allowance races trying to avoid tougher horses," she snarled back at him.

"Oh, what the hell are you talking about? The goddamn horse made himself," Ted stated and started walking away. "As I said before," waving his arms in the air, "I never signed any papers. It's just my word against yours."

Maggi stared at him for what seemed like hours.

"Yes, that's right, Ted. Just your word. And I thought your word was good. Beau was right! That's why you haven't been around and didn't give your colts to him this year."

"Look, Beau made plenty of money on Searcher. Besides he has those millionaires he trains for now. He doesn't need a little two-bit stable like mine anymore . . . I'm late, I have to go. Good-bye."

Maggi told Beau the story.

"The rotten son-of-a-bitch—the dirty mother fucker! The cock sucker!" Beau stormed. "I knew it! I knew it when he didn't want me to train his horses this fall. He

417

didn't even have the guts to come and tell me to my face."

Maggi felt bad, and it hurt her to see Beau being cheated. That's what it all came down to: Ted just screwed them out of their twenty thousand dollars. "The rotten, sneaky bastard," she turned to Beau "He did promise you ten percent when he sold Searcher. You could take it to court," she urged.

"Forget it, forget it! Let the mother fucker have it. It's too late now! Besides, how can you sue for a thing like that without anything in writing? He's got me by the balls, and he knows it."

She knew Beau was right and knowing Beau's ways, she dropped the matter and decided not to mention it again. Maggi also knew she had talked with Ted Bryon for the very last time!

25

Sportsman's Park — Year Seven — Was Over

Beau and Maggi had just shipped home. Arizona Downs was the first meet. Beau was busy with getting horses in and out. Maggi was getting her home and the office in order. She pasted a large clipping in the thirty-fifth scrapbook. It read:

Chicago Tribune

Beau Witlow—GRAND SLAM

RECORD SMASHING SEASON FOR TRAINER BEAU WITLOW

It can be firmly stated that—for one man anyway, 1972 has been a banner year of unique proportions:

That man is trainer, Beau Witlow, whose pleasant features have adorned well over 100 winner's circle photos taken at Prairie State tracks this season. What a year he had!

Witlow has already saddled the winners of more money in a single Illinois campaign than any trainer ever. Now, with three weeks to go at Sportsman's Park, he is nearing yet another unprecedented achievement: A *grand slam* of trainer titles in a number of victories at Chicago area meetings.

The stocky round-faced Arizonan began by saddling 32 winners at the Hawthorne season. Then came 43 tallies at Arlington Park, followed by 24 at the National Jockey Club session here.

His conquest of Chicago had placed Witlow third in the national standings in number of winners with 149, while also firmly establishing him in the top 15 money winners with $697,171. After warming up last winter on his "home court" Turf Paradise in Phoenix, plus a few successful sallies to Santa Anita, he began. His 1972 wins for Illinois, 112.

For the past five-year period, his stock has risen to this extent: 1967—79 wins and $241,411 in purses; 1968—96 wins and $388,367; 1969—131 wins and $426,881; 1970—118 wins and $426,220; 1971—133 wins and $571,168 and 1972 of course, is the best yet.

No other trainer has ever dominated the Chicago circuit. If Witlow manages to complete his sweep, he is expected to be honored in a special ceremony here closing day.

Sprawled on a trunk in his stable tackroom at Sportsman's the other morning, Witlow reviewed his bonanza year:

"We came here with 70 head in April," he recalled. "I'd say we've gone through 40 horses or so. It seems like Hal Bishop claimed most of them," he laughed.

"Right now we've got 32 head here. That's three stakes horses and 29 claimers. Well, no, some of the 29 actually fit races other than claiming."

Witlow's ability to "fit" his stock to races they can win is one of his major attributes. And this modest Westerner has talent as a judge of horseflesh. He is

420

adept at claiming horses he can improve,
as well as being as shrewd as they come
in selecting yearlings for his various
clients.

"What about your goals?" I asked
"Do you ever dream about winning the
Kentucky Derby?"

"Naw," he drawled, "I don't think
much about stuff like that, I just want to
keep rolling along!"

Maggi closed the scrapbook. She daydreamed after
reading the clipping once more. The years had been good
to her and Beau. They had their good health. True, she had
gotten too fat these past years, but now she had lost thirty
pounds and she never looked or felt better. Beau was still
overweight, but he was not one to cut out starches. Steve
had never had more than a bellyache or the flu. She was
glad Steve was doing well and liked his job running and
managing a fine resort in northern Wisconsin. Yes, she
thought, life was good to them. But . . . her thoughts
changed quickly. If only Beau would quit drinking and not
torment her with his too-often nights out with the boys.
This, she thought, was the only thorn in their marriage. Of
course, they had differences. Those she could handle, but
this drifting apart was gnawing at her from within.

Arizona Downs — Meet Thirteen

During the summer, Michael's father had died
quite suddenly. Even Beau and Maggi knew nothing

of it until they read about it in the *Racing Form* weeks after he was buried.

The stockholders of the Arizona Downs Meet voted Michael, against his wishes, to be the new president of the Downs Meet. It was at the beginning of Michael's meet that he confronted Beau.

"Look, Beau with me being president now and you the leading trainer, people are going to think I'm playing favorites. So, we will have to kind of cool our relationship here on the track," he continued. "You understand?"

Michael loved Beau, but he certainly didn't know Beau or he would never have made a statement like that!

"That son-of-a-bitch!" Beau told Maggi that night. "Who in the hell does he think he is? 'Don't talk to me or be over-friendly,' He can go fuck himself!"

Maggi tried to console Beau, but she couldn't get close to Beau these days — there seemed to be a screen between them. And now, Michael added to the thickness of it. Beau was pulling into a shell of his own.

Turf Paradise: Number Seventeen

That winter and spring, in spite of Beau's successes, were not the happiest. Michael and Jill were going in another direction of higher society. There seemed little time for Beau and Maggi, and because of their different roles they held in racing each time they got together a bitter argument over racing matters arose. It was on such a visit that one of their worst disagreements came about . . Michael was telling Beau that the handle was down . . . The holidays took their toll on the track attendance according to Michael. "It is beginning to pick up now that everyone has settled down," he said.

"Gosh, Michael, I never realized the problems involved in running a race track. I was so busy with our barn and our problems it never occurred to me just what problems you have in putting on a meet."

"Christ, it's about time you bastards knew just what we have to do," he said, looking straight at Beau. "Our utilities on the grounds and backside are astronomical because your goddamn grooms don't turn off the lights and heaters they have in their tack rooms," he ranted.

"I will have to agree with you, Michael, and the water we waste. Gosh, how many times I have seen water hoses just lying on the ground running endlessly after some person went off to do another chore," Maggi added.

"Shut up, Maggi, you always have to be running off at the mouth," Beau retorted.

Michael continued to explain. "Stop and think, Beau. We have to hire men to maintain the backside, pick up trash and manure daily, plus the mutuel clerks, parking lot attendants, officials, stewards, office personnel for the racing office and main office, and the security guards. There is also insurance for the jockeys and public and for the money room. We have to borrow a million or more each season to operate and hire a man and bond him to survey the money room; a state auditor has to be there to keep tabs and count the money spent and earned. Christ, all you have to worry about is a barn full of horses, you bastard," he smiled at Beau.

"We lease the clubhouse concessions on percentage but we still have to hire someone to read the register daily to make sure we don't get shafted on the count.

"The way I look at it, we break down our operation into four parts: Racing in itself which includes the backside; Operation of seating, clubhouse and concessions; Mutuels, the machines, clerks and totalizer board; Administrations, income of the business, taxes, overhead and the horsemen's bookkeeper we have to maintain.

"I haven't even mentioned the complaints and lawsuits yet. Come to my office some day and I will show you stacks of law suits from the racing public. Some lost money at the races and want to prove the races are fixed. Others trip or fall and want to cash in on the accident. Some claim they were pickpocketed in the racing crowd and it's our duty to see that these undesirables are not allowed around the track. Christ, I could go on and on," Michael gasped.

He was worked up now and there was no stopping him once he got started. He was wanting an argument from Beau.

He kept on about how all he ever heard was about the goddamn horses and how the management doesn't take care of the horsemen. "Well the goddamn horsemen don't worry about our problems as far as I can see. All they want from us is to up the goddamn purses, up the purses. It looks easy from the other side of the coin," Michael spat out.

"Hey, you guys, calm down, no need to work yourselves into a frenzy," Maggi spoke.

"Well, that goddamn Beau. He only thinks of himself and his goddamn barn and his owners."

"Hey, I know what in the hell goes on around the race track, you bastard, I was racing before you threw away your security blanket. Don't tell me about racing," Beau remarked. "I have been around it since I was eight years old. You don't have a clue what the horsemen have to put up with . . ." he ranted at Michael. "The goddamn owners on your back wondering why their horses haven't won or aren't running every damn weekend . . . Or you think you got the best damn horse on the grounds and the bastard

424

breaks down," he continued. "Plus we have all the headaches with shipping and begging for stalls . . . never knowing from one meet to the next if we can get all the stalls we need, and the trying to get good help to move with you . . . So don't tell me about your damn problems. You never did see our side of it, only your side . ." Beau stated and then got up and left the room.

Maggi spoke up, "Look, let's drop talking racetrack business from here on out, it always leads to an argument every time . . . Let me fix you another drink . . .

"Okay, where did the little fat bastard go off to?" Michael laughed. "Come back in here you little shit . . ."

Beau came back grinning and changed the subject and the four sat down to the dinner table.

But thoughts went through Maggi's head as she passed the food around . . . it was a shame that management and horsemen couldn't meet on better terms . . .

Sportsman's Park Meet — Eighth Year; Hawthorne — Seventh Year

When spring shipping time came, Maggi stayed back until the last shipment of horses, and flew in with them to save Rip being put in a crate. She was in awe of how calm the horses were during the short flight! They periodically picked at their hay nets and dozed! She enjoyed sitting behind the pilot in the huge cockpit, viewing all the instruments on the panel and the preparations before taking off, and responding to the plane roaring down the striped runway and to the thrust of its engines. As the huge craft lifted up ever so gently, not a horse seemed the least bit concerned.

Maggi giggled. "What's so funny?" the pilot asked.

"Oh, I was thinking how we used to haul our horses around the fair circuit . . . and now we're flying eighteen head at a time."

She was disappointed that Beau was not at the cargo terminal to meet her. After the first nine horses were unloaded, she rode the first van load to Sportsman's Park. Beau made no fuss at her arrival.

"Come on, let's get these horses off the van," he told the grooms.

Maggi didn't like the way things looked around the barn. It looked terribly messy. A card table was set up in the tack room, and a card game was in session. Lonnie and some of the boys were playing race track rummy. She could see an empty stall.

"How come you haven't set up the barn yet?" she asked Lonnie.

"We've been busy," he told her, in a curt way. "Can't you see?"

She didn't like it as she looked at him and the uncleaned tack.

"Get the hell out of there," Beau snapped at her. "It's none of your damn business what we do here."

Maggi left for the car.

After a few seconds in their motel room, Beau made her forget the whole issue . . . for that moment!

Fans and bettors at Hawthorne and Sportsman's Park loved Beau. Even the parking lot attendants waited on him hand and foot. Beau was free with his money and often tipped the valet parking attendant well. In return, the attendant always saved Maggi a special place for her car. Little did she know that Beau was paying well for this service.

As Maggi put the fifth gold watch into a drawer, she

wished they would give something different at Sportsman's Park instead of the same award every year. But, she rationalized; "How do they know that Beau is going to win it again and again?"

Arlington Park for the Eighth Time

The Webbers surprised Beau by moving his stable over to the Millionaire Row, Barn Four — eighty stalls, the whole barn was his, with twenty-four tack rooms, and two bathrooms and showers at each end. The grooms loved it! There was even a special phone at the end of these barns with a direct wire to the racing secretary . . . a convenience so that trainers could enter their horses and save a trip to the office during the busy morning training.

Mr. Webber had become closer to Beau and Maggi since Mrs. Webber got so involved with the hotel. Maggi suspected that he was lonely. He came over every morning, asking them to come join him at the Inn for breakfast. Always, Beau said, "No," almost before Mr. Webber had time to ask. Maggi went once without Beau, but she felt ill-at-ease without Beau being there too. Only because she refused to go unless he did, Beau gave in. He was not a social climber; he cared nothing for this structure of the racing game and made it clear to Maggi after a few mornings at the Inn.

"Don't ask me to go anymore," he told Maggi. "I don't like it, and besides, I eat too damn much," he grinned.

Since the big flood, Mr. Webber had begun to replace the old flume and widen the creek. But Chicago winters delayed the construction. Huge ditches exposed grotesque figures of steel and concrete. It gave the backside an ugly look.

Maggi and Beau found it harder each spring to find a house or apartment to rent for such a short stay. And when Mrs. Webber told them she had built a motel complex right behind the grandstand, they rented two of the rooms. It was handy, and one would have to admit, very unique. But living around all the noise and construction only added to the depression of Maggi's feelings.

Harry and Hilly couldn't have picked a better time to come. They rented a room next to Beau and Maggi. Harry was like Heidi — he gave the barn a lift, kidding with the grooms and exercise boys and walking one of his horses for a lark. As one groom put it, "Mr. Obrien, you're the only hot walker I know who drives a Rolls Royce."

It was Hilly's birthday, and Harry had planned a small party for her. Robert and Rosie couldn't come; they had other plans. The evening was one of the finest for the other four — good food, good wine, and good friends. Suddenly, Beau turned to Maggi and spoke in a thick tongue.

"I can't stand your fucking guts!"

She looked at him in shock. Everything she had just eaten and drunk threatened to come up at any minute.

"What was that all about?" she asked, as Harry and Hilly looked on in total confusion.

"Oh, come on now, Beau," Harry spoke. "It's Hilly's birthday."

"I don't care whose birthday it is," Beau answered.

"What have I done?" Maggi asked.

"You jus' make me sick," he slurred. He was drunk!

Harry paid the check. No one said a word during the long drive back to the track. As the big car rolled to a stop in front of the motel, Beau went from the car to his truck and drove off.

"Goodnight, Harry and Hilly," Maggi murmured.

"Goodnight, honey," Hilly answered. "See you in the morning."

Beau came back about four a.m., but when Maggi woke, he was gone.

Harry and Hilly came for coffee and breakfast; they were leaving that morning since Beau could not get any of Harry's horses in that week. Maggi told them of how Beau had been drinking and staying out.

"Maggi, why don't you stay away from the barn? You have Lonnie now," Harry reminded her. "You have enough bookwork and things to do. You don't need to be there anymore. I think Beau hears too much from everyone about how it is *you* that really made him. And he resents it. I know I would."

"On, Harry, I don't run everything. Beau runs that barn. All I do is keep it clean," she added.

"Yes, that's just it. You're always after someone to do his work, and that's good, but people see that and tell Beau, and he resents it. You see?"

"Yes. I'm afraid I do," she answered.

After Harry and Hilly left, Maggi tried to visualize not going to the barn. She would miss it terribly! She loved working with the horses, watching the new colts they had brought at Keeneland developing into full-fledged racehorses, making sure that each night blanket was mended during the cold spring, doctoring the horses, helping Beau. She had always loved animals, but horses had been her whole life. It seemed unfair that she couldn't be a part of the one thing she enjoyed the most.

During the races that day, she didn't see Beau even once. By ten that night, she called Rosie.

"Yes, he was here and ate with us and left," Rosie told her.

She couldn't sleep so she took a warm bath, downed two

Bufferins and by midnight, finally fell into a fitful sleep. She woke at one a.m. She could not sleep. She had taken more than enough Bufferin. She lay in the darkness of the big room, trying to think where Beau might be. Why hadn't he come home?

The phone rang. It made her jump. She grabbed at the instrument and knocked it off its cradle. She heard a frantic voice, "Hello! Hello! *Hello!* Maggi Witlow, this is the hotel operator. *Your barn is on fire!*"

"On, no! Oh, God, no!" She ran to the annex door and looked down toward their barn. Flames! Yellow, red, blue — shooting hundreds of feet into the night darkness . . . *it was their barn!* She was numb for a few seconds. She couldn't think. She didn't know what to do first . . . go out without dressing, or dress first. She threw on her clothes after quickly deciding she would be no good in a frilly nightgown and slippers. She pulled on her riding boots and finished buttoning her shirt as she dashed out the door.

She headed the big white Cadillac toward their barn. Sirens were wailing everywhere now! She could hear others in the far distance coming from the small towns close by.

Fire trucks were already at the barn, their light beams shooting through the billowing smoke. As Maggi got closer, a band of thirty or more horses came trotting toward her car.

Faster they trotted. Soon they would break into a run, she thought. Quickly, she snapped off the headlights, knowing they would blind the horses and that maybe they would run head-on into the car. She began to honk the horn incessantly. The horses kept on coming, trotting faster and faster! She kept on honking the horn as they came closer. She yelled out the window: "Yah! Yah!! Yah!!!"

The horses brushed so close they moved the big car,

shaking it on its huge frame. Maggi crouched on the floor. She had seen horses hit cars before. They always crash over the hood into the windshield. She was frozen with fear as she waited for a hoof to come poking through the windshield . . . and then, the clippity-clip began to fade away. The horses had bypassed the car and were heading toward the motel complex and saddling paddock. They too were bewildered.

She started up the car and headed for the barn. Hundreds of backside people were running around frantically trying to catch the loose horses that were running everywhere.

A fireman signaled her to stop!

"Sorry, miss, you can't get any closer. You'll have to park over there," he commanded.

"But I have to get through! That's my barn!" she blurted out wildly.

"No way," he stated calmly.

She dropped her head down on the steering wheel and broke into sobs. Then she started to turn the car around. She looked up toward the raging blaze and couldn't believe her eyes!

IT WAS NOT THEIR BARN!

"It's not our barn!" she blared out. "Oh, dear God," she prayed thankfully. She was so relieved . . . until she realized it was still *someone's* barn and horses; then she was ashamed of her relief.

During all the chaos — she kept thinking — that goddamn Beau! It *could* have been his barn and he wasn't even here to save one horse — the ungrateful bastard!

She stood helpless with countless others watching the eighty-horse barn burn into a grotesque skeleton. It heaved and swayed and collapsed into sparks and sputtering amber coals. The heat was incredible even from where she was standing! The heat blistered the paint on cars within fifty feet, and they burst into flames, giving the firemen some added problems!

Horses were running wildly throughout the barn area. Several had fallen into open ditches, breaking their legs and necks, lying there in twisted contortions. Several vets were hurrying to every spot to administer the humane shots that would put the animals out of their agony.

Maggi noticed that a groom had caught a horse on the parking lot and was waiting for a vet as he spoke. "The poor devil hit one of those big dumpster manure bins and broke his hip — and he's a good horse — worth two hundred thousand!"

There was talk everywhere! "Thirty-nine head burned up in the fire." "I can't get over how fast the thing burned down." "I could see the flames five miles from here — that's where I live." "Those poor horses" is what she heard most often.

From where she stood, she could see that their barn seemed to be all right. Lonnie came by leading a loose horse. "Our barn is okay. We locked the top doors in case our horses tried to jump out," he told her and left with the loose horse.

Maggi thought of the thoroughbred horses. All they had ever known from the day they were born was their stall. There they were secure — safe — cared for! They were totally dependent upon man. No wonder, she thought, they went right back into their stalls. It was the only place they knew that would be safe.

She was tired, and sick from the nightmare. What if it had been their barn? How would Beau feel with no barn — no horses? Just a charred mess! She wasn't quite sure at that point what Beau felt — or if he felt at all!

The phone was ringing when she got to their room.

"Hello, Maggi?"

"Yes, Mr. Bullington," she said, in a daze now.

"Are the horses okay? Where's Beau? I want to talk to him."

"He's not here, Mr. Bullington. Everything's all right with the horses."

"Good! Have Beau call me when he comes in."

"Sure."

The phone kept on ringing and the calls were all alike. Finally, daylight came, and the phone was still, and thinking that Beau might be at the barn, Maggi went there.

The grim sight was not new to her. It was the fourth fire she had seen on the backside, but it still had a profound effect on her. Twisted carcasses lay everywhere!

Beau was nowhere in sight and no one had seen him. Maggi went back to the room.

Around noon, she called Rosie and was told that Beau was over at Jinx's — Robert's agent!

"Still sleeping, I guess," was all that Rosie said, and then she hung up.

It was late in the afternoon when he finally came in, and Maggi demanded, "Where have you been?"

"None of your fucking business!" he answered.

"Look, I have a right to know where you've been — and why you're treating me the way you are!"

"You don't have any goddamned rights over me at all — get that?" He walked to the refrigerator with Maggi right behind him, firing questions, one after the other. He shoved her aside and made his way toward a chair by the coffee table.

"Don't you shove me around, you son-of-a-bitch!" she screamed. "Keep you goddamned hands off of me!"

He shoved her hard at that, and she hit the edge of the

screen. Furious now, she grabbed the waste paper basket and hurled it at him. Blood spurted from a gash on his forehead. He put his hand to the wound. When he saw the blood, his eyes turned to Maggi. She was terrified! She ran for the bedroom, knowing that she could lock the door against him and be safe. She felt his hands around her neck and he took hold of her long hair. She struggled desperately to free herself, and turned to face him. Blood was running down his face.

"Look what you did to my face, you cock sucker!" He was livid with rage. She struck at him but was stopped by his steel grip on her arms. He hurled her across the room where she fell between the coffee table and the chair. She hit one of the huge claw feet of the coffee table and immediately, a sharp pain ran through her back. She felt nauseated. She tried to get up but the pain had made her helpless as he came toward her.

"You burly bitch!" He stopped and glared at her as he wiped the oozing blood from his face. "Get up! You're not hurt," he commanded.

"You son-of-a-bitch, this is the last time you'll ever lay a hand on me."

"What the fuck — I hardly pushed you away. You were trying to claw my eyes out," he muttered. "You just fell."

"Well, I've had enough!"

He suddenly stopped in his tracks and thundered, "I want out too! Go on home — I've had it!" With that, he slammed out of the place with such force that the walls shook.

Maggi lay where she was, welcoming the sudden peace and quiet. She managed to drag her aching body to the bedroom and very carefully, eased herself onto the bed, lying very still.

When Beau finally came home, he quickly changed

clothes and left. She was alone again, and this went on for the next four days. Unable to bear the loneliness, she called Rosie.

"Let him alone for a while," Rosie advised. "He wants to show everyone he can run the barn. I told Beau he wouldn't be where he is without you, and it's true. Beau knows it, too, but he says he's fed up with your bossiness. Look, it's something you two will have to work out; I don't want to get involved. I will say one thing though. He's wrong, too — and I would never let him talk to me the way he talks to you." Then she said that she had to go pick up Robert and hung up the phone.

Maggi was totally confused. Why? If she knew all these things, then why was Rosie making it so convenient for Beau — letting him come to their home instead of telling him to go home to his wife?

Maggi moped around for days. Then, just to keep from being alone, she began to go out — anywhere — with friends, to movies, to cocktail lounges, till *she* was the one coming in late hours. Beau didn't like it one bit and demanded, "Where in the hell have you been?"

"None of your business," she answered. "That's the answer I always get from you!"

She hated that sort of thing. She had never believed in playing games and wanted it to stop. Before she could say it to Beau, he surprised her.

"Look, you had better make our plane reservations to Kentucky. The Keeneland sale starts next Tuesday," he told her, with a sheepish grin.

"I'll be glad to do that for you, Mr. Witlow," she smiled back, reaching for the phone — and thinking to herself, "It's over, thank God. This nightmare is over."

Keeneland Sale

At Keeneland, Beau was showing a yearling colt to Maggi when a long-time friend greeted them.

"Boy, I'm sure proud of you guys!" he said, slapping Beau on the back. "You two have come a long ways — Beau, you've really made a name for yourself! Every breeder here speaks highly of you!

He shook Beau's hand and then turned to Maggi. "But here's where the real brains are . . . right, little lady?"

Maggi looked stunned as Beau turned sharply and disappeared into the sale pavilion.

When they returned to Chicago, Beau reverted to his old dressing habits. He avoided the clubhouse and visits with clients, leaving Maggi in an awkward position.

Bullington bluntly asked one day, "Are you and Beau having troubles?"

"Yes," Maggi admitted. "I love Beau, and I want to be a good wife to him. And I'll do anything to save our marriage."

Beau hit a second slump. Quite suddenly, he was no longer the leading trainer. Nothing went right. His races wouldn't fill. The extras didn't fit his horses. He ended up on the also eligible more that he drawed in. Out of disgust, he told Maggi, "Call Delaware Park for stalls. I'll starve to death here!"

Delaware Park for the First Time

Delaware Park was hot, sultry and sticky! Maggi's blouse stuck to her skin from the moisture. The little track had the same aging nostalgic air as Miles Park. Quaint green little stables, looking more like summer cottages, with their narrow shedrows . . . everything was painted a deep olive green, with windows trimmed in white.

"Green for the DuPont money." Maggi said, for DuPont was the word in this town. The impressive DuPont Hotel, with its beautiful Italian hand carvings in the dining room showed the DuPont wealth. But to Maggi's surprise she heard that the State of Delaware was going broke.

* * * *

Turf Paradise — Eighteenth Time
Arizona Downs — Fourteenth Time

Delaware wasn't Maggi's favorite place. By November, it had rained more in the one month than it rained in Arizona in the last ten years. Mosquitoes were alive . . . and hungry! When the first fifteen horses were being shipped home, Maggi and Rip were on board the plane.

It was a tiring run, stopping off in Kentucky to drop off two horses and pick up two, then a stop at Chicago to pick up the remnants of their stable and tack at Sportsman's Park, then a stop at Oklahoma City to change flight crew, then — last stop, Phoenix . . . after ten hours!

Michael and Jill met her at the plane. She was surprised and happy to see them. Over two bottles of a good domestic Beaujolais, she told them of the troubles between her and Beau. They were both saddened to hear the story.

Harry came to the barn with a new MG . . . "Hey Harry is that what you carry around in the trunk of the Rolls?" one of the grooms hollered out . . . .

The bookwork continued and increased. Maggi began to pall from all the commitments. She hired a part-time girl to help with the payroll. It was the worst — always demanding every Monday.

Beau ranted, "What in the hell do you need a girl for? You don't have that much bookwork!"

"How in the heck would you know? You've never stuck your head in a ledger since the day we were married," she said, then continued, "It takes time to keep track of all the horses moving around and to keep it straight . . . and the payroll."

"Well, you don't keep anything straight. You're always making mistakes," he quipped.

"And you don't, Dr. Cyclops?" she smarted back.

"Ok, go ahead and hire someone. I don't care," he said drily.

It was hard for her to wean herself away from the barn but Maggi made every effort. She loved the early mornings that were so much a part of her life. To make it worse, Beau hired three girl grooms. It seemed wrong for another girl to be at their barn.

But she understood that with good men grooms hard to find, girls were filtering into the backside more and more and making very good hands. She had no objections as long as they behaved like ladies, and she saw to that they did. She thought, how fast racing and the style of it was changing — too fast for her!

Santa Anita for the Third Time

Beau sent Lonnie back to Santa Anita with ten horses. During the meet, Boomerang won the $25,000 Juvenile Stakes for Mr. Bullington the day after Christmas. It was that very day that Beau was notified by the racing secretary that:

"No horse claimed at this meet can run anywhere else in California until the Santa Anita meet is over.

"And that horse cannot leave the state until the meet is over."

The new ruling prevented any more trainers from coming in and claiming horses and taking them away from the Santa Anita meet.

They even called it the *Witlow ruling* later on.

This put a serious cramp in Beau's plans. If he claimed a horse, he was compelled to keep the horse at Santa Anita till the meet was over. That was Beau's last winter for shipping horses to Santa Anita. Maggi was happy at his decision, for on the books it cost the stable far more than the little profit they made. Splitting the stable always took more tack, long distance calls, endless trips . . . yet she realized, too, that it could not always be avoided.

Arlington Park — the Ninth Year

Maggi and Beau were surprised at the changes — a new cement barn of 150 stalls replaced old Barn 1A. The little creek was widened and reinforced, and two steel bridges crossed over the parking lot.

The grandstand had had a major face-lift, with beautiful terrazzo tile covering the once ugly gray cement walls. A glass elevator skimmed up the outside of the walls to the clubhouse floor and down to the main saddling paddock level. It gave everyone a shot in the arm: new meet, new clubhouse, new hopes! The Inn was as glamorous as ever . . Mayor Daley, Frank Sinatra, Jimmy Durante, Kup from Kup's Show . . . even Dear Abby! The days were full and the time went fast!

439

Beau was at his finest hour. Defending his title well. Boomerang was making the headlines every time he won, as *the hot horse in the Witlow stable.*

Everything Beau touched turned to gold . . . even *Ole Rob.*

Beau had bought the two-year-old at an Illinois-bred horse sale for $1,200. Robert and Rosie went along to the sale that night, and Robert spoke up. "Why don't you name him after me?"

"Okay, I will. We'll call him Ole Rob, how's that?" Beau laughed.

"Why 'Ole Rob'?" Robert asked.

"Because that's what Rosie has been calling you all these years . . . Ole Rob," Beau laughed again. "Since the day you two got married when you were nineteen!"

Maggi sent the name request in to the Jockey Club, and within a few weeks it was official: "Ole Rob . . . bay colt."

Beau remarked, "I hope he's not as lazy as Robert!"

Omaha: Second Visit to Ak-Sar-Ben

Boomerang was nominated in the Ak-Sar-Ben $20,000 Juvenile Stakes for two-year-olds. Bullington insisted that they fly to Omaha in his Lear Jet. Beau had Ole Rob in the second race and wanted to stay until he ran, then catch a commercial plane. Bullington said, "Go ahead and run him, and we'll wait at the airport for you." Since the small private airport was close to Arlington, it would take Beau and Maggi only twenty minutes to get there from the track.

Ole Rob won, and they headed for the airport.

At the Omaha airport, a rented limousine was waiting for all of them.

Boomerang came through and won easily. A huge silver

bowl was presented to Bullington, and a champagne party was held in the VIP room afterwards.

"Here's to Ak-Sar-Ben," Mr. Bullington said, raising his glass. "What does that word mean anyway?"

It's Nebraska spelled backwards," a lady spoke up.

"I'll be darned!" he said.

Beau checked Boomerang at the test barn. He came back pleased and reported, "He pulled up good, not a sign of any shin-bucking."

"Fine. Then are you ready to fly back to Chicago?" Bullington asked.

"Yes."

The limousine whizzed them back to the luxurious jet.

Ten p.m. . . . . they were in bed; they had made love! And as Maggi listened to Beau breathe deeply, she recapped this incredible day!

Won two races at Arlington Park!

Flew to Omaha!

Won the $20,000 Juvenile Stakes with Boomerang!

Back home in bed by ten!

A tiny smile curled the edge of her soft full lips.

It took Maggi a few days to come back to earth. She could get used to that kind of life very easily, she mused.

Sportsman's Park — Ninth Year

Somewhere in the move, River Spy's papers got lost! Beau had planned to run him the following Saturday. He was furious!.

"The son-of-a-bitch!" he stormed. "I told him to take those papers right over to the office."

"Look, don't get all in a dither. I'll get a duplicate set right away," Maggi promised.

441

"How in the hell can you get a set of registration papers in two weeks?" he asked doubtfully. "It'll take a month!"

"Just leave it to me," Maggi replied, recalling her encounter with the identification man in Detroit.

She called the New York Jockey Club and explained her problem. They informed her what to do, and she got right to work. She wrote a letter stating that the papers were lost permanently and had it notarized. Then she took four shots of River Spy's body . . . left, right, rear, front. And because he was marked with a white spot on his belly, she took a picture of that, too. She thought that of all the horses they had in the barn, they *would* lose River Spy's papers — he had so damn many white markings. She had to write his full description. She remembered that on his original papers there were at least ten sentences describing his markings. She carefully put all this in an envelope and mailed Special Delivery to New York!

In less than a week a duplicate set of papers arrived.

"Only you could have done it!" was Beau's comment.

The Quells congratulated Maggi for getting the papers back in time, especially when River Spy won the race. Maggi had no idea how the impact of her being so efficient affected Beau.

Beau was being totally consumed in the aura of success, becoming over-abusive from the pressure, and taking all his vengeance out on Maggi. He was constantly apologizing after each new outburst.

Maggi was deeply concerned about the way their life was going and suggested he go see a doctor. This only sent him into a higher rage!

"Look, I'm sorry. I don't know why I jump on you. Without you, honey, I would be a bum. I know it better than anyone. I'm just a bastard."

442

"No, you just have a lot on your mind these days, and I understand that. But I still think you should see a doctor," she countered.

"No way!" he snapped and stomped out of the room.

Beau thought as he drove to the track that she was probably right. He knew he was being stubborn, and maybe he *should* go to a doctor. Oh, to hell with it! He pushed the thought from his mind.

They saw less of Robert and Rosie each year as Robert was in Atlantic City. He could do no good in Chicago except when he rode for Beau. Beau knew that Robert was more overweight than the scales showed and rode Robert only when his horses were assigned that much weight. Maggi thought of Robert like the weather: he came in like a tornado and left like one — leaving everything in a turmoil! Since they had become parents of a son, Rosie began to lag behind more and more, staying at home in El Paso.

Harry and Hilly came in at the last of the Sportsman's meet. After viewing the gray, dismal motel and the smoke belching from the Cicero dump, Hilly remarked, "My God, this has got to be the most depressing place in the whole world! How do you stand it, Maggi?"

"It's our living and making a big fuss over something we can't control doesn't make it any better," she quipped.

"Well, my hat's off to you guys," Hilly added.

"A few years back," Maggi began, "we even thought of buying a small house. But with the different race meets we would have to drive back and forth everyday. And in this big city and the traffic, it would not be worth it," Maggi explained. "Living in the motel is better than an apartment on this side of town. We tried that too, one year. And the noise and the filthy mess I had to clean up were all I wanted. We're fairly comfortable here, and the owners treat us nice. With being at the track all day, all we need is a bed anyway," she finished. "That's why we are always so glad to see you and Harry. It gives us a lift and helps us pass the dreary days."

Maggi and Beau both hated to see Harry and Hilly leave.

Hawthorne Park for the Eighth Time

During the second week of the Hawthorne meet, Beau said, "I'm flying to Denver this Sunday to try and buy some horses. I'll be back Monday."

Maggi thought of going also but she had been with Beau looking at horses, and he never made it very interesting for her. He shut her out completely during the whole time. And she wasn't in for anymore of that treatment!

Maggi made no fuss about this weekend. She knew a man had to run his business the best way he saw fit. And like a good wife, she would wait for his return.

"Want me to pick you up at the airport?"

"No, I'll just catch a cab," Beau answered, pecked her on the cheek, and left.

On Monday, when Beau had not come back, she thought that had she known he was going to stay two days, she would have gone along. She felt so alone. Even though she walked Rip and visited with the motel owners, she still missed Beau. He came in early Tuesday morning, changed, and headed for the race track.

Rain only added to her dismal feelings. She welcomed the phone call that told her Rip was a father, and she asked for the pick of the litter. Another Rip!

The following weekend, Beau repeated his Denver stint. This time, Maggi said, "I want to go too."

"No, dammit, you make such a big deal out of it,

444

packing two suitcases, having to take Rip to the kennel . . . hell, I'm coming right back," he snapped at her.

"Okay, okay — fuck Denver," she said, and went into the other room.

Late November. Maggi hated this time of year in Chicago. It was cold and snowing and Beau was running only one or two horses a week. He had sent Lonnie back to Arizona with one load of horses, and he was to come back with the plane to stay with the few left. When Beau told her he was going to Denver again, Maggi decided she would drive home.

"There's no use me sitting here in this goddamn motel room alone every Sunday! I can do that at home and in better surroundings," she told Beau.

Beau didn't take her seriously. She had spouted off before! By the time he returned from Denver late Sunday night, Maggi was packed and ready to go. He couldn't talk her out of it. Her mind was made up. He had never seen her this way. So set in her ways. Even when he tried to embrace her, she withdrew. For the first time, Beau was scared.

26

Maggi drove home like a wild person. She was so unhappy. She thought to herself . . . what in hell was the matter with Beau? Christ, they should be the two happiest people in the world. But they weren't; at least, she wasn't. She was tired of his putting her down constantly. Thoughts continued to race through her mind.

Their little Spanish-style home never looked better to her than when she pulled into the long driveway. She felt better already. When she realized she had driven home in two days, it horrified her!

Rip was glad to be home, too, she mused as she watched him check out the big yard. "He's getting old, he's so stiff," she said to herself.

As she walked through the cozy, warm house, she recalled how happy they used to be in this house . . . all the fun parties. And the good times she and Beau had in the lazy afternoons when there were no race days. She visualized Beau lying on the huge davenport. She remembered how he liked sleeping there during the day. He was so afraid he would miss something if he were back in the bedroom, she chuckled to herself. She fixed herself a soda and Tia Maria over ice and sat down in the big soft chair, and looked East toward Chicago. "Wonder what Beau is doing this minute?" she asked Rip.

Beau paced the small room the morning after Maggi left. Then he went to the races and didn't come back until after ten that night. He took two grooms to eat with him. He hated being alone! "Yet I'm always leaving her alone," he admitted to himself. "That's it. She has got tired of being alone." He got angry at the thought and threw his keys on the desk. They skidded off and behind the chest of drawers. "Goddamn it to hell!" he spewed as he fished for them.

He missed Maggi. Suddenly, he missed her very much. The quiet room was like a tomb. He went to Arizona with the next plane load of horses, leaving Lonnie to bring the last eighteen head in December.

When the plane touched down, he was pleased to see Maggi standing by the loading ramp. She greeted him with a warm hug and kiss. It felt good to him, and he liked the way she smelled . . . her perfume . . . she had never worn another brand in all these years. "Hell, I can't even remember the name of it," he quarrreled with himself.

They held hands driving home, and as he held her close to him in bed, he knew he would never love anyone but her! Maggi cuddled closer to him as he squeezed her. She felt ashamed of her recent thoughts of him.

*   *   *   *

Spring. One morning after tracking all his horses, Beau made sure that the grooms did up the horses and checked on those that needed to be shod. He was feeling guilty and he took his remorse out on his saddle horse, gigging him with his spurs for no reason. He even hated himself for doing that. He was going to Golden Gate tomorrow and had not told Maggi because he had no intentions of taking her along. He wished he didn't have to go home to gather

447

up some clothes before he left. He didn't want to face her.

"No, you don't need to go!" he told Maggi. "I'll be back tonight." He stayed two days. Maggi cried that night as though she had dammed a whole wall of water behind her eyes. As the tears wet her pillow, she kept asking, "Oh Beau why didn't you at least call me? Why? Why?"

The next evening Maggi fixed one of Beau's favorite meals—a broiled fryer with rice and Caesar salad. They had just finished eating when Beau asked, "Where is Rip?"

"I thought he was in the bedroom," she answered. They soon found him lying quietly on his pad.

"Gosh, he looks like he's sleeping," Maggi said as she stroked his soft pelt and tiny tears began trickling down the side of her nose, dripping off onto the dog. "I didn't think he acted right since we got home. He has been sleeping more than usual, but he was eating okay, so I figured he was just tired."

"Well, his son, a new Rip, will be flying in with the horses. I talked with the people at the races just before I left," Beau told her.

Two graves lay under the big eucalyptus trees—Rip and his Dad. Maggi thought of how much the two dogs had gone through with her and Beau.

During the shipping to Chicago, a magazine asked Maggi for a story, in her own words of how a big, successful stable like Beau's was run. She sat down to a typewriter and wrote:

WITLOW WONDERS
By Maggi Witlow

For newcomers to racing, here's a picture of one aspect of the racing scene that proves you can never "pull up." It's

April—shipping time—and we have all this work to do, as though we'd never been through it before. . . Beau has spent weeks planning how many horses he will have to make arrangements for (and how many stalls they'll let him have in Chicago), how many exercise boys he'll need, and hot walkers . . . He must talk to the foreman about getting all tack up to date and in good repair. Do we have enough screens? Better order 10 more, and we need about 20 feed tubs as the others have been bent and broken. . . Do we have enough night blankets? We'd better check, because it's cold back there now. We can have the old ones mended. Some of them have been mended so many times they're more patch than blanket, but they'll do.

We must be sure to tell the grooms to pack the tack boxes good and tight so nothing spills out all over things . . Also, tell them the shipping date so they can get all their business taken care of and their cars in good shape (if 'they're going to drive back.) The others must have their bedding and belongings ready to load on the plane (we make a note of how many will be traveling with the horses). . . Foremen Lonnie and Jim are busily checking and rechecking the lists of horses and owners so there will be no mix-up getting the information to the brand inspectors and to the vets for health certificates.

We must get clearance slips and the horses' registration papers from the track office, and don't forget the colors (jockeys' silks, if you're not up on racetrack lingo) . . . Get this, get that. It never ends.

We must call the airlines and make sure of the time of loading, and ask Dr. Trotter to be there in case he's needed on our arrival. . . Check that the stalls will be leveled and bedded beforehand . . . check whether VEE (a virus injection preventive) slips are necessary this year . . . . Check with the van lines there. . . Check, check, and check again. At least farewell dinners with the Willis Ruckers, the Michael Hansens and the Harry Obriens are brightening these hectic days.

All horses now on farms must be brought in if they're to be shipped, and horses which aren't going back must be sent to the farm. . . We'll be running 6 or 7 head before we leave so we must leave a bridle or two and some tack here, which will go in one trunk on the last plane load. . . Must get the van driver's name in case we have to call him regarding a possible change in plane schedule. . . Order 6 dozen doughnuts and coffee for everyone while we're loading the planes. . . Pack car and office supplies . . . Get payrolls ready so that the payroll will be there next Monday. Close all office accounts and send them to the proper addresses . . Send to the Post Office for a box number which Beau will pick up when he gets there . . . Did we forget anything?

Our foreman, Lonnie, has driven his car back, and will return by commercial plane to ship with the horses. The assistant foreman and secretary went on ahead this week. Beau has gone back for Chicago's opening day, on which he wins 3 races; he plans to return here for the Phoenix Futurity on Saturday, April 21. On Friday, ROSENKRANZ kicks him on the shin bone, fracturing it and requiring 16 stitches. Saturday, when Beau runs 2nd with ROYAL RUKEN in the Futurity, is a rough day. His leg is very bad Saturday evening, but he doesn't pay much attention to it as there's so much to do.

Monday morning he goes back to Chicago on a commercial flight at 7:00 a.m. I stay here to close up things. Five loads of horses are planing out today, with the last one scheduled to leave late at night. Lonnie and Jim are working their heads off folding awnings, packing the last of the tack, boxes, screens, and so on. No time for lunch. We have a last minute inventory. . . NO LEAD SHANKS! What has happened to all the lead shanks? We had 30 of them! It's the same old story. Some of them went to Chicago, and the rest of them, no doubt, went the way of all lead shanks. So we go to the tack shop and get 25 more so we can lead the horses onto the plane. Also 10 more water buckets, as we find we're short on these.

At 1:00 a.m. on Tuesday morning, the horses are airborne and heading for Chicago. They will arrive in 20 degree weather, where it is snowing. There will be much scurrying around getting them off the plane and into the vans, with cold hands grabbing cold lead shanks, and horses edgy from the trip. It will be 4:30 in the afternoon before things begin to look normal again and the horses are settled down. The grooms will be exhausted after a day of frantic unpacking and getting the tack in its proper place.

Meanwhile, back at the ranch, I'm closing up, loading the car, calling Dr. Raymond to take care of the horses at the ranch for the summer, getting a driver for the car, giving keys and last minute instructions to the caretakers . . . walking . . . answering the phone . . .trying to think of anything I've forgotten. Finally, the last cover is over the last chair and I lock the door, with a last backward glance at our home until fall. It's our 18th year, and the harder we work, the luckier we get. But, it's work!

Turf Paradise for the Twentieth Time

It had been ten years since Beau began to use metal stall screens. He liked them, but at shipping time, they are a pain-in-the-neck. They were heavy and took up a lot of space on the plane. And banging them around three times a year bent them and broke the welding loose at the corners. It was a full-time job to keep them spot-welded and painted. He often thought how much easier it was with just the simple chains.

A lot of things were easier a few years back, he mused. Horses were plentiful. . . if you had the money. Now, money was plentiful, but horses were scarce. A new breed of horse trainers were on the race track now, young, educated, ambitious! The majority didn't know anything about racehorses. . or about horses—period! But they were smart enough to admit that and to hire a competent trainer as foreman. This man had the ability, he just never got lucky or got the right breaks. He ran their barn for these conglomerate trainers while they wined and dined the owners. With his ability and their money, they were successful.

Racing calendar days were being extended at every major race track in the States. More new tracks were being built. Even the Texans were still fighting the Baptist Church for legal racing in Texas. God knows how high the horses would go if they did get racing days in Texas. Horses were in such great demand, Beau kept on thinking, it was hard to claim useful horses these days. And Bute (phenybutazone) was now legal at major tracks. And he had gotten suspended for using it just a few years back.

He had to be careful now in claiming a horse. The son-of-a-bitch might not be able to walk the next day after the pain killer wore off! He began to think of the Keeneland sale coming up. The horses were selling too damn high last summer—what in hell would they bring this year?

The door opened suddenly. As Maggi entered, she spoke. "Well, I found a high school boy who will paint all the screens for a hundred dollars."

"That's good," he said, "for sixty screens."

451

"But we buy the paint," she added.

"That figures," Beau sighed. "God, it's sure good to be home," he added as he fell back on the huge divan and soon dozed off. Maggi covered him with his favorite soft afghan and went quietly into the kitchen to take stock of what she needed to buy at the store.

27

Hawthorne Meet for the Ninth Time

Maggi hated Chicago's extending its racing dates. Each spring they left Arizona two weeks earlier, and each fall they came home a month later. They were home only four months now—only four months, she thought.

Nevertheless, she was troubled when Beau remarked, "Hell, we're back there more than home! Why in hell don't we sell this damn place and live in an apartment?" he asked.

"You're kidding!" Maggi answered, "This is our home! God, that's all we have that is pleasant, a place to come and rest. You can't be racing all the time, you get sour!" she replied. "In an apartment? You'd die . . . you'd be all choked up in one."

"Yeah, I guess you're right," Beau answered. After he stopped talking, Maggi thought, "I wonder why he brought that up?"

* * * *

July. Keeneland sale.

The *Racing Form* had a front page picture of Beau and Bullington and the headline:

LEADING TRAINER BEAU
WITLOW HERE
TO BUY NEW RACING HORSES

Right after the evening sale, Beau asked Maggi, "How would you like to go to Europe?"

"Oh, Beau, I would love it . . . and we could go see all the horse farms there," she enthused.

"Oh, I'm not going. The trip's a gift for you—sort of," he said. "You know me, I don't care anything about traveling."

Maggi knew he was right about that. "Well, then, I won't go either. It's no fun going alone, so forget it," she snapped.

Back in Chicago one morning, Beau hurried from the saddling paddock. He saw Maggi walking toward it and he slipped into the racing office before she could see him. He hated himself for being like this. But he had the office girl call and make plane reservations for him to Denver. As he came from the office Maggi saw him.

"Come on, let's go watch your horse run," she suggested.

They sat in one of the many vacant seats in the reserved section. No one bothered them for a ticket or a pass. The horse won easily.

"You going down to the winner's circle?" Maggi asked.

"Hell, no," he snapped back. "It's too damn far down there. We couldn't make it if we wanted to."

She turned around and looked straight at him. "What's the matter with you?" she asked curtly.

"Nothing, goddamnit! Just leave me alone," and he got up and left for the paddock to saddle his next horse for the fifth race.

That night when Beau left in a cab for the airport, Maggi

454

picked up the phone and dialed a number. "Hello! Reservations, American Airlines," came a pleasant voice.

"Yes, I would like to make reservations to Scotland, please," Maggi told her.

* * * *

October. Europe only made Maggi feel more in despair and more aware of her terrible loneliness. She cut her stay two days short. She was even more saddened on her return to find Beau aloof and engaged in constant card games every night.

Beau watched her as she fumbled through her bookwork, making a fuss. She had never done this before. She had fired the part-time girl. I wonder why, Beau thought. I should have gone to Europe with her. Wonder what she is thinking, he thought, as Maggi took Rip out for a walk.

As she watched Rip going from one spot to another, the cold wind, biting around her face, she asked herself, "What is wrong with me? I'm so down. I wish Beau would go to a movie. I wish Harry and Hilly could come for a few days. It has been a month since we have seen anyone. I think I'll go home."

Beau hated himself as he watched her pack, yet he knew he would make no attempt to stop her. Even before she drove off in the car, he could barely speak a kind word. He was a miserable bastard. He had gone too far, and he knew it. If only he could tell someone! Anyone! He snatched up the *Racing Form* tried to study the races his horses were in. He soon gave that up, showered, shaved, and went to the track. It was only noon. Maybe Jim and the boys would be there playing race track rummy, he thought.

Arizona Downs for the Sixteenth Time

Even though he had done well at Sportsman's Park and at Hawthorne—a record-breaking year and another gold watch, plus the seven nice new well-bred colts he had bought at the Keeneland sale—Beau was more concerned about Maggi. She wasn't the same Maggi—strong, sure of herself! He felt so guilty . . . guilty of all the things he had said to her, the vicious things. No one should be treated like that, he said to himself. He couldn't think of anything else but her. All of a sudden it came to his mind, "I'll call Harry and Hilly. She likes them. They can go over. I'll call Michael, he has a way with words, maybe he can find out what's wrong." It seemed a good idea and he reached for the phone to dial Harry's number.

As Maggi hung up the phone, she thought, "That's funny. Michael just called—and now Harry. Both wanted to come by and take me to dinner. How nice," she thought, "it is to be home and to have your friends come by." But deep inside she was thinking how nice it was just to be quiet and alone. No hassle, no commitments. Suddenly, she thought of the holidays coming. Christmas! How nice it would be to be far away, no cards to mail, no shopping, no wrapping. The ringing telephone broke the spell of her thoughts.

It was Doc Trotter. He wanted her to come over to the barn He had to do minor surgery on Boomerang and he wanted her to help him. Maggi had loved helping Doc the past fifteen years and she had done all the doctoring after each operation. As Doc always told everyone, "I'd rather have Maggi take care of the horses, she does it so well, and I've never had any infections set in."

As she rode her saddle horse over to the barn, the smells

of the backside area filled her nostrils. The combination of liniment and horses and tack smelled so good to her. She liked it here. A tranquil euphoria seemed to float through the barn area. Until now, she hadn't realized how much she had missed being there.

Boomerang had a breathing problem that had been getting worse. It was caused by a saccule in his throat that obstructed his breathing when he extended himself running. Consequently, he didn't get enough air and it would stop him from running at the finish. This difficulty is a common problem with racehorses and often a lagynogotomy and sacculectomy (roaring operation) can rectify it. A cut is made right into the windpipe under the jaw at the base of the throat (larynx). A wire snare is slipped into this area, and the saccule is snipped loose. The incision is similar to a tracheotomy and can be performed with local anesthetic, on a horse while he is standing.

The operation is considered minor surgery by the vet. But caring for it afterward is very important. The wound has to be kept from healing too fast from the outside and closing up too soon. It must heal from the inside first. A lot of mucus and so forth from the clipping of the flap has to slough off and drain, and the three-to-four-inch incision has to be kept open. This was to be Maggi's job.

Every day she swabbed out Boomerang's throat. She marveled that the horse could still eat hay. Even though some of it came right out of his esophagus, he managed to get some down to his stomach.

She was doctoring Boomerang and applying the medication the vet had left. "It's healing nicely," she thought, as she finished wiping the area.

Beau came up behind her and saw that she was doctoring the horse, and asked, "What in the hell are you messing with him for?"

"Because Doc asked me to," she answered back.

"Oh, hell, the groom can do that. You just leave him alone, do you hear?" he said, scolding her in front of the groom.

Maggi withdrew from doctoring Boomerang. She slipped off his halter and quietly put everything away. She could hear Beau. His words were muffled as she washed her hands. She untied her saddle pony, put her foot into the stirrup, eased up into the saddle, and urged the horse toward the ranch.

"Goddamn him, goddamn him, the son-of-a-bitch, the bastard!" she cursed. The saddle pony's ears twitched back and forth at the hostility in her voice. "I was good enough to help him muck all those stalls, cook breakfast in that lousy tack room . . and now the son-of-a-bitch tells me to get the hell away from *his* barn! Fuck his barn!" she sputtered, waving her arms about and scaring the pony so that he jumped to one side, ducking from her waving hand. She gently stroked his neck and assured him everything was all right.

As he saw Maggi leave the track, Beau was overcome with a sudden wave of self-loathing, "Now, why did I jump all over her like that?" he questioned himself. "Christ she wasn't hurting anything, and doing a good job on the horse too." He felt sick inside. How much longer could he go on like this—and how much more could she take? "God, she has to be strong," he thought, "to put up with a miserable son-of-a-bitch like me. And I know she must love me to keep on doing it." He felt a great urge to take off for home.

She saw Beau as she unsaddled Chappo. He was coming toward her.

"Here, let me put him up for you," he offered.

"No, I can do it myself," she snapped at him.

"Hey, look—I don't blame you for being mad at me," he answered. "I'm sorry." And he held her in his arms.

She wanted to bury her head in his chest and cry her heart out. She felt so alone . . . even with Beau holding her. "Oh, Beau, please help me, please, please!" she prayed silently.

"Do you want a divorce?" he asked, as he held her.

"No, no! Why do you ask something like that?" she answered, pulling away from him now.

"I know I've been treating you terrible. I don't know why I do it. I'll do anything to make it up to you."

* * * *

As she walked into the doctor's office, Maggi thought, "What am I doing here? Why am I seeing a psychiatrist? There is nothing wrong with me."

She found it hard to say anything against Beau. She was shielding him even to the doctor. But it was good to be able to talk to someone, to just have a person listen as she poured out her soul to this total stranger.

"I'd like to go away for a little while and just think things out," she told Beau.

"Then why don't you?" he suggested. "I think it would be good for you." He handed her five thousand and said, "Here, take this and go wherever you want to," all the while wondering why he was sending her away without him. Why didn't he insist he go with her? Yet, inside he was glad she was going away. It would let him have some time for himself!

* * * *

Spain was cold and damp as Maggi made her way down

the narrow street to the phone station.

"Maggi Witlow, booth 8, please!" She picked up the receiver. "Hello, Beau?"

"Hey, what in the hell are you calling at three a.m. for?" he snapped.

It's noon here and the only time I can get a call through. They close these stations after five," she explained. She could hear him grumbling. "How are you, Beau?"

"I want out!" he answered.

She felt sick inside. She felt weak.

"Look, this is costing," he snapped. "I'll talk to you when you get home."

When she returned and entered the dark house, Rip was overjoyed to see her. She fell to the floor and hugged her dear friend. The house was so quiet. She heard Beau's truck.

He entered the room. "Well, you're back," he grumbled and sat in the first chair.

"Yes, I feel much better. And how are you?" she asked.

"I want out. I'm a mean son-of-bitch and I'm going to stay that way," he snapped.

It was as though she could see him but not really hear him. As his words finally came to her, she felt as though she were falling.

Beau watched her as she stood so still. He knew he had hurt her. He had shot off his mouth now. He couldn't back up anymore. He wanted to go over to her and hold her close, yet he couldn't move. He just stared at her blank face. It was three a.m. before they made a move to get some sleep. Then Beau lay down on the couch. As Maggi crawled into their king-size bed, the cold sheets had no effect on her as she dozed off into darkness.

She heard the part-time girl in the office. She got up and made some coffee and spoke to the girl. Mail was stacked on one corner of the desk. By noon, she had opened most of it and then Beau came in from the track.

"Hey, you just stay out of this! I'll take care of it," he snapped at her.

Maggi sent the girl home because she wanted to talk.

"What in the hell is the matter with you?" she challenged Beau. "*Your* business—*your* horses—*your* barn!"

"That's right!" he told her, "I don't need you to run things, I can run it now, and I'm moving out today!"

As he grabbed his hat and drove off, he figured he would stay just one night. He'd show the boys, by God, that he was a macho man! Show her, too! He was surprised he had managed while she was gone.

As she watched Beau drive out, Maggi couldn't believe this was all happening to them. She thought, "He'll be back."

Not so! Beau was a stubborn man and he could lose himself in his work very easily. So, he plunged into long hours of training his horses.

Weeks later he was riding back to his barn and saw Maggi riding in on the saddle horse. She looked good on a horse. She seemed thinner, he thought. It was hard to believe he had been away so long. He missed her. Deep inside he missed her terribly. Yet, he forced himself to think about his horses, and what he was going to take to the track next. He didn't want to think about Maggi. He rode quickly around to the other side of the barn so that he wouldn't have to talk to her either.

Maggi had seen Beau as she got off her horse and tied him up. She thought it a good idea to ride over to the track. Maybe she could talk with Beau. She started to walk to the tack room.

Even Jim, their assistant foreman, watched her as she came closer. He thought, "She's going to try to talk with Beau today. I'll get the boys together for another card game after we're done here."

Jim was always the card player in the barn . . . and now Beau was eager these days to play long hours in his motel room, and apparently he had no intention of giving up that little leisure time. Jim liked it that way. Maggi wasn't around the barn much these days. It gave him a free hand. He knew Beau didn't care whether he folded the coolers and saw that everything was clean and well taken care of. He could do as he pleased. Yet he, too, felt guilty. Maggi had always been good to him and taught him all he knew and how to get along with the crew. That was why, when he took the payroll hours over to the house, he spoke only the necessary chatter. As Maggi came closer, Jim quickly ducked into the tack room.

Maggi waved to Jim. She felt he deliberately didn't acknowledge the greeting as he slipped into the tack room. She walked directly to Beau. "Hi, I brought a list of all the horses for shipping, for Doc, and the van drivers," She said pleasantly.

"Yeah? Well, just leave it there on the trunk. I'll handle it."

A sickening knot formed deep inside her stomach. She felt like an outsider as she untied her saddle pony and led him toward the track kitchen.

Shipping Time to Sportsman's Park—Eleventh Time

All during shipping time, Beau would not let Maggi turn a crank. She was frantic now that he was getting ready to

462

eave. Finally, she turned to Michael.

"Let him alone, he just wants to show everyone he can un the barn. You know how everyone has kidded him all hese years about you being the ram-rodder. Just wait. 1e'll come around," Michael assured her.

Maggi was willing to do anything to get Beau to come ack, but it took all her will to stand by and do nothing. It vas all she could do to stay away from the airport the night hat Beau left with the last plane of horses. But Beau had isisted, "Now, don't you come down to the plane."

It was midnight. She couldn't believe he had gone and ft her behind.

* * * *

July. By midsummer, Maggi was in utter despair. There as no communication between her and Beau. Nothing as working out at all. She decided to go to Chicago, and ooked a flight to O'Hare Airport. Beau knew she was oming, she had called and laid it on the line: she was oming to talk.

She met him in the grandstand at Arlington Park. As she ached over and kissed him gently on the face in the glass evator going up toward the clubhouse, Beau didn't seem mind. She was glad she had come. They met Rosie as ey came out of the elevator. Beau went on to the ubhouse table.

"Hi, Maggi—what brings you here?" Rosie asked, niling in her angelic way, Maggi thought.

"To see my husband," she said.

Rosie continued talking, "You know, we've grown so uch closer to Beau now than we ever have been before," e chuckled.

"What's wrong with him?" Maggi asked, sincerely this

463

time.

"I don't know, Maggi. He says he wants a divorce." Rosie replied.

"Is there another woman?" Maggi asked, before she even realized it.

"If there was, I'd be the first to tell you—you know that, Maggi," Rosie assured her.

"I'm glad to hear that," Maggi answered. "It's just that I don't understand what's wrong with him."

"Oh, you know, Maggi, you ran everything all these years, and he wants to show everyone he is the man."

* * * *

As Maggi boarded the plane to return to Phoenix, she recalled the last two days. It hadn't gone as she wanted it to. Beau didn't really give her a chance. He wouldn't even take her to dinner so they could talk. Robert and Rosie were at his beck and call. How could he get lonesome for her, she thought, with all those people pulling at him from every direction. She wanted to stay. That was where she belonged . . . with Beau . . . and with their horses . . . their barn and crew! It was her life too—one she had learned to love so well. Then why was she flying nineteen hundred miles away from it?

28

Maggi had just doctored one of the horses in the paddock and was hanging up the halter, when a tall, bearded man stepped out from nowhere. It frightened her, for she had just heard on the morning news that a man wanted for murder was in the vicinity, she was sure it was the suspect.

"Maggi Witlow?" he asked.

"Y-yes....?"

"I'm to serve you with this . . . sorry," he added, and left as quietly as he had come.

Maggi unfolded the sheaf of crisp legal papers.

PLAINTIFF. . . . . .Beau Witlow
DEFENDANT. . . . . . . .Maggi Witlow
DISSOLUTION OF MARRIAGE

Tears blotted out the rest of the words. She felt numb and sick inside and anger against the grim injustice of it all! "He did it! He finally went ahead and filed!" ran through her head, over and over. "I never thought he would do it!"

* * * *

When she heard that the first load of Beau's horses had

come in, she hurried to the track. There was nothing for her to do now; she simply felt she had to be there. Maybe she could persuade Beau to come home, or go away somewhere . . . anything to save their marriage.

But it didn't work. Beau had no intention of giving her a shot! She could see that now. She felt helpless and licked, and like an intruder at a barn she was once a part of. The few times she was at the barn, always ended in tongue lashings between her and Beau.

"What have I done? Why are you doing this?" she prevailed upon him. "There must be another woman!"

"Hell no!" he snapped back.

The next two months were sheer hell for her, and she was in complete despair, but still totally against the suggestion of a close friend who insisted:

"Look, it doesn't add up. He must have a girl or he wouldn't be acting this way. You hire a detective, and I bet what I say is true," she stated.

Against her better judgment, Maggi engaged the services of a private detective. She hated this sneaky approach to things, but managed to tell the man about Beau's usual daily habits.

He had been watching her closely as she spoke, and now asked, "Are you sure you want to know?"

"Yes," she insisted, but she felt sick inside.

It took only two days.

"There's a woman he stays with at night," the detective told her. The words burned deep down inside her soul. She paid him his fee and never saw the man again.

Now for the first time she felt she had hit upon something that made sense. Beau was having an affair. It wasn't her after all! She felt somehow relieved. All these years she had let others intimidate her into believeing that everything was her fault. "Macho man, my foot!" she thought bitterly. "He's been screwing around all this time." She decided to talk to him.

"Now I understand why you've been saying all those mean things," she told him at their next encounter. "It's because you're guilt-ridden. The problem wasn't me at all!"

"Oh, fuck your guilt bullshit! I don't have to answer to you," he snapped and went raging out the door.

As he drove toward the track, he thought, "I am a mean son-of-a-bitch . . .she's right. But I'm glad it's all out in the open now, no more goddamn worrying and stewing over it. I feel like a rotten bastard. I suppose I should go back there and say I'm sorry." But he was too stubborn. He had shot off his mouth too much. He decided he would have to take time to think things out. Right now, he had five horses running though, so it couldn't be today. One horse was in the first race so he had only thirty minutes to get dressed and get over to the track.

The racetrackers picked up on the gossip, and it spread like a brushfire. Irma, the local hot-line at the tack shop, took full advantage of the opportunity to let everyone know of the problems between Maggi and Beau. She could not be said to have a malicious nature, but all forms of gossip intrigued her, and aroused her insatiable curiosity. Maggi was deeply hurt to discover that on top of the burdens she was already carrying, she must now take on the people she had once considered her staunch supporters. She felt conspicuous and humiliated—like something in a sideshow. She could feel everyone's eyes upon her as she passed, and imagined all sorts of conversation once she was safely out of earshot.

While she had still been considering Irma as someone she could confide in, she was shocked to hear her say, "Well, after all, Maggi, it's just one of those things . . . " It was the sort of superficial sympathy she had always despised, glossing over problems, making light of everything, reducing everybody to statistics . . .

To make matters worse for Maggi, Beau hit an all-time high in achievements and ability. Boomerang won two $100,000 handicaps in Chicago and two $50,000s in Hollywood Park and was syndicated for a million dollars. Beau's ten percent immediately drew a wall of "go-fer" boys, hustlers, and women. Maggi could not penetrate that wall.

Harry made every effort on a man-to-man basis to sway Beau to wait a while, with no luck. Beau wouldn't let up; he was constantly badgering Maggi for the divorce. He threatened to let the court handle their affairs. He pushed and pushed, continually nagging her, "This is what I will give you. . . "

"What in hell are you talking about . . . *give* me?" Maggi snapped back. "I have put in the same twenty years that you have in this business, and it is just as much mine as it is yours! I'm not going to fight you any longer," she stated, "So, get your goddamn divorce."

She was surprised when he agreed to everything, plus he wanted to lease the horse facilities on the ranch. Within two weeks of the outburst, Beau had gone to court . . . alone!

On the same day the divorce was granted, Maggi pasted two more clippings in scrapbook number thirty-eight.

* * * *

She called Harry and Hilly and was shocked to hear

Harry had sold all his horses. "Can you two come over?" she asked.

"Sure! We'll be right there," Hilly answered.

Maggi burst into tears as Hilly put her arms around her and said, "Maggi, you've got to get hold of yourself."

Harry added, "Quit blaming yourself, Hell, Maggi, Beau's a chaser."

The words burned deep in her mind, and she spouted back, "If you knew all this, why didn't you tell me years back?"

"Because I was Beau's good friend," he retaliated. "If you knew I was cheating on Hilly would you go and tell her?"

She looked at Harry, dumbfounded.

"Of course you wouldn't," Harry went on, "No one wants to stir up trouble for a man and his wife."

"He's had the best of two worlds for a long time, and it finally caught up with him," Hilly broke in, "Beau let you have everything you wanted in material ways, but he never gave of himself. He was a very thoughtless person."

"I've gotten Beau out of a lot of jams that you know about," Harry continued, "and a lot that you didn't know about. And he hasn't called or talked to me since last summer. I can forgive him for that, but when Hilly was sick, he never even tried to get in touch with me. I'll never forgive him for that."

Maggi hated hearing Harry talk about Beau like that. She never wanted anyone to dislike Beau. She just couldn't believe that she had been that dumb and naive. She thought of the old cliche: *The wife is always the last to know.*

29

When shipping time and April rolled around, Michael, Jill and everyone were getting ready to leave. Life went on despite her problems, and it plunged her into a deep depresssion. Friends were kind and sympathetic toward her, but they had their own lives to live too.

The night Steve called her, she reached out to him across the miles with a troubled mind and an aching heart.

"Did you know all of this was going on?" she asked in a faltering voice, very close to tears.

"I-I'd rather not say," Steve told her in a way that made it obvious that he knew far more than he cared to discuss.

"I'm sorry about everything, Mom. And Dad will be sorry too—later."

Harry and Hilly suggested she go somewhere different, get a job and let it take her mind off of everything. She decided to take their advice and sought a job as a riding instructor at a mountain resort. After all, she had decades of horse riding knowledge stored up, and this was what she knew best and liked most.

It was a good tonic for her. The beautiful mountain surroundings and hard work did wonders for her figure and her mind . . . until she got a phone call early one morning before class.

"Hello, Maggi—this is Lonnie."

"How did you know where to find me?" she asked.

"I got your number from Harry."

"W-What for?" she asked, thinking deep down that Beau must have asked him to call. He wanted her to come to him! Her heart was beating fast as she listened.

"Beau got married yesterday . . . "

"Got married! *Got married!!*" repeated itself through her mind like an echo chamber.

"Yeah, and get this. Bullington was the best man. And Rosie was the matron of honor," he told her. "If Beau had any class, he would have told you himself. He's treated you like shit, and you deserve a lot better," Lonnie continued. "He seems to have forgotten all the times you held that damn barn together when he was off boozing it up. Well, I'm sorry to be the one to bring this kind of news to you."

"Oh, that's all right," she said mechanically, "I thank you for calling." After that, there was nothing else to do but hang up.

She wouldn't repeat the words in her mind, yet *Rosie* burned deeper than any word she had heard just a few seconds ago. Rosie knew all the time . . . burned through her brain.

Maggi plunged into her daily work with a vengeance until the summer resort closed. She couldn't face up to going home so early . . . with no one there, it would only depress her more. She forced herself to visit relatives in California. Then she took a small cottage on the beach close to Harry and Hilly's summer place.

The beach was good for her. She slept most of the time . . the ocean was so soothing. She read several books a week. Harry and Hilly offered to take her to the races at Del Mar.

"No, it would only stir up old memories," she insisted.

471

"Look, Maggi, why don't you claim yourself a horse and get back into the business? You're a good trainer, and you like it," Harry suggested. "Beau's Dad is at Pomona. I bet he would claim a horse for you, if you asked him. You have to do something. You can't just mope around like this," he added "What do you say?"

"Okay, I'll call Buck Witlow and ask him," she agreed.

It didn't take her long to load up Rip, and within a few hours she was driving into the Pomona fairgrounds backside. It felt so good to be around the track again, the smell, the action, the whole atmosphere! It was like coming home.

She found Buck. They talked about what price horse she wanted to claim. They studied the *Racing Form* all of that morning, sitting on a bale of hay in front of Buck's barn. They finally picked out a nine-year-old gelding named Paper Clip, who was dropping down in price. He had earned $30,000 the previous year. He was a consistent runner on his past performance charts. All they had to do now was check him out tomorrow.

Maggi gave Buck six thousand dollars to put in the office and filled out a claiming blank. Buck signed it and put it in his pocket to wait for the sixth race. They followed Paper Clip over to the saddling paddock, Buck's watchful eye scanning for any leg problems.

"He looks okay to me . . . outside of being nine years old—can't see a damn thing wrong with him," he told Maggi.

"Well, it's okay, let's drop the claim in," she said.

"It's your money, you have to make that decision," he grinned, "You know how claiming a horse can go."

"Oh, hell, Buck, I believe in your judgment. If he looks sound, I'll take the risk. Go ahead and drop the claim in the box."

Paper Clip hadn't run for some time. He had just come back to the track from a lay-up period. The trainer was trying to get a race or two in him before going on to Golden Gate.

The horse ran a creditable race for his first out in three months. He was tired as his groom led him into the saddling paddock after the race. Buck waited there with a halter, waiting for the steward to okay the claim.

Everyone was glad to see Paper Clip cool out, *sound*! He was a beautiful bay horse, no white markings of any kind. And his long thoroughbred lines showed class in the old horse.

It wasn't until he was put into his stall, and when an "Ah uuuggg Ah. ." sound came from him that Maggi and Buck realized they had claimed a stump sucker, a cribber—(a horse that grabs at anything between his teeth and sucks in air). Such horses keep up this aggravating habit by the hour.

"Have you a cribbing strap handy?" Maggi asked.

"No, I don't," Buck answered.

Maggi went over to the tack shop and bought the last cribbing strap they had.

A cribbing strap is made up of a double two-inch piece of leather about a yard long. A piece of steel is sewn between the strips on the bottom half. The strap fits a horse's throat like a dog collar and is buckled in place. Each time the horse grabs hold of anything and clenches down hard, his throat muscles expand and hit the hard surface of the steel and leather. After a few attempts, his throat will get sore from this, and he will quit cribbing to avoid the pain.

After the collar was made secure, Maggi made arrangements with Buck. He would see that Paper Clip got shipped back to Phoenix when he went home. She thanked him for his help and left for the beach cottage.

Maggi enjoyed the two months on the beach, the rest was good for her. She had never had that much time to herself in all these years. She passed the days reading, sleeping and lazing on the warm sand.

> *The lowest ebb is the turn of the tide.*
> *Henry Wadsworth Longfellow*

* * * *

As Maggi turned into her home driveway, she saw that Paper Clip was there. He looked good standing in the big paddock, sunning himself and hardly noticing her at all. She thought, "Nothing like the good old Arizona sun to thaw out the body soreness."

She had a look around the ranch, touched base with the caretakers, picked through the mail, and finally sank into the comfortable chair by the fireplace, thinking "It's good to be home."

She dialed the phone "Hello, Harry—well, I'm home." As she hung up the receiver, she was glad they were coming over. She didn't want to be alone the first night back.

Harry looked Paper Clip over very carefully. Maggi was surprised he knew so much of his racing background.

"He's been a real old class horse for years," he told Maggi. "You can claim a horse for me anytime," he kidded. She felt good, for she valued his opinion very much.

The van loads of Beau's horses came in from Chicago. It gave Maggi a strange feeling that Beau was renting his own place. She realized, too, that Beau being at the ranch was not going to be easy for her.

Paper Clip was a gentle horse to train, and Maggi could gallop him herself on the track at the ranch. After a week she realized that galloping made him body sore and so she changed to ponying him instead. She studied his racing charts and saw that his best races were over a distance of ground . . . the farther the better.

The third week of the meet she entered Paper Clip in a mile and a sixth race. He ran second for $6,500 claiming. She bathed him herself and cooled him out, loaded him in the horse trailer, and hauled him back to the ranch. She knew he would do better sunning in the paddocks during the day. She put him up at night in a nice, bedded stall and give him a hot bran mash. With Paper Clip at the ranch, she wouldn't have to worry about the track closing at ten, but the main reason was she wanted to avoid being at the track. It was very painful for her to see Beau under these conditions.

Eleven days later, she entered and ran Paper Clip again for $6,500. He ran another second and was claimed! As she pulled off his bridle in the saddling paddock and watched him being led off by his new owners, she felt depressed. She had grown to love the old horse in the short time she had owned him.

As she walked back to the barn, she heard someone call her name, "Hey, is that you, Maggi?"

"Why, hello Dick," she smiled.

"What'd they do, take your horse?" he asked, viewing the halter in her hand.

"Yes."

"Did you want to loose him?" he asked.

"No, not really, He was going to make me some money if they had left me alone," she added.

"Boy, you sure look great! Lost a lot of weight, haven't you? Looks good."

"Thanks," Maggi smiled.

"Listen, I've got a two-year-old you might be interested in."

"No, I don't want any two-year-olds," she answered.

"Well, he'll be three in just a few more weeks, and has all the conditions in the world and can run a lick, too." he told her persuasively.

"What's his name?"

"King of Summer," Dick answered.

"Oh, okay . . . let's go look at him," Maggi relented.

King was a powerful built large gray colt, seventeen hands tall at least, she thought. His legs looked clean and sound, and he showed a good conformation all over, even to his long slender, thin neck and find handsome head. Maggi liked him at a glance.

"How much you asking for him?"

"Ten thousand," Dick answered, without blinking an eyelash.

Maggi shook her head and repeated the figure. "That's a lot of money . . ."

"I know, but he is worth it . . " he stated. Maggi knew he wouldn't take less.

"Come over tomorrow morning and watch him work," he insisted.

"Okay, I will, But if I decide to take him, I want the vet to check him out, okay?"

"Sure, I'd want you to," he said.

The next morning as she watched the powerful gray horse swallow up the track with his long reaching strides, she knew she had to own him. She also knew she had no business spending ten thousand dollars on any damn horse. She began to figure up her money: the amount Paper Clip had won and the amount she lost him for was in the office. She had the ten thousand already. That night, King of Summer was in Paper Clip's old stall. And Maggi lay awake long into the night thinking, "What a dumb thing I did . . . "

King of Summer was the opposite of Paper Clip. He was an extra tough horse to gallop. He could run away with the average exercise boy easily. Maggi found the best exercise boy who worked for Beau, and he agreed he could gallop King around nine o'clock after he was through at Beau's barn. She had no choice but to wait for him. It was the only way she could get this big horse fit and ready to run.

Even the exercise boy took a liking to the big gray colt, and took extra pains in galloping him slow and easy. Maggi followed Beau's way, always galloping his horses slow. He didn't believe in letting them "twenty-two" it around the race track every time they came up there . . . and neither did she.

Maggi had to endure the backside gossip that she had paid too much for the colt. It didn't help her morale a bit, but she made up her mind that if she had to, she would run the big gray colt where he could win, even if it was for five thousand! She wouldn't try to hang on.

King of Summer had one advantage. He was an Arizona-bred colt. Outside-bred horses were excluded from an Arizona-bred allowance race, cutting down the stiff competition. She entered King in the Arizona-bred Allowance, and he finished second and was beaten by just a nose. She felt much better after this race, for she knew she had a horse worth ten thousand, and his best year was coming up. He would turn three on January first.

By April, King had run four seconds. He was just getting ready to run, and the meet was over.

477

She decided to take King to the California fairs where, she had heard, the minimum purses were $3,000 and that it wasn't too tough. The better horses went to Hollywood Park. Just before she left, her old gyp friend, Jiggs Madders, asked if he could go with her.

She explained, "I couldn't afford to pay you, with only one horse." Jiggs didn't seem to care about that. He wanted to go anyway.

"Look, I want to bring my old horse along, so I'll do the work, you do the training and we will split the feed bill."

"You got a deal!" she answered.

Having Jiggs was a godsend. Now she had no fear about sending King on the van alone. Jiggs left on the van with their two horses and would meet her at Golden Gate in a few days. This gave her time to close up the ranch and make the long drive without any worries.

Golden Gate seemed dismal and cold as she passed the closed-in, gray-painted barns. She pulled up to the barn after the gateman told her where her horse was stabled.

Jiggs was sitting on a bench. "Well, come on in and I'll buy you a drink," he grinned. "How do you like the cold weather?" he asked her.

"Not bad after the heat at home," she replied. "How are the horses?"

"They shipped fine—no trouble, and they never missed a bite of hay or grain since they got here," he told her. Maggi looked into King's stall. He looked okay to her. Then she glanced at Jiggs' horse.

"But . . . they're on strike here," Jiggs sputtered. "The damn janitors want more money. Hell, they are getting sixty dollars already," he grumbled.

"A strike! That's all we need! I wouldn't have come had I known that," Maggi snapped.

The strike lingered on. Pleasanton was past . . Maggi tried to get stalls at Longacres in Seattle, but it was full up because of the strike in California. Everyone was shipping out. Some, who couldn't afford to wait out the strike, turned out their horses. Rumors about a strike settlement continued, and finally, after three more weeks, the Vallejo Fair meet started.

Maggi knew that King of Summer and Jiggs' horse Misty would be short (not fit) from not racing. King ran third, and Jiggs' little horse ran second. The purses were good; King got one thousand and Misty got twelve hundred.

Next, at the Santa Paula Fair, the two horses were winning enough to keep them out of the red, but there was no doubt that the strike had cost them a shot of winning a race or two.

Bay Meadows was the final leg of the northern part of the California fairs. Maggi loved this little plant. It was unique from the backside to the pleasant clubhouse surroundings. Everything was clean and well kept.

She entered King of Summer the next day. He finished second. By the time he had cooled out, Maggi noticed he had pulled his rump muscles. The track was so deep and sandy that King had a hard time getting hold of it. It cupped out.

Maggi got the vet to inject King with a muscle relaxer. "Half the horses here have the same problem because of this deep heavy track," the vet told her and advised her not to race King for ten days. That shot the rest of the Bay Meadows Fair meet.

Maggi decided she would run King one more time at the Stockton Fair, then take him home and turn him out for a few months rest. After all, she thought, the horse had run twenty-two times this year. That was a lot of races. Jiggs had a cold so Maggi insisted he stay in and rest. She would ride over with the van driver.

Bay Meadows Fair allowed horsemen to keep their stalls as a home base and van back and forth to Stockton, because Stockton did not have enough stalls to accommodate all the fair-circuit horses.

The little, dirty Stockton fair brought back memories of the fair-circuit days in Arizona. Maggi was surprised to see many old gyps from Arizona at Stockton.

The van pulled in by the receiving barn to unload all the horses that were vanned in. Thirty stalls were already bedded––compliments of the Stockton Fair. As soon as King came off the van, she led him into an empty stall and got him a bucket of water. She hung up his bridle on the stall door, turned over a bucket, and sat down in the narrow shade of the barn, watching others unloading and getting their horses ready for their races. The surroundings were depressing: Dust boiled up from every horse hoof, car, and van. Water hoses were running constantly, no one caring to turn them off. It was every man for himself! By post time, the wind had come up suddenly. This discouraged Maggi from watching the races from the rail on the backstretch. She went back to King's stall to wait for the call for the sixth race. King was in for $6,500 claiming. She wondered if she would lose him.

"Bring your horses to the paddock for the sixth race. . ." the loudspeaker blared.

She borrowed a brush to clean King up, put his nose band on first, then the bridle and started to lead him over to the saddling paddock. It was a long, hot walk. King just lowered his head and followed like a saddle horse.

After the race, she picked King up and turned back toward the barn area. She was disappointed that he had run sixth. She wished someone had claimed him.

By the time she got back to the barn, there were three other horses waiting ahead of her for the one and only water hose. By the time she got her turn, King had quit blowing, but he liked the cool bath and stood nicely as she hosed him off. The hose was only a few feet long and Maggi had to stand in a mud hole ankle deep until she finished giving King his bath. She scraped him off and proceeded to cool him out. The dry dust stuck to her muddy boots. She was so disgusted, she snarled out, "Son-of-a-bitch!" She thought of Beau—goddamn him for putting her in this position, having to grub around these fairs again, putting up with all these shoddy conveniences! She visualized Beau in Chicago, with lots of good help . . . grooms . . . clean shedrows . . . nice wash racks . . . sweet-smelling stalls! She stopped and let King sip, he was so thirsty. He drank a whole bucket of water. She slapped his long neck and asked, "You ready to go home, ole feller?"

After King watered out, Maggi cleared the caked dust from his eyes and head, brushed him, and combed out his mane and tail.

"There, you should feel better," she assured the big horse. She stole a flake of hay from the next stall and threw it to King. He rooted toward her and blew a gust of air from his nostrils, spraying muddy mucus all over her shirt.

"Goddamn you, King!" she railed, "I look bad enough without you adding to it!" She tried to brush the crud off, but only made it worse. She sat down on the bucket in disgust. Having to wait on the van didn't help either.

It was nine that night when they unloaded King back at

Bay Meadows. Jiggs had his stall ready and a bran mash mixed. All it needed was the hot water added. He had a pot of beans, coffee and doughnuts in the tackroom. His little Sony TV was blaring the olympic games as Maggi turned the dial down so they could talk. She told him of King's race, and after the second cup of coffee, she said, "Pack the tack . . we'll go home as soon as we can get a van ride out."

"I'm ready to go right now!" Jiggs replied.

Maggi figured the horses were in good hands with Jiggs and that it would be four days at least before he and the horses would get a ride home. The next morning, she headed the big Cadillac with Rip in the back seat toward Phoenix.

She had time to get the house opened and a good two days rest. When she looked out on the third day, at five a.m., King of Summer and Misty were in the paddocks, and Jiggs had his cot and bedroll set up in the shedrow of the barn. They had come in sometime during the night, she thought, and went out to greet Jiggs and invite him in for coffee.

30

Maggi put her heart into training the horses and kept to herself. One morning after the chores were done, the phone was ringing off the hook as Maggi came into the house.

"Where in the hell have you been?" Mr. Maddox asked. "I haven't seen you at the track for so long that I got to wondering if something was wrong."

"Oh, I'm all right," she assured him. "I just stay away from the track 'cause its a downer for me to go over there."

"To hell with that, Maggi. Damn it, forget all that stuff. Look, I want to talk to you about training two horses that I just bought in California. They should be here in a couple of days."

"Oh, Bert, I don't want to train any other horses right now. I can't afford to hire any help."

"Oh help, my ass! You and Jiggs can do the work. Don't be so damn silly," he said jokingly.

"Okay, I'll come over and see you in the morning and meanwhile, I'll put in for two more stalls," she added. "No use talking tomorrow if I can't get stalls," she laughed. "What are the two horses' names, so I can tell the racing secretary?"

"Rhoda's Girl and Foxation," she was told. "I'll send the horses to the track," Maddox added.

"Good."

The horses arrived the next day and as they were unloaded, Maggi noticed that one of the horses had a slight bow on his right tendon. Maddox hadn't mentioned that the horse had any problems. The three-year-old filly, on the other hand, had just been broke and galloped thirty days. She was still a maiden but looked okay.

As soon as she had tended to them, Maggi hurried to call Mr. Maddox and advised him of the bowing problem.

"Are you sure?" he asked. "He wasn't supposed to be bowed when I claimed him."

"Well, he is. I wanted you to know it right away so that you wouldn't think I had done it."

Maddox stopped by and examined the horse's tendon closely. He saw that she had diagnosed the problem accurately enough and asked for her conclusions.

"Well, if he were mine, I'd get rid of him as quick as I could because it won't hold—he'll tear it loose. Run him for the bottom claiming price and pray someone takes him."

"Okay," he said. "You're the boss."

She put off taking the horses to the track as long as she could because it was easier at the ranch and she didn't have to worry about the track closing at ten o'clock.

By the middle of February, she could not avoid going to the track. She put King back in training. He looked fit; the long rest had done him good. After thirty days of slow gallops, he was ready for a 3/8s of a mile workout. She planned to run him six-and-a-half furlongs the first out. She trailered him over to the track, had Dick the shoer put new plates on him, and then had Doc Trotter worm him. She put King in the first stall of her barn and went back to get Maddox's horses.

As she arrived with the second load, she saw Beau from

a distance. She felt a sudden change in her pulse as she avoided any eye contact. As she drove to her barn, she knew she still cared for him. The very next morning, she met Beau head on, and they exchanged polite hellos.

Mr. Maddox's bowed horse was training well, but Maggi knew the bow would not hold with too much strenuous training. She planned to run him in a $2,500 claiming race the next weekend. From the day she got the horse, she and Jiggs rubbed his tendon each day with Ica gel brace to tighten the bow down. After a while, only a skilled eye could have detected the slight bump on the tendon.

Jiggs bragged, "Maggi, that bow is better now than it ever was. Why, you can hardly see it!"

"The heck you can't!" Maggi warned, "It's there, don't kid yourself. A little bow is like—like being a little bit pregnant."

Jiggs' little horse began to come around. He won his first out for five thousand claiming. Ten days later, they moved him up in class, and he won for six thousand. The horse was running so well, Jiggs was afraid he would lose him. He insisted that Maggi run him for seven, and to her surprise, he won for that. In the short span of a month-and-a-half, Misty had won more than five thousand dollars.

"It couldn't happen to a nicer guy," Maggi told Jiggs.

Mr. Maddox's filly was training well and began to show some speed, but she was a poor doer. She picked at her food and refused to eat any bran mash. Sweet feed was practically all she cared to eat. After a time, she began to clean up and put on a little weight.

Maggi had planned to run Rhoda's Girl cheap, but Mrs. Maddox insisted that she not run for less than $5,000 claiming, and her husband was going along merely because her health had not been up to par and he didn't want to upset her.

Maggi had the filly in for $2,500 and Mrs. Maddox called her on the phone and chewed her out.

"Damn it, Maggi, I don't want to run my little filly for $2,500. I told Bert that! He don't have a damn thing to do with her."

Maggi was livid as she listened to her spouting off.

"Okay, Rhoda, I'll get a vet to scratch her out of the race. Now, don't get yourself all upset over her," Maggi answered smoothly.

"Good, and I won't run her for less than $5,000 do you understand that?"

"Yes," Maggi affirmed.

"Good," she answered and hung up.

Maggi was still livid as she walked toward the office and thought, "I must be crazy to let her talk me into running her for $5,000! Hell, I couldn't lead that one-gutted thing around this track and get $500 cash for her. No one is going to claim her for $2,500. And then they have a fit 'cause she hasn't won a race."

Maggi got the mare scratched from the race . . . and entered her the following week in a $5,000 claiming going five-and-a-half furlongs . . . The race went for Monday!

On the day of the filly's race, Maggi put out a cooler, halter, and shank and had Jiggs get some hot water. Before she left for the paddock, she told Jiggs, "Don't forget the breast collar. She's so one-gutted (an extremely skinny barreled horse), I don't want to risk the saddle slipping back during the race."

The filly broke straight from the gate and was laying second. She made the lead at the 3/8s pole and was two in front as she turned for home. As she came down the lane, Maggi could see that the horse was tiring and other horses were closing the gap. As they crossed the finish line, you could have thrown a blanket over the four horses. The time was: 56.

"I think we won!" Jiggs hollered.

"I don't think so," Maggi answered as she watched the tote board for the results to be posted. Then the numbers flashed into place. She finished fourth.

While washing off the filly, Jiggs commented, "Too bad they didn't let you run her in that $2,500 maiden claiming. She'd have won it and no one would even have looked at her."

"I know," Maggi said, "But that's owners for you."

The next morning she went over to enter King since it was getting close to ten o'clock.

She was coming out of the entry booth, when a trainer grabbed her by the arm. "Come here, I got something funny to tell you about ole Marble Head and Beau," he grinned, as they drew aside from the other trainers.

"Just before Beau left Hawthorne he had made a bet on an 8-9 on the Big Q, and it paid $2,000 for the two-dollar ticket. So Beau gave Marble Head the ticket to cash and was going to give him a couple of hundred bucks so Beau wouldn't have to pay the ten percent income tax . . . you know?" He continued to tell the story. "Anyway, Marble Head cashed the ticket and left town. Beau's never seen him since! Ain't that something?"

Maggi laughed but inside she felt a twinge of victory. How many times had she told Beau that Marble Head, and the dozens of other hangers-on were just hanging around him for what they could hustle or mooch off him. She thought to herself, "I bet that killed Beau more than losing the money—that I was right!"

King's race didn't fill, Maggi was let down because the horse needed to be run. She didn't want to keep working him every few days. The racing secretary promised he would write a non-winners of two races for her horse the next weekend.

He kept his word, and the race went. King of Summer drew the number 5 position in the eighth race for a $2,900 purse, going six-and-one-half furlongs.

He won by four lengths and ran in 1:17:3, beating a horse worth at least $15,000. Then the backside gossip was: "Guess Maggi knew what she was doing all along. That's a damn nice horse!" "Hey, that son-of-a-gun can run a lick!" "Hey, he's a nice colt."

All these compliments helped Maggi's ego. She needed the boost, but she took it with modesty and felt just as Beau had many times, she was sure: she'd got lucky!.

Luck was holding out. Ten days later, Maggi entered King in "Non-winners of two races going a mile," a cheap allowance race. He won it . . running it in 1:36:1. Now, the backside talk was that if she ran him for ten thousand claiming, a Canadian trainer was going to take him! Maggi knew this was a true rumor, because King was worth ten right then.

She realized for the first time she was like all other stupid owners. She was already hating the thought that she would have to run King for a higher claiming price, for she knew she would lose him otherwise. She knew that the horses in the last two allowance races she had won were not worth any more than ten or twelve. Now she had to make up her mind to be practical about the horse.

She read the Condition Book over and over. There weren't many races that fit King's conditions without running him for ten or more claim. Arizona-bred races were her best bet, and King had a good shot as there weren't too many Arizona-bred horses on the grounds.

The Cactus Wren Stakes for Arziona-bred three-year-olds caught Maggi's attention. King would have a shot in that race, she thought! She talked with the racing secretary to see what would go in that race. After he looked over his charts and records, he found only nine horses eligible for it and that there was one outstanding horse that would be tough to beat.

"You don't think I'd be nuts to enter him in that race?" Maggi asked.

"Hell you look as good as the rest of them, that's about what they are worth—ten to twelve thousand—except Cellar Boy. He's the horse to beat. The nomination fee is fifty dollars and is due next week," he told her.

"Okay, thanks. I have a week to think it over," she said and left for the track kitchen for a cup of coffee.

As she paid for her snack, she noticed a big pickle jar that had FOR MEXICO printed on a card and taped on the jar.

"What's that all about?" she asked the cashier.

"For Mexico's funeral," she answered.

"Mexico! When did he die?"

"Yesterday."

"Why, I just saw him the night before," Maggi said, still stunned.

"Well, Charlie said he don't have any relatives or nothing, and the HPBA is donating a hundred dollars toward his funeral, and they still need another hundred!"

Maggi pulled out a few bills, picked out a five, and stuffed it into the stock of crumpled bills already in the jar.

As she sat down to eat her doughnut and coffee, Maggi thought back to when Mexico worked for her and Beau. He was a big hulk of a man, puffy-faced, not too bright. And she was sure he had never taken a bath, ever! He came along when hot walkers were getting hard to find. He just showed up one morning, riding a big sorrel horse. He called the horse Mexico because that was where he came from . . Mexico! The horse looked more like a work horse—big feet, a big head, and a thick mane and tail that would have taken weeks to comb through. He carried his master well and loved him equally.

Maggi remembered that she had hired the man on the spot. His name was Frank. She hired him and Mexico for seventy-five dollars per week and hay for Mexico.

The horse followed Frank everywhere and would wait patiently for him outside the track kitchen or restrooms. The horse would even nicker to him through the rest-room window as though he were talking with old Frank!

Frank and Mexico looked like the Man from La Mancha . . . with the gaudy saddle and its huge *tapaderos*. (stirrup covers) hanging from each stirrrup. No one could remember Frank's name, and several grooms began to call him, "Hey, Mexico, come here . . . " and the nickname stuck. Poor old Mexico, she thought, never had a thing but that old horse. And when the horse died a few years back, the old man just kind of gave up . . . Someone let the screen door slam. It startled Maggi and broke her train of thought. She swallowed the last gulp of coffee and got up and headed for her barn.

Maggi had learned from Beau that taking the horses over to the ranch periodically, letting them sun themselves for a few weeks, and putting them up in a stall at night, gave them a new lease on life. She thought it would be good for King to take him home for a few days and do just that.

She hurried home, hooked up the horse trailer, and jumped into the truck, as Rip leaped into the back of the pickup bed. He loved going anywhere. King loaded easily and in ten minutes Maggi was putting King in one of the large paddocks. He rolled and rolled, then reared and

490

pawed at the air, striking out, bucking and pitching and jumping in the air and kicking out his hind feet. Maggi thought, "I bet it feels good to get out of that stall."

"Hi, what you up to?" spoke Lar, the exercise boy.

"Where did you come from?" she asked.

"Oh, one of your boarders wanted me to gallop his colt, and I just got done," he smiled as he spoke. "Boy, you sure got King looking and running good."

"Thanks. How about a cup of coffee?"

"Sounds great."

They got off onto track reminiscences and jokes. After a second pot of coffee and a plate of snacks, Lar said suddenly, "Do you realize how much you've changed?"

"How do you mean?" Maggi asked.

"Well, you're a lot more quiet—more tolerant. Hell, the first time I met you, you were always in some fucking hurry," he stated. "Hell, you're a lot of fun! . . . You were so busy before, kissing all those damn owners' asses . . . And where are all those damn bastards now?" he asked. "All they care about is what you can do for them, and if you're not winning races, they'll quit you. Have any of them ever called you?"

"No . . . . " she answered.

"Hey, you have a lot of friends over at the track, and they think you got a rotten deal. I bet Beau misses you, too," he stated as he got up. "Well, I gotta go. I have five more horses to ride today," and he headed for the door.

Maggi felt good after he left . . . the thought that someone liked her and respected her . . . just for herself.

She had just finished doing up Bert's filly when he came up to the stall. "Hello, how are the horses going?" he asked.

"Okay," she answered.

"Maggi, I can get you another owner if you're interested," he stated.

"Bert," she answered thoughtfully, "you know the days of the small stable are over. It's too hard to compete with big stables like Beau's. You can't get the good jocks or platers, and even the racing secretary isn't going to knock himself out too much . . You know that."

"Yeah, I guess you're right. It's not easy anymore," he answered. "Every year they are squeezing out the little public stable."

"Yeah, they make it hard on them to get stalls. You know all the hassle. I fought all that kind of stuff for years, and I'm not up to starting all over again," she said. "At least not right now."

The loud speaker blared out:

"Maggi Witlow, please come to the steward's office!"

"Wonder what that is all about?" she asked Bert.

"Now what did you do?" he asked, kidding her.

"Well, I'd better go and find out," she said and left. As she entered the office, she saw the steward and asked, "What do you want to see me about?"

"The gateman reported you had a dog in the barn area yesterday . . . that right?" he asked.

"Yes, but he was in the truck," she replied. "He never got out."

"You know the rules, Maggi. No dogs allowed in the barn area."

"But he was never out of my truck," she pleaded.

"I'm sorry, but you're still breaking the rules, and we're going to fine you fifty dollars," he declared.

"*Fifty dollars!* Why, you don't fine that much when you're late to the saddling paddock!" she ranted. "That's a dirty, rotten deal!" She stormed out of the steward's office slamming the door and thinking, 'Now, they will probably fine me another fine for that!'' She was livid. By the time she got back to the barn, Jiggs was sitting talking with Maddox. She began to tell them what happened.

"Why, the sons-of-bitches," Maddox burst out. "Hell, there's dogs all over these barns. I'd take it to the HPBA if I were you."

"Oh, to hell with it. It just makes me mad. This is the first time I ever had a ruling against me," Maggi stated as tears welled up and fell down her face. "I just can't seem to stay out of hot water," she added.

Maggi brought King of Summer back to the barn, making sure that Rip stayed home. King was entered in the Cactus Wren Stakes to run the next Sunday, and she wanted to get a 5/8s mile work before the race. He had drawn the 5 hole. The Cactus Wren was the seventh, the co-feature race. The feature was the eighth race, the Gold Cup. As she read the other horses in King's race, she thought, "I bet Beau thinks I'm crazy running him in here, and he is probably right!"

She worked King that morning . . . five-eighths. As she led him off the race track, she asked the clocker, "What'd he work in?"

The clocker called down, "58.2."

"Damn," she said to the jock. "I didn't want him to work that fast."

"Wow! It didn't seem like he was going that fast," the jock replied. "He is so powerful and has such a long stride."

"Oh, don't let it worry you," she said, as she grabbed King by the bit to keep him from dancing around and stepping on his coronet band (just above the hairline around the hoof.)

493

Sunday! Maggi was extremely nervous. The tension had built up. She worried about King . . . making sure he was right. As she was finishing up her work, she thought, no wonder Beau was uptight . . . and all the horses he had. She could relate to it now more than ever before.

"Well, Jiggs, I guess we're done," she told him as they put away the last of the tack and swept out the room.

"Now, let's get King cleaned up and his feet painted, and then leave him alone until race time."

Another trick she had learned from Beau was not to worry your horses, and not to fuss with them all morning and afternoon before their race. Let them rest and relax. She remembered old Langly Queen, a little black mare who would go bananas if she saw her bridle hanging on her stall door, because she knew she was going to run . . . Especially if they took her out of her stall and brushed her in the afternoon, she would get all shook up and wash out before the race. She would be wringing wet by the time she was led to the saddling paddock. Maggi remembered how Beau had figured out this problem. On the day Langly Queen was to run, they would clean her up as soon as she came off the hot walker and then leave her alone. Beau would give her groom specific instructions: "Don't bother her . . Don't even stand in front of her stall . . . let her alone!" And she ran like a haint (ghost) for Beau.

Jiggs broke into her daydreaming.

"Well, I'm gonna bet ten dollars on your horse today," he told Maggi, "I think he'll win."

"You better keep your money in your wallet," she kidded him back. After she had painted King's last hoof, led him back into his stall, took off his halter, she told Jiggs, "I'm going home to get ready. See you at one."

"Don't worry. I'll have everything ready," he stated.

Maggi could sense that he was uptight also.

494

Maggi picked through her wardrobe. She wanted to look special today! As she stepped back from the mirror, she was pleased with her image. Her freshly washed hair lay in a mass of dark soft curls against her white pant suit. As she drove to the race track she made herself calm down and gain some composure.

As she came around the corner of her barn, Jiggs was sitting in a lawn chair, sunning himself.

"Jiggs, you look like the mayor of Phoenix," Maggi kidded him as she noticed his white hair combed back neatly, a new clean shirt with the collar buttoned, fresh, clean jeans, and polished shoes.

"Well, you look like a movie star yourself," he answered.

"Thank you," Maggi replied. "Oh, damn, did you find the pony boy about taking King to the gate?" she asked.

"Yep, I took care of that right after you left. He'll be here right after the sixth race," Jiggs confirmed.

"Thank God, you remembered. I had forgotten all about it," Maggi spoke out. "You're a good man, Jiggs. I don't know what I would do without you."

"Well, Maggi you remind me of my wife . . . I lost forty years ago. she made me clean up and look like a gentleman. You know Maggi, the day she died, she made a bum out of me." he said, with a gleam in his pale blue eyes.

"You'd never be a bum, Jiggs, not in my book," she answered. "I'm going up to the clubhouse. See you in the paddock. Don't bring King until they call for the horses the second time."

"Okay," he answered as he dropped his hat to shade his eyes from the bright sun.

As Maggi sat in the clubhouse waiting for the seventh race, she was tired of answering all the questions from

495

everyone:

"Hey, you gonna win today?"

"Think you got a shot?"

"How do you like your horse? I'm thinking of putting him into the double."

"What do you think?"

"Who's the tough horse in your race?"

She was glad she had kept her table. It gave her a chance to get away from the crowd. The sixth race was in the gate when suddenly a horse broke through the gate. The outrider standing in front of the starting gate broke his pony into a full run. In seconds, he was running parallel with the race horse and in just a few more jumps he grabbed hold of the bridle reins and pulled the horse to a stop.

"Good job," Maggi thought. Old Roy was one of the best outriders in the business. Runaway horses hardly ever got away from him. In just a few seconds the horse was reloaded, and the race was started.

Maggi got to the paddock just as King of Summer came walking up into the saddling ring. Jiggs led him into the 5 stall. King stood very still, just looking at the track.

King was a good sixteen hands tall, Maggi figured, and it made it hard for her short body and arms to pull up on the billets. As she tugged and pulled, she had the disadvantage of no leverage! Then came the overgirth as she crouched down to secure it into the buckle. She pulled the tiny stirrups down and tucked in the end under the overgirth. She tightened up King's noseband and ran the leather through the little keeper. She took the reins from Jiggs' hands, threw them over King's head, and let them hang loose as Jiggs got another hold on King's bridle reins. She tucked King's forelock under the brow band as she had seen Beau do many times. He was saddled. The jock's valet said, "Good luck," and left. She heard the buzzer in the jocks' room. She knew the jocks would be out in just a few minutes. So she started toward the walking ring and stood by the number 5 stake.

"Try and make the lead if you can, but save some for the lane," she told the jock. She legged him up on King, patted his leg and said, "Good luck!" As Jiggs handed King to the pony boy, King jumped and kicked out . . . he was feeling good, she thought.

And then the announcer yelled, *"They're off!"*

King broke out in the lead by two lengths. Maggi looked up at the tote board. Fractions flashed on the first quarter . . . 23 . . . a slow pace. That's good for us, she thought. King can gallop like that all day. If they held this pace until the half mile, she knew he had a good chance of winning.

At the half mile pole, a .48 flashed on the tote board. King was neck and neck with the horse Maggi figured was the one to beat. The jockey hadn't asked King to run yet. She figured he would make his move soon.

Then she saw the jock raise his stick. Now! He's getting into King!

" . . . *and it's King of Summer taking command . . . by one,"* the announcer continued, " . . . *and turning for home, it's King of Summer by three lengths, pulling away . . . "*

"Come on! Come on, King!" Maggi screamed.

" . . *at the wire it's King of Summer by four lengths . . "* the announcer blared for his final call.

He win!

After the race, Jiggs was the first one on the track, to pick up King.

"Go get your picture taken!" everyone yelled at Maggi. "Go on—you won it!"

The public—old friends, and gyps from the fair circuit

days joined in. "Hurry up, get on down there!" she heard from all sides.

She hurried toward the winner's circle. Although she had been there many times before, this was the first time she was going for herself. She had bought the horse—herself, trained him—herself, and now she had won! As she approached the circle, a crowd of eight people were waiting and pushed her into the center of the group, while they all waited for King to come to be led into the circle.

"Ladies and Gentlemen, entering the winner's circle, King of Summer , winner of the Cactus Wren Stakes. Trained by Maggi Witlow and ridden by jockey Jim Cavaro."

Maggi listened to the announcement and vowed to remember this moment forever. As Jiggs led King inside the circle, his crafty blue eyes scanned the odds board. Jiggs grinned from ear to ear. As he squared King off into a good standing position, a huge pewter trophy was presented to Maggi. Even the Gold Cup wasn't that big.

As Jiggs led King off toward the test barn, and as Maggi stepped down out of the winner's circle, she caught sight of Hilly.

"Hilly! Did you see the race?" Maggi asked.

"We got here just in time," Hilly told her. "But we couldn't make it down for the picture, because of the darn elevator."

"Where's Harry?" Maggi asked anxiously.

"He went to cash his ticket. He'll be here in a minute."

"Come on, Hilly, walk over to the test barn with me," Maggi insisted.

"Do you think Harry will know where we are?"

"Sure, he's been around the track enough to know a winner goes to the test barn," Maggi laughed.

As she looked up she passed Beau . . . a magnetic pull and sensation ran through her veins.

"Good luck, Beau," she spoke before she knew it!

"Thank you," he answered curtly.

"My God, he's gotten fat!" Hilly stated, "I haven't seen him since last year," she added.

"Yes, I know," Maggi answered, "It doesn't seem that long, does it?"

"We heard his marriage isn't working out too well," Hilly went on.

"Oh?" Maggi picked up, "I've never heard anything myself."

"Well, Harry said it wouldn't last, and Beau should have waited and not gotten married so fast. He would have come to his senses, but too many people were pushing him. And he couldn't back up," Hilly said.

By the time they got to the test barn, King had his halter on and Jiggs was giving him a bath.

"Well, you're getting to be a regular in here," the pee catcher said, kidding Maggi. "That makes three in a row, this old horse has won for you," he continued. "You made everyone eat their words. He's a nice horse and you'll do good with him."

"Thanks, Heinie," Maggi answered.

"Hey, congrats . . . " the state vet called from his car as he headed for the starting gate.

"Come on, Hilly, the Gold Cup Race is about to start." They hurried up toward the railing, found an empty spot to stand and glued their eyes to the starting gate across the end field into the quarter chute.

Maggi watched the horses approaching the gate as her mind drifted back two years ago.

499

Beau won the Gold Cup for the third time, and Mr. Bullington got to keep the Gold Cup permanently. Mr. Bullington was ecstatic! What a red-letter day for all of them! She thought how happy they were that evening celebrating, and their tender lovemaking later that night.

How they had loved one another through all the hardships of their early marriage, the fair circuits, dingy motels, the cold mornings, the water fights, and the tussles in a clean bedded stall. Detroit! . . . their fears of the Mafia! The hicks from the sticks . . she mused. Chicago, the Bullingtons, the Ruckers, Harry and Hilly . . . their home! Beau leaving . . . the divorce.

Funny, she thought, all their effort and struggle to be successful only destroyed their marriage . . . and then Beau remarrying! The sting of that thought jarred her back to reality.

"Hey, where are you?" Hilly asked.

"I'm here," Maggi said.

Baggy Pants went to the lead. It was a speed jam of twelve evenly matched three-year-olds battling it out!

Baggy Pants began to pull away at the 3/8s pole. Maggi knew by the way the big red colt was running that he was going to win, unless he fell down! The jockey hadn't even uncocked his stick yet, and he had tons of horse left. As they turned for home, the colt widened his lead by four lengths. He glided over the finish line with no sweat! He won!

Maggi was happy for Beau. He was a good trainer and earned every bit of his success, she thought.

"Come on, Hilly, let's go back to the test barn. I have to sign the test slip yet," Maggi said. "Where's Harry?"

"He'll be here. He went to get something," Hilly answered.

Jiggs had taken King on back to the barn. They got the pee test fast. Maggi and Hilly, too, walked back to the barn.

Harry showed up with a big bottle of champagne under one arm and a packet of plastic glasses under the other. Michael and Jill drove up.

"Hey, Super Trainer!" Michael yelled.

"Oh, Maggi, he ran a beautiful race," Jill added.

"Thanks, but I just got lucky," Maggi insisted.

"Luck, my foot! A horse doesn't run in 1:36 4/5 by luck. That's damn good training, I'd say," Harry interrupted, as he snapped the cork off the bottle and poured the golden bubbly liquid into the plastic glasses sitting on the tack trunk.

"Okay, everyone grab a glass," Harry said.

Michael, Jill, and Hilly each picked up a glass and Harry took a glass over to Maggi and Jiggs.

"*To the trainer!*" he expounded grandly. "We all love you, Maggi!"

Tears welled up in Maggi's eyes. She tried to fight them back. She was overcome with the joy of having such good friends and thought of the many good times they had shared.

She swallowed the hard lump in her throat and brushed away her tears.

"Now, *I'd* like to make a toast," she told them suddenly.

"To all us racetrackers. . .
Keep yourself in the best of company,
And your horse in the worst. . .
And—*NEVER LOOK BACK!!*"

The Meet's Over!

There is nothing either good or bad,
but thinking makes it so.
William Shakespeare

502

Racetrack Jargon

He's just a gyp . . . . never got any better.

Watch he don't paw you on the head . . . . warning of a horse that will strike with his front feet.

We got outshook for him . . . . more than one claim in for the horse.

He pulled up bad . . . . meaning a horse came back lame after a workout or a race.

He broke out again . . . . a horse began to sweat again after he was put in his stall.

He's a stall walking S.O.B. . . . . when a horse runs his stall constantly weaving back and forth and in circles.

He's head shy . . . . a horse that slings his head and won't let you bridle him without a struggle.

He laid down his soul coming for home . . . . when a horse is really giving his all.

He can run a lick . . . . a horse that can light the board, finish 1-2-3-4.

He's knodding . . . . when a horse favors a leg from soreness.

Muzzle him . . . . trainer or groom muzzling the horse the night before his race so he won't fill up on hay or bedding.

He runs down on all fours . . . . when a horse burns his heels during the race.

He refused his last race . . . . when a horse won't break out of the starting gate.

I'm going for him . . . . putting in a claim for a horse.

We haltered him . . . . claimed a horse.

He got clipped . . . . when a horse's front feet clip the horse's hind feet in front of him, cutting his legs and sometimes causing a spill.

He speedy cut . . . . a horse actually cuts himself with his own feet, front as well as back. Corrective shoeing usually can stop this.

Did you do up? . . . . rub the horse's leg and bandage him with leg wraps.

Did he water out? . . . . get all the water he wanted before you put him up.

Muck sack . . . . a sheet of canvas or burlap, 10 x 10, used to carry manure and straw from the stalls.

He lost his pedal . . . . when a rider lost his stirrup.

He broke his cross . . . . a horse breaks the hold on the reins from the jock.

He's a stump sucker . . . . a horse that grabs hold of something with his upper teeth and sucks in air constantly all day long.

He is a parrot mouth . . . . a horse with an extreme over bite.

He runs like a haint . . . . referring to a saint, a ghost.

Drop him down . . . . lower his claiming price.

What equipment does he run? . . . . bit, snaffle, ring or dee bit, blinkers, overcheck, nose band, shadow roll, tongue tie, run out bit, rubber bit, prong bit?

He is on the muscle . . . . horse feels good and ready to run.

He never cocked his stick . . . . jockey never used his whip.

He came from the bushes . . . . when you have raced on the fair circuits and small league tracks.

Set chilly on him . . . . a trainer telling the rider to not move or whip the horse and wait until they turn for home.

He will be 8 to 5 . . . . meaning the horse is a cinch to be the favorite.

He's too cheap for me . . . . runs for bottom claim.

Let's blister this horse . . . . a strong brace of medicine that will scurf the skin, this increases circulation.

He spit it out at the turn . . . . a horse quits trying.

About the Author

Marge Hazelton was born in Eureka, California, daughter of a blacksmith. She was raised in Southern California, her father having created much of the ornamental wrought iron for homes in fashionable Beverly Hills and Bel Air.

She came to a sparsely populated Arizona in 1949 as manager of a small horse ranch in the Phoenix area. Soon, Arizona had become one of the fastest-growing states in the country and a magnet for people seeking the "Western lifestyle" that has always been Marge Hazelton's life. But few people have been born to it the way Marge Hazelton was . . . and even fewer live it the way she does today.

She has trained show horses and quarter horses since coming to Arizona and for twenty years was married to Richard Hazelton, one of the leading horse trainers in the world. She was Champion Girl Calf Roper in 1951-1952 and was jumping instructor at Stevens College in Steamboat, Colorado. An artist and author was well, her paintings have been sold throughout the United States and in Australia. She has contributed numerous stories for Arizona newspapers and Arizona Horse Breeders magazine.

Backside *is the product of a lifetime's experiences and first-hand knowledge as only an insider would know it . . . and as only Marge Hazelton could tell it.*

"BACKSIDE"

This title can be ordered directly from the publisher.

Teeny Weeny Publishing
Route 2
P.O. Box 2672
Seymour, MO 65746